# SCANDAL, SECRETS AND SENSUAL CONFESSIONS . . .

for Holly —
A Dr. Ruth favorite . . .
ISSIQUAN 2024

love Naomi

On Newsstands Now:

**TRUE STORY**
and
**TRUE CONFESSIONS**
Magazines

*True Story* and *True Confessions* are the world's largest and best-selling women's romance magazines. They offer true-to-life stories to which women can relate.

Since 1919, the iconic *True Story* has been an extraordinary publication. The magazine gets its inspiration from the hearts and minds of women, and touches on those things in life that a woman holds close to her heart, like love, loss, family and friendship.

*True Confessions*, a cherished classic first published in 1922, looks into women's souls and reveals their deepest secrets.

---

To subscribe, please visit our website:
**www.TrueRenditionsLLC.com** or call **(212) 922-9244**

To find the TRUES at your local store, please visit:
**www.WheresMyMagazine.com**

# SCANDAL, SECRETS AND SENSUAL CONFESSIONS . . .

From the Editors
Of *True Story* And
*True Confessions*

Published by True Renditions, LLC


True Renditions, LLC
105 E. 34th Street, Suite 141
New York, NY 10016

ISBN: 978-1-938877-61-2


Visit us on the web at www.truerenditionsllc.com.

# Contents

# LOVE HOSTAGE

As I walked up the steps of St. Joseph's Hospital, tears blurred my eyes, and I felt their wetness on my cheeks. I stumbled, and Dr. Calvin slid his hand under my arm. "Brace up, Mary," he said. "We don't know yet how bad it is, but I'm sure Dr. Finch is doing all he can for your brother. You must be brave for your mother's sake."

I nodded my head numbly. Everything still seemed like a bad dream that couldn't have really happened.

I'd been busy in Dr. Calvin's office when I got the news. I was the receptionist, and I was always busy, because Dr. Calvin was the best baby doctor in town. I liked my job, although at first I'd felt bad about not going to college right out of high school. But Mom was a widow and we needed the money so much for Matthew, my only brother. He would be finishing high school that year, and afterwards he wanted to go to the seminary to become a priest. Having Matthew become a priest was the most wonderful dream in Mom's life, and mine, too, so I hadn't really been unhappy about making a small sacrifice. After all, I was going to be married as soon as I could stop working. That was a greater sacrifice . . . waiting to marry Neal Monroe when we were so in love we could hardly stand it. But Neal was a good Catholic, too, and he understood and was willing to wait.

Then this happened. A teenage boy coming back from the football game . . . a kid driving too fast, probably drunk, because a half-empty flask had been found in his car, smashed into our old car that Matthew had been driving. He was coming home after taking the orphanage kids on an afternoon hike.

Dr. Calvin had received the call from the hospital, he'd tried to break the news to me gently but there was no way to ease the blow. The other boy had been killed but Matthew was still alive. That was all the doctors could say.

I bit my lips as Dr. Calvin pushed open the door to the waiting room. Oh, surely God wouldn't let Matthew be hurt badly. Not Matthew, who was so good and gentle and always kind.

Mom flung herself into my arms as I entered the room. She looked so little and old and shrunken. I tried to comfort her, holding her close while looking over her shoulder at Father Douglas, our parish priest.

He sighed. "I know this is hard to bear, and there's nothing I can say to make it easier. Matthew is badly hurt . . . he may die. But he has lived a good life. His faith is strong, and he has received the last rites.

1

The other poor boy lived without faith and died alone. Pray for his soul if you can, Mrs. Sinclair . . . when you pray for your boy's life."

Mom shook her head. "All my prayers are for Matthew," she said. "How can I waste even one of them? God's got to hear me. All my life I've sacrificed for Matthew and prayed for him. I dedicated his life to God before he was born!" Her eyes filled with tears and a burning fire gleamed from them. "God has called Matthew to the priesthood. He wants Matthew to live for Him, not die for Him!" She cried out.

Father Douglas placed his hand on Mom's shoulder. "None of us can say what God wants or what He thinks is best. His will is often difficult to understand. But Matthew has always loved and trusted Him, and we must trust Him, too."

I don't think Mom heard. She turned away and dropped on her knees in front of a little statue of the Blessed Virgin that was set in the wall of the waiting room. Father Douglas watched her for a moment and then drew me into the hall.

"You're a brave girl, Mary," he told me. "You can know the truth. I couldn't let your mother hope for too much, because the doctors say Matthew's chest is crushed and he can't live more than a few hours." He patted my arm. "Go back to your mother. Pray with her and try to help her to remember the words of the Lord's Prayer . . . Thy will be done."

I nodded, unable to speak. He gave me a comforting smile. "I'll go up to your brother's room now, Mary." He walked toward the elevator. I started back into the waiting room, my head bent, tears streaming down my face. Suddenly I heard Neal calling. Then he was beside me, his face twisted with sympathy.

"We just got the news, Mary. Father Douglas's housekeeper called me. Oh, Mary, why did it have to be Matthew?"

Clinging to his hand, I went back into the waiting room. It helped just having Neal beside me. He had always been someone to lean on, ever since I'd first met him in junior high school years ago.

For hours of that long night, Neal sat near me and held my hand as we waited. Mostly Mom prayed. I took out my rosary and tried to pray, too, but my prayers were all mixed up with thoughts of Matthew.

He was born only eleven months after me, and a lot of people asked if we were twins because we both had the same blue-black hair and white complexion and Irish-blue eyes. But I had always stayed in the background. In our home, every thought was of Matthew, of the time when he would become a priest.

Ever since we could remember, the Church had been the center of our lives. St. Anthony's Church was just a block away from our little brown house. My earliest memories are of the way Mom made us dress up to go to Mass. I remember the special processions and

2

the wonder of Midnight Mass at Christmas. The church was always ablaze with hundreds of tall white candles and fragrant with the smell of fir and candle wax and incense. One year, when I was going to the nuns' school, my class was chosen to fix the crib scene for the church. I'll never forget the thrill of unpacking the big box with the Christmas figures, of building a tiny stable where the little cows and donkeys looked almost as real as life. And, oh, the moment of putting the Christ Child in the crib! How beautiful He was in His new dress of white silk that Sister Victoria had sewed herself!

Yes, those were happy memories. The Church was the center of my life . . . a place for worship, meeting your friends and neighbors, and doing the most interesting and wonderful things all year long. Father Douglas was my best friend. He almost took the place of my father, who had died when I was seven.

I guess we were brought up to feel the Church was so important because Mom was very devout. She had thought she'd be a nun, like her sister Agnes, but she'd met Dad and fell in love with him. However, to ease her guilt of leaving the convent, she vowed to dedicate at least one of her children to God. How often she told us about that vow . . . although Father Douglas reminded her many times that while it was fine to dedicate all your children to God, no one had the right to say a child should be given into the orders of the Church. That was out of human hands. God chose the ones he wanted for holy orders.

For a long time it looked as if Mom and Dad weren't going to have any children at all. After going through two miscarriages, Mom was finally able to bring a baby to term five years after they married. She was disappointed because I was a girl, especially when the doctor told her she probably wouldn't have another child. But she told Dad that at least I could be a nun. I've often heard how Dad tried to reason with her by reminding her, as Father Douglas had, that no one could force a young person to become a nun. That God might choose many other ways for me to be dedicated to Him. But Mom was stubborn. "God Himself will supply the desire in Mary's heart for the religious life," she told Dad. "Unless, by some miracle, I have another baby."

Well that miracle happened, and when Matthew was born, all of Mom's dreams fastened on his becoming a priest. Over and over, Father Douglas warned her about not forcing a child into a vocation, and I know she really tried not to influence us. But she felt so strongly that naturally we became aware of it when we were very young.

The wonder of it was that without any real forcing from Mom, Matthew grew up wanting to be a priest. He wasn't completely pious by any means . . . he was strong, and full of fun, and got into his share of mischief. But there was a gentle goodness about him. He loved people, his family, and God. He didn't make much of a show of it, but that love was there. Finally Father Douglas admitted that perhaps Matthew should be a priest.

I thought the world of Matthew, but sometimes I felt a little insignificant because I didn't have a vocation. Neal Monroe felt I was very important, though, because he loved me.

Neal's folks lived in a shabby farmhouse that was run-down looking, not because they were lazy, but because, as Neal's mother said, she was like the old woman that lived in a shoe. She had so many children . . . however; she knew what to do. She put her kids' happiness above everything else, and they were a wonderful, laughing, strong, and loving family.

I dated Neal all through high school, but we really fell in love the last summer of high school when I was working for Mrs. Monroe at the farm. She was pregnant again and not very strong.

Neal and I were together every day that wonderful summer and it became so much more important than just dating. It was a beautiful, clean kind of love, yet it was exciting, too. Our kisses made my whole body glow with the knowledge that I was a woman at last, in love and eager to make love. I knew Neal had even stronger feelings, but we both fought the excitement of that desire. We couldn't get married for a long time because I had to work and help pay for Matthew's schooling.

Matthew was sorry I had to sacrifice for him, but Mom thought it was only right. After all, she pointed out once, Matthew would be pledging celibacy for his entire life; surely I could wait for Neal a few years.

But Neal and I still had our glowing plans for the future. After Mrs. Monroe's new baby was born, I started to work in Dr. Calvin's office, and Neal went to work on a farm at the other end of the valley so he could save money to buy a small farm for us. Even if it was a little rough waiting for marriage when we were so much in love, we were still happy with our hopes and dreams.

But now our safe, lovely future had crashed around us. Matthew was hurt, maybe dying. I clung to Neal's hand and looked at Mom, who was praying frantically. Surely she was right . . . Matthew couldn't die. His life had been pledged to God even before he was born.

At just about sunrise Dr. Finch and Father Douglas came in, their faces told us even before they put it into words. Matthew had died.

Mom completely fell apart. She turned on Dr. Finch and actually tried to hit him. "It's not true!" she cried. "It can't be true. I prayed!" Her face was very white. She gave one more shrill, heartbroken cry, then she sagged unconscious in Dr. Finch's arms.

They kept her in the hospital a couple of days. When I took her home, she looked like a broken old woman.

Mom was really sick the next few weeks. I gave up my job to take care of her. After all, a job didn't matter much now that we didn't have Matthew to send to seminary. We could get along on her little pension. Mom never wanted much for herself, and she'd brought me up not to expect much, either. Matthew had been our whole life. Now what was the use of anything?

For days I did nothing but take care of Mom and fight my own wild grief. It would have been easier if Neal could have been near, but Mom couldn't stand to see him around . . . Neal, so strong and handsome, when Matthew was dead. Every time he came over she'd get just hysterical after he left. Finally one evening I followed him out onto the porch, with my heart breaking, I told him it might be better for Mom if he didn't come around for a while.

He nodded. "I understand, Mary. But, honey, try to get your mother to snap out of it. It isn't good for her to shut herself up and do nothing but mourn. It isn't good for you, either." His face was troubled. "Sometimes I have a kind of crazy feeling about it. What if your mom won't ever let you go?"

"Why, Neal Monroe!" I cried. "You know Mom would never do a thing like that! Of course she clings to me now, but Father Douglas says time heals everything, and I guess we just can't rush her. It would be cruel to think of ourselves now."

Neal sighed. "Sure. But I love you so much that I couldn't take it if something broke us up. Promise nothing will . . . ever. Promise, Mary!"

I nodded, and his lips pressed down on mine. We stood in that embrace for a long time. Then I heard Mom calling, and reluctantly I slipped from Neal's arms. "I've got to go now," I said. "Oh, honey, be patient. Try to see how my mom feels. Don't make things harder for me."

"God knows I wouldn't do that, darling." He gave my hand a squeeze and went down the steps. I took a deep breath and went inside.

Mom was standing in the hall with tears streaming down her face. "I saw you kissing Neal!" she cried. "Your poor brother hasn't even been in his grave a month and you're ready to forget all about him and go on with your selfish plans."

"Mom, you know that's not true!" I said.

Her tears became wild sobs. "I guess I do know it, Mary, but it's so hard to see Neal so full of life when Matthew is dead." Her lips quivered. "You and my faith . . . that's all I've got now."

I couldn't leave her while she felt that way, but I told myself this first stage of sorrow would pass gradually. For now I did everything she wanted me to. The only time we left the house was to go to church, and we went there every day. Even though I'd always loved the beautiful service of the Mass, I used to hate to get up almost before daylight and walk in the chill dawn in time for the six a.m. service. But now I was glad to leave our dark, sad house and go into the freshness of a new morning. There was comfort in kneeling in church and listening to the familiar prayers, their Latin chant rising and falling like music. I knew the words so well I didn't have to follow the English translation in my prayer book: "I will go unto the altar of God. To God, the joy of my youth. Why art thou sad, my soul, and why dost thou trouble me? . . . Our help is in the name of the Lord. Who hath made heaven and earth."

Yes, it was good coming to the altar of God . . . and surely it did seem that only God brought any joy to me. Even Neal seemed very far away then. My life, once so full and happy, had become narrow and filled with tears. And kneeling there in church, I found the only peace I knew during those days of conflict and despair.

The thought that perhaps I shouldn't get married, that I should be the one to enter the religious life now that Matthew was gone, drifted into my mind and heart so gently I don't even know when it first came to me.

I guess every Catholic girl thinks about becoming a nun at one time or another. When I was twelve, I'd daydream about myself in the sweeping robes of some religious order. It was a stage I passed through, like the stage of wanting to be a nurse and then wanting to be an actress. All those daydreams had finally sifted down into the one wonderful dream of becoming Neal's wife. But in those days after Matthew's death, the old daydream came back to me stronger than ever.

I can't say why. Maybe it was because I was still in a state of shock and grief. Maybe it was the long hours of listening to Mom talk about how she'd prayed for a vocation for one of her children. Matthew had been the answer to that prayer. But me . . . I was such an ordinary, everyday sort of girl. Mom wasn't ashamed of me, but naturally she couldn't be as wildly proud of me as she'd been of Matthew, and that thought hurt. Sometimes it hurt so much that I would cringe inside.

Well, Matthew was gone and there could never be a priest in the family. But maybe it was my turn to give my life to the Church. Mom had promised one of her children to God. Now that I was the only one left, perhaps it was my duty.

When I reached that stage of thinking—and it took several weeks—I just went cold with dread. Oh, no, I'd tell myself, I can't! What am I thinking? I have my life planned. I'm going to be Neal's wife. How can I give that up?

Neal! My mind always twisted in sorrow when I thought of him. But he was so dreamlike now. Somewhere I'd lost the strong, sure feeling I had for him. I'd lost it in days and days of almost hysterical praying and mourning. Neal didn't understand anything about the way of life that had become so natural to me . . . the darkened house, the long prayers.

It didn't take Mom long to see I had something on my mind. I knew I was acting strangely, but I couldn't help myself. Some days I wouldn't even want to go to church. I was afraid of church. It was drawing me closer and closer to a decision I didn't want to make. I'd stay at home for two or three days, and even Mom's begging and scolding wouldn't move me. Then, suddenly I'd get an awful hunger to fly to the very comfort that had caused me to draw away before, and I'd go every morning with Mom. When we had the novena services, nine consecutive days of praying, I'd go in the evening as well. I'd sink into such deep prayer that I was hardly aware of what was going on around me.

It was hard to eat, and hard to sleep. And I was so nervous I'd scream at Mom over any little thing. But my worst problem was Neal.

Twice, paying no attention to what Mom thought, I called him at his home. He was out in the fields both times, so his mother said he would call me back. But when the call came, I just couldn't take it. Once I ran right out of the house and left Mom to say I wasn't there. Another time I told her to tell him I couldn't talk then and I'd call him back. But I didn't. When he drove in to see me the next night, I saw his car stopping and ran up to my room. I told Mom to let him think I was asleep. Later, when I heard his car leaving, I ran to the window and called to him. But he was already gone.

It was all so mixed up and strange for me. I knew I loved Neal, but my desire to leave him—and the world—forever was tearing me apart.

Finally I couldn't stand to keep my doubts and hopes and fears to myself any longer. One evening after Mom and I had finished saying the rosary, I went and sat on the floor by her and rested my head against her knee. And then I told her that I'd been thinking about becoming a nun.

She was silent for a long time. When I looked up, her face was glowing with joy, and on her lips was the first smile I'd seen since Matthew had died.

"How I've prayed for this, Mary," she said. "You were my first . . . the baby I prayed for first, long before you were born. When you were a girl, maybe I was a little disappointed, but then I thought you could be a nun like my sister Agnes. I couldn't wish anything better for my baby than a pure, happy life like that.

"Then, when Matthew was born and you grew up and never showed much desire for a vocation, I put that dream to the back of my mind. But it was always there." Her hands tightened on my shoulders.

7

"Perhaps God had chosen you first, but you might never have realized it if He hadn't taken Matthew."

She sighed. "You know how I've suffered over Matthew's death. But Father Douglas is right. God's will shall be done. I have lost my son, but somehow I feel that just now I'm finding my daughter."

Every word she said made me more and more sure I was right. I was supposed to enter a convent and give my life to God. That's what I wanted to do. But how could I stand to give up Neal?

Mom thought it would be better for me not to see him again . . . to just write a note and tell him what I'd decided. But I couldn't do that. I did write him a note, though, and told him I'd like to see him that Saturday night.

The minute Neal got it he called me up. I'd almost forgotten the sound of his voice. It had been six weeks since I'd talked to him. Now tears came to my eyes because he sounded so happy.

"Do you mean it, Mary? You really want to see me?" he asked. "What does your mother say?"

I gripped the phone so hard my fingers hurt. "She . . . she'd rather I didn't," I said. "But I've just got to anyway."

"Me, too, honey. If you hadn't got in touch with me, I'd have come to your house pretty soon and broken in!" His words were all tumbling over each other. "I'll be at your house at seven." He laughed. "Let's make it six-thirty. Even an extra half hour is too long to wait."

I slowly got ready to go out with Neal. I remembered all the times I'd dressed for dates with him. Tears stung my eyes again. This was our last date. It wasn't really a date, of course, but I had to be alone in order to talk to him. I couldn't tell him what I had to here in our living room, with Mom hovering around . . . not exactly listening, but near. It would be hard enough just to tell him.

Funny enough, after being away from Neal just those weeks, I'd forgotten how bright and tender his eyes were, how strong and safe his hand felt over mine. As we walked out to his car, he smiled down at me. "It was so hard to stay away from you, honey. But I tried to be patient. You're worth waiting for, Mary."

I tried to smile back, but my lips were stiff. I twisted my fingers together as I sat in the car beside him. Oh, Neal! I thought. I hadn't realized how difficult it would be to tell him when he was so close to me . . . when I could reach out and touch him. For a second the thought ran through my mind: Maybe I'm wrong. Maybe I don't have a vocation. Perhaps I should just go on and marry Neal, no matter what.

But I put that thought behind me quickly. A true vocation couldn't be that easily lost.

"Neal, I don't want to go anyplace tonight," I said. "Let's just drive up to the bluff."

8

He gave me a swift, teasing grin, and I knew he thought I was hungry for his kisses, just as he was hungry for mine.

The first stars of evening were just dotting the sky as he stopped the car under some pine trees. It was the most romantic place and time for lovers. Neal slid his arm around my shoulder and pulled me toward him, but I jerked away. If he kissed me now, I'd never have the courage to part from him. Every nerve in my body screamed for that kiss. I squeezed my eyes shut so I wouldn't see his face. "No," I whispered.

"But, Mary . . . why?"

I edged away from him and sat as near to the door as I could. My tongue was numb as I formed the words. "You can't kiss me, Neal. I . . . I just asked you to drive up here so I could tell you. . . ." I was trembling. My body seemed wrapped in an icy chill. "I'm not going to marry you, Neal."

His face went white. "Is this some kind of a joke?"

"No, oh, no! I'm not going to marry you because . . . I'm going to become a nun."

I don't like to remember what followed. At first Neal couldn't believe it. Then he begged, and finally he got angry. He said that I was hysterical, that my mother had forced me into this. He said he'd been afraid something like this would happen when he left me shut up with Mom so long, but he'd thought I had better sense.

He raved on and on, but I didn't say a word. I sat like someone turned to stone. There was no way I could answer him or make him understand. I was so heartsick that I just wanted to run away from his hurt and anger. I forced my thoughts to the quiet church, to the burning candles and the prayers. It seemed like a refuge now. I wanted to get back to it. I wanted to get away from Neal before my heart was torn right out of my body.

Finally he took me home. I've never seen such a hopeless look on anyone's face as the one he gave me when he walked me to the door.

"I can't reason with you," he told me. "But you'll have to talk to Father Douglas before you go off to any order. Maybe he can show you what a crazy idea this is."

His words stung through the wall I'd built around myself. "It isn't crazy to be a nun!" I cried. "How can you, a good Catholic, say that?"

"Of course it isn't crazy . . . for lots of women. It's just that it is for you." A little muscle twitched in his jaw. "Mary . . . Mary. . . ." His voice broke, and I saw the tears in his eyes. Suddenly he hurried back to the car. I knew he couldn't take it anymore, and neither could I. Oh, dear heaven, why did I meet Neal? If it wasn't for him, I could enter a convent free and happy without any heartbreak. As it was, I had to hurt him as well as myself.

I felt all lost and mixed up, but Neal hadn't changed my mind.

He had become a temptation. No matter how either of us suffered, my love of God came first.

Of course, I had to discuss my intentions with my confessor . . . Father Douglas. After I'd told Neal I felt free to go ahead with my plans, and after Mass the next day I went to Father Douglas's study to wait for him.

"Well, Mary!" He smiled at me as he came in and sat down at his desk. "Now what can I do for you?" He poured himself a cup of coffee from the breakfast tray his housekeeper brought. "Can I offer you some coffee?"

I shook my head.

"No? Well, child, what is your problem?"

"It isn't exactly a problem," I blurted. "I . . . I've decided to enter a convent."

He picked up an orange from the tray and began to peel it slowly, evidently searching for words. There was a wise, compassionate look on his face when he said, "I'm not surprised, Mary. I rather expected you to feel this way after Matthew's death. But, my dear, you must realize no one can enter a convent because of an emotional storm, any more than one would marry for their emotions alone."

"It isn't emotions alone!" I cried. "I do have a vocation . . . I do! You didn't doubt that Matthew was meant to be a priest. Why do you think I'm just overly emotional when I want to be a nun?"

He smiled at me. "I was with Matthew from the time he was a little boy. I saw his reactions to every situation. I was his friend, just as I hope I've been your friend, Mary. Yes, I'm sure Matthew had a real vocation for the priesthood. But vocations for the religious life are rare and precious. You can't force them." He leaned toward me. "Mary, you can't be Matthew, and you can't demand that God give you the gifts he gave Matthew. God will give you the gifts meant especially for you."

"This is my gift," I said.

"Is it?" Father Douglas asked while raising one eyebrow.

I didn't answer. He sighed and said, "Perhaps. But I know you well enough, Mary, I know that nothing will stop you once you've set your mind to something. You're that much like your mother." He tapped his fingers on the desk. "But I am going to demand one thing," he went on. "I must insist that you wait three months before you do anything more. I want you to be absolutely sure in your own mind that this is what you want. If, at the end of that time, you still feel you have a vocation, you'll enter the convent as a novice. For several years you'll be given the opportunity to live the life of a nun and to further test whether it's meant for you. If you discover it isn't, of course there'll be no stigma attached to leaving the novitiate than

10

there would be in breaking a human engagement. However, if you go ahead and accept your final vows as a nun knowing that it is not the life for you, it will be as wrong as if you married a man you knew was not the man for you . . . only it would be worse."

I nodded my head, but I was hardly listening to his words. I didn't want to listen. Because he hadn't doubted Matthew's vocation, it hurt that he doubted mine.

"Many are called," Father Douglas reminded me, "but few are chosen. If you are not chosen, you must not go against His will, no matter how hard it is for you to admit your mistake."

Those three months seemed endless to me. It was almost like Mom and I were pulling from one side, and Neal and Father Douglas from the other. Father Douglas didn't say any more, of course, but I knew how he felt. Neal didn't give up, though. He kept calling the house, and at first it was hard refusing to talk to him. But Mom stopped even calling me to the phone, and with each day of not seeing or talking to him, of shutting him out of my thoughts, the terrible pain and loss dwindled to an ache, and then to only a dull twinge.

Finally my time of testing was over, Mom and I went to Father Douglas again and he didn't try to argue with me anymore. Instead, he said that if my mind was made up he'd help me all he could.

Mom and I had decided I'd join the order of the Sisters of St. Margaret. We'd talked about my entering the same order that my Aunt Agnes had entered, but the Sisters of St. Margaret was a smaller order and the mother house was in a town not far from my home. The order was divided into three groups . . . the nurses, the teachers, and those who led a cloistered life, never leaving the convent.

"Wouldn't it be wonderful if you decided to lead a cloistered life and devote your life to prayer?" Mom said.

I'd been thinking the same thing. I liked the idea of remaining sheltered from the world in the peaceful convent. Yes, that was what I wanted.

The next weeks passed quickly. There were the personal interviews at the mother house, the shopping for the necessary clothing and equipment for my new life, and all the many other things that had to be attended to.

The night before I was to leave, Neal came to see me. My clothes were packed and I'd gone to bed early, but when I heard the familiar sound of his old car stopping before our gate, my heart gave a lurch. "Mom," I cried, "I don't want to see Neal! I can see him!"

"Of course you can't," Mom said. I heard her go down to answer the door.

Even though I buried my head in the pillow, the murmur of their voices came to me. It seemed that Neal wouldn't leave. How much longer can I stand this? I thought. Sending Neal away was bitterly hard, but hadn't God said we must each carry a cross?

After he had gone, I lay there crying quietly and thinking. I didn't dare think of Neal though, so I thought of Mom and of her joy because I was going to enter a convent. I thought of my own joy and finally peace came to my heart, and I fell asleep.

It was seventy miles to the town where the convent was. My bus got in just before noon. I had to take a cab to the convent itself, which was about a mile outside the city limits. My hands were moist with excitement as the cab turned in through the big wrought iron gate and drove up to the circular driveway to the front door. The convent itself was a big, old-fashioned house that must have once belonged to some wealthy person. It had sprawling porches and a lot of fancy trim, and it sat on a wide green lawn. In the back I caught glimpses of a large, well-tended vegetable garden and a cluster of neat chicken houses and duck pens.

The cab driver carried my bag up to the door, and I gave a sigh of happiness. For me, this was coming home. Then I rang the bell.

A small white curtain was pulled back from the door window, and a nun's round, placid face gazed at me. Then she opened the door, and when I told her who I was, she nodded. "Mother Mary Francis is waiting for you in her study. This way, please."

I followed the little nun down the long hall. The walls were covered with soft yellow wallpaper and the wooden floor creaked beneath my feet. Two or three religious pictures were hung along the hall, and a little statue of the Virgin sat on a hall table with a candle burning before her. There was the good smell of baking bread coming from the back of the house. Everything was peaceful and quiet.

The nun tapped on a door near the end of the hall and a soft voice told me to enter. A moment later I was standing before Mother Mary Francis.

I'd met her before, of course, during my interviews. She was a tall, pleasant-faced woman with bright blue eyes. She wore the stiff, pleated white coil, covered by a black veil, and the sweeping black robes of the order. She nodded for me to sit down, and we talked for a few moments. Nervous and excited as I was, she made me feel at ease almost instantly. Then she repeated to me a little about the founding of the order and its aims, things I already knew, and again I told her that I'd like to be a cloistered sister.

She smiled slightly. "You're very young to make such a decision," she said. "That's the reason there is a five-year novitiate before you take your final vows. Your first year will be spent doing simple homemaking tasks in the laundry, kitchen, and garden of the convent. There will be long hours of study and prayers. The second year you will work six months in the nursing home and six months assisting the teachers in the parish school. Although you don't have the education to become a teacher yourself, we can find many duties for you if you work best with children. There is office work in the school, playground supervision, and work in the nursery school.

"The third year you will start your real training for whichever task we decide is best for you," Mother Mary Francis went on. "There will still be the hours of study and prayer and the work of caring for the convent, for all nuns and novices have to help with that. However, in the first three years you have a vacation once a year, when you may go home."

I shook my head. "I'd rather stay here all the time."

Mother Mary Francis smiled again. "How eager you are to forsake the world! But we aren't just being good to you when we insist you leave our company for awhile during these first years. Vacations are to help you prove that you do wish to leave the world for good. The first year you are sent home for a month, the second year for two weeks, and the third year for one week. After that, there will be no more visits home until after your final vows."

In her firm, gentle voice, Mother Mary Francis went on to tell me more of the rules. As a novice I was allowed to write and receive only one letter a month. As a nun I could write as often as I'd care to, with my superior's permission. The cloistered nuns, however, were allowed to write only one letter a year.

"It's a hard life, you see," Mother Mary Francis told me. "But it's a very happy life for women who have a true vocation. You must not get the mistaken idea that the cloistered nuns are better than the sisters who work outside as nurses or teachers. They just have a different gift to offer God. He has a place for every creature, and we are here to help you find your proper place. Perhaps it will not even be in a convent. But although we can advise and help you, only you and God will really know what is going on in your heart.

"No one wants you to stay here if you do not wish it. In fact, we urge deeply that you be sure. To a woman who has a real vocation, the restrictions of a convent are not restrictions at all, but a warm and protecting wall that keeps the distractions of the world away and allows her to give all her time and thoughts to God. The nun's vows of poverty, chastity, and obedience are a natural and loving gift for her to give. They seem no more difficult to her than the earthly bride's promise to take her husband for richer or for poorer, for better or for worse, in sickness and in health."

I felt a strange ache when Mother Mary Francis mentioned the wedding vows. But I ignored my feelings. I knew it was natural for every girl who had once been in love to suffer some regrets. But my new love, my intensified love for God, was all I needed or wanted now. . . .

There was a lot I liked about the life in the convent. My room was a tiny white cell that I shared with another novice. It was very bare, with just the two narrow white cots, a cross that hung on the wall, and two small chests for keeping our simple clothing.

I liked my novice's habit of gray and matching veil with a white band across the forehead. When I took my final vows I would exchange it for the black habit and white calf which I would wear all my life. I also gave up the name of Mary. I was called Novice Perpetua. When I became a nun, I would become Sister Perpetua and discard the name of Mary for always, just as I had given up my worldly clothes.

The novices' work was hard, but I liked that, too. We were awakened at four forty-five in the morning. There was always a great scurry to be ready for five o'clock Mass. After Mass we had a simple breakfast in the dining hall, and then Sister Sophia, the Mistress of Novices, gave us our tasks for the day. Sometimes I was put to work scrubbing and cleaning, at other times I worked in the garden.

At ten o'clock, lessons began. In the classroom we learned more about our religion and studied the lives of the saints. At eleven-thirty we went to the chapel for prayer. Lunch was served at twelve-thirty, then came more work, more study, and more prayers. At four o'clock we were given thirty minutes as a recreational period. If the weather was good, we spent the time in the garden. If it was raining, we gathered in the main hall. This was always a time for conversation, for we weren't supposed to talk much during our daily duties.

There were six other new novices besides myself, and they were like girls anywhere. It didn't take me long to realize that nuns and novices aren't a strange breed of people, but very human, with human faults and virtues. One girl, for instance, Novice Cecilia, was real mischievous. It was hard not to call her Sissy, because that fit her so much better than Cecilia.

Those thirty minutes a day were always filled with giggles and chattering as we tried to crowd all our talking into such a short period of time. Sometimes one of the girls would play the piano while the rest of us sang. They weren't religious songs, either, but were more popular tunes. And once Novice "Sissy" started doing a tap dance, until Sister Sophia heard the racket and came to the door with raised eyebrows and a smile she tried to hide.

After the recreational period there was supper, and then everyone gathered in the chapel for evening devotions. Mother Mary Francis usually gave us a short talk afterward, followed by an hour's study and required religious reading in our room. Then there was another rush as we washed and hurried into our long white cotton nightgowns. Each of us said our night prayers kneeling beside our own bed. Then we just tumbled into those beds, eager to sleep, because we knew the bell rang awfully early in the morning.

But my sleep was all too often filled with dreams of Neal. I'd wake up ashamed, as if even my dreams were an awful sin. How did I dare dream about Neal's kisses when I had vowed to put such thoughts behind me forever? And I had put them behind me. But even so, I was tortured by a feeling of unworthiness, and I worked harder than ever to fit myself into the convent life.

I lost weight and became nervous and tense. Mother Mary Francis seemed to sense something was wrong and she had several talks with me, but I always denied that anything was bothering me. Two novices had been sent home already because she had discovered they didn't have a real vocation, and I was terrified that she might misinterpret my unhappiness.

Toward the end of the first year, the senior novices took their final vows. It was a very solemn occasion, but a happy one, too, for it was what they had been working toward for five long years. The other novices and I sat in a group on one side of the church and watched the ceremony in tense excitement and reverence. Someday we would be standing at the altar rail repeating our vows, just like these girls. Tears swam in my eyes, and the figures of the young new nuns blurred before me. How beautiful they were, each of them dressed in a white wedding gown and long white veil. They were clothed as brides, the brides of Christ, with the Church their home, and the needy of the world their family.

I watched them as they passed back down the aisle, their faces glowing, gold wedding bands gleaming on the fourth fingers of their left hands. In a few moments they would come back into the church dressed in their new nuns' habits, the black robes they would wear for the rest of their lives. They would kneel at the altar rail and take Holy Communion, true brides of heaven, from then on removed from the world.

Tears crept down my cheeks, and my hands clenched over my prayer book. To say those vows and live that life took great courage . . . and great love. Someday Mom would sit in this chapel watching me take my vows. It would be the proudest moment of her life. And it would be a wonderful and happy moment for me, too. I would be transfigured by the peace and joy those girls today must now know. . . .

When the year passed and it was time for me to go home on vacation, I didn't want to leave. I begged Mother Mary Francis to let me stay in the convent.

"Are you afraid the world will attract you too much?" she asked me. "This is not the time for you to hide, my dear. In fact, a convent is never a place to hide."

15

Well, of course I had to go home. When I went in the house in my novice's habit, Mom hugged me excitedly. "Oh, Mary, you look like a nun already!"

But I felt ill at ease. I knew first-year novices were allowed to wear their regular clothes while they were at home, but Mom was delighted with my habit, I felt it would be a shame to change into a dress. Besides, I was more comfortable in it. It made me feel like I was a nun already.

I stayed strictly at home that first week. Father Douglas came to see me once and asked how I liked the convent. When I finished telling him how wonderful it was, he looked at me sharply but didn't ask any questions. He did tell me the church was having a bazaar, and he asked me to come. I didn't give a direct answer, but I knew I wouldn't go. I would have felt strange and uncomfortable. Besides, it would be embarrassing if Neal was there.

Mom said she'd heard Neal was working on a farm in Maple Grove. She saw Mrs. Monroe at church often. Mrs. Monroe was expecting another baby in about a month. Mom clucked her tongue. "It's a pity the way that family has children! This will be the eighth! When I see her so thin and worn out, I just get chills, thinking you might have been in her shoes someday if you'd married Neal."

"It's silly to talk that way, Mom!" I said. "You know children are one of God's greatest gifts."

Mom sniffed. "Well, yes. But it's easy enough for nuns to talk. Oh, I agree having children is wonderful, and I always thanked the Lord for mine. But it's hard, too. Many a time when I was so sick during my pregnancy, I thought of Agnes never having to know that kind of pain. There are the money worries, too. Not that we suffered want, but we had our times of trouble. Often I'd look at you and Matthew and wonder what it would be like to have to worry about more than two."

Her words made me angry. "The Monroe kids have never gone hungry," I snapped. "They get food, shelter, and love."

Mom shrugged. "Of course, but I can imagine the struggle Melvin and Fiona Monroe go through to give them that." She sighed. "Oh, the world's a hard place, Mary. You're lucky to be out of it."

I wanted to say it wasn't that easy to forget worldly things, but her next words made me silent with a crushing hurt.

"Of course Neal never looks ahead enough to realize he's headed straight toward a life that's as hard as his parents' life has been. No, he's crazy for a wife, that one. First you . . . now Molly O'Brien who sells tickets at the movie theater over in Maple Grove."

A stab of pain went through me. I felt hot and then cold. I hoped Mom couldn't see the stinging tears in my eyes. But what had I

16

expected? That he'd stay away from all women and pine for me?

"She's a good girl, as far as I know," Mom went on, "and she's pretty, too . . . that blond hair and those big blue eyes. But just think what she'll look like after eight babies. Huh!" Mom shook her head.

I had to get away from her words. "I'm going to my room." I jumped up. "We . . . we're supposed to read in our book of devotions at least an hour a day."

I tried to read, but the slow tears ran down my cheeks and kept dropping on my page. Oh, I wanted Neal to be happy . . . I was glad that he wasn't brooding over me. . . .

Even later, when I found out from Mom that he'd only taken Molly out a few times and wasn't serious yet, it still hurt. He'd taken up with another girl already. I knew he'd loved me, but he was warmhearted. He needed affection. I understood, but every beat of my heart was a throb of pain.

Mom and I went to early Mass that Sunday. I didn't want to see any of the Monroes. I was sure they wouldn't want to see me, either. But when I looked out of the window Monday morning when I heard someone's knock, I saw Mr. Monroe standing there.

Mom hadn't gotten up yet, so I called down that I'd be there in a minute, and hurried into my clothes. My heart was pounding, my mind whirling with curiosity.

"I'm sure sorry to bother you," he said almost shyly when I opened the door. "But I didn't know where else to turn, Mary, and Fiona said maybe it wouldn't be too much to ask you." He took a deep breath. "Fiona's sick. Dr. Calvin told her Saturday she'd have to stay in bed until the baby comes. She called her sister and asked her to come and stay with her, but she can't come until next week."

My hands twisted together. It was painful just watching Mr. Monroe. He was thin and stooped, but his eyes were bright blue like Neal's. I forced my voice to stay calm.

"Do you want me to go out to the farm and take care of her and the children?"

He nodded, embarrassed. "I know it's awful to ask you when you don't have a lot of time at home. But Fiona reminded me you two had been mighty good friends. And you always liked the kids, too." He cleared his throat. "We've tried to get a hired girl, but you know how scarce they are around here. And . . . well . . . Neal won't be around. He never gets home till weekends, and Fiona's sister should be here by then."

I was cold with shock. I could see how worried Mr. Monroe was, but he just couldn't ask me to do this. How could I spend a week in Neal's home with his family? I shook my head.

"I'm sorry, Mr. Monroe," I said. "I couldn't leave Mom when I have such a short amount of time to spend with her. There must be somebody else you can get. Maybe Father Douglas can help you find someone." I wet my lips with the tip of my tongue. "You understand that I can't help out, don't you?"

Mr. Monroe gave me a sad look. "I guess I didn't have any right to ask you." His thin shoulders slumped even more. "I'll go see Father Douglas."

He went slowly down the steps. I went back to my bedroom, feeling sick and ashamed. Mom came out of her room then, still brushing and braiding her hair. "Who was that, Mary?"

When I told her, she flung out her hands. "Whatever was he thinking of?" Her frown fumed to a pout. "I have you for such a little amount of time, and then you'll be gone from me forever. Of course it's what I want, and I don't begrudge giving you up, but it's only normal to want you with me all the time I can have you. Melvin Monroe's plain selfish not to realize that. After all, the Monroe family's problems aren't your business."

I nodded slowly. Mom was right, but I still felt I'd shirked my duty.

Father Douglas thought I had, too. He came storming in while Mom and I were having breakfast. "Pat Monroe came to me," he said, sitting down across the table from me and refusing Mom's offer of coffee. "Mary, I'm surprised. Of course you don't have much time with your mother, but you've decided to spend your whole life in the service of others. Isn't this a good time to put that self-denial into practice?"

Mom started to say something, but he waved her silent. "Mary, I can read you like a book. You don't want to go out there because they're Neal's family. But no matter what you've decided about your personal life, this is an act of Christian charity."

"Oh, they can find someone else." Mom smiled nervously.

"Don't you think they've tried?" Father Douglas thundered. "It wasn't easy for them to ask Mary to go out there, either." He banged his fist on the table. "Fiona Monroe is sick! Do you want her to risk losing her unborn child and perhaps her life by trying to do all that work now?"

My cheeks burned with shame for myself. I stood up. "I . . . I'm sorry, Father Douglas. Of course I'll go."

"Mary!" Mom cried.

"I have to go, Mom," I told her, then went to my room to pack a bag. I couldn't let Mrs. Monroe down in her great time of need. Her life was more important than Mom's wishes.

The shabby little farmhouse looked just as I'd remembered it. Children's feet had worn the yard free of grass. Toys were scattered everywhere. Yet when Father Douglas's car stopped, I forgot the dingy first impression, because the Monroe children who ran to meet us were scrubbed and healthy in spite of patched jeans and faded dresses.

"Mary! Mary!" they cried, and thin, strong little arms hugged me tightly. I bent over them, loving every one. Kaitlyn, thirteen and serious; Barry, eleven, a smaller Neal with twinkling blue eyes; Garret, ten, freckle faced and snub nosed; Megan, a seven-year-old charmer with black velvety curls and eyes like blue stars; Tara, a chubby four-year-old; and Allan, the two-year-old baby of the bunch.

"I'm so glad you came," Kaitlyn said with a deep sigh of relief, and I knew how heavy the burden of taking care of the family must have rested on her thin little shoulders. "Dad said you couldn't come, but I just knew you would."

"Kaitlyn prayed for you to come," Garret piped up.

Megan's eyes were round as she looked at my severe novice's habit, so different from the dresses I had always worn. "That's a funny dress," she said.

"That's her church dress," Garret cut in, important with knowledge. "She's a nun now. That's why she can't marry Neal."

My face felt on fire. Father Douglas placed his hand on my shoulder. "Mary isn't a nun yet," he explained. "She's just learning how to be one." He gave me a warm smile. "I have to get back to town now. If you need me, call, but I know this gang will help you. Won't you, kids?"

"Sure, Father!" they chorused.

As soon as Father Douglas's car left, the children scattered in all directions, back to their various duties. Kaitlyn took me into the house. "Mother's been so sick," she said as she opened the door. "I've been awfully worried."

Mrs. Monroe was on an old cot in the kitchen. I was shocked by her drawn, paper-white face, her thin arms, looking so strange folded over the great bulk of her body. But she greeted me with her usual cheerful smile. "If it isn't my Mary," she said, as warmly as if I was her own daughter. She gripped my hand in her thin one. "Bless you, darling. It's almost worth being sick to get to see your pretty face." She turned to Kaitlyn. "Honey, run upstairs and make the beds like a good girl. Mary's going to fix us both a cup of tea, and we're going to have a nice visit, just like old times."

"I didn't come to be treated like company," I said when I had the kettle boiling and the cups set out.

Mrs. Monroe laughed. "There's plenty to be done, and I know you'll do it. But now we'll relax a minute and sort of pull ourselves together, as my mother used to say." She smiled at me as she sipped her tea. "Having a baby brings all sorts of nice things you don't expect. For instance, it brought you here to me now."

19

I shook my head. "But you shouldn't be having this baby," I blurted. "When you were pregnant with Allan, Dr. Calvin said—"

Mrs. Monroe waved her hand. "Lord love that doctor! He's a good man, but he says a lot of things." She laughed a little. "Sure, he told me having this baby might be dangerous and that at my age I shouldn't have become pregnant at all." She gave me a confident smile. "I told him that was in God's hands. I've never planned when or when not to have babies, and I'm not going to start now."

Her faith, trust, and happiness were so deep and devout that I was surprised. I had always felt that only nuns could dedicate themselves to God's will that fully. But here was Mrs. Monroe with her loving husband and her house full of noisy, happy kids, being just as dedicated to God in her own way as any nun in a cloister. It made me feel all mixed up.

And in the next few days I felt even more mixed up, especially when I took care of the children. When I was feeding or bathing or holding one of the little ones in my lap, I felt such a lovely warmth, almost a sacred feeling . . . just as I was supposed to feel when I was saying my prayers in the convent. But in the convent I had never felt quite that way.

There was a lot of work to do. It rained almost all of that week and the younger children were in the house all the time. There were three large meals a day to be cooked, cleaning to do, and never-ending laundry. Mrs. Monroe tried to help me, but it seemed she got weaker every day. She was still cheerful and just as excited over the new baby as if it were her first one, but I worried about her.

Dr. Calvin came out once and examined her. "You seem to be a little better now that Mary's taking over, Fiona. But I suggest you go to the hospital anyway. If this rain keeps up, it might be hard to get you into town in a hurry. The roads are bad now, and I've never seen the river so high."

Mrs. Monroe shook her head. "No. An extra big hospital bill would just put too heavy a burden on my poor husband's shoulders."

The doctor couldn't change her mind, either. But after he left, I looked at her sweetly stubborn face and wondered if just the bill was keeping her at home. Maybe she didn't want to go to the hospital yet because she wanted to be near to talk to me.

Mrs. Monroe had been a bit against my entering the convent because, she said frankly, she didn't think that was the place for me. Now, watching me with the children, she'd dropped hints about what a natural born mother I seemed to be. I admit it bothered me, and finally I couldn't stand it any longer. One rainy afternoon when the children were having naps, she started another of her little talks, and I knew that was the time to put a stop to them.

20

I sat down by the cot and took her hands in mine. "Mrs. Monroe," I said as firmly as I could, "I know you mean well, but I've made my choice. I'm going to be a nun. If I'm so good with children, maybe my Mother Superior will decide I should work in the school. That way I'll be doing what I'm supposed to do."

Mrs. Monroe was equally firm. "For some girls that would be the right answer. For you, no. I've watched you, Mary." She shook her head. "I know you think I'm just pleading Neal's cause." I winced when she said that, and she nodded. "Yes, Neal. I've been careful not to mention his name, but now I've got to. In spite of the girl he's been dating, it's you he loves . . . and you he's always loved."

A sharp, sweet pain shot through me. "Oh, please don't say that!" I cried.

"I have to." She took a deep breath. "Mary, I'd never deny a daughter of mine the right to go into a convent if she really wanted it. But I feel a girl can be just as dedicated to the Lord if she marries and raises children of her own. Somewhere along the way you've forgotten that marriage itself is a sacrament of the Church." Her eyes searched my face. "I'm convinced you still love Neal, and for you to enter a convent with that love still in your heart would not be what the Lord wants. It would hurt Neal and you, too, and it would deny life to the children that perhaps the Lord wants you to have."

I couldn't keep the tears back any longer. I covered my face with my hands. "I've made my choice." I sobbed. "You can't change my mind. And you've got to stop talking like this or I'll have to leave you."

"All right. I'll say no more," Mrs. Monroe promised. But the look on her face told me my tears had done nothing except make her even more certain that I loved Neal and shouldn't enter a convent at all.

The next day it was really raining. I hadn't slept well the night before, and I looked as tired and miserable as I felt. It was one of Mrs. Monroe's bad days, too. She could hardly move from the cot. The children were tired of the week of rain, and at the breakfast table they were loud and unruly. I sighed as I tried to cope with them. I just didn't see how I was going to manage.

Mr. Monroe noticed. "I'll take this bunch of wild ones with me today," he said. "I promised Mr. Thorton, our neighbor to the south, that I'd help him mend some harnesses. The Thortons have three kids of their own, and the whole bunch can play in their attic."

I smiled. "That sounds like quite a load for Mrs. Thorton to take."

Kaitlyn laughed. "Oh, she likes to have us. I'll stay here if you'd rather . . . only she's been promising to teach me to make nut bread, and Mother said she'd like some." There was a droop to her mouth.

"Oh, run along." I smiled. "The nut bread can be your project for

21

supper tonight while I catch up on the laundry."

When they were all gone, the house seemed strangely quiet. Mrs. Monroe took a nap while I cleaned up the breakfast dishes. The need to get out of the stuffy house was strong within me, too. I decided to go to the barn and look for hens' nests. Mrs. Monroe was still sleeping. I could be back before she needed anything.

It was fun poking around in the fragrant hay. Finding the nests was like a treasure hunt. But no matter how I searched, I could only find a few eggs, and I knew there should be more than that. I was sure the big speckled hen had been coming in there every day to lay her eggs.

I was bending over a manger; my hands busy rustling through the hay, when a deep voice said, "Try looking under the ladder. That's where I always found the best hens' nests."

I wheeled around, a sudden wild pulse beating in my throat. Neal stood there, his face flushed, his hair plastered to his head from the rain. We looked at each other . . . just looked. Suddenly I grabbed my veil, which I'd taken off and hung over the edge of the manger because it was damp. I couldn't wait to throw it over my head, as if it were a kind of armor I could hide behind. Neal went pale when he saw the veil. For the first time he seemed to notice I wore the severe high-necked habit, with the skirt that came almost to my shoes and the black rosary clasped at my belt.

"You look like a nun," he whispered. "Oh, Mary . . . have I really lost you?"

I was trembling so I could hardly stand. "I'm going to be a nun. You've lost me. You should know that."

"But you're not a nun yet!" he cried.

"Don't think that way," I begged, my voice shaking. "Don't try to get me mixed up and unhappy. If I'd guessed you were going to come here . . . if I'd thought I had to see you . . . oh, why did you?"

"You won't like this, Mary," he said. "Mother had Dad call me up this morning and told me you were here. They knew I'd waste no time getting over here."

"How dare they?" I gasped.

"Because they know we love each other, Mary. And we do, darling . . . you know we do. Think back, Mary. Remember how it always was with us. . . ." His deep voice went on and on, forcing me to remember moments that I'd spent months trying to forget. I moaned and half turned away from him. It seemed I'd been trapped forever in the dimness of that barn with the sweet smell of hay around me and the rain pouring down outside . . . a gray curtain that cut me off from Mom and the convent and all the things I clung to with such desperate determination.

22

"Look at me, Mary," Neal begged. "Listen to me. Do you understand what a great mistake you're making when you think our love is less wonderful than it is? No matter what you say, you belong to me." His voice quavered a little. "That doesn't mean you can belong to God, darling. We're both God's children. They say marriages are made in heaven. Who are you to decide this marriage isn't the will of Heaven?"

Slowly I turned to face him. We stared at each other in a kind of desperate fear. "Oh, Mary!" he burst out. "You're acting as if you're a nun already, one who's taken her final vows. But you haven't! You're still free. I have every right to try to win you back!"

Suddenly he pulled me into his arms and kissed me. For a second, my lips responded with a frantic hunger. This was Neal, and we'd been apart too long. But then my shocked mind screamed the truth. I'm a novice! I belong in a convent. The kiss, so filled with love, seemed like a terrible sacrilege. I struggled with him frantically while screams tore from my throat. Then I broke free and ran to the door of the barn.

But I stopped there in sudden horror. Mrs. Monroe was stumbling down the long flight of back steps. Oh, dear Lord, she must have heard my screams and come to see what was the matter!

I didn't even have time to call to her, everything happened so quickly. She lurched with weakness as she came down the wet steps. The wind was blowing very hard, and it tangled her long cotton robe about her feet. She stumbled, and before either Neal or I could reach her, she pitched forward and fell full length onto the rocky path. There she lay, quiet and grotesquely sprawled.

"Mother of Mercy, save us now!" I prayed as I raced toward her, but Neal got there first. By the time I got there, he had his mother scooped up in his arms.

We got her back to her bedroom, and I rushed for dry clothes for her while Neal wrapped her in a blanket. She tried to smile at us. "No bones broken," she whispered. "I just got shaken up some. It's my own fault. I . . . I guess I was dreaming, I thought I heard somebody scream. The next thing I knew, I was out on those stairs, and then— bang!" Her laughter was a wisp of sound.

I turned away, tears pouring down my cheeks. What a fool I'd been! Neal didn't mean any harm when he kissed me. But no, I had to act like I was too holy to touch! And Mrs. Monroe had paid for my foolishness. "Dear God, let her be all right," I prayed under my breath. But the prayer wasn't out of my mind when her hands clenched on the covers.

"Mrs. Monroe, the fall . . . did it hurt you?" I bent over her.

Her lips curved faintly. "Darling, we can't blame all this on my tumble," she whispered. "That twinge I got just now wasn't bruises . . . it was the baby. Oh, I know that kind of pain well enough." Her breath drew in sharply. "Neal, your father had better get the doctor. We'll be needing him pretty soon, I think."

I followed Neal into the other room. His face was white, and I know mine must have been, too. "Why get the doctor?" I said. "Shouldn't we drive her right to the hospital?"

Neal shook his head. "There's too much chance in this rain that the car might get stuck or slide into a ditch someplace. Mother has sense enough to know that. The baby will have to be born right here at home." My panic must have showed, for his voice softened. "Mother will be okay for a little while yet, I think. Dad and I'll get Dr. Calvin and come back just as soon as we can."

I was terrified when I was left alone with Mrs. Monroe. Never in my life had I been so close to life and death. I stood there shaken and cold for a long time before I could get up the nerve to go back into Mrs. Monroe's room.

I'm ashamed to admit it, but of the two of us, Mrs. Monroe was the calm one. In a low, even voice, she told me what to get ready for the doctor . . . the things to sterilize in a pan of alcohol, the things to sterilize in boiling water, the layers of newspapers, the clean old sheets . . . all of it. I hurried back and forth, finding things. The most unreal part of all was getting the clothes basket and lining it with blankets. A baby would soon be placed in it! Panic touched me again, and once more I whispered some prayers to myself. Now I knew what praying was really like. You had to pray at a time like that.

I prayed for Mrs. Monroe, the baby's safety, and for myself to remain calm so I would be able to do what I had to do. And, oh, how I prayed for the doctor to come! My prayers got more and more frantic, for even my inexperienced eyes told me it wouldn't be long. Mrs. Monroe couldn't give me directions any longer. She twisted back and forth on the bed when a labor pain hit her. Her teeth would clamp grimly down on her lower lip, but even so, she moaned once, deep and hurting. Between pains she lay like she was dead, limp and gray faced. I couldn't stand to see her suffer that way. I wanted to leave the room, but I didn't dare. The doctor just had to get here soon.

Then I heard steps on the porch. I ran to the door. But it wasn't the doctor who stood there . . . it was Neal. His face was white with worry, his clothes soaking wet. He stumbled to a chair.

"Dad's gone after the doctor," he gasped. "But the bridge has collapsed over the river. I had just crossed it, coming back from the Thorton farm, when it happened. For a minute I thought I was going down, too. If I'd been a second slower—" He shuddered, then took a deep breath and looked at me. "Mary, do you know what this means? There's no way the doctor can reach us now. We're going to have to deliver the baby by ourselves."

24

I stared at him. Then I found my voice, and when I spoke, new courage flowed into me. It seemed that at last all my prayers returned to give me strength. "Yes, Neal." I moistened my dry lips. "There's nothing else we can do."

We went into Mrs. Monroe's bedroom and told her what had happened. She must have seen that we were frantic with worry, and she tried to smile. Then another pain caught her, and she twisted in an agony that shocked us both. When it had passed, she whispered, "It isn't always this bad. In fact, after the baby's born you forget it was bad at all."

For almost an hour longer we worked . . . Neal and I. We no longer thought of ourselves, of how afraid we were. I still prayed, but the prayers were whispered bits of words in my mind. Mother of All Mothers . . . Mary help us now. You who had your baby alone . . . alone in a stable with no doctor to help you . . . guide my hands. Show me what to do.

And my prayer was answered. For a moment I thought we were losing Mrs. Monroe, that she was slipping from us into the shadows and taking her unborn child with her. Then suddenly it was all over. The baby, a strong, wiggling bundle, was in my hands. It cried, and Mrs. Monroe made a sound halfway between a moan and a laugh. She opened her eyes and they were full of concern.

"It's a girl," I whispered. "She's fine, I think."

"Good." Mrs. Monroe's lips barely formed the words. "I . . . I knew she would be."

And strangely, I knew Mrs. Monroe had been sure her child would be all right. I wanted to drop to my knees and sob out my gratitude, but I didn't have time. There was still so much to do.

It was three hours later when Dr. Calvin got there. He'd had to find a boat to take him across the river, and everybody had told him he was risking his life to chance crossing the swollen, angry water with its mass of swirling debris.

But he didn't act as if he'd been brave. As far as he was concerned, it had been the only thing he could do. But when he got to the house, he'd found that another Great Physician had been on duty, for surely only God Himself had saved Mrs. Monroe and taught me to do the right thing at the right time.

It seemed a lifetime later, but it was only that evening when the house was quiet at last that Neal and I could be alone. We sat by the fire and talked in low voices. Mr. Monroe was with his wife. The new baby slept in her basket, which I'd placed on the kitchen cot so I could keep an eye on her. She was a darling baby. Neal went over and pulled the blankets away from her face so he could look at his new sister.

"She's a doll," he whispered. He turned to me. "Mother told me

25

she was going to name her Mary because you saved her life."

I shook my head. "Not just me. I was praying awfully hard for the help of the Virgin, Neal. I'd like the baby to be named Mary for her, not me."

Neal gave me a strange look. "You really are awfully devout, aren't you? It's not just something you're putting on to please your mother." His face was quiet and resigned. "I guess you do belong in a convent after all."

I looked up at him. "I don't know how devout I am, Neal. I . . . I make lots of mistakes, but I guess almost everybody does. But there's one thing I'm sure of now, and I know I won't make a mistake about that any longer." I took a deep breath. "Neal, when the baby was born . . . when I held her in my arms and heard her cry . . . well, I knew I'd seen a real miracle . . . a miracle of life." My words stumbled awkwardly. "I . . . I guess I knew the truth then. I can never be a nun. You see, I want to be a mother very much."

Neal stared at me, and then he put his hands on my shoulders. I knew he wanted to take me in his arms, but I drew back. The time wasn't right for that yet. I had to make him understand.

"First, before I promise to be your wife, I've got to free myself of old promises," I said. "I'm still a novice. I have to make a clean break first and tell my Mother Superior. I know she'll understand."

Neal's eyes held both a bleak fear and new hope. "You have to go back to the convent?"

I nodded. "Yes. But I'll be back, Neal. Oh, I'll be back!"

I told Mrs. Monroe what I'd decided, but I didn't tell Mom. I couldn't, not yet. I knew there'd be scenes and hysterics, and I couldn't face them until I had the approval of Mother Mary Francis. And in spite of my new, brave resolutions, I was still scared when I stood in her office and told her that I was sure that the life of a nun was not for me.

But I had no reason to be afraid. Mother Mary Francis understood, just as I'd told Neal she would. "It won't be easy to go back into the world," she reminded me. "Lots of people will forget that a novice has spent that time in the novitiate to find out if she is suited for convent life of not. Many of them will feel you're a quitter, a coward. Others will feel that you have actually broken sacred vows." Her cool, quiet eyes looked deep into mine. "Many will laugh at you, actually seem to despise you," she told me. "But be brave, my child. You have chosen the way that is right for you. You will be doing God's will. Remember that, no matter what anyone says."

Mother Mary Francis was right. If I had broken a nun's final vows, my mother wouldn't have acted more shocked and ashamed. Many of our neighbors were the same. They whispered and gossiped until I actually felt an outcast with many who had been my friends. But of course it was worse to face Mom. "Why, Mary?" she kept saying brokenly. "Why? Why?"

Well, she understood why, and so did everyone else . . . or at least they thought they did . . . when less than a month after I'd left the convent I announced my engagement to Neal. Mom went almost wild then and said many bitter things that will always leave scars on my heart.

"It's only a carnal, wicked desire that caused you to leave the convent," she screamed when Neal and I stood before her. "Matthew was my true son, but you're no longer my daughter!" She clenched her fists at her sides. "Leave my house! Leave it now. I'll not have a wicked, ungrateful girl like you under my roof another night!"

She meant it, too. Alone and struggling with sobs, I packed my clothes while Neal waited by the car. When I came out, Mom had shut herself in her room. She wouldn't even say good-bye.

It nearly broke my heart to see my mother suffer like that. The only thing that kept me from feeling guilty was the sure knowledge that I was doing what was right . . . the thing that God wanted me to do. Neal took me to his own home, and Mr. and Mrs. Monroe took me in as if I was their daughter to love and comfort.

The next day Father Douglas came out to see me. He told me he'd tried to reason with my mother but she wouldn't listen to him. "You are right, though, Mary," he said. "You've been brave and strong. Don't weaken now. Sooner or later I'm sure your mother will see that you were right."

I didn't weaken. Three weeks later Neal and I were married. We had a very quiet wedding. Only the Monroes and some of their close friends were there. My mother didn't come. I wore a simple white dress and a white veil that Mrs. Monroe had made. As I whispered my sacred vows my eyes filled with tears. They were bittersweet tears . . . half happiness because I was Neal's wife at last, half sorrow because my mother wasn't there to witness the greatest moment of my life. I'd heard that she was telling everyone that she had two dead children, because I was dead to her as well. Only she said Matthew had died in honor and her daughter had died in shame.

Neal and I didn't have a honeymoon . . . or at least we didn't go away on a honeymoon. There was a little fishing cabin on the land that Neal's boss owned. He let us fix it up as a home. It was a shabby little place, but after Mrs. Monroe and I had scrubbed it and put up buttercup-yellow chintz curtains, and after Neal had painted the old furniture a silky forest-green . . . well, it seemed like a palace to me. That's where we spent our wedding night, the most beautiful night of my life. The river murmured outside our bedroom windows. There was a great silver-disc moon to give light to our little room, and Neal's arms around me, Neal's lips on mine, were a benediction and a fulfillment. Our love was filled with joy, not shame, and the sharing of it as man and wife was a sacrament, created by the love that God had meant us to have for each other.

In the weeks that followed I was very happy in my little home with Neal, but my mother's hard feelings were a thorn in my heart. It was even worse when I became pregnant a few months after our marriage. I had an easy pregnancy, but I was so unhappy about the way Mom still refused to have anything to do with me. I wanted her with me then, as every girl wants her mother at a time like that. Mrs. Monroe did all she could. She even went to see my mother, but Mom slammed the door in her face. Mrs. Monroe tried to comfort me, and Neal was angry because I'd been hurt so badly.

"Forget your mother, darling," he said. "Forget her like she's forgotten you." But as much as Neal loved me, he still couldn't understand. No daughter could put her mother out of her heart just like that.

My baby was born in the summer. I went to the hospital, and thanks to Dr. Calvin's good care, I knew none of the agony that Mrs. Monroe had gone through. Or maybe, as she said, I just forgot it once I saw my beautiful little daughter. And when I held her in my arms, it seemed worth any suffering or any sadness. But, oh, how I wanted her grandmother to see and love her, too.

We named her Fiona, after Mrs. Monroe, but I held a secret wish in my heart that I could have named her after my own mother. Only I didn't dare, because when Father Douglas went to give Mom the news that she had a granddaughter, Mom said she couldn't have a granddaughter because she had no daughter or son. Her children were dead.

Father Douglas reported this sadly. "You can't be angry with the poor woman," he said. "She is very, very wrong, but she is almost sick with her own unhappiness."

When the baby was three weeks old, we took her to the church to be baptized with her official name of Fiona Marie. It was a great and wonderful day for all the Monroes and most especially for me. I dressed little Fiona carefully in the hand-sewn dress I had made, and put her crispy white bonnet on her. But my eyes misted with tears. Something was missing. It was Mom . . . had I been wrong all along? I thought of Mom in her dull, sad house, and the tears spilled over or my cheeks. No, I knew I'd done the right thing. Fiona Marie, a soft warm bundle in my arms, was the answer to that. But I had been brought up to honor my father and my mother, and when I cuddled my baby close to me I realized the full measure of Mom's unhappiness.

It was the middle of the afternoon when we gathered at the

church. The Monroes were all clustered around, their faces bright with happiness. But as Father Douglas took the baby in his arms, he must have seen the misery on my own face. He hesitated.

"You've been hurt enough, Mary," he said at last. "But we must make this one last try to get your mother to see reason. Do you feel well enough to come to your mother's house with me, now?"

Neal's arm tightened around my shoulders. He started to protest, but Mrs. Monroe put her hand on his. "I know how Mary feels," she said. "A mother is a mother . . . and no one should know better than me. We've got to try again."

I nodded, leaning against Neal. "Oh, please. . . ." My voice trailed off.

Neal looked down at me and sighed. "Okay, Mary. Anything you want." But his eyes were still full of anger, and I knew he was bewildered, because no matter how much I got hurt, I'd keep sticking my neck out. Anything to make up with Mom. Well, maybe a man couldn't understand that. But Neal loved me, and I knew he'd comfort me if my heart got torn open once more.

We walked the long block and a half to Mom's house, and I guess we were a strange-looking group. Neal held my hand tightly. Mr. and Mrs. Monroe came along behind us, and in front Father Douglas walked briskly, his black cassock flapping about his ankles, Fiona Marie held firmly in his arms.

When we came to our little house, he walked up and rang the doorbell. He had to ring twice before Mom came to the door. When she opened it, her face turned white and she tried to slam the door in his face, but Father Douglas had his foot wedged in to keep it open. He held up Fiona Marie. "Woman," he thundered at Mom, "this child's parents have been united in the sacrament of holy matrimony. This afternoon this child, born of a union blessed by God, is to receive the sacrament of baptism. In your selfish, sinful pride are you going to deny a baby and a marriage that God and the Church accept?"

Mom moved back a little. She stared down at the child as if she expected to see a monster. Fiona Marie yawned broadly, her baby face crinkling up. "She . . . she looks a little like Matthew did when he was a baby," she whispered, almost to herself. No one said a word. Actually, Fiona Marie didn't look a bit like Matthew . . . no more than any baby looks like other babies.

There was a moment of silence. Then Mom began to cry . . . great, heartbroken sobs. But they were tears of healing, and Father Douglas began to smile.

"Come on," he said gently. "We're late now. But we had to come and get you, because you know a baby's grandmother should be at the baptism."

29

That day Mom started to accept my marriage at last. Oh, her resentment didn't end right away. It took months and years for us to become close again. But we are close now, perhaps more than we have ever been before, because Mom adores her grandchildren so much.

Neal and I have been married seven years, and there are four of those grandchildren. We still don't have our own land, and living on a farm as hired help isn't easy. But I know I've found my proper vocation. And when I look at Neal, my heart warms as it warmed when I was a bride, and my heart and soul know again the truth of the words that Father Douglas spoke at our marriage service: "What, therefore, God hath joined together, let no man put asunder."

THE END

# THE STORM THAT
# WAS MY LIFE

When I was fifteen, my mother died, and it was like the end of the world. She was all I really had . . . the one person who made life bearable and fun, even in the most desperate hours of our lives. Sure, I had a father. He came and went, boasting of big dreams that never materialized, making promises he would never keep. Still, Mother would make excuses and say he was trying, trying to better our lives.

Mother was a cleaning lady, working in motels, offices, and banks. On Saturday afternoons when she did the big bank on Main Street, she'd go down to the diner and bring home a big dinner in one of those carryout cartons. It was her treat to us.

But one Saturday she didn't come home.

I remember Dad came strolling in through the kitchen door, asking me, "Abby, is your mother home yet?" Then, looking in the other room, calling out, "Vicky? Vicky, where are you?"

He'd driven by the diner before coming home, but hadn't seen her anywhere. Suddenly, his face went chalk white, and he leaned against the wall and swallowed hard. "There was an accident on the corner . . . I noticed it on my way home. No one called, did they, Abby?"

I remember a sinking feeling went through me then. I looked around the empty, quiet living room and at the dining room table where I had just placed a freshly ironed tablecloth and a vase of flowers from Mother's garden. The rooms were spotless, everything polished and sparkling. It was my gift to her, and how she'd praise me for the work I'd done!

I started to cry because I knew intuitively what had happened. I knew before Calvin Hobbs, the police chief, stood in the back doorway, fumbling with his hat as he glanced at Dad and me and sort of whispered out the news.

Mother's sister, Faye, came down from Washburn where she lived. She came with two big suitcases and told Dad that she would stay till things settled down. I would hear them at night as I lay in bed weeping for my mother, hear Faye telling Dad that he'd have to be more responsible now that Vicky was gone . . . that he'd have to find someone to come in and take care of the house until I was older. Dad would just cry and tell Faye he couldn't be bothered with that now, and how could he get on without his Vicky?

Well, Faye finally went to the county social service agency

before returning to Washburn, and she arranged for a woman to come in three days a week, on Mondays, Wednesdays, and Fridays. Her name was Diana and she would take care of the laundry and the shopping and help me with a lot of the cooking.

Dad carried on something terrible. After Faye left he was crying all the time, saying he didn't know how he could get along without Mother's cleaning money. And he was lonesome, he said.

Didn't I know that? That Mother was always there for him, that he could depend on her and now he had no one? Well, I had no one, either, but he never thought about that.

Mother wasn't dead six months when Dad came home with Jean Galen and told me that they were getting married. Jean was a big woman, loud and brash, the complete opposite of mother. But she also owned Galen Dry Cleaners and Laundry and the big house behind it. I guess Jean was what Dad needed. She had a business head and Dad could lean on her.

They went away and got married and Diana stayed with me the week they were gone. The day they returned, our house went up for sale and we moved into Jean's house. I had one of the rooms upstairs and Dad and Jean stayed downstairs.

Jean assured me that we'd get along just fine. I could work at the store and earn some spending money . . . and I could clean house just like I'd done at home.

Dad was completely happy. He had a new car, nice clothes, and he always had money in his billfold. And now Jean had someone to take her out to dinner and to do things with. It was a good arrangement for them both.

But me . . . I was lonely. I had no one but Nikki Hagan, who'd been my friend since first grade. Nikki lived in a small house with her mom and dad and ten brothers and sisters. She was never lonely like I was, but she was as alone. We were outcasts in school, down on the bottom rung of the social ladder. But we had dreams. That's what we had to look forward to . . . dreams without reality, just pictures in our minds of the good days ahead: a husband, a real home, maybe clothes and jewelry, and anything we'd want to eat.

I was a senior when Seth Barton came in the store and applied for a job delivering laundry. There'd been an ad for it in our local paper. I remember that it was late December, snowy and cold. He came in, stomping his feet and looking sort of apologetic because of the wet floor. His eyes met mine, steady and friendly.

"Sorry about the mess," he said. "I guess it doesn't make a good impression when I'm looking for a job."

My face felt warm. I shrugged. "It's okay. The floor will get a lot wetter than this before the winter is over."

Seth looked around, then leaned toward me and asked, "How is it working here?"

"Okay, I guess," I said. "The owner is married to my dad. But she's all right. No fooling around, though. Do your job, that's all she expects."

"I bet she had a lot of people apply for this job," Seth said.

Before I could say anything more to him, Jean came in, looking at me. "You'd better get in the back and finish loading the truck, Abigail," she said loudly.

Well, I always did what Jean said, but I managed to come up front enough to hear her tell Seth that she had a lot of applications to consider, and then I heard him almost begging for the job. His voice trembled and caught in his throat. "My mom's alone and she isn't well. She needs me. You wouldn't be sorry, I promise. I'd work hard for you. . . ."

Jean was opening and shutting the drawers to her desk, making a lot of racket like she did when she was nerved up about something. I saw her stare long and hard at him, and then heard her say reluctantly, "Well, I'll give you a chance. But if you goof up . . . and I don't care what sob story you have . . . you'll be out!"

Seth was thanking her and standing in the open doorway, waiting while she told him to be there at five-thirty Monday morning to start out on the route with Elmer Davies, who was retiring. Elmer was getting too old to travel on winter roads, too old to put in the long days that Jean demanded from her employees.

I felt warm inside just knowing she'd hired Seth. I don't know why really, except that I thought he was cute and nice, not really cocky like most of the fellows I knew.

I was up at six o'clock Monday morning. I made my bed and went down to fix breakfast. Jean expected a big breakfast ready and waiting for her when she got up, and it was one of my duties to get the bacon and eggs and hash browns ready. Dad was grumbling because the morning paper was wet, and Jean was staring out the window with a frown because the snow was coming down in thick, heavy flakes.

She glanced at Dad. "I wonder if I made a mistake, hiring that young kid to take over Elmer's route," she said. "Maybe I should have given the job to someone more experienced and not messed around with him."

Dad looked at her absently, mumbling, "Give him a chance. If he doesn't work out, let him go."

That's how it was. Jean always talking to Dad, my dad always agreeing with her, and no one saying anything to me. I was like hired help, not family.

As I was doing the dishes, Jean reminded me that the sweaters had to be packed that morning and ready to go on the route. The high school sent all their letter sweaters over for winter cleaning and they had to go out that morning. I'd forgotten. I glanced at the clock, knowing I'd have to rush to get everything done and get to school on time.

I practically ran to the shop, tearing in the back door, grabbing all the cellophane bags, and placing them on the corner table so when Betty Lynn, the woman who worked the press, brought the sweaters I could package them. It was hot and steamy in the corner and I felt the perspiration trickling down my back. I didn't see or hear Seth until he said hello. Then I turned around and he was grinning at me, looking friendly.

"I see being one of the family doesn't give you any privileges," Seth said.

I shrugged, feeling warmer, aware of my red face and sweaty hair. "No, it doesn't. But then, I'm not really family," I told him.

Just then Jean came stomping in the room from out front. "Listen, we don't have time for dillydallying around," she warned. "Abigail, do you have the sweaters ready to go? This is a business, not a meeting place for singles."

I went back to bagging sweaters and Seth followed behind Elmer to the delivery van. I heard Jean call after him, "If you think you're going to be flirting around and working for me, you won't last! I can afford to be fussy with my help."

After the truck pulled away, Jean came over and put a firm hand on my shoulder.

"There's something I don't like about that new fellow," she said. "You watch out he doesn't try any funny business with you!"

The words hurt my pride. Seth wanted to be a friend . . . just a friend. Why couldn't Jean see that?

Overhearing Jean, Wade Jenkins peeked around the laundry tub to leer at me. "Any guy would like to make out with Abby," he said. "She's a beauty, just like her mother was."

It was the wrong thing to say to Jean. We never talked about my mother . . . ever. Jean was jealous, Dad said, and he warned me that it was best for all of us if we just kept our memories to ourselves. After all, we had it pretty good living under Jean's roof.

After that incident, Jean didn't like me. She really didn't. I felt her eyes watching me during quiet times in the evening or even at work. It was like I had become the enemy, a threatening reminder of things she wanted Dad to forget.

I told Nikki all about Seth, what little there was to tell, and she said that maybe sometime he'd ask me out. But I knew he would be afraid to because of Jean. Still, it wasn't all that long before I would graduate, and then maybe I could get a place of my own. Maybe Nikki and I could be roommates. We planned to work at the new factory a few miles out of town. In fact, we had already put our applications in through the employment program at the high school.

Nearly two months passed before I finally got to go out with Seth. Jean's sister in Valley City got sick and Dad had to drive her there. Seth came around when we were loading the van the day they left and quietly asked me if I'd go along with him on his route. My heart pounded with excitement as I glanced around. There was Wade, peering from behind one of the pressers, listening.

"I can't," I whispered.

Seth turned his back so Wade couldn't see him and whispered back, "Listen, I'll make the in-town deliveries . . . that'll take a good two hours. Then I'll swing down by the railroad tracks like always. You know that big billboard on the corner? I have to make a stop right before tracks, and you can just run out, hop in the truck, and keep your head down until we're out of town. Then we'll be home free."

My mind whirled. "Okay," I managed to say. Then I turned around and smiled innocently at Wade before going back to my packing.

Wade edged over to my table. "He tried to make out, didn't he? Like I told Jean, he's a wild one, Seth is. I was asking around. He's been in trouble before. Over in Mandan, he ran with some of those bikers, real wild types."

Betty Lynn usually just listened to everyone without saying a word, but this time she stared at Wade with a look of contempt in her eyes. "Shut up, Wade. Just shut up," she ordered.

Betty was the oldest employee at Galen Dry Cleaners, and she carried a lot of weight with Jean. One word from Betty and you could be out, no matter who you were.

Well I got my work done and sort of loitered around, drinking a soda so I wouldn't look suspicious. I helped Betty with some of the cleanup, then went home and changed my clothes. I combed my hair and dabbed on some lipstick and eye shadow. Jean never let me wear makeup, but I bought some anyway, and I carried it in my purse so when I left the house I could put it on.

Once I was off of Main Street, I ran down the alleys to the railroad tracks and sat behind the thick bushes that grew around the billboard. There weren't too many cars on the road and my heart started to pound wildly when I saw not Seth, but Wade Jenkins come around the corner in his bright blue car. He was driving slow, looking all around. I lay flat on the ground and never moved. Finally he drove out of sight.

I sat up, brushed myself off, and waited. Then the van came, edging to a stop at the tracks. I ran out. Seth had the door open when

35

I got there and I hopped in, closed it, and lay down like he'd said.

We drove way into the country before I sat up. Seth looked at me, and then his hand touched my arm gently. "I was afraid you wouldn't come. Really afraid," he said.

I felt excited, thrilled. "Why? Why'd you think I wouldn't come?"

Seth shrugged. "Why should you? I'm just a bum, a nobody."

I leaned back against the seat, finally relaxing. I watched the countryside pass by as Seth slowed down, feeling needed and wanted for the first time since Mother died.

"You're not a bum, Seth. You're somebody nice," I told him. "Don't put yourself down. My mother always said a person should have respect for himself or no one else ever would."

Seth seemed to relax, too. He was looking at me, smiling. "Your mother sounds like she was a good person. Like you, Abby."

After that, the two of us couldn't quit talking. By the time we were done with the route, we practically knew each other's life history. I told Seth all about my mom, about my dad marrying Jean, and how I wasn't part of their family. I was just part of Dad's past, an obligation he'd rather not have.

Seth told me about his father, a musician who'd gotten into drugs, liquor, and women. He had beaten Seth and his mother until she finally got up the courage to leave him. She had hidden away enough money so that they could move here to Medina, where her sister Candice lived.

I knew Candice Gordon. She lived in a little white frame house down by the fairground, and she worked at the gas station just off the interstate. Candice's husband had died of a heart attack and she always kept to herself.

Anyway, Seth was sort of like me. He didn't have a lot of friends in high school because he never had a car or clothes or money to run around. Then he got a job at a garage in Mandan and earned enough to buy a used motorcycle.

That's how he got to running with the motorcycle gang. At first he hadn't known they were a gang. And then he didn't care. They had become his friends, they accepted him, no questions asked.

Seth told me that he never meant to harm anyone, never meant to actually steal. But he had known that Rick Egan, one of the gang's leaders, was stealing tires from another local garage. Seth had ridden along in the van with Rick one time. He didn't steal the tires, but he did drive and keep watch for police on the service road.

But without Seth or Rick knowing it, the police had followed them back to the farmhouse Rick rented and they found all kinds of stolen items. Seth got off because he'd never been in trouble before, and because everyone in the gang said he was clean. But the incident almost killed his mother. That's when she finally left her husband and they moved to Medina.

Seth pulled up to a truck stop then and looked at me. "Let's go in for a snack," he suggested. "I've eaten here before . . . food's good."

I smiled and nodded in agreement.

When we were inside and the waitress had taken our order, I glanced around. There were three other young couples in a corner booth, laughing, enjoying themselves, and I thought about how this was the first time I'd ever been out with a guy. This was the first time in seventeen years that I had been attracted to anyone.

I looked at Seth; he was watching me. "Of course, my aunt wasn't exactly glad to have us come to town," he said, continuing his story. "Well, not me at least. She laid down the law on day one. She's respectable, you know . . . a good church member and all. She tells everyone that my father is dead. As far as we're concerned, he is."

The waitress brought our order then, and when Seth picked up his cup of coffee, his voice got quiet. "Maybe knowing all this, you won't want to see me again, Abby," he said.

I touched his arm. My eyes burned with quick tears and my breath came hard. "Seth, I want to see you. I like you. Your past has nothing to do with you now. You couldn't help any of it."

Our eyes met. His glowed bright with promise. "Abby, you don't know how glad I am we came here to live," he said. "You just don't know how scared I was coming here. But now I have a feeling that everything is going to look up. I'm going to keep my nose to the grindstone . . . now that I have you."

It was pitch-black when we got back to Medina. I slunk down on the front seat as soon as we got to Main Street, and in the alley alongside Jean's store, Seth stopped slowly and I got out and ran through the darkness to the house.

I fumbled with the key in the back door, turned the lock, and went inside the house. It was dark and quiet. Only fingers of light from the corner street lamp shone in on the dining room table. I reached for the kitchen light and switched it on. Suddenly the telephone rang, breaking the silence. I ran to answer it, breathless.

"Hello?" I said.

It was Jean. "Abigail? Just where have you been, young lady?" she roared.

My heart pounded, my mind raced for an excuse. "Well, Nikki was baby-sitting and I walked over to see her. Then when I came home I had to go over with my keys to open up the garage so Seth could put the van away."

"He has his own keys. So why were you traipsing over there?" she demanded. "Look, don't try to put anything over on me! Wade's been keeping an eye on you . . . and the house. And that reminds me: Wade tells me that Betty is taking two weeks off, so yougoing to have to run the press."

The press? I thought. It was hard work, hot and exhausting. I'd done it a few times, but I got sick from it. Even Betty said it was no job for a kid and certainly not for someone as small as I was.

I tried to make some excuse to get out of working the press. I mumbled that I could hardly take time off from school with graduation only a few months away.

Jean snapped back angrily, "You're not an honor student, are you? Just skimming along. And you owe me something, Abigail. I put a roof over your head, didn't I?"

Dad came to the phone. I was crying then. "Please ask her if I can't call Helen Mathers in so I won't have to take off from classes, Dad," I begged. "I want to graduate. My average isn't that good. I'll flunk out, and you know Helen Mathers always fills in for vacations," I cried.

But Dad wasn't about to be moved by my tears. Jean was yelling in the background that he was running up a phone bill, and he cut me short with a firm, cold answer. "Listen, Abby. You do like Jean says. She's the boss."

I hung up then. She was the boss, all right. She had bought and paid for Dad and I was just a liability that happened to come along with my father.

I called Betty and asked her if she would be at work on Monday morning so I could go to school and talk with Mr. Walters, the principal. She told me she'd stay till noon, and then she asked, "Why isn't Jean calling Helen Mathers in?"

All I could say was that I didn't know why.

Monday morning, Mr. Walters sat behind his big desk, completely disinterested as I told him that I was concerned with getting an excused absence and graduating on time. He leaned back in his swivel chair and glanced at me through his glasses and shrugged. "I can't do anything for you," he said. "That's up to your teachers." Obviously, I didn't matter to him, either.

I was on my way back to the store when I saw Seth in the van. He pulled over to the curb and I got in. I was crying.

"Hey, what's up?" he asked gently.

He stroked my arm with his hand as I blurted everything out. "Don't worry, Abby. Someday I'm going to take care of you," he said. "I mean that. I know it feels like the end of the world right now, but I love you, if that means anything."

It meant everything to me. Seth's words were the light at the end of the dark tunnel of my life. I looked at him, at his caring expression, and I knew that he meant more to me than anyone. He was my friend.

He was someone I could love who loved me in return.

Seth let me off by the alley, leaned out the window, and called, "See you tonight?"

I just nodded, and he said he'd meet me in the alley around nine.

Betty worked with me till noon, and then she left. Somehow I kept up with the pressing for the rest of the day.

Seth came in just before five with the van. He pretended to ignore me . . . we both knew Wade was watching us, that he was reporting to Jean.

Wade was locking up, swinging his keys with authority and standing by the door as I was leaving. Suddenly he reached out, grabbing my arm.

"Going home now?" he asked.

I nodded, staring straight ahead. "My friend Nikki is coming over tonight to help me with the classes I missed," I said.

"Just Nikki?" he questioned suspiciously.

I swallowed hard, fighting to control my voice. "Yes, Wade. Just Nikki."

He held the door open. "Well, you know Jean asked me to look in on you, so I might stop by."

I was trembling inside, but outwardly I tried to look calm. Anyway, I said in a firm voice, "Wade, my dad said I was to not let anyone into the house. And he meant it." Then I walked away.

His voice followed me. "Your dad is a kept man," he sneered. "Does he work? No. He just keeps Jean happy. We all know that."

The words stabbed through me. It was true. Even I couldn't deny that. It was also true that Wade had had visions of moving in with Jean before my dad came along.

I called Nikki as soon as I got inside the house. She said sure, she'd stop around and that she'd bring over her books from the classes I was missing. I could read up on things. I could try to study so maybe I'd pass the finals.

As Nikki and I sat by the living room window studying, Wade drove slowly by the house. Then Seth called. As he was driving over, he'd seen Wade, too. He suggested that I walk with Nikki part of the way home. He'd pick us up and take us the rest of the way.

Wade was nowhere around as we walked down the street and around the corner where Seth was waiting. He took Nikki to her house, then we rode out into the country in his old pickup.

I loved being with Seth, loved sitting close to him, feeling his arm around me. We were so alike, so happy together! I didn't care about the outside world as long as I had Seth and we could have our dreams: a home one day, children, living like other people, and mostly just being together.

I'll never know how I managed to work the press while Betty was gone. The work exhausted me, and by the end of the shift I'd feel sapped of energy and my arms always ached. But that never stopped me from seeing Seth. Just the thought of being with him perked me up.

I was with Seth every night that Dad and Jean were gone . . . slipping in beside him in the pickup, driving out to little cafes in nearby towns, falling in love. I'd come home after midnight, try to study, and feel just too tired to concentrate.

Then one day in March it all came to an end. Dad and Jean came home, earlier than expected. I didn't even see Jean's car from the store . . . I was too busy struggling with the press. But after work, the minute I opened the porch door I heard her sharp voice on the telephone.

I walked softly into the kitchen, feeling the guilt mounting, along with the fear of being found out. Inside, I reasoned with myself: I do the work that she wants done. I don't hurt anyone. And what's wrong with loving Seth?

Jean hung up the telephone with a bang and turned to glare at me.

"How's your sister?" I asked.

"Fine. Just fine. And what have you been up to?" Jean demanded. "Wade tells me you've been out every night."

I was searching my mind desperately for an answer when Dad came in and stood in the doorway, filling the empty space with his big frame. "Well, answer Jean when she asks you something," he ordered.

"I've been working at the store and studying with Nikki . . . studying so I can graduate and get out on my own!" I said.

Jean's face momentarily softened. She believes me! I thought.

"Well, I tell you, it will be a relief when you are out on your own," she said. "It hasn't been easy for me, putting up with you, Abigail."

Her words stung me, but it didn't matter. I hadn't been caught and I felt the tension slip away from me.

Dad was overly nice to Jean that evening . . . waiting on her, touching her each chance he got. Even Jean looked puzzled.

Nikki was going to be baby-sitting that night and Seth was picking me up there. I got my books together, making it look like I'd be studying, mumbled an explanation to Dad while Jean was in the bedroom, and rushed out the back door.

Fifteen minutes after I arrived at the house where Nikki was baby-sitting, Seth came to the back door and I left with him. On the way to his car, he said that Wade had confronted him about seeing me. Wade told Seth if he didn't watch it, he would tell Jean. I got in the car beside him.

"Do you think he will?" I asked anxiously.

40

"Listen, you'll graduate soon. After that, who cares? You can be with me then. We can even get married, can't we?"

I stared at him, love flooding through me. "Seth, do you mean that?" I asked.

"Of course I mean it," he said. "I love you, Abby. I'll never love anyone this way. I don't care if we are young and I don't care what people say. I'll never love anyone but you."

That night with Seth I learned what love really was. I knew what it was to belong to someone, to feel his strength and warmth and gentleness. . . .

Later, Seth and I made plans. Plans for our life together. We had big dreams, but we never expected to have them all come true at once. It didn't matter . . . as long as we could be together.

I managed to be with Seth during the next two weeks. Jean and Dad seemed to be busier than usual, going out of town, taking weekend vacations, leaving me more or less on my own.

Betty had come back and I returned to school. It was evident to me immediately that I could not pass my classes. In the first place, learning came hard to me. And in the second, I'd let everything slide to spend time with Seth. But still I kept on plugging along in my classes, hoping against hope.

All of a sudden everything seemed to happen at once. Every day after school I had came home, changed into work clothes and went to the store to work until at least six o'clock. Then one Wednesday afternoon when I was walking home from school I noticed a strange car parked in front of the house. I tentatively entered and heard a stranger's voice in the kitchen. I set my books on the closet shelf and paused, listening.

But Jean heard me and shouted, "Abigail, don't sneak around. Come in here. There's someone I want you to meet."

My legs felt wooden, but I went. A man stood there, taller than my father, a tough-looking man dressed in a plaid shirt and trousers that looked new.

"This is Jake Monroe. A friend of the family from Valley City. He's going to be living here," Jean said.

Jake Monroe's mouth was a thin, tight line; his eyes burned into mine. "So you're Ray's kid. You must look like your mother," he said, glancing at Jean.

She sighed heavily, her lower lip jutting out angrily. "She does!" she snapped. "She's not at all like Ray. But she's a hard worker, I'll say that much for her."

I stood there awkwardly for a moment until Jean glanced at me and in a gruff voice said, "Well, get changed and get to work."

I swallowed hard, noticing through the kitchen window that her

41

car was gone. That meant Dad had it. I turned and ran to my room and got into my jeans and went out the back door without another word to them.

The work was piled up again. Betty looked tired and impatient. Wade sauntered over to my table, grinning. "Where'd the boyfriend get the money for the new wheels he's driving?" he asked.

I swallowed hard. "I didn't know he had a new car." And that was the truth.

Wade threw his head back and laughed. He'd unnerved me and that's what he wanted. "I thought you knew everything about each other," he sneered before strolling back across the room.

My face was burning and I felt eyes on me from all over. I blinked hard to hold the tears back and kept working with trembling hands.

Around five-thirty Seth came in. His eyes met mine. "Hi," he said, and that one word sent shivers through me. "See you before I go home. Maybe you could get away tonight?" he asked.

I just nodded. Wade made a low, insinuating whistle just as Jake Monroe came walking in through the back door. Wade disappeared and the rest of us kept our eyes on our jobs like Jake was some kind of general passing through.

Jake stopped by Betty, watched her for a moment, then edged on over to me. "You're supposed to come home now," he said. "Jean wants to talk to you."

He walked with me through the plant and out the door. Seth was standing outside the store by the van, fiddling around, trying to look busy. I knew he was waiting for me but I couldn't say anything with Jake there.

I was tired, so tired and weary, I felt old. Even older than Jean. Jake walked with confidence and speed, and my heart pounded hard as I followed him into the house.

Jean was standing with a big black purse over her arm. Dad was nowhere in sight. Her eyes met mine. "I had company today," she snapped. "On top of everything else, Mr. Walters was here from the school. You're not going to graduate! So that's the thanks I get, taking you in. Humiliation and insinuations. Talk that I make you work too hard. Isn't that a joke? After all I've done for you."

I felt hot and dizzy. The room seemed to be spinning. I sat down on the nearest kitchen chair. Jean took this as an insult, and she crossed the room and slapped my face with a swift movement that stunned me. Her voice was shrill and out of control. Words ran together . . . threats. Her last words were that my dad and I were on our way out of her house and her life! Then she and Jake went out the door and drove off.

I don't know how long they were gone before Seth came. I'd gone

42

upstairs to wash my face, to hold a cloth soaked in cold water against my cheek with the imprint of Jean's hand. Seth knocked and called my name. I went down and told him what had happened.

Seth held my face between his hands and kissed me, and he told me he loved me and that he would always take care of me, that I didn't have to worry because I'd always have him. Then Seth said he had a surprise for me . . . a nice surprise.

I locked the house up and we went to the parking lot behind the store. We walked to the only car left on the lot, an older car that was polished and shining, as nice as a new one.

"Isn't it something?" Seth asked, grinning proudly as he opened the door for me to get in.

Inside, I looked at him, at his confident smile as he started the engine. "My mom gave me the money. Said she'd been saving it for years. A little bit every week," Seth explained excitedly. "She said she wanted to be around to see me enjoy it. We need a car, don't we, if we get married? Something nice like this, I mean. They even gave me two hundred bucks on my old pickup."

Well, naturally I got excited about the car, too, and it almost made me forget what Jean had said and what her threat would mean to Dad and me if she followed through on it.

I didn't dare stay out late, so after we'd eaten at a little diner the next town over, I had Seth drive me right back home. As soon as we turned onto our street, I noticed all the lights were on downstairs at our place and Jean's car was parked in the alley. But Jake's car was nowhere in sight. My heart pounded as I got out and ran through the darkness of the alley to the house. Even then, I remember hearing Seth's voice calling out, "I love you, Abby!"

The porch door was open and so was the kitchen door. I walked in quietly, but no one was in the kitchen. I called out nervously for my dad.

He came out from their bedroom, pale and haggard, his forehead beaded with perspiration.

"Where's Jean? She isn't with Jake Monroe, is she?" he asked.

I shrugged. "I guess so. His car is gone."

Dad sat down heavily on a kitchen chair, looking at me like I could help him. "He's trying to take her away from me, Abby. I knew that up in Valley City, the way he waited on her hand and foot. He's not so dumb. But what would I do without her?" he whined.

My throat was tight and dry. I felt sorry for my father. He was like a child . . . helpless and weak, with not even enough gumption to stand up for himself.

Suddenly Jean came in from nowhere. She was just there. Her eyes were cold and heartless.

43

"Pack up, Ray," she ordered. "Get your things together and get out!"

Dad started crying like a baby, pleading without shame, telling Jean that I would be leaving soon and that they could be together like they'd always wanted . . . together, alone.

Jean just walked away from him. "I'm tired of you, Ray, tired of footing the bill for your company. Frankly, it hasn't been worth it, and now I'm getting rid of you . . . and your pain-in-the-neck kid. I have the divorce papers all drawn up," she added. "And you'd better believe they'll be signed and sealed before the month's out!"

Dad was still crying, and finally Jean said he could stay until Saturday. That would give him time to find a place to live. Then she went into the living room to talk to Jake.

Dad looked at me then and asked if I had any money. I told him that I had very little.

"Well," he said, "is there enough to get up to Faye's? Maybe we could stay there—"

"We're not going anywhere together!" I yelled, unable to control my hurt and anger any longer. "I'm staying right here in Medina with Seth. He loves me like you never could or wanted to," I said, and then I turned and rushed upstairs.

I slammed the door to my bedroom and quickly began piling my clothes on the rocker so that all I would have to do the next day was bring home some boxes from the store and put everything in them. I didn't know where I would go, but I wouldn't be caught here, begging Jean for help!

Jean and Jake left the house very early the next day. The sun was just beginning to rise when I heard the porch door slam shut, and I got up to see them crossing the alley together. Then I heard Dad rummaging around downstairs. I figured he must have slept on the living room couch.

I showered, dressed, and went down to make breakfast. Just as I entered the kitchen, a police car turned in the alley. Jean and Jake came rushing from the back of the store toward the house. Dad went white. "Oh, no," he mumbled shakily. "What's wrong now?"

The police officer, Jean, and Jake all arrived at the door at the same time. Jean glared at Dad.

"We've been robbed!" she spat out accusingly.

"Jean," Dad stammered, "you—you don't think I'd do a thing like that?"

Jean's face was set like stone. "You've been taking from me all along. Why not? Why wouldn't you? You don't believe in working for what you get."

Maybe my father was shiftless and lazy, but he wasn't a thief.

And I knew Dad hadn't left the house since last night.

Jean turned to the officer. "Check his billfold and the bedroom, it's just down the hall to your right," she said.

Dad handed the policeman his billfold and I noticed his hands were trembling. Inside were two dollar bills, a Social Security card, and a picture of Mother and me. Nothing more.

Jake shouted down the hall to the officer, "Better go up and search the girl's room."

I was numb, too stunned to think straight. Finally the search was over and Dad looked at me, beads of perspiration standing out on his forehead. Then he sort of crumbled together, grabbed his chest, and collapsed. I got on the floor beside him, touched his face, and heard him take his last breath.

The ambulance came. Then Betty and Wade came over, and in the background stood Seth. Our eyes met. He came toward me, put his arm around my shoulder, and held me close as I watched them take Dad away.

Betty gently touched my arm. "You want to come home with me?" she asked. "Jean said she was moving you and your dad out."

I couldn't think. I just went along with Betty, going to her car, telling her to call my aunt, agreeing I would spend the night with her. And Seth walked with us until Jake called his name. Seth told me he'd be in touch with me soon, then went back to where Jake was standing with Jean and the policeman.

Betty unlocked her car and sat me inside it then said she had to turn the press off but that she'd be right back. Then I saw the officer questioning Seth and Wade watching from across the alley. Seth got his billfold out and they went through it while Jean stood there with that masklike face and spoke through those tight lips. Seth glanced my way and I could see he was scared. Then he and the officer walked to the police car.

Betty came back, got in the car, and started it. "I know it seems like the end of the world," she said softly. "But you've got the best of your life still ahead of you Abby. Once you get away from here you can start over. Graduation isn't that far off."

I couldn't think of the next hour, much less the weeks ahead. "Why did they take Seth?" The words stuck in my throat and fear gripped me like grief. All my thoughts were hurting ones.

Betty sighed. "When you started up with Seth, I had this feeling that it wouldn't be anything but trouble and heartache. You knew he ran with those bikers. They're rough characters. Abby, think about it. Where did Seth get the money to buy that car and pay cash?"

"His mother," I said. "She saved the money over the years. Seth told me that and I believe him!"

Betty parked next to her house and turned to look at me with pity. "Listen, Abby. You haven't had much to believe in and I don't blame you. You needed someone to lean on, someone to care. But not someone like Seth. If his mother had any money at all, don't you think they'd have had some decent clothes and furniture?" she asked gently. "Don't you think she'd have a winter coat and some boots? Staples, not luxury items. Sooner or later you're going to have to face it. Seth is a thief and he's headed for jail."

I got out of the car and followed Betty into her house. It was small and spotless, everything polished and covered with embroidered tablecloths. There were plants covering all the windowsills and walls that were cluttered with pictures. It reminded me of our old house.

Betty called my Aunt Faye and they talked for some time. When Betty hung up she said that my aunt would be driving down so I could go home with her if there was nothing else for me to do. She'd arrive late, but she was coming.

That afternoon Wade came over with my things from Jean's house. He carried them all into the kitchen and set the boxes on the floor.

"So the boyfriend's in jail!" he said. "You'll be missing his loving, won't you, kid?"

Before I could think of an answer, Betty came in the room and Wade stepped toward the door. She thanked him for his trouble and I was very relieved when he left.

Betty tried to be nice. She fixed a big supper and tried to make conversation. She told me Nikki was welcome to come over if she wanted. I sure needed a friend, so I called her and she came. She kept telling me not to worry. That Seth would be cleared soon and we could get married. I sure hoped she was right, but I'd long since learned not to count on good things happening for me.

When Faye arrived that evening, she looked tired and impatient. "Have you made any plans for after graduation?" she asked.

My mind felt too numb to think. Plans? No, I had no plans, just a lot of dreams that were shattered. Sure, Nikki and I had talked of going to work in a factory, of getting an apartment together. And Seth said we were getting married. But it was all talk. There was no job waiting, no place to live, and now, no Seth.

The next morning the pastor came and Faye helped me make funeral arrangements. Faye was nice on the surface, but in little ways she let me know this was inconveniencing her, that she had her own family to care for and plenty to do at home. She went on about how my dad always passed his responsibilities onto someone else, and even now he was doing the same thing.

I remember riding around in silence, watching the world as we

46

drove around Medina, seeing homes where real families lived. Faye said it wouldn't be fair to stay at Betty's for our meals, so we went to eat at the little diner on Main Street . . . the one where my mother used to get our special dinners.

I just had some soup and a glass of milk and when I was finished Faye said, "Anyplace else you'd like to go, Abby?"

I looked away from her. "If you wouldn't mind, I'd like to walk around the corner to the jail . . . to see Seth."

She put her hand over mine. "Abby, forget him. Betty told me all about Seth. He was nice to you when you were lonely. Can't you see that he met you at a bad time in your life and took advantage of the situation?"

Just then the waitress brought our bill and Faye reached in her purse for money. As far as she was concerned, the subject of Seth was closed.

I didn't say anymore. I walked with her to the car and we got in. Then I looked down the street toward the jail and I just couldn't help it . . . I burst into tears. Faye sighed and leaned back tiredly.

"All right," she said. "Go on down. I'll wait. Maybe you need to see him to cut free of him."

The jail was situated behind a bottling plant. It was a little brick building with two rooms to house prisoners until they could be transferred to Jamestown where the county courthouse and a larger jail were located.

I remember feeling weak as I entered the front door. Deb Whal, the dispatcher, stood up, recognizing me. She was my mother's age and she'd lived in Medina for as long as I could remember.

"I suppose you want to see Seth," she said. Her face was set and her tone was unfriendly. After I nodded, she shrugged. "Well, you came just in time. They're taking him to Jamestown at one."

I followed her down the narrow hall. Seth was sitting there on a cot, looking scared. Deb opened the door and told us I could only stay a few minutes.

I went to Seth. He put his arms around me, held me tight, and our tears ran together. He held my face in his hands. "Abby, I swear I didn't take anything!" he said. "Not one cent. I wouldn't do anything like that. Mom gave me the money, and when the officers came and questioned her, they didn't believe a thing she said. Abby . . . you've got to forget me," he pleaded. "I'm headed for the state penitentiary. Five years at least. There's no way out."

I kept saying if he was innocent . . . and I believed he was . . . there was no way he'd be locked up. But there wasn't time to talk, to rebuild shattered dreams or soften the grief inside. Deb had come back.

"Come on," she ordered. "No time for nonsense. They're here for him."

Seth held me close until the officer came, a big, burly man who jerked him up by his arm. Seth didn't resist, but the officer still treated him roughly.

I stood outside the jail and watched as they drove away. Seth kept looking back, and our eyes locked until he was out of sight. I turned and walked toward Faye's car. It had started to rain a slow drizzle from an all-gray sky. Faye rolled down her window. "Abby, you're going to get wet," she said. "Hurry!"

I remember thinking: Wet? Who cares? But I hurried anyway so Faye wouldn't get mad.

On the way back to Betty's, she talked incessantly. Advice. It came easy. And questions like: "Have you given serious thought to your future?" "Is there anyplace you could live in Medina?"

When we were parked in front of the house, Faye turned and looked at me . . . just looked, not with affection or caring . . . just sizing me up while she talked.

"It's a good thing that this happened," she said. "Someday you're going to be glad that you never married Seth. Got saddled down with a kid, maybe, and its father off to jail."

"Seth didn't take the money," I whispered bitterly. "He said so and I believe him!"

"Listen, if he was so honest, why didn't the police believe his mother when she said she gave him the money? A likely story," Faye said sarcastically. "She's as poor as a church mouse. Let's not talk about this anymore. I don't have the patience and I've got enough on my mind."

My father's funeral was very small. Nikki came over and sat with me. I saw her mom and dad sitting toward the back. There were some old neighbors, a few of my dad's friends from way back. One of them was old Uncle Sid. We were related somehow through my father's side, I couldn't remember the exact lineage . . . just that I grew up calling him Uncle Sid. The flowers on the casket were pretty. Faye had lent me the money for them, after I'd promised to pay her back.

After the funeral, Betty returned to Jean's store and Faye said she wanted to go over and see an old friend. Nikki walked back with me to Betty's. She mentioned that she saw Jean at the funeral, but I hadn't seen her and that was just as well.

I felt like a stranger in Betty's house, not even a guest but an uninvited intruder. Nikki said that maybe we should walk to her place. We could have some coffee or something. So I left a note on the dining room table that Nikki had invited me over and that I would be back later in the day, but if Betty or Faye wanted me, they could call her house and I wrote the number down.

We were almost to Nikki's house when she told me that she had won a scholarship to a school for nursing in Dickinson, a city almost two hours away from Medina. She had been waiting to find out for almost three weeks without anyone knowing except the teachers at our school who had helped her apply for the scholarship, and now she knew she would be able to start in September. The scholarship would pay for nearly everything as long as she lived in the dorms provided for the nursing students. The money she saved working part-time at a local cafe would pay for her books and other expenses.

Nikki was so excited, but I felt like my world was getting smaller and smaller. "Nikki, I thought that maybe you and I were going to do something together after graduation . . . like we always talked about," I said.

"I know, Abby," Nikki said softly, taking my hand. "But I can't pass up the opportunity. You know how much I want to get ahead, to make a better life for myself, and this may be the only chance I get."

I knew Nikki was right. She had worked hard all through high school, always determined to do her best and get good grades. She deserved this scholarship, even if it did take her away from me.

We'd walked quite a while before I realized that I hadn't said anything to Nikki. Not a word. Finally I turned, touching her arm gently and swallowing hard. "Nikki," I said, "I'm glad for you, honest. I just can't think clearly right now. Too many things on my mind, I guess."

"Listen, Abby," she offered, "my mom said that if you wanted, you could stay with us until after graduation. You'd have to sleep with my sister and me, but we could do it."

I thanked her and said I'd think it over. Of course I wanted to accept her offer, but I knew what a hard time her parents already had making ends meet. The last thing they needed was another mouth to feed.

Nikki's mom invited me to supper that evening, and I took my place at their big oak table. I ate little, but gratefully accepted their words of sympathy. Nikki's father said some kind words about my dad . . . that maybe he wasn't ambitious but he'd been a good man anyway and he'd loved my mother and me. And that was something to remember. I guess he was the only person who offered me any comfort at all.

I called Betty's house, and Faye said I could take my time coming home. They wouldn't be doing anything anyway, so if I felt like staying for the rest of the evening I could.

Only, I sort of felt like I should have been going. Nikki needed to study and help her mother put her brothers and sisters to bed. There was nothing for me to do but thank Nikki and her folks for dinner and be on my way. But before I left, Mrs. Hagan took me aside and told me again that I could stay with them until graduation.

"With as many as we have now, one more won't make too much difference," she said with a warm smile. "At least not for a little while."

I wanted to hug her then. Instead, I thanked her and said I'd let her know in the next couple of days if I needed a place to stay.

Outside in the cool night air, I felt reality hit me as I looked up and down the street and faced the world . . . alone. I just stood still a moment, looking up into the sky and wondering about God, about my folks. Then, I don't know why, but I decided to walk over to Seth's house.

It was almost a mile from Nikki's to the little cottage on the edge of town where Seth's mother lived. The house sat on the edge of some farmland, and there was no sidewalk, just a gravel path to the front door.

I knocked lightly on the door, noticing a dim light in the living room. Finally I called, "Mrs. Barton? I'm Seth's friend. Can I talk to you?"

She opened the door then, just a crack. "Are you Abby?" she asked hesitantly.

I nodded.

Right away she started to cry, sobs that shook her whole body. Holding her face in her hands, choking the words out, she told me how the police questioned her, trying to trap her, trying to make her change her story. When she was all cried out, she took my hand and said, "I brought Seth up to know stealing is wrong, and I don't think he ever did. He wasn't like his dad, not my baby. He was always so good to me, bringing me treats when he got paid, buying me little surprises. Now they say they're going to lock him up and what can I do? Nothing!"

"Mrs. Barton, you did give Seth money for the car he bought?" I asked.

"Of course I did," she said. "I saved it over the years . . . kept it in a little strongbox I hid away. . . ."

"But did you tell that to the police when they came? Did you tell them?" I persisted.

She shrugged, going limp. "I told one officer and he just laughed, said they expected me to make up some stupid story like that. They wouldn't listen to me. They just took my Seth away."

I was alive with renewed hope. I held Mrs. Barton's hands, promising that somehow, some way, we'd get a good lawyer and we'd get Seth free. She listened but she didn't hear. She didn't believe.

I almost ran back to Betty's, tearing in the back door, spilling it all out to Faye and Betty.

50

They just looked at each other, and then Faye sighed deeply.

"Abby, I talked to Seth's aunt, Candice Gordon," she said. "I saw her at the grocery store. I didn't know her, of course, but she came over and said she was sorry about what had happened and that Seth's mother always protected him, always got him out of scrapes. She says he's like his father . . . good looking, cunning, and no good."

Anger whipped through me and I lashed out at Faye, shouting, "Why? Why can't you give him a chance to prove he's innocent?"

Her face reddened and she quickly retorted, "Because he's a criminal and he had his chance. And now the taxes I pay will help support him while he's in prison. People who work hard get tired of freeloaders!"

I said no more. I'd gotten the message. Faye wasn't just talking about Seth. She meant my father and me when she used the word freeloader. Well, I'd show them all! One day I'd be independent and respected.

Faye stayed two more days and then she said she had to be getting home. I'd told her about the offer the Hagans made for me to stay with Nikki until graduation, and I felt her relief. She was brighter, friendlier. It was evident that she didn't want me to go home with her. She said I didn't have to pay her back for the funeral flowers. And she would even leave some money for Nikki's mother.

Faye went and talked to Mrs. Hagan and took my boxes of things down there. I felt so guilty moving in with them, but I wanted to be in Medina in case Seth was released. I was sure that a miracle would happen . . . that they'd find the real thief and set Seth free.

Nikki was serious about her schoolwork, so I studied in the bedroom upstairs with her and I helped with the work around the house. I'd do the dishes and cleaning and ironing. I ate very little and I tried to be cheerful. But in the quiet of the night, I cried a lot. And I prayed.

It was the week of graduation when Mr. Hagan came up to the room I shared with Nikki and her younger sister, Lindsey. He came in and sat on the edge of the bed and watched me putting their clothes in the dresser drawers. His eyes were soft and gentle and he sort of smiled.

"I was wondering if you'd like to ride out to the new factory to check on a job. Nikki says you had put in an application through the school and they're hiring now," he explained. "You're welcome to stay on here for a month or so, Abigail. Until you get some money to get a room. And I hear that Mary Duncan is renting rooms since her folks passed away," he added.

I knew about Mary Duncan. She was a widow who lived in a big three-story farmhouse on the outskirts of town and had spent the last few years caring for her ailing parents. It scared me to think of moving that far out of town. I don't know why. Everything scared me. I felt sick again. My stomach churned and rolled around and I felt hot. But Mr. Hagan was waiting for an answer.

"I guess I should go out and see what they have to say at the factory," I agreed.

"Well, how about going in a half hour?" he asked.

I nodded, but I didn't want to go. My heart raced and perspiration poured out of me. Seth, where are you? Mother? Dad? Anyone? I thought helplessly. But there was no one.

Nikki's dad went downstairs and pretty soon Mrs. Hagan came up with a freshly ironed white blouse. "It's mine," she said, "It's new but you can wear it to go out for your job interview."

I thanked her, but I felt like saying I wished she could give me some courage, too.

The receptionist at the factory office said many seniors at the high school were applying for work. I waited while she took my application from the file and brought it to Mr. Bellow, the personnel manager. Then she returned and sent me in to see him.

Mr. Bellow was a big man, sitting behind a huge desk that was stacked with folders and loose papers. He didn't smile. He didn't offer me a chair. He just straightened his shoulders a little and said, "You aren't going to be graduating, I understand. Well, one of the requirements for employment here is a high school diploma, so obviously we can't consider you. I'm afraid, young lady, that without a diploma you're going to have a difficult time finding a decent job. . . ."

I remember turning and running, tears streaming down my face. I remember a sound like a scream echoing around me as I ran out of the building to the car where Mr. Hagan was waiting.

"Abigail, what happened?" he asked when he saw the state I was in.

I told him everything, and he tried to make me feel better. He said I could always get a waitressing job someplace.

At that point, it didn't matter what he said. I felt violently sick. I just had no idea how to straighten out my life.

When we got home, Mrs. Hagan stopped ironing to come and sit on the couch with me. She took time from her busy day to tell me that her life hadn't been an easy one, either, but that now she was happy with her large family, even if they didn't have everything they'd like.

Okay, I thought, maybe you're happy . . . but you have people that belong to you, people that care about you. And I have no one. I'm just in the way wherever I go.

Then Mrs. Hagan said I could easily remedy the problem of not graduating by signing up for fall classes at the Vo-Tech school after passing a high school equivalency test and getting my diploma signed. So it wasn't the end of the world, it just seemed that way.

The next morning I was sick again and I told Lindsey to tell her mother I'd be down later. Then I lay in bed and let the tears fall and felt the nausea keep coming.

Everyone had left the house except for the two youngest children, and they were downstairs watching TV when Mrs. Hagan came into the room. Hesitantly, she approached the bed, sitting down on the wooden chair by the window.

"Abby," she said, "Abby, you couldn't be pregnant, could you? I've noticed that you're sick a lot. Of course you've been through a traumatic time and I don't mean to be nosy, but. . . ."

Now it was out in the open. I guess I'd been burying that fear along with many other fears. I looked away. My period was late, by over two months. It was more than likely that I was pregnant with Seth's baby.

When I admitted this to Mrs. Hagan, she made an appointment with Dr. Thompson, their family doctor, for that afternoon. She went down with me. Dr. Thompson was gentle and understanding and he didn't try to pass judgment on me. He just sat back behind his cluttered desk and said, yes, I was three months pregnant, did I know who the father was, and was I going to carry it to term or was I going to take a trip to Fargo to have an abortion?

I was shocked. "I'd never do anything to hurt this baby," I said. "I know the father. We love each other."

Dr. Thompson smiled, nodding. "That's more than half the battle. You'll be all right. Take care of yourself, eat well, get exercise and plenty of rest," he advised, before sending me off with a handful of pamphlets on things the expectant mother should know.

I don't know why, but I felt a sort of calm after I walked out of his office. Warmth flowed through me, a feeling of Seth being there. I had to see him now!

In the car, I turned to Mrs. Hagan and looked at her. "I hate to ask you another favor, but do you think we could drive over to Jamestown?" I asked. "I feel like if Seth knew about the baby, maybe he'd fight harder for freedom. I know he loves me Mrs. Hagan. I don't care what the whole world says . . . we love each other."

Her face was like a mask . . . set and controlled. She didn't want to take me to see Seth. She didn't approve! I looked away. How much could I expect of them? Not this, too. It was too much.

"I'm sorry," I said. "I've imposed enough on you already."

"Abby," she said then, "I'll drive you over. I guess Seth has a right to know about the baby. Maybe he can help you make the right decision."

The right decision? I wouldn't even let myself think what she meant.

We didn't speak all the way to Jamestown. She had her thoughts, I had mine. When she stopped just down the street from the courthouse, I told her I'd go in alone and she didn't offer to go with me. I looked at the large pale building and felt a little scared. It looked cold and heartless.

I went to the first desk I saw and blurted out that I was there to see Seth Barton. The lady behind the desk nodded and called to a man who stood down another hall. "She wants to see Seth Barton," she announced.

He mumbled something about my coming just in time . . . that they were about to lock up for the day. He glanced at me. "This isn't a hotel, you know. I don't know if he'll even come down. He just got word about his mother. She had a stroke. Are you family?"

The lady behind the desk kept looking over some papers and talking at the same time. "He hasn't any other family besides an aunt. This has got to be a girlfriend. How these guys manage to get girls to wait for them, I'll never know."

The man disappeared and the lady behind the desk looked at me. "This isn't the visiting room. I'll take you there. Your boyfriend will be brought in."

I waited for a long time. Finally Seth came in. He was thinner than before. His face was gaunt and his eyes were red. He just sat down where they told him to sit and only glanced at me.

"Why did you come, Abby?" he asked.

"Seth, I love you. Remember? I—I'm sorry about your mom," I said.

"Yeah. They went to see her again and she couldn't take it. When I think of how many times she's been raked over the coals because of this, and I didn't even do it! You know what, Abby? I hate this world. I can't love. I don't know what it is."

"You love me. I know you do," I said. "Everything can still work out . . . just keep believing that Seth. I . . . I'm going to have your baby. We're going to be a family."

Seth got up, kicked the chair and looked at me with fire in his eyes. "Abby, how dumb are you? We aren't going to be anything. I'm going to be sent to the state prison in Bismarck, and you're going to give the baby to some nice couple. Then you're going to start over and forget we ever met. That's what's coming up for you and me. You know, my mom can't talk or walk or eat by herself, she's going to a nursing home," he yelled. "See, Abby, there's a place for each one of us in this rotten world."

Seth was crying and I was crying, too. Then the man came and took Seth by the arm and said he had to take him back to his cell. Seth looked at me one last time and then turned to follow him.

"I'll be back," I called out to him. "Just as soon as I can!"

Mrs. Hagan looked at her watch as I got into the car. "It's getting late," she said with a sound of weariness in her voice.

"I'm sorry," I apologized as we drove away.

I fixed supper and when the family sat down to eat I went upstairs, saying I'd be down to do the dishes. And lying up there in that room, I knew that my welcome was wearing thin. I kept thinking of Seth's last words to me and that everyone has a place. But there was no place for people like me, no nursing home or jail. No place at all.

I wrote to Faye that night asking her if I could please go up there and work for my keep, and I asked if she could spare money for a bus ticket for me to come. I told her I'd sleep in the room above the garage and work in the fields or the cabins at the little resort that they owned. I'd do anything to have a roof over my head and earn my own way. Then I borrowed a stamp from Nikki and walked downtown to mail the letter.

The day of graduation I didn't go to school. Nikki understood how hard it would be for me, so I just congratulated her before she left. Her folks were having a little party afterward and they invited me to stay but I just couldn't.

I decided to walk down by the local creamery because I knew Uncle Sid worked there, and I used to hang around a lot down by the place when I was a kid.

Sid's wife, Gloria, had died six months ago and his daughter had been killed in an accident about a year before that, so I figured he must be lonely, too.

Sid was sitting on a milk can outside the intake door, staring down at the ground. He jolted his head up with surprise when I called his name.

"For goodness sakes, Abigail. What are you doing down here?" he asked with a happy smile.

I almost started crying right then. "I've got no place to go, Uncle Sid."

He leaned back against the building and suddenly I was telling all my problems to him, like he was my father or something. When I was finished, he put a hand on my shoulder.

"Listen, kid, in one hour my shift is over and then you can come on over to my place. It's not much without Gloria to keep things up, but you can have some supper with me," he offered. "Sandwiches and some strong coffee. How's that sound to you? And I'd like the company. It gets mighty quiet being there alone all the time."

So I walked home with Sid, across the vacant lot, over the wooden

55

bridge to his little house on the banks of a little creek. It wasn't much of a place, but it had a friendly feeling to it.

I hadn't realized it but I was hungry. The cold milk tasted good and I thought about the baby needing calcium and nutritious food. I told Sid all about Seth, and he offered to drive me over to Jamestown in the morning because he was off the next day. I couldn't thank him enough, and when I left for the Hagan's house my spirits were lifted. Sid had even told me that if Faye let me go up there to live with her, he'd buy the ticket if I promised to come down and visit him sometime after the baby came.

In the morning I got up bright and early. I told Mrs. Hagan that I'd written Faye and that Uncle Sid Taylor was buying me a ticket as soon as Faye said I could come. I added that he was taking me over to see Seth. She just shrugged her shoulders and said nothing.

I was on my way out the door when she said, "Abby, it isn't that I wouldn't like to keep you on. But with the baby coming and as crowded as we are, it's just impossible. There's just got to be a limit on what we can expect of other people."

"I understand," I told her. "And I'm grateful for all you've done for me."

Sid was standing on the stoop outside his front door. As we walked toward his old car he said, "I heard this morning that Mrs. Barton died last night. So I guess it's a good thing we planned to go over. That young man needs someone."

I cried all the way to Jamestown. When Sid stopped outside the courthouse, he said, "Abigail, you've got to get hold of yourself. You can't help Seth by crying and making him feel worse."

I knew Sid was right, so I went to the bathroom in the courthouse and washed my face, combed my hair, and dabbed on some lipstick before going to ask for Seth.

The same lady sat behind the desk. "Well, you came just in time," she said. "His mother died, you know. They're letting him go to the services and then they're taking him directly to the state prison. You might as well know," she went on, "he confessed. Why not? His only alibi died."

I stared at her, thinking she must be hollow inside. She acted like she was talking about a TV program, not someone's life. Seth's mother was dead and Seth was being sent to prison for something he hadn't done, and this woman couldn't care less.

"But he's innocent," I insisted.

She smiled at me like she felt sorry for me. "Honey, they all say that."

She left to tell someone to bring Seth, then came right back. "He doesn't want to see you. He said for you to just go away and forget him," she said. "That boy's going to be locked up for five years and he wants to be free when he gets out. He said to be sure and tell you that. So my advice to you is—"

"I want to see him!" I interrupted coldly. "Take me to where he is."

"I can't do that," she told me, "so you might as well leave. I can't take you beyond this section. That's the law. And I can't make him see you."

"When is his mother's funeral?"

"Day after tomorrow. It's going to be out west someplace. It won't even be a funeral, I hear, just a committal service."

Poor Sid. All the way back to Medina he tried to cheer me up with stories about years gone by, tales about Gloria and his daughter, Sally, about my dad and my mother. But it was all just words that skimmed my mind and never touched what I was feeling inside.

I stayed at Sid's place all day, and after supper I walked back to the Hagan's house. Mrs. Hagan said that Faye had called and said I could come and that she'd already sent some money down for a bus ticket and for postage to mail the box of my things that I had upstairs. I nodded and said I'd leave the next day if I could.

That was fine with Mrs. Hagan. She'd already checked and found that there was a one o'clock bus leaving from the old hotel. Since Mr. Hagan had to work the day shift, she had called around and found that Betty could drive me downtown. I wanted Sid to take me, but then I remembered that he worked the seven-to-three shift the next day.

At twelve-thirty Betty's car was out front. I carried out one small box of my things, and when I got to the car I saw that Wade was behind the wheel. He got out grinning.

"Betty got sick so she asked me to give you a lift," he said.

I wanted to walk away.

"Get in," he said, reading my mind. "You don't have all day. Buses don't wait."

I got in because Mrs. Hagan was at her front door waving me on, glad to see me go.

Wade tried to put his hand on my leg but I shoved it aside.

"I hear the boyfriend is getting sent to the state prison. No wonder you're leaving town. Of course, I could have helped you out until he got released," he said with an ugly smirk.

I stared ahead. In just a few minutes I'd be on my way and I'd never have to look at Wade again. Never have to hear his filthy talk. I'd live on memories . . . of Seth's arms around me. I'd dream all those old dreams until he got out, and then I'd find him again. . . .

It was a long ride to Faye's. The interstate wound around Bismarck and I remember thinking it wasn't that far from Washburn

57

to where Seth would be. Not that it mattered how near or far it was. I wasn't going to get to see him for a long, long time.

Faye was waiting at the bus depot in the old pickup from the farm. I was feeling dizzy and nauseous, but I knew I'd have to cover that up. I wanted to wait for the right time to tell her about the baby.

"Well, come on," she said impatiently the minute she saw me. "We have fields to tend, and when we get home you can hang some sheets out. They'll be dry by nightfall and you can take them over to the cabins."

I just nodded and remembered coming here as a child with my folks. Then, Mother helped with the work and I spent my days walking along the shore, wading in the water, pretending the big lake was the ocean.

Mother always said that Faye worked like a man, and it was true. And she expected the same from her help. The migrant workers that came up from the South worked from dawn until dusk, and I worked beside them. They got paid. I got room and board, and some clothes Faye bought at a rummage sale at her church. It figured out, she said, to more than what the other help got.

On days that it rained, I ironed clothes, cleaned, or packaged produce picked the day before. There was always something more to do . . . never a night when I'd go to bed and think we were caught up. We never were. Never. The migrants spoke mostly Spanish and so I couldn't talk to them while we worked. I didn't care. I liked the quiet . . . liked to think about how it would be after the baby came and Seth got out of jail.

It was the hottest summer in years. Hot, dry, and dusty. I'd perspire in the heat of the relentless sun, and the dust would cake on my face and burn my eyes. Sometimes I'd be so sick to my stomach I'd put my face down between my knees to keep from fainting. But I kept moving because Faye's husband, Paul, was talking about letting some of the help go so he could raise his profit and still lower the prices on his produce. He was the biggest truck farmer for miles around, selling off a wagon on the highway and delivering fruits and vegetables to neighboring towns. He and Faye also had the resort his father had left him years ago. I was sure they had a lot of money. Not that they lived like they did, because they were too busy to spend any. They just kept piling it up and figuring out how to make more.

It was August and corn-picking time. Paul was always checking the fields, his eyes squinting in the hot sun, searching the sky for rain clouds. When it didn't rain, he'd put on the sprinklers to save the crops, complaining about how much money it cost.

I remember sitting in the wagon at the end of a row of corn one day, checking the ears for rot, tossing the bad ears in the big bin for silage. I remember feeling sick, looking at the big open door of the shed and longing to go inside and lie down. Then, suddenly, I felt the baby move. It was like it was saying, "I'm with you. Remember?" Hot tears burned my eyes and I said a little prayer for our baby and for Seth.

A feeling of loneliness overwhelmed me whenever I thought about Seth. His eyes and his face seemed hazy in my memory but I remembered his love. I'd always remember that.

Paul came from nowhere just then, erasing my thoughts. "Abigail, help me cover this wagon and then head for the shed," he said. "A storm is coming. It's going to hit any minute."

I looked up, feeling the sudden cool air. The clouds were black and edged with lacy white. They were whirling about in the sky as I struggled with the heavy canvas sheet, pulling it over the wooden nails Paul had fitted into the side of the wagon. Then he grabbed my hand and pulled me with him toward the shed.

We made it just before the storm hit. As the rain pounded down, I cried softly to myself, holding my stomach. My baby was still moving, still talking to me with its gentle flutters of life.

After the storm was over, Paul went over to check out the cabins. Everything was all right except one cabin that the rain had damaged, and he repaired that the next day.

The heat returned, but now it was humid from the rain and the air was suffocating. Paul decided now was the time to paint the outside of the cabins, and he came and got me from the cucumber patch. Earth and sky whirled as I got to my feet, and I felt so tired and sick. The big old shirts I wore over jeans concealed my condition, but I couldn't count on hiding it much longer.

While I was painting, I felt faint. I leaned against the side of a big tree and closed my eyes, feeling the sweat on my face and on my body.

"Couldn't you find a better day to paint?" a voice asked.

I opened my eyes and saw a tall man standing by a utility truck. He was young, around twenty-four, and nice looking.

"I work out of Williston. Lots of lines down around here. Do your folks own these cabins?" he asked.

I explained that it was my aunt and uncle's place and that I lived with them. He'd heard of Paul and Faye's truck farm, he told me. His folks drove out to get fresh fruits and vegetables there.

I felt faint, so I slid down to sit on the ground, wiping my face with my hand.

As I rested, the man told me his name was Tim Laurelton. He asked me my name and if I was married or had a steady boyfriend.

I shook my head no to the last two questions, but Seth's face flashed in my mind and I felt guilty, like I was cheating. Words caught in my throat.

"In a way, there's someone." I admitted. "But we're separated now. Something neither of us can help."

"Well, if I came to take you for a ride or a movie, would you go?" Tim asked. " I mean, just as friends," he added.

"I don't think you'd care to have me for a friend," I said softly. "I'm going to have a baby."

There was silence, a time while he thought it all over. Then he looked at me and smiled again. "None of that matters to me," he said. "I'm not asking you to go steady . . . I just said we could be friends. Right now, I'm a little short on friends. How about you?"

I wanted to cry. Tim was right. There was not one person I could call a friend here. Not one!

Tim came to the farm that night, driving a nice car, dressed in fresh jeans and a plaid shirt. I'd cleaned the kitchen up, taken a shower, and when I saw Tim in the yard talking to Paul, I dabbed lipstick on and went out. Paul liked him right away because Tim knew how to get on his good side by complimenting him on the farm and telling him that his folks came regularly to buy Paul's produce.

That's how I started going with Tim . . . as friends. We went for walks along the shore of the lake, to the movies, for long rides. And then one day I asked him if we could drive to Bismarck . . . just for fun, I told him.

It was a rainy day and the work was caught up on the farm. Paul and Faye had gone somewhere right from church. I said a ride to Bismarck was a good thing to do on a Sunday afternoon.

Tim wasn't the least bit suspicious. We drove all around Bismarck and then I casually asked where the jail was. Tim drove out to a long stretch of country and suddenly high barbed wire fences loomed up and there it was . . . the prison. A terrible yearning to see Seth again welled up inside of me, but I didn't say anything about it to Tim.

That night when we got home, Tim kissed me. Then he said that after the baby was born and everything was settled he'd take me home to meet his folks. That scared me a little. After all, I wasn't a typical teenage girl. I hadn't graduated from high school and soon I would be a single parent. I didn't agree or disagree with Tim about his idea. My feelings about him were all muddled up with my past. Still, it was nice to feel his arms around me and nice to be kissed again. It made me feel special . . . even loved.

When Tim left me at the door Faye opened it. The lights were bright in the living room and she glared at me angrily.

"I want to talk to you," she said.

My heart pounded with fear. I felt sick again.

"Why didn't you tell me you were pregnant? Why, Abby? Why did I have to find it out from one of the field hands? That Teresa

Castillo had the nerve to come up to me today after church and tell me you shouldn't be working in the fields . . . not in your condition. I had to pretend I knew all about it. Isn't it enough that we have to take you in without our being disgraced in this way? Why didn't you have an abortion?" she screamed.

I suppose I should have known that Teresa or one of the other women would guess I was pregnant. But since we never talked or got friendly at all, it hadn't occurred to me. But now, when that word "abortion" registered in my mind, I began to cry. I sobbed out to Faye that I wanted the baby, that Seth was innocent and I still loved him, and that one day we'd be a family.

Faye raised her arms in a gesture of helplessness. "I don't believe it!" she sneered. "I don't believe that anyone could be as stupid as you are. If you love Seth so much, what are you doing out with Tim? Letting him fool around with you? You certainly can't be so stupid as to think there's any other reason why any man in his right mind would go around with a girl who's carrying someone else's child, can you?" she asked.

It was like I was dying inside. I wished I could die! I stared out into the darkness of the night. "We're just friends. Tim's going to take me home to meet his folks soon," I said.

"Oh, sure. Sure he is," Faye snapped. "I'll believe it when I see it. The Laureltons are respectable people. Don't think for one minute that Tim's ever going to let them see you with him. His folks belong to a country club and they live in the nicest section of town. Get down to earth where you belong, Abigail. You aren't the kind of person someone like Tim takes home to meet his parents!"

She said a lot of other things . . . hurting words about how bad and unworthy I was. How I was just like my dad. Finally she ran out of words and I started for the stairs. But she called my name again.

"Abigail," she said coolly, "I hope you aren't thinking of keeping this child, because you're not going to. We don't need another ward of the state in this family."

I rushed upstairs, escaping Faye's cold ultimatum. Once in bed, I lay under the quilt and said my prayers. I asked God to guide me, to keep Seth and my baby safe. That's all I wanted. Not anything fancy or special, just for all of us to be together.

I woke up at dawn to the sound of Faye downstairs yelling about something. And then it all washed over me, all the words from the night before. I got up slowly. My body ached. The baby was growing inside moving a lot. One day at a time, Abigail, I told myself as I made my bed, washed up and went downstairs, wishing the earth would open up and swallow me whole.

Faye looked at me angrily the minute I walked in the kitchen.

61

"Don't think you're going to get off doing your share of the work just because you're pregnant!" she said. "It would be a blessing if you miscarried!"

I swallowed hard. "Want me to go out and feed the chickens and gather eggs?"

Faye's eyes were like steel, and I remembered suddenly that Mother said she was always bitter because she couldn't have children. The story was that Paul had gone out on her and there was a woman up north, near Canada, who contacted Faye and said she'd had his child. There was a big to-do about that, and Paul paid the woman off and Faye didn't divorce him. But after that, things weren't right between them. They just lived to make money.

"Of course I want you to go out and feed the chickens," she told me now. "And do all the other chores, too."

I was halfway to the chicken coop when she yelled, "Another thing, Abby. I don't want that Tim coming around here any more. When he comes again, you tell him you can't see him."

The whole day was extra hard for me . . . feeling sick from Faye's words, sick from my pregnancy, forcing my legs to move, my hands to do the work expected of them, trying to keep my mind clear and hope in my heart.

We had supper and I was doing the dishes when the pastor and his wife drove into the yard. Faye got all nervous. "Don't hang around while they're here," she told me. "Go out back or to your room." And then she said to Paul, "Change into something a little nicer. You look like a bum!"

I ran out the back door and headed toward the road where Tim would come if he was stopping out to see me that evening. I sat under a big oak tree and waited. Cars started whizzing by, filled with people dressed up to go to the corn roast and dance on the other side of the lake. The Indians from the reservation were having a fall festival.

Finally Tim's car came around the bend slowing. I got to my feet and waved to him, motioning for him to turn onto the service road that ended in a thick pine grove.

He was grinning. "Thought we'd go for a ride, not park! But that's all right with me too!" he kidded.

I started bawling, not caring if I looked a mess or if my eyes swelled or how I looked, just telling Tim all the things Faye had said. He listened without interrupting, and then he said, "Abby, I like you a lot. We're friends, remember? But I don't know how I'm going to feel after you have the baby. I just don't know. Do you know how you're going to feel? What if Seth comes around . . . then what? What about me?"

I ignored his questions. I was the one who had to know

62

something. "Would you take me home to meet your folks? Would you, Tim?" I asked.

"Not now . . . I told you that," he said. "They wouldn't understand."

I sighed. "Then Faye was right," I said. "I'm just a tramp to you . . . someone to fool around with."

"That's not true," Tim protested. "I—I think I love you. Maybe I'll want to marry you sometime. But I'm just not sure. . . ."

I began running back toward the house. Tim came after me. When he caught up, he pulled me to him and kissed me.

For a moment I leaned against him, feeling his strength. Then I remembered Seth and I pushed him away. "I don't think we should see each other again," I said. "This is good-bye!"

I heard his car leave, and I knew he'd look for someone else . . . someone good enough to meet his family.

I opened the back door and sneaked in, listening. The pastor and his wife were leaving. The pastor was telling Faye and Paul what a charitable act it was, taking in a poor, homeless girl in trouble. The voices faded as they all walked outside. I ran up the stairs to my room and closed the door. The trap was tightening. Time was flying and I had no plans for the future . . . for my baby or me.

Faye came upstairs after a while. "Abby? Abby, are you home?" she called, her voice gentle now.

"I'm home," I said.

She came in my room and sat on the chair by the dresser. "Abby, I feel much better now that I've talked to the pastor," she told me. "I know everything is going to work out all right."

"Good," I said, wondering what she meant.

She stood up and walked to the window. "Paul's going to town . . . he needs to get out a little," she said. "We've all been working too hard. When the baby comes and you're free again, you can have some fun, too. Go to the movies, join the young adults group at the church. There's a lot you can do with your life. . . ."

I knew what she was getting at; life could be beautiful if I gave my baby away. Well, I didn't say anything, but I knew I'd never do that. No way would I give my baby away.

Time had wings. Soon the air had a chill to it, and Paul and I would go into the woods and cut up fallen trees and haul the logs back to the little shed attached to the house. The summer help was long gone and after wrapping up the nightly chores I'd go in the house and sit with Faye while Paul went into town . . . for a beer, he said.

In December, Faye took me in to see Dr. Henri. It was obvious she'd called him before we came, because he had a nice little talk all ready for me. He examined me then smiled and said, "Somebody is going to be very happy to get a healthy baby like yours. I know people myself . . . people who could give a child everything. A mother and father . . . a beautiful home . . . a fine education."

I made myself speak calmly. "You've got it all wrong, Dr. Henri," I said. "I'm keeping my baby!"

Then I put on my coat, buttoned it up, and walked out into the waiting room. Faye went in and talked to the doctor. She came out looking peeved. All the phony kindness was gone from her eyes.

It snowed all the way back to the farm, big thick flakes that frosted the ground in innocent white. I was feeling heavy and full of aches. Tired. When we got to the farm, Faye noticed that Paul's pickup was gone. She sighed. "Paul's going out more and more," she said. "Guess he gets tired of the crowd in the house."

"I won't be staying much longer," I told her. "Just give me a chance to find a new place . . . a room is all I need."

She slowed the car and looked at me. "You sound so stupid!" she said. "You can't live in one room! And certainly not with a baby!"

I shrugged. I knew there was no point in arguing with her.

We trudged through the unshoveled snow that had formed drifts up the hill from the garage to the house. The wind took my breath away. Faye unlocked the door, then turned and glanced back down the road. Our tracks had already been covered by fresh snow. It was the first real blizzard of the season.

We carried logs in to the fireplace and to the little wood-burning stove that was in the archway between the bedrooms and the living room. The wood crackled as it burned, filling the air with its fragrance, and the flames flickered with a warm golden glow as daylight blended into night. We had soup and sandwiches. Faye seemed restless and nervous. The phone rang. I answered it. Surprisingly, it was Tim. Once in a while he called . . . to keep in touch, he said.

I told him I'd been to the doctor and that it wouldn't be much longer before the baby came. Tim said he would be glad when it was all over . . . that maybe we could start dating again. I wasn't thinking clearly. It had been an unnerving day and Faye kept looking at me, frowning, wanting me off the phone. Finally I told Tim I had to hang up.

Around ten, Faye started calling all the places that Paul frequented. At the last place she called, she evidently got some clue to where he was. She listened, then whispered a thank you and hung up. "He's with friends," she told me, glaring at me like it was all my fault.

I knew he was with another woman. I was honestly sorry, but what did Faye expect? She never fixed herself up. She went around dressed like a hired man. Even her hair was cut like a man's, and she never wore makeup or made herself desirable and attractive. And she could have been pretty if she had just made a little effort, taken a little time. Her attitude toward Paul was all wrong, too. If he tried to touch her she'd shrug him off and tell him she was tired or behind in her work.

I finally went up to bed and lay awake listening for Paul, listening for the sound of the county plow on the highway. It wasn't till around five a.m. that I heard the plow coming up the long, winding drive. When I peeked out the window, I saw Paul's pickup following behind it.

I went back to bed and slept for a little while. Then sounds of a terrible fight downstairs woke me up. Faye was really letting Paul have it and he was giving it right back to her, telling her that if she was any kind of woman maybe he'd stay home more.

After that, he left right after supper every night and came home when he was good and ready. Faye looked like she was really suffering, but she didn't say anything more.

Two weeks before Christmas, Paul went out and cut a pine tree for the living room. "Where's the tree stand?" he asked Faye. "We could put this up tonight, couldn't we?"

"We aren't putting up a tree," Faye told him. "Why have a Christmas tree in a house that's full of hate?"

Paul dragged the tree back outside and left it leaning against the side of the house. Then he came in, showered and shaved, and put on a nice sweater and slacks. It was pretty obvious that he was going to someone who appreciated him more than Faye did. Just before he left, he turned to me and said, "When your time comes to go to the hospital, I'll take you if the weather is bad, don't worry. I talked to Lenny, the man who drives the plow, and he'll get us there."

I just nodded. I wasn't used to anyone giving me that much consideration.

Well, my time was that night. Around midnight the pains started. I got up and went to the window and saw that the pickup wasn't home. The night was blustery, the wind howled against the house, and snow blew in sheets of white powder. I remembered reading it was important to relax in labor, so I lay down and prayed that Paul would come home before I had to go to the hospital. But he didn't come home, and finally at three in the morning I went downstairs and woke Faye.

She got right up, grumbling, but she called the doctor and the hospital. Even though the car started hard, it got us into town.

I kept thinking about Seth . . . and the new life I was bringing into the world, but the pain kept getting worse until it consumed me and there was no room in my mind for anything except suffering.

When Dr. Henri came, he examined me. Then he called for a nurse and said something to her that I couldn't hear. She left, then came back with a sheet of paper on a board and a pen in her hand. "Sit up, Abigail," she said. "You have to sign some papers."

The pain was deep and the room was whirling around me. I leaned on one elbow and held the pen in my hand. "What am I signing?" I whispered.

Dr. Henri moved between the nurse and me. "Abigail, we're having some problems," he said. "You have to sign these consent papers for surgery. You want the baby to live, don't you?"

The words shocked me into action. I signed several papers, and then they moved me to another room and put me to sleep.

When I woke up, the pain was gone, my stomach was flat, and everything was still and quiet. My bed was next to the window and outside I could see pine trees with Christmas lights blinking in them.

A nurse entered. "You had a little girl. A beautiful little girl," she told me.

A glow went through me. "When can I see her?" I asked.

The nurse told me that they didn't move the babies for at least twelve hours after delivery, but she said I could cross the hall and see my baby if I was strong enough. Better still, she said, she'd bring a wheelchair and take me.

She did that, and I stood up and looked through the glass and saw my baby . . . a dark-haired little doll with a tiny turned-up nose and plump little cheeks. I thought: thank you God. And then I began to cry . . . tears of relief and joy.

Suddenly another nurse came and said something sharp and cross to the nurse who'd brought me. Then I was wheeled back to my room. I felt dizzy and scared. The first nurse left and the second one stayed.

"I'd advise you to stay away from the nursery," she said. "No sense making things harder on yourself."

"What do you mean?" I whispered, some deep instinct telling me my baby and I were in terrible danger.

"When you're giving up a child, you don't want to have the memory of it haunting you," the nurse said, almost sympathetically. "It's better to make a clean break. I can't understand why Nurse Johnson didn't use better judgment."

"I'm not giving my baby up!" I protested. "I never said I was!" My heart pounded wildly.

The nurse shrugged, her expression turning wary. "You signed the papers. It's all perfectly legal. You had nine months to make this decision."

When she left, I called Faye. I begged her to help me. She listened and then said, "Abigail, I told you before that I won't take a baby into my home. I have enough problems of my own. If you have someplace else to go with the child, okay. But don't look to me for any help or money."

I don't remember hanging up, but I guess I did. I lay back, feeling weak with fear. Who else did I know to call? Tim! I'd call Tim.

I dialed his home number and a pleasant sounding voice answered. I figured it was his mother.

"Could you please have Tim call Abigail at the hospital and Washburn?" I asked. "It's urgent."

She wanted to pry, but I said I had to hang up.

It was seven before he called. He was angry. "Abby, what are you calling my home for?" he demanded.

"I just need someone to help me," I said. "I had my baby, Tim. She's a beautiful little girl—"

"Sure, sure," he cut me off impatiently. "Look, Abby, I like you. I want to see you when you get your problems worked out. But if you're looking for someone to play Daddy, count me out. In fact, if you're thinking about keeping the baby, we'd better say good-bye right now."

I hung up without saying another word.

As I lay there in my bed, I saw proud fathers passing my door on their way to the nursery . . . candy stripers delivering roses and plants to new mothers . . . grandparents congratulating each other . . . and down the hall the carolers came. It was the season of birth . . . of love . . . but I had no one.

It was eight o'clock when Paul came. Paul, not Faye. He brought me a box of chocolates. "How are you doing, Abby?" he asked.

I didn't want to burden him, but I had to talk to someone. I told him what had happened.

He looked pained and embarrassed. "Abby, if I could help you, I would," he said, "but I honestly don't know how. I'm divorcing Faye. I'm not even planning on going back to the house. I've found someone who really cares about me. Someone I love. I can give you a little money to tide you over, but that's it."

I told him about Seth and I gave him the Hagan's name and telephone number. He listened, but he didn't promise anything.

The hall lights dimmed and it was announced that visitors were to leave. Paul got up right away . . . glad to be going, I guess. I got out of bed, pulled the hospital robe around me, and said I wanted him to see the baby. We walked to the window and looked at her, and then Paul went on his way.

When you're on the county welfare roll they keep you two days for having a baby and then you're released. Well, at noon a nurse came in and said it was time for me to get dressed and she'd take me down to the lounge. My aunt was waiting there for me, she said.

I dressed slowly, and when I was ready, I said, "Will you get my baby for me?"

"I thought we had this all straightened out," the nurse said impatiently. "Your baby is gone. You gave her up for adoption."

I started to scream, and Dr. Henri came racing in. A nurse came with him.

"Abigail, get yourself under control!" Dr. Henri scolded. "Now, I'm going to give you a shot so your aunt can get you home. . . ."

The nurse shoved a needle into my arm and then she helped me into my coat and set me down in a wheelchair. By the time I was in Faye's car, the world was whirling around and around.

I was only half aware of the drive home. Faye helped me out of the car and into the house to her room. When I woke up it was night and the house seemed so cold and empty. Then I remembered my baby and I began to cry. Faye heard me and came in the room.

"Listen, Abby, you've got to pull yourself together!" she said impatiently. "I've had about all I can take of your hysterics. It was all this trouble with you that chased Paul away!"

I wanted to tell her that he had left her because she was a cold, mean, money-loving person, but what good would it do me to hurt her? We were both hurting enough already.

Christmas came and it was just another day. A day of work and silence and tears. But then the next day Paul came in his pickup. He'd brought the woman he'd told me about and her two children along. They stayed in the pickup while he came to the door and asked me to come outside. He introduced me to the woman . . . her name was Amy . . . and then he shocked me by saying, "Amy says you can come and stay with us. Her house is two blocks from the vocational school. We both figured it would be smart for you to go there and learn some kind of trade."

I cried. But it was a good cry because someone cared about me! I went upstairs and put my few belongings in a box and pulled it down the stairs. When I came down, Faye was right after me, telling Paul he had nerve coming there with "that woman" and her "brats." And where did I think I was going? Paul said I was going with them, and Faye began begging me to stay, pulling my arm and crying wildly. But I went with Paul and Amy.

I liked Amy and her children, Suzy and Sam. They were all so good to me. It was better than I'd had it since my mother died. I told Paul I'd get a place of my own as soon as I got on my feet, and he said there was no big rush . . . to just take my time.

I thought about my baby all the time, of course. But I also kept my mind on my studies. Over the months, I earned my diploma, took a secretarial course, and got a good job with an accountant.

But I wasn't happy. Memories of Seth and my baby haunted me. Amy could see that, and it worried her.

"Abigail, you should go out and have some fun," she'd tell me.

"Forget about Seth. By now you surely realize that he was giving you the oldest line in the book. . . ."

At first I'd be mad, hearing things like that. But gradually doubts began to creep into my mind. Why hadn't I heard from Seth? One letter, just one line!

Amy kept telling me that I had built a shell around myself, that I didn't try to make friends. But I did! I went to church functions, but I felt out of place. I was the only one without a girlfriend or boyfriend. It was the same at work. All the girls I knew there were engaged or married or having their first baby. Where did that leave me? What did I have to talk about? My baby was gone and the man I loved was being held in prison for a crime I just knew he didn't do.

One day in late spring I was walking home from work. I came to the house and noticed an unfamiliar car out front. I walked past it and went in the house . . . and then I heard Seth's voice! I screamed and he came down the hall toward me. He was older looking, thinner . . . but it was truly him. And his eyes were shining with love.

Seth explained it all to me in a rush. Wade Jenkins, the man who'd worked with us in the laundry, had gotten drunk one night in a bar and started bragging about how someone else had taken the rap for the robbery he'd committed. It didn't take long for somebody to pass this information on to the police, and after a hearing and subsequent indictment, Wade was jailed and Seth was released. Wade was awaiting trial, and Seth was cleared.

Paul had contacted him in jail months before, offering to act as a go-between if Seth ever wanted to contact me, and that was the first call Seth made when he got out of prison!

Four days after we were reunited, we were married. We stayed with Paul and Amy until Seth got a job in a new service station outside of town. Then we rented an apartment. But we didn't even look at apartments until we had gone to Social Services about our baby. The woman there was not very friendly, and she went to the file and her eyes skimmed the papers in the manila envelope and she looked at me and said, "Well, you put 'father unknown' for one thing; and, for another, you signed the three necessary papers. It's a little late to be changing your mind. Your child has a father and mother, and there's nothing you can do."

"I was told I was signing for surgery," I protested.

The woman closed the file. "Oh, yes I've heard that one before," she said.

From there we went to an attorney. Seth's voice broke as he related everything to the tall, cold, professional-looking man. The lawyer leaned back in his chair, lit his pipe, and glanced at me. "Who was your doctor?" he asked.

"Dr. Henri," I said.

This seemed to get his attention. "Oh, yes, Dr. Henri," he said. "He's a personal friend of mine. A dedicated man. Frankly, this isn't the kind of case I care to get mixed up in. At any rate, I would advise you to drop it. You don't have a legal leg to stand on. . . ."

Back in our car, I clung to Seth. His arms held me tight and he promised me that one day we'd find our little girl. I wanted to believe him.

I loved Seth so much! It was as though I hadn't really known him before. Now I was getting acquainted with the man I loved. He was gentle, patient, and kind. He was more than all the dreams I ever had. Life would have been so wonderful if we had our child.

It was all I thought of. We had a small room in our apartment that the lady before us had used as a sewing room. I bought nursery paper and hung frilly curtains at the window, and over the spot where the crib should be I hung a picture of a little girl walking hand in hand between her mother and father. Eventually I even bought a crib and dresser at a secondhand shop, and I refinished them one evening when Seth was working. When he came home and saw them, he said, "Abby, are you pregnant?"

I felt scared inside. I shook my head.

"Then why are you doing this?" Seth demanded. "Why, Abby?"

"Because you promised me that someday we'd find her," I said weakly.

Seth went to the window and stared out into the darkness. "Everything that happened was my fault . . . I know that," he said. "But it's hard enough for me without this. . . ."

I ran to him and put my arms around him, but he stood motionless, closing me out of his private world of pain.

The next morning was awkward, but we both tried to act normal. But all day there was a heavy feeling inside me . . . a feeling of dread.

It was about three o'clock that afternoon when the phone rang. A woman introduced herself to me as Faith Myers. I didn't know her. She spoke nervously, words tumbling out of her. She worked for Social Services. Her best friend was Dr. Henri's nurse, and she was also acquainted with the secretary to the lawyer we had been to see. She wanted to talk to us. She said she knew where our little girl was.

My heart almost pounded out of me. I arranged to have her come over that evening, and as soon as we hung up I called Seth at work. He was supposed to work the evening shift, but I said he had to come home. Our prayers were being answered.

Faith Myers came a few minutes after seven. She seemed very nervous.

"I wouldn't be doing this," she began, "but Dr. Henri did the same thing to me. By the time I found out what had happened, I also

70

learned that my baby and his adoptive parents had been killed in a car crash. There was no hope for me, but maybe there is for you. No lawyers around here would ever go against Dr. Henri, but you could go to Fargo maybe, and find one that will take your case. Anyway, I wrote down the name and address of your little girl's adoptive parents. I don't know anything about them, but if you do go to court, I'll help you all I can. Maybe that will stop Dr. Henri's lucrative baby business."

After Seth and I thanked her and she left, I looked at the name and address she'd given us: Barbara and Bill Engle, 215 Oak Street, Breckinridge, Minnesota.

Seth called his employer and said a family emergency had come up and he had to be going out of town. I called my boss and told her I wouldn't be in the next day. Then we just sort of collapsed in each other's arms . . . out of shock and joy.

We didn't sleep all night, making plans. Seth wanted to drive to Fargo, see an attorney, and go to Breckinridge from there. But I couldn't stand it and I guess he couldn't, either; so we left for Breckinridge at dawn.

The long drive seemed endless, but we finally made it. The first gas station we came to in Breckinridge, Seth pulled in and went inside to ask directions to the address we had. The man told him it was a street in the nicest part of town.

When Seth got back in the car and told me that, he added, "I suppose they have money, money to pay Dr. Henri and money to hire a good lawyer to fight us."

"Don't talk that way," I begged. "Don't start giving up . . . please!"

"Okay honey," Seth agreed. "But don't get your hopes up too high."

Oak Street was a lovely winding road along the Red River. We finally came to a sign that said Private Road.

Seth drove slowly, glancing at house numbers, then nodding at a large house on the right-hand side of the road. He stopped next door and we stared at the house. They had everything!

"Well, now what do we do?" Seth asked.

I leaned back against the seat, feeling less able to deal with it all now that we were here and my baby was so close. "Maybe we could call them . . . ask to come up," I said. "I don't know, Seth—"

"Well, we can't just sit here," he said. "We need to think this out."

We found a motel and checked in. Seth looked in the phone book and found the Engle's telephone number and a listing below the home address for a business number. He went to the phone. "I'm going to call him and lay it on the line," he said.

He dialed, and then when someone answered, he said, "Is Mr. Engle in? This is a matter of extreme importance."

I felt like our life was on the line. I listened to Seth as he fumbled with his explanations and the reason for our visit. I waited and prayed until finally he hung up.

"He's coming right over here to see us," Seth told me.

In fifteen minutes Mr. Engle arrived. He drove a big car, was slim, and well dressed. Seth opened the door for him and said, "Are you Mr. Engle?"

The man nodded, and I saw the fear in his eyes. "Dr. Henri assured my wife and me that Kaitlyn's mother didn't want her," he began, "but I always had a premonition that this might happen. We love her like our own . . . like Justin and Ryan. . . ."

Their own! They had children! Why should they have mine, too? Surely this fact would strengthen our case in court if it came to that.

Seth was busy discussing our side of things . . . how I'd been tricked into signing those papers. Finally Mr. Engle said, "Why don't you come to the house . . . meet my wife and Kaitlyn. Just a casual visit. I'd like to buy a little time to prepare Barb. . . ."

I stared at him. Why would a woman with a home like that and two sons and a fine husband need time to be prepared?

"All right," Seth was saying, "we'll come. But we'll play it by ear when we get there. I want you to understand that whether it's tonight or next week or next month, we're going to go to court and get our little girl back. Neither of us wants to hurt you and your wife, but I don't see how that can be avoided."

We had agreed to be at the Engle's house at eight that evening. When we got there, all the outside lights were on. Seth rang the doorbell. A tall, attractive woman opened the door. "Did you come to see Bill?" she asked.

Seth just nodded, but I spoke up. "Are you Barbara Engle?" I said.

"No, I'm a neighbor," the woman explained. "But come in. Barbara asked me to run over and stay with Kaitlyn. I expect her to call me as soon as she can."

We followed the woman into the living room. A fire was blazing in the fireplace and the room was furnished like a picture out of a magazine. On one table there was a picture of two young boys.

Resentment filled me as I looked around. They had everything! A lovely home, two sons, and my daughter.

The neighbor's voice went on as she invited us to sit down. And then Kaitlyn came toddling into the room, a plump little body taking uneasy steps. She only glanced at Seth and me and reached for the woman who had led us in.

Seth restrained himself, but I crossed the room and reached out to touch Kaitlyn's arm. "She's so beautiful!" I gasped.

Seth spoke up then. "Well, where are the Engles?" he demanded. "He said we should come over." There was irritation and nervousness in his tone.

"I know he planned on someone coming," the neighbor said, "because he came home from the office early and told Barbara not to make plans for the evening. Then he went upstairs and collapsed. Another heart attack. . . ."

Seth paled, and the woman stared at him . . . at both of us. "Are you Kaitlyn's birth parents?" she asked quietly. The question hung in the air.

"I saw the resemblance right away," she went on, "and Barb always feared something like this would happen. She always said she loved Kaitlyn too much. But how could you help but love her?"

"I was tricked into signing papers," I stammered. "I never intended to give up my baby. . . ."

The woman looked away. "Maybe not—"

"They've got everything!" I protested. "They've got two sons, so why do they want to keep my baby?" The words caught in my throat as I struggled to hold back the sobs.

The woman glanced toward the picture of the little boys. "They're dead," she said tonelessly. "One from leukemia and the other from complications during the bone marrow transplant . . . they died a few months apart. First Justin, then Ryan. After Ryan died, Bill had his first heart attack . . . and Barb gave up. A cousin of Barb's came down and told her about Dr. Henri . . . how he placed babies quicker than the other agencies. And Barb was told it was all legal. That they'd be giving a home to a child who had neither home nor parents. This house was just a shell of memories before Kaitlyn came."

She kept watching me, weighing her words. "I think I know how you must feel," she said, "but Kaitlyn is their life. They adore her. Living here, she would have the best of everything . . . and certainly just as much love as you could give her. Maybe you would win in court if it comes to that, but sometimes justice has to come from within ourselves."

Seth asked if she thought Barbara knew why we were coming to the house, and she shrugged. "Barbara told me that Bill was really troubled," she said, "and she couldn't understand what would upset him so much unless it has something to do with Kaitlyn. Then she said that everything was in God's hands . . . that He could take both of them from her if He wanted, just as He had taken Ryan and Justin."

I tried to pick Kaitlyn up, but she pulled away from me. Seth got up and headed for the door, saying we'd call the house in the morning.

He also asked what hospital Bill Engle had been taken to.

I cried all the way to the motel and Seth said nothing. We went inside and when Seth closed the door, he put his arms around me and held me tight, our tears blending.

"We aren't going to fight for her, are we?" I whispered.

"No," Seth said brokenly.

I felt his heart beating against mine and our tears flowed together. There was nothing more to say. Even if all the courts in the land would return our baby to us, we couldn't take her away from the parents she loved, the home they provided, and the need she fulfilled in their life.

We were awake all night. Around seven in the morning, Seth went to the telephone. "I'm going to call Barbara Engle," he said. "I want to tell her what we've decided. It might save her husband's life."

I nodded.

He dialed, and then she was on the phone. He stumbled through the explanation of what we had wanted and that we'd talked it over and decided we weren't going to try to take Kaitlyn away from her. He asked her to give that message to her husband, and he asked how her husband was. Apparently, from what Seth said then, Bill Engle was out of danger and doing well.

Barbara Engle talked to Seth for some time, and then she wanted to speak to me.

"I don't know how to thank you," she said. "Only God knows how much this means to me. I pray that He will bless you both. We love Kaitlyn so much . . . she's everything to us. We'll always be good to her and always see that she is cared for . . . just as our sons were. . . ."

I managed to ask if they planned to tell Kaitlyn someday that she was adopted, and when Mrs. Engle said yes, I asked her if she would please tell her then that her real mother and father loved her very much.

She took our name and address and then we said good-bye. We packed up our suitcases and took one last ride down Oak Street, staring at the house where our daughter lived. All the way back to our own home, I prayed for strength and peace . . . for all of us.

A month later we received a long letter from Bill and Barbara Engle. He was home from the hospital, doing well, and they wanted to thank us for our decision and for the joy it gave them. They also extended an invitation for us to visit them if we ever wanted to.

I didn't answer the letter until four months later . . . after I'd been to the doctor and he had confirmed that I was pregnant. When I wrote the Engles, I said that Seth and I felt that perhaps it was in everyone's best interest if we did not return to their home. But I assured them that I was thankful for their very selfless and kind thought.

74

After our son was born, I sent a hospital picture to the Engles with the birth announcement. A week later a gift from them arrived. A little blue bunting set and a prayer that God would bless us all. There was also a note that said how much our son looked like Kaitlyn in her baby pictures. Maybe it was God's way of giving to both of us, Barbara Engle said.

Seth read the note and then he held me close. In his arms, I said a silent prayer of thanks for my husband and my little son. And in that moment it was like I'd freed Kaitlyn to give all her loyalty to the fine man and woman who loved her so much.

THE END

# ADDICTED

There was only ugliness and dirt, freezing in the winter and sweltering in the summer on the streets of my city. We lived in a dark, cramped apartment . . . Ma, me, and my stepfather, Sal. I was just a baby when Ma married him. You'd think he might have treated me like I was his own, but he didn't. He despised me. He beat me every chance he got, and I learned to keep out of his way.

Sal worked in a factory. He drank a lot of beer spiked with whiskey, and Mom drank right along with him. When Sal was drinking, he always started in on my mother.

"Dirty tramp!" he'd yell at her, pounding his fist on the table. "You don't even know who the kid's father is. At least if you did, you could get some money out of him. Instead, I'm the one who's stuck with her. I've got to feed her."

Tears would run out of my mother's eyes, and then she'd turn on me. "Get out of here!" she'd yell, as though it were my fault that I'd been born. "Get lost! I don't care what happens to you!"

Then, she'd push me out of the apartment and lock the door. In the summertime it wasn't so bad. There was a park nearby where I could sit on the grass and watch the sparrows. They were cute with their bright eyes and fluttering wings. If I shut my eyes and listened to their chirping instead of the traffic noises, I could pretend that I was out in the green country, which I'd never seen.

In the winter, though, Mom or Sal would lock me out when I didn't even have a coat. The smelly halls were drafty and freezing cold. I'd huddle in a corner behind the stairs for hours until I'd hear Sal stumble out. Then I'd sneak back into the apartment.

Nobody had ever tried to help me. The other people in our building had their own troubles, and, besides, they were afraid of Sal's violent temper.

Once, I'd gotten very sick. I'd been absent from school for so many days that the school nurse had called my mother. She'd reprimanded my mother for not keeping me clean and warm.

My mother had been drunk at the time. "Maybe you'd like to take Pamela and raise her yourself," she said. "You'd be more than welcome to her!"

After that, the nurse had tried to be especially kind to me at school. But, I wouldn't talk to her. I was ashamed that she'd had to hear my mother speak that way about me, and that she knew what kind of mother I had.

School was no good for me, anyway. The other kids didn't have any more money than I did, but for the most part, their parents loved them and did the best that they could for them. They all knew that I was just an accident from one of my moms many affairs, and the mean kids teased me. They yelled at me on the playground and called me names. I didn't have enough courage to fight them. And so, I took the abuse silently . . . the same way that I took Sal's curses and blows.

The teachers didn't like me because I was never properly bathed, and I never knew the answers when they called on me. They thought that I was stupid, but I wasn't . . . not really at least. I was actually fairly intelligent, but I was afraid to say anything in class. When I got into middle school, I couldn't keep up with the class because Sal wouldn't let me bring my books home.

"What do you need with books?" he'd roar at me. "You're going to turn out to be a tramp, anyway, just like your mother!"

Then, he'd hit me on the side of the head with such force that I was thrown clear across the kitchen. My head would ring for hours.

When I was fifteen, I made my first friend. Somehow, I'd scraped through middle school and had begun attending a trade school to learn industrial sewing. Rosalie sat at the next sewing machine. She was a little older than I was, and she had a graceful way of walking that I admired.

We became friends right away and I started going to her room after school, staying as long as I dared. Rosalie lived alone, and though it was just a tiny room in a rundown boardinghouse, I didn't care. But I couldn't understand how she got enough money every month to go to school and pay rent. I didn't ask any questions, though, I was too humbly grateful to the first person that'd ever liked me.

Rosalie seemed to enjoy doing things for me. She styled my hair and showed me how to do it myself. She bought me makeup, and one day, she brought material to school to make a new outfit for me. We worked on it together after school, and when I had it on, with my new hairstyle and makeup, I couldn't believe how pretty I looked.

I threw my arms around Rosalie. "I'll pay you back," I promised. "I'll pay you back with the very first money that I earn."

"Forget it," Rosalie said casually. "It didn't cost me a cent."

I looked at her wonderingly. "It didn't?"

She grinned. "The fabric was on the remnant table, with a lot of women pushing each other around, fighting over it. I just eased it up under my jacket and held it with my arm. No problem."

I wasn't shocked or horrified. Sure, I knew that you could be sent to jail if you were caught stealing, but that didn't mean that it was wrong. In a world where I'd been beaten and pushed around because I was too weak to fight back, how could I have had any standards of right and wrong? I cried because Rosalie had liked me enough to steal for me.

I was afraid that Sal would get angry when he saw me fixing myself up, but his reaction was just the opposite. He began to treat me nicely, for a change. He talked to me about my work at school, and he even gave me a little money now and then. He told me that it was for doing the housework, because my mother had been sick.

There was something terribly wrong with my mother. She took pills all the time to help the pain, and still, she just kept on losing weight. She sat there all day in her rocking chair, waiting for Sal to come home. And, if he came back late, they'd have a big fight.

One night, when I was doing the dishes, Sal came over to the sink. I was so used to dodging him that I moved away, but suddenly, I felt his hand brush across my hip. Mom made a choking sound and when I looked at her, she was staring at me with pure hate in her eyes.

"Get out of this house!" she screamed. "I saw that! You've been after Sal for a long time, haven't you?"

"Shut up, Lori," Sal snapped.

"You shut up, you pig!" Mom yelled. "Don't think I don't know that you've got other women, now that I'm of no use to you . . . now that I'm sick and dying. And now, you're after my daughter!"

I ran out of the apartment and down the stairs to the street. I felt sick, scared, and I was trembling uncontrollably. All I could think of was getting to Rosalie . . . the only friend that I had on earth. I knew that she spent her evenings with a group of friends at a club called Changes, so I went straight there. She'd asked me to meet her there before, but I'd always been too afraid of Sal to sneak out at night.

Changes was located in an alley. A dim light seeped through the windows and I heard loud music inside. I hesitated in front of the door. I was worried that Rosalie wouldn't want to see me . . . but then, I thought of Sal and Mom fighting over me, and I went in.

It was dark inside the club. I stood there, waiting until my eyes got used to the gloom. The air was filled with an unfamiliar, sort of sickly sweet scent. It was a small club, with a bar on one side and a single row of booths on the other. Beyond them was a larger room where couples were dancing. I saw Rosalie at the same time that she saw me.

"Hey! Pamela," she yelled while rushing up to the door.

My heart filled with a great surge of happiness because Rosalie was glad to see me. She led me to a table in the back room and introduced me to her friends.

There was Gary, a guy in his thirties, who glanced at me and nodded his head slowly, like somebody in a dream.

"Gary's mine," Rosalie told me, stroking his hair. "You can have these other two characters, but stay away from Gary. He's a great musician, and, someday, we're going to be rich. Right, honey?"

Gary stared straight ahead, not answering. I felt a little embarrassed, but Rosalie didn't seem to mind. She introduced the others. There was a young, good-looking guy named Bruce, a well-dressed girl, older than Rosalie was, who gave me an unfriendly look. Her name was Sonia. And last . . . there was Mark. He was sitting beside Sonia and their hands were on the table, close together . . . like lovers' hands.

Mark was about twenty, and very handsome. He got up to greet me, drawing out the empty chair beside him. I sat down, feeling shy, but nobody paid any attention to me. Rosalie and Gary got up and began to dance. Bruce was drinking, staring straight in front of him. His eyes had a blank look, as though they didn't see anything.

I looked away from him with a shiver and found Mark smiling at me.

"Don't mind Bruce," he said in a low voice. "He's high. Want to join him?"

I didn't know what he'd meant until I saw that he was holding out a cigarette. It was funny looking, thin, with the ends pinched in.

"Thanks, but I don't smoke," I said politely.

Mark laughed as though I'd said something cute.

"Leave her alone," Sonia said angrily. "Don't you know that it's girls like her who get you in trouble?"

"Her kind of trouble I might like," Mark said flirtatiously, and turned his back on Sonia. "Try it," he coaxed, holding out the cigarette. "You'll like it."

His eyes were warm, and a little thrill of happiness ran through me. Mark likes me! I thought. He wanted to be my friend, so I took the cigarette and he showed me how to smoke it in very short puffs, so that it wouldn't make me cough.

Rosalie and Gary came back to the booth, and Rosalie giggled when she saw me smoking. "Didn't take you long to wise up, did it, honey?" she asked.

I smiled at her, not understanding what she'd meant. I sat there, smoking slowly, feeling the tension and the fear ebb out of my body as the sweet smoke filled my lungs. It made me a little dizzy, but it was a pleasant sensation. I heard myself talking to Mark, laughing and making jokes. I felt so smart and confident. I'd never dreamed that I could be that way.

Suddenly, Mark was holding my hand. I felt warm and content . . . and I almost felt like going to sleep. Then, somehow, my head was on his shoulder, and I was smiling into his eyes.

"I'm a loser," he said suddenly. "Did you know that, Pamela? I flunked out of college."

The note of unhappiness in his voice cut through the fog that I was in and I snuggled closer, wanting to comfort him. "That's not so bad," I told him. "I don't even know my real last name. I mean, I don't know who my father is . . . from what I hear it could be any number of guys."

"So you're a misfit, too," he commiserated. "We're a couple of lost souls in a world that doesn't want us."

"Oh, please, listen to that!" Sonia cut in. "Mark's happy now. He's got a new shoulder to cry on. Come on, everyone; let's go over to my place. I'm sick of this music."

We all got up. Sonia looked at me coldly. "Not you, honey."

Mark's arm was still around me. "I won't go unless I can bring her," he protested.

Sonia gave me a murderous look, but I didn't care. All I cared about was staying with Mark.

Sonia lived in a two-room apartment in an old building. She went straight to the bathroom and Rosalie told me all about her. Sonia was divorced, with a two-year-old son that lived with her mother. She worked as a personal trainer and got alimony from her ex-husband.

"Don't let her scare you away from Mark," Rosalie advised. "I can see that he likes you, and she hasn't got any hold on him. She's too old for him, anyway."

We went back in the living room and it was full of that same sweet smell that I'd noticed at Changes. A stereo was playing softly, and everybody was sprawled on the floor around it, listening and smoking. Mark gave me another cigarette and I leaned against his shoulder, smoking in short puffs. A kind of cloudy feeling drifted around me, and I was suddenly very peaceful and happy.

After awhile, I noticed that Mark was restless. His shoulder jerked under me and suddenly he got up, so quickly that I fell back against the wall. He went into the bedroom, Sonia followed, and they closed the door.

I didn't know what to think. I was miserable until Mark came out again, about five minutes later. He sat down next to me and the feeling between us was the way it had been at Changes. We didn't even need to talk. Just being close, our bodies touching and our hands clasped together, tight and warm, made me happy in a way that I'd never known before.

I'd been lonely all my life. I'd always felt unwanted and worthless. Mark had suddenly given me something wonderful . . . the feeling of being wanted and needed by another human being.

I didn't think about Sal, or my mother, or having to get home.

"Pamela, honey, do you know what time it is?" Sonia asked finally. "Two o'clock. Time for schoolgirls to be in bed."

I jumped up, my heart pounding in terror. Two in the morning! I thought. Sal will kill me . . . beat me to death!

"I've got to get home right away," I said. "Oh, Rosalie, I'm scared!"

She soothed me, telling me that they'd drive me home. She got Gary to his feet, shaking him and slapping him lightly across the face until his eyes had lost their glazed look. I'd hoped that Mark would come with me, but he just said good night at the door of the apartment. He didn't even try to kiss me; he just rested his cheek against mine for a second. All the way home in the car, I held my hand over my cheek, reliving the wonder of his touch.

I told Rosalie about the way that Sal had been acting. She told me to tell him that I'd call the police if he got rough.

"Tell him that you'll tell the cops that he tried to rape you," she advised me. "That'll keep his hands off you. Statutory rape is no joke, and he knows it. Stand up and fight for your rights. I'll see you at school tomorrow."

I'd felt brave enough when she was talking to me, but after Gary's car had vanished down the street, I began to shake.

I crept up the stairs to our apartment and tried the door. It was unlocked, which should have warned me. As soon as I got inside, the lights went on and there was Sal, grinning at me like a devil. He was sitting at the kitchen table, and I could tell that he'd been drinking for hours.

He stood up. "Where've you been?" he asked.

I saw his hand clenching into a fist and I broke out in a cold sweat. "It's none of your business," I told him.

"I'll show you whose business it is! You're going to turn out just like your rotten mother, aren't you?" He grabbed for me, but I dodged and slipped behind the table.

"Don't you touch me!" I warned. "If you do, I'll call the police. I'll tell them that you tried to rape me. I'll . . . I'll have you sent to jail."

"Why, you dirty—" A flood of terrible words poured out of his mouth. I took the verbal abuse without flinching. I could see that I'd bluffed him, just as Rosalie had said I could.

Finally, he tramped into the bedroom and slammed the door. I heard Mom and him fighting for a long time after I'd made up my bed on the couch in the living room. It didn't bother me, though. I felt as though I didn't live in their ugly world anymore. I stepped into the world where Mark lived, with his warm eyes and his soft voice.

I slept soundly and woke up so late that I had to dress and rush off to school without breakfast. Sal had left for work and Mom was still in bed when I left. I was glad . . . I didn't want to talk to anybody. My head felt like it was blown up like a balloon, and my hands were shaking.

81

"I feel terrible," I whispered to Rosalie as we sat down at our sewing machines. "I must be coming down with the flu."

She laughed and gave me a knowing look. "That's not the flu, honey. You smoked three joints last night. That's pretty heavy going for a beginner."

"What do you mean . . . joints?" I asked. "They were just cigarettes, weren't they?"

"They were joints," she hissed, glancing over her shoulder at the instructor. "You know, weed . . . marijuana."

"But, joints are drugs," I said. "You can get sent to jail if you're caught smoking marijuana."

"Oh, give me a break," Rosalie scoffed. "Supposedly, you get sent to jail if you beat your wife, too, but lots of guys do it, anyway. Okay, it's a drug . . . so are pain relievers. You take pain relievers if you've got a pain, and you smoke a joint if you want to feel good. What's the difference?"

The class started then and we couldn't talk anymore. I had a terrible morning. The instructor made me rip out everything I'd stitched, and by noon, I was ready to cry. Rosalie had promised that we'd cut the afternoon class, and after our morning class had ended, she took me to her room and fixed me a good lunch. Then she brought out two joints and we smoked. I didn't think any more about whether it was wrong to do it . . . or dangerous. Rosalie was my friend, and I loved and trusted her.

After that, I felt fine and we talked about Gary and Mark. Gary didn't have a regular job with a band. He just filled in now and then when somebody needed an extra musician.

"I pretty much support him," she admitted. She must have seen the question in my eyes, because she laughed. "Don't ask. I've got ways to make money. And, I can always get a few hundred from my old man, back in Texas. He pays me to stay away."

I admired her for feeling that way about Gary. I knew that I'd have done the same for Mark, if he'd needed money. She told me that Mark's parents were terrible to him. One of his brothers was a doctor, and the other was a lawyer. Mark worked in a garage, and his parents were ashamed of him. As I listened, my heart almost burst with pity for him. He'd been pushed around, just as I had. Nobody could have understood him or loved him the way that I could.

I hung out with Rosalie all day. In the evening we had dinner and then went to Changes. The whole group was there again in the same booth . . . Gary, Bruce, Sonia, and Mark. Mark's face brightened when he saw me. He took my hand and pulled me down beside him. I saw then that there was a stranger at the far edge of the big table. He was an older man.

82

He grinned and smiled at me. "A new one?" he asked. "Who gets the credit, kids? The same offer stands."

"Shut up!" Mark snapped. "You talk too much. You know where that might land you someday," he warned.

"Maybe so," the man said. "But I won't go alone. I'll take all my friends with me."

A strange silence fell over the table then. Everybody seemed to stop breathing . . . to listen for something that he or she was scared about. Then, the man stood up.

"I'll see you again, sweetheart," he said to me. "We'll get to be good friends, you and I."

Gary gave him a hard shove away from the table. Then, Mark, Bruce, and Gary followed him across the dance floor and through a door in the back. I didn't know what it was all about, and I didn't care. I was with Mark again . . . and he liked me. I could tell he did by the way that he'd acted, and by the way that Sonia was glaring at me, as though she'd like to cut my throat.

After the boys had come back, we all smoked marijuana and sipped beer. That wonderful, free, and happy feeling had come over me again. Suddenly, nothing mattered . . . as long as Mark was near me. We ended up at Sonia's place and listened to music until midnight, then Gary and Rosalie took me home.

The apartment door was locked, but I was feeling brave enough to face anything. I banged on the door until Mom came and opened it. She was cursing and muttering cruel things to me . . . furious that I'd been out so late. I walked past her without a word. She couldn't hurt me anymore. She couldn't touch me. For the first time in my life, I had friends. And, I had Mark.

I wasn't really sure of Mark, though, until the night when he'd said that he'd take me home. I knew that there'd been something between him and Sonia at one point, and I knew that he was choosing me.

Mark didn't have a car. We walked all the way home, but it didn't feel like a long walk at all. I was all keyed up from the marijuana that I'd smoked. I felt as though I were floating a foot above the sidewalk, listening to Mark talk, and looking at his handsome face. He told me a lot that night . . . about his family wanting him to be a doctor or a lawyer like his brothers, and how he'd failed every subject during his first year in college.

"I knew that I didn't have it in me," he said, "but they made me try. They've never forgiven me for failing. I've never forgiven myself either. My life fell apart then. It crashed into little bits, and I've never been able to put the pieces back together."

"Maybe I can help you, Mark," I murmured timidly. "I . . . I love you."

I wasn't sure that I'd said the words until Mark turned to me, right there on the street, and put his arms around me. "Do you really, sweetheart?" His voice was husky. "You're such a baby. You don't know anything."

"I'm not a baby!" Tears flooded my eyes. "I love you in a way that nobody else could . . . more than Sonia!" I insisted.

I threw my arms around his neck, pressing my body fiercely against his. He kissed me, hard and deep, and we stood there for a long time, locked in each other's arms.

"I love you, too," he murmured, "but I'm no good for you. If you're smart, Pamela, you'll run a million miles away from me."

That sounded like a crazy idea to me. Mark couldn't be bad for me . . . not when we loved each other, when just being near him filled me with joy.

Mark had insisted upon walking me up the dark stairs to the apartment. The door was unlocked and as I opened it and turned on the light, Sal came charging out of the bedroom. I stared at him. I realized that I was swaying, and that I was still a little dizzy from the marijuana.

"So, you're coming home drunk now," he bellowed, "and bringing your men with you. I'll have you sent to reform school, girl," he threatened.

"She's not drunk," Mark told him. "She hasn't done anything wrong."

Sal let out a roar of rage. "Who asked you, you bum?" he yelled. "Now, get out of my house or I'll throw you down the stairs!"

He started toward us furiously. I grabbed Mark's arm and somehow, we got down the stairs, and were finally out on the street. Mark was sobbing . . . a dry, rasping sound. It hurt me to listen to him.

"Why haven't I got any courage?" he asked. "Why didn't I force his words down his throat?"

"Don't, Mark. Please?" I begged. "We don't care about him. I wouldn't want you to fight him. I love you, Mark."

I tried to put my arms around him, but he stepped back. "You're a fool to love me," he said. "I've ruined my own life . . . do you want me to ruin yours, too?"

"If we were together, I wouldn't care what happened to me," I told him. "Oh, Mark, please, don't push me away!"

He took me in his arms then. "I can't help myself, Pamela," he whispered. "You're the only one who's ever loved me. My parents and Sonia . . . they don't count. They just wanted what they could get from me. You're different, Pamela. You take away the loneliness."

Tears stung my eyes. "You do that for me, too, Mark," I assured him. "You're all that I've got . . . all that I'll ever want."

The darkness hid the dirty street . . . the ugly, crumbling buildings. We even forgot about Sal. For a moment, we were just any boy and girl, lost in the thrill and the wonder of our love.

"I'll get you out of this situation, somehow," Mark promised. "Just hang on for awhile longer, Pamela, until I can figure out what to do."

He left then, and I went up to the apartment . . . alone, but not afraid anymore. Mark's love had made me feel protected. Sal was sitting at the kitchen table, drinking a beer.

I had to walk around the table to get to the living room. I watched him out of the corner of my eye. He made a move, as if to stand.

"Don't try to touch me," I warned. "I'll do what I said before; I'll yell until the police come."

His face twisted in a vicious sneer. "Do you think that I want you after he's had you?" he said. "You're a disgusting, dirty—"

I ran from his words as though he were throwing filth at me. Later, I heard him trying the knob of the living room door, but I'd wedged a chair under it. He stood there cursing and threatening me with the horrible things that he'd do to me if he could. I whispered Mark's name over and over, like a prayer.

When I went into the kitchen the next morning, Sal was sitting at the table. He squinted at me from puffy eyes.

"Go in and look at your mother, Pamela." His speech was so thick that he could hardly get the words out. "Go and look. I think that your mother's dead."

"Mom . . . dead?" My voice was a scared whisper. Sal was scared, too. I could see it in his face.

Slowly, I opened the bedroom door. The window shade was drawn and it was too dark to see anything. I stumbled over shoes and dirty clothes that had been thrown on the floor. When I pulled up the shade, the gray morning light poured in.

Mom lay in the middle of the old, battered bed. She'd got so thin that she hardly lifted the blanket.

I'd never seen anybody that had died before, but I knew immediately that my mother was gone. Her eyes had sunk way back in her head and her skin was a strange color. She looked like a wax doll . . . like a tired, old wax doll that'd never really been alive. I didn't cry.

How could you cry for someone who had hated you all of your life? I wished that I could grieve, but all that I felt for Mom was pity.

Mom never had anything, I thought. Nobody ever loved her, and she never really loved anybody. And, no one cares, now that she's gone.

A sudden rush of panic was like ice water in my veins. This can happen to me, I thought. I could have lived and died that way, if it wasn't for Mark. Oh, Mark . . . Mark!

85

I ran out of the bedroom, dodging Sal as I made for the door. "Don't leave me, Pamela," he begged. "I don't want to be alone with her. Stay here—"

His voice followed me like the howling of a scared animal. Blocks away, I could still hear it echoing in my ears. I could still see the empty shell of my mother's body.

I was almost hysterical by the time I got to Mark, but I managed to tell him that my mother was dead, and that I couldn't live at home any longer. He tried to be reassuring, but I could see that he was worried.

"We can get married," he said immediately. "I want to marry you, Pamela, but how can we live?" he asked. "I don't earn enough money for us to survive. If my parents would only be decent and let us live with them, we could manage until you found a job, and we'd saved some money."

"How do you know that they wouldn't understand?" I asked. "I'll bet they're sorry for the way that they've treated you, and that they'd like to make up for it. Maybe, when they see how much I love you, they'll be glad that we're getting married. They'll want to help us."

"Maybe," Mark said hesitantly.

I moved in with Rosalie, and a few days later, Mark took me to meet his parents. Their house was in a neighborhood that wasn't fancy, but it was clean and respectable. My knees started shaking as we went up the front steps. Mark's mother opened the door. Her eyes moved from Mark and then to me, her gaze was hard as a blow.

"What is it this time, Mark?" she asked bitterly. "More trouble?"

I couldn't have spoken a word to save my life. The arm that Mark had around me was trembling and his face was pale.

"I didn't tell you before, Mother," he began, "because I knew what you'd say. This is Pamela. We love each other and I want to marry her. We were wondering if we could live here for a while."

His mother's figure blocked the door. "What's the rush?" she asked. "I've never even seen this girl before, and you're asking me to take her into my home? Is she making you marry her?"

"No!" Mark insisted. His face was red with fury. He told her about my mother's death, and about the kind of man that Sal was.

She listened without a flicker of expression on her face. Then she'd turned her eyes on me and I shriveled under the scorn that I saw burning in them.

"Disgusting," she muttered. "You bring me a girl who's been raised in filth and ask me to take her in as my daughter. All your life you've been a disappointment to your father and me. Your brothers have made us proud, but not you, you've only made us ashamed. It would've been better if you had never been born!" She stepped back and closed the door in our faces.

86

"Oh, Mark!" I burst into tears. "I'm so sorry. This is all my fault. I've done this to you."

Mark was staring at the closed door. "It's not your fault, Pamela," he insisted. "My mother's always despised me . . . my father, too. They think that their sons must be better than everyone else's . . . stronger and smarter. But, I'm weak and I make mistakes, and so, they hate me." He grunted an angry laugh and said, "They disown me? Well, I disown them, too!"

"Don't talk like that, Mark," I begged. "They're your parents . . . your family."

He looked at me with tenderness in his face that drove away the darkness and the despair that I'd been feeling. "Not anymore, Pamela. You're my family now. You're the only thing in the world that I love. Don't ever leave me, Pamela."

"There isn't anything that could separate us, Mark," I assured him.

We were married soon after that. Rosalie and Gary drove us to a justice of the peace out in the country somewhere. On the way there Mark had seemed nervous, and I was worried about him. He'd asked Gary to stop at a gas station, and when he got out of the car, Gary had handed him a small, flat box.

"You need it bad, huh?" he asked, grinning.

"Is Mark sick?" I asked as he'd walked away from the car. It had seemed to me that he was walking strangely . . . weaving back and forth.

"He's okay," Rosalie told me. "After we get out of town, we'll all smoke a joint. Getting married is enough to make anyone a little nervous."

Why did I smoke marijuana when I knew that it was a drug? Because Rosalie and Gary were my friends, and Mark was the man that I loved . . . and whatever they did, I wanted to do, too. I didn't realize the danger of it then . . . but, even if I had, it might not have stopped me. Honestly, my life had been too miserable to risk losing the only happiness that I'd ever experienced.

After I smoked a joint, I felt good again. Mark was happy, too, so we started singing, sitting with our arms around each other, and feeling as though we owned the world. We were all laughing when we went into the justice's office. I was a little dizzy, but the feeling went away as I listened to the marriage service.

Perhaps it wasn't the wedding little girls dream about . . . it wasn't even a decent one, with all of us high on marijuana. But, I truly loved Mark, and that made our wedding beautiful to me. I listened to every word, holding tightly to Mark's hand. When it was over and he kissed me, I cried with happiness. Finally, I belonged to someone . . .

someone who wanted me. I'd never be alone again.

We smoked more marijuana on the way back home, and I felt that flying-in-a-cloud feeling. Buildings, cars, people . . . everything had flowed past me in a pleasant blur with Mark's arms holding me, and his breath warm on my cheek. Once, a traffic cop had chased us when Gary had run a red light, but we'd managed to lose him. Afterward, we treated Gary as though he were a big hero. We acted as if it was a game. It was the marijuana . . . we all felt so smart and important.

Gary and Rosalie had treated us to a nice dinner, and then we went to a club where Gary would sometimes play with the band. I'd never been in a place like that, with live music and people all dressed up. It was exciting. We couldn't smoke out in the open there, but some women were smoking in the ladies' room. Rosalie and I shut ourselves in a stall and smoked a joint. When we went back to the table, Mark and Gary were gone . . . but they came back a little while later with the older man that I'd met at Changes.

Mark seemed to like him all of the sudden. He told me that the man's name was Wilbert.

"Wilbert's giving us a wedding present," he told me. "He owns a motel on Front Street, and he's going to let us live rent free in one of the cabins for a while."

Somehow, that struck me as wrong. I didn't like that older man. He kept staring at me and nodding knowingly.

"We can pay rent, Mark," I protested. "You're working, and I'll have a job in a few days. Nobody has to give us anything for free."

Mark scowled at me. "What's the matter with you? An old friend wants to do us a favor, and you throw it back in his face."

I began to cry. I couldn't stand to have Mark mad at me.

"Stop picking on her," Rosalie said quickly. "It's not her fault that you're so on edge. Help him out, Wilbert. Don't hold out on him on his wedding day."

"Okay, I'm a nice guy," Wilbert said. "Just remember how good I've been to you kids and don't change your connection."

It was like they were speaking a foreign language, but I didn't think about it much. I supposed I was too naive to understand everything that they were doing. Mark went out with Wilbert for awhile, and when he came back alone he was himself again . . . gentle and sweet.

Gary played his guitar around midnight. Nobody else played . . . it was just Gary, standing there in a circle of light, playing music that made your blood run hot and fast. Rosalie was watching him eagerly, her lips parted, and her eyes gleaming. I moved closer to Mark, and he slipped his arm through mine and hugged it against his side. I remembered how it was just a few months before . . . I was lonely and friendless. But now I thought that I was the luckiest girl in the world.

When Gary and Rosalie dropped us at Wilbert's motel, it was three in the morning. Our cabin was just a shack . . . one room for cooking and living, and a tiny bedroom. The springs on the bed sagged and the place looked dirty, but I wasn't used to anything better. That little cabin was our home . . . Mark's and mine. We could close the door on the world and be happy together.

There wasn't even any indoor plumbing. I went out to use the public toilet and when I came back, Mark was in the bedroom. I locked the door and turned out the lights, feeling nervous and excited. The bedroom was dark. I slipped into bed beside Mark and, when he didn't move or speak, I whispered his name. His breathing sounded strange . . . very slow, and so quiet that I could hardly hear it. I put my hand on his shoulder, but he didn't stir. I cried a little then, because it seemed strange for Mark to be asleep on our wedding night. But, finally, I fell asleep myself . . . curled up against his warm back.

When I woke up, it was dawn and a gray haze filled the room. Mark was standing by the window. I must have dozed off because when I woke up again, I was in his arms and he was kissing me. We made each other very happy, but it was a lot more than sex. We were two lonesome people, filling our hearts with warmth and love. It was a time that was good to remember.

That same day, I got a job at a diner down the highway. The pay was good, counting tips, and from then on I was the one who supported the two of us. I bought all the food, I paid for the laundry and cab fare, and when we went out with Gary and Rosalie, I paid for our half of the bill. Mark never seemed to have any money, though he was still working at the garage. I couldn't imagine how he spent that much money every month.

Once, I'd suggested that it might be a good idea for us to work out a budget. Mark had been furious, and he wouldn't even talk about it.

I didn't want to fight with him, so I never said anything more about it. I even loaned him money . . . it seemed to become more and more of a habit. I began to worry about his health. No matter how carefully I'd planned and cooked a meal, he hardly touched the food. It seemed to me that I could see the pounds falling off him, but when I asked him to go to a doctor, he flew into a rage.

"There's nothing wrong with me!" he yelled. "Do you have to nag me all the time? I should've listened to Sonia. She told me that I was a fool to marry you."

That hurt a lot and I cried, but Mark didn't seem to care. He told me that I'd have to learn to mind my own business. I was very confused. Suddenly, Mark was changing, and I didn't know why. That wasn't what I'd expected our marriage to be. I thought that Mark loved me and needed me. And sometimes, he was so sweet that I'd forget my worries and be gloriously happy.

We hadn't seen much of our friends since the wedding. Mark didn't seem to want to smoke marijuana anymore. I was glad, because it gave me a headache in the morning, and I knew that I had to keep my job. Then, one day, Rosalie had dropped by the diner to invite us to a party. She and Gary had agreed to start living together, she said, and they wanted to have their friends over to celebrate. They couldn't get married because Gary had a wife somewhere in another state. I wasn't shocked. Rosalie was my friend, and I thought that whatever she did was fine . . . as long as she was happy.

Mark had looked sick on the night of the party. I suggested staying home, but he silenced me in that harsh way that had always frightened me. Sonia was at Rosalie's party, and so were Bruce and Wilbert. Wilbert left soon after Mark and I arrived. As he was leaving, he'd patted me on the cheek.

"How's the little bride?" he asked.

Mark's laugh was unpleasant. "Nothing new. Sorry to disappoint you."

"Oh, I can wait," Wilbert said. "I know I'll have a new customer, one of these days."

I didn't understand what he'd meant. I thought that he was just a fool.

"Let's get going," Rosalie said briskly. "The kitchen's open for business. Wilbert's giving us a good price, because it's a special occasion. Get your hit and crash anywhere. As long as we keep the music low, we won't have any trouble with the neighbors."

Rosalie had looked very pretty that night. Her eyes sparkled and she was full of life.

"What do you mean?" I asked her. "He's giving us a good price on weed?"

She giggled. "Listen to her, everyone. Pamela thinks that we're getting a good price on pot. That's kid stuff, honey. We don't smoke pot anymore. We've found something better now. Show her, Mark. How come you've been holding out on Pamela?"

"Yeah, Mark, why have you been holding out?" Sonia put her arm around his waist, pressing her body against him. "Don't you trust your child bride?"

I didn't understand, but I felt that I was fighting for Mark's love . . . that Sonia was trying to take him away from me.

"Of course, he trusts me!" I told her. "I'm his wife and I love him. I'd do anything for him."

"No, you wouldn't," Sonia said. "You're boring. You don't know what's happening. Would you do what Rosalie does for Gary . . . take money from other men so he can get the high he needs?"

I stared at her, confused and frightened. "I don't know what you mean."

"Heroin!" Sonia laughed scornfully. "Crank . . . whatever you want to call it, we're all doing it now. Come on, Mark, I can see you're dying for a hit. Let's show the little girl how we do it."

She opened a small box and took out a loop of string, a bent and blackened spoon, some cotton, and an eyedropper with a hypodermic needle fastened to the end. Rosalie handed her a capsule and she broke it open. Then she dumped the white powder in the spoon. She added water, lit a match, and held it under the bowl of the spoon until the mixture had bubbled and the powder had dissolved. After that, she dropped a bit of cotton in the spoon to absorb the liquid and put the needle into the eyedropper.

"Ready, Mark?" She smiled at him, and he nodded eagerly and held out his arm to her. He was trembling and his face glistened with sweat. He'd put the string around his arm and pulled it tightly so that the vein on his forearm stood out, big and blue. Sonia punched the needle into the vein and I looked away, feeling sick.

They all used the needle. They acted as if I wasn't even there. I watched Mark, who was leaning against the wall and nodding his head dreamily in time to the music. Suddenly, he looked fine . . . relaxed and happy.

The group had started drifting from the kitchen to the living room. Sonia had whispered something to Mark and slipped her arm through his, then they both laughed. I couldn't stand it. They were purposely excluding me. Mark had forgotten all about me. A smothering wave of fear swept over me. I just couldn't lose Mark. I just couldn't. He was the only thing that I had in the whole world. . . .

"I want a hit, too!" I blurted out. "Why doesn't somebody give me one?"

"Listen to her," Sonia mocked. "She'd run a mile if you shoved a needle at her."

"I would not," I protested. "I want whatever Mark wants."

"Good girl." Rosalie patted my shoulder. "Why should Pamela miss out on the fun? Come on, Mark, give her a hit."

Mark straightened up and brushed Sonia's hand off his arm. He stood close to me and looked down into my eyes.

"This is big time stuff, Pamela," he warned. "Not like smoking a joint. Are you sure that you know what you're doing?"

"I want to try it," I repeated stubbornly.

Mark glanced around at the others. "You remember, Pamela's married to me. I get the cut."

91

It wasn't until later that I understood the meaning of his words. Wilbert gave a bonus of free heroin to whoever brought him a new customer . . . and Mark was making sure that he got the credit for me. But, Mark hadn't been born that way . . . cold and calculating. I couldn't bear to remember him if I didn't believe that the man I loved had once been a clean, fine, human being. Drugs had killed the goodness in him.

I rolled up my sleeve and let Rosalie tighten the string around my arm. Mark had filled the needle and I gritted my teeth as he'd plunged it into the swollen vein. I was scared . . . but not scared enough. I was too dumb to have been scared. I thought heroin was like marijuana . . . something that I could take or leave alone. When we went to those parties with the group, I'd smoked up just to keep the closeness between Mark and me.

The sting of the needle had vanished quickly and a hot flash had run through my body . . . a kind of pins-and-needles feeling. I felt good all over . . . as though everything in the world was fine, and couldn't have been any better. My worries about money and Mark's health had disappeared.

Mark and I sat in the same chair . . . daydreaming, and listening to the soft music from the stereo. Nobody talked much. There were sodas to drink, and around midnight, we all had another shot of heroin. If I did any conscious thinking, it was to tell myself that I was happy.

In the morning, I was shaky, but no worse than if I'd smoked marijuana. Mark gave himself a hit the minute he awakened. It was then that I saw his bare arms for the first time in daylight. They were crisscrossed with raised welts, and there were ugly scars where the needle had pierced the vein. I tried to hide the revulsion that I felt when I saw it.

"I have to have at least two fixes a day," he told me. "That's why I've been so broke."

"But, why do you use so much?" I asked. "Why don't you save it for parties, or special occasions?"

I could still see his face . . . drawn and old looking. "Because I'm hooked," he admitted. "So are Bruce, Gary, and Sonia . . . and Rosalie's pretty far along. It gets so that you have to have it, just to keep going."

I didn't believe him. I thought that, because I hadn't needed a fix that morning, I could take heroin, or leave it alone. I didn't understand the terrible hunger for the drug that grew stronger every time the needle entered your flesh.

We had several more parties at Rosalie's place, and sometimes, everyone came to our place, too. I went hit for hit with Mark. I wasn't going to give Sonia any excuse to push me aside and wedge herself in between us. Soon, I had scars on my arms, and I wore long-sleeved blouses at work, explaining that I got cold easily.

One morning, I was watching Mark give himself a shot and I found myself wanting one, too. Every square inch of my body ached for the prick of that needle . . . I yearned for the hot flash, and the sensation of all my muscles and nerves letting go, and relaxing into a sense of peace. I felt as though I'd scream if I didn't get a hit right away.

I forced myself to look away and fixed our breakfast on the hot plate. Coffee was all Mark ever wanted in the morning, and I hadn't had much of an appetite myself lately. I tried to eat a piece of toast, but it scraped my throat and I felt sick. My eyes were watering so I dabbed at them with a paper napkin and picked up my cup of coffee. My hand shook and the scalding coffee spilled into my lap, burning through my dress to my skin. I hardly felt the pain, though. I was panicking—trembling with terror—and I didn't know why.

I muttered something about going to work early and put on my coat. I stumbled out of the cabin. It was a crisp, autumn day, but I began sweating the instant that the cold air hit me. I staggered down the driveway to the street and stood there, swaying dizzily. The sound of the cars passing by made a deafening roar in my ears. Something fell from my hand and I saw that I'd dropped my purse. My hands and my whole body were dripping with sweat.

"I've got to have a fix . . . I've got to," I heard myself whining in a high, thin voice.

I stumbled back to the cabin. Mark was drinking his coffee.

"I feel terrible, Mark," I told him. "A hit . . . fix me a hit, or I won't be able to go to work."

It hurts to remember the look of cruel satisfaction that I saw on his face.

"Look who's talking!" he said mockingly. "I thought that you were too smart to get hooked. It's only been a few weeks, and already you're begging for a fix."

I ripped off my coat and pushed up my sleeve. "Please, Mark!" I begged, so lost in my suffering that all I could think of was getting relief.

He opened the kit and filled the eyedropper. The needle sank into the blue vein in my arm and I stood there motionless, waiting for the effect. My eyes cleared and I felt the sweat drying on my body. I took a deep breath of relief. The trembling was gone and I felt calmer almost immediately.

"You better start thinking about where you'll get the money for drugs," Mark told me. "I need a few hits every day now, and you're going to want them regularly pretty soon. Wilbert will give us some free because you're a new customer, but after that, we're on our own. It's not cheap, baby. How are we going to get by?"

I stared at him, suddenly terrified again. "I won't need it every morning," I protested. "I just didn't feel good today. I'm not hooked!"

"Yes, you are," he said. "You're no different than the rest of us. You can't play with heroin without getting hooked. That's what you've been doing . . . playing, and thinking that you could take it, or leave it. It doesn't work that way, honey. First, you take it because you like the feeling that it gives you. You feel superior to the rest of the world. You don't care what happens, because you're way above it . . . floating on a cloud. Nothing matters, and nothing can bother you. But, eventually, it takes more and more heroin to get that good feeling, until you find that you've got to have it every day, to keep going at all. It's no fun anymore, but you've got to have it. If you don't get it, you fall apart . . . you go to pieces, like you did just now. That's when you know that you're hooked."

I burst into tears. "I'm not hooked," I insisted. "Oh, Mark, let's both quit! We can do it . . . we'll help each other."

I tried to put my arms around him, but he pushed me away. "You're talking like a fool!" he yelled. "You can't kick the habit once you've got it! I got picked up in a raid last spring. I didn't have anything on me, so they couldn't hold me for too long. But, they kept me in a cell for a while, just to torture me. I stayed in the county jail for three days, getting the cold turkey treatment." He paused, his eyes dark with the memory.

"Do you know what that's like?" he asked. "Your nose runs, and your eyes run. You yawn and you sweat like you've got a fever, and then you shake with chills. You can't sit still, and you can't sleep. Then, your muscles start jerking, and the cramps begin. You wouldn't believe the pains in your stomach and legs. It's like being torn apart! Then, you vomit until you feel as though you've been turned inside out. You get so weak that you're sure you're going to die . . . you want to die! Don't talk to me about kicking the habit . . . I'd kill myself before I'd try it," he vowed.

Then, he rushed and left me lying on the bed, moaning and sobbing. After a while, I pulled myself together and went to work. I didn't dare lose my job. I did my work mechanically, remembering to answer when I was spoken to, and smile when necessary. Finally, I understood what had happened to me, and my despair was a black curtain that stood between the rest of the world and myself. Other people were shadows. I was a shadow myself. The only real things were the heroin, and the needle.

It was a life without love or tenderness or joy . . . a life utterly without hope. It was an endless nightmare, filled with lying, stealing,

94

and doing unspeakable things to scrape together enough money for the fix that our bodies screamed for. I watched Mark's personality and character change before my eyes . . . he was warped and degraded by his hunger for drugs. I knew that the same breakdown was happening in my own mind and heart. Drugs weren't like alcohol. I guess I thought you could be an alcoholic and hurt only your body . . . but drugs crushed your body and soul at the same time.

The free heroin that Wilbert had given Mark for hooking me was soon gone. Mark was shooting up three or four times a day, and I couldn't get by without two hits. I began to steal from my boss, tearing up order slips and pocketing the money from customers. Mark stole, too, from the garage where he worked.

Rosalie taught me how to shoplift. It was winter by then, and we made big pockets of cloth that we tied around our waists under our coats. We stole the small, valuable things like jewelry, evening bags, compacts, and perfume. Bruce knew of a place and sold the stuff for us, taking a cut for himself. We didn't buy any clothes or a lot of food, either. I lost interest in eating, just as Mark had. I was really thin and not as pretty as I'd been, but I couldn't worry about that. Every spare cent went for heroin, and all we ever thought of was when we could get the next hit.

We often spent the evening at Rosalie's place, shooting up, and lying around listening to soft music on the stereo. I wasn't even jealous of Sonia anymore. Finally, I understood drug addicts, and I knew that their sex drives weakened and finally disappeared altogether. Mark hadn't touched me in a long time. I didn't care much. You didn't have normal feelings when you were hooked on heroin. You didn't love or hate the way other people did. You just existed, from fix to fix.

One night, Mark brought a man to me. The stranger had waited outside the cabin while Mark had explained to me why he was there.

"Rosalie does it for Gary," he pleaded. "He'll pay good money if you let him stay for a while. Just think of how much we can buy with the money, Pamela!"

I shut my eyes to block out the sight of his face as he begged me to sell my body. I knew that I was going to do it, and I didn't know who I hated more . . . Mark or myself.

The man was old, fumbling, and impotent. It was over almost before it began, and I got rid of him. Mark went away with the money to find Wilbert, and fix us up for another few hours. Just a few, short hours out of a lifetime.

Why don't I just kill myself? I thought. It seemed like the only way to end the nightmare.

There were other men. It was such an easy way to make money, Mark told me. I couldn't fight him. I wanted the drug too much myself.

I suppose the mind had a way of forgetting things that were too horrible to endure. I couldn't remember any of the men who'd used my body . . . except the last one. He was a nice-looking guy . . . not much older than I was. He came into the room and laid some money on the dresser. I stood there . . . waiting. I wasn't thinking of anything but the heroin that his money would buy.

"You're a junkie, aren't you?" he asked suddenly. "I can see it in your eyes."

I didn't answer him. He was staring at me as though I was something vile. "I wouldn't touch you with a ten-foot pole," he snapped. "Keep the money. You look like you need it."

He left the cabin, and I opened the window and passed the money out to Mark. He was the second man that night. Mark had enough money for two hits . . . one for him, and one for me. We were skating on thin ice, always terrified that we'd be left without enough drugs to quiet our screaming bodies.

I took the shade off the lamp and studied my face in the cruel, strong light. I was only seventeen, but I looked like I was in my thirties at least. I stared at my gaunt face, yellow skin, and the circles under my eyes that were dark and deep.

I turned away quickly and paced back and forth, my nerves twitching while I waited for Mark to come back with the drugs. The past week, I'd fainted twice at work. The other waitresses had teased me, hinting that I was pregnant. In my mental fog, I'd hardly listened. Suddenly, though, I began to wonder. I tried to think back, but the days and weeks ran together in a gray blur.

Mark came back with the heroin and we both had a fix. Mark took his shot in the jugular vein now. He'd worn out the veins in both arms and they'd collapsed. The vein in one of my arms was gone, but the other was still good. It made me sick to see the needle plunge into Mark's throat, but I knew that if I had to, I'd do the same thing.

Mark fell asleep soon after that, and I went to see a doctor. Because I was scared and worried, I didn't give him my real name.

"You're pregnant," the doctor said after he'd examined me. Then he glanced at my arms and shook his head. "And, you're on heroin, I see. You know that your baby will be an addict, too, don't you?"

I tried to speak, almost choking on the horror of his words. "You mean . . . the drugs get through to the baby?" I asked.

He nodded, studying me with stern eyes. "Right now, your baby is an addict, just like you. When it's born, it'll have to go through a withdrawal period. If you don't lose it before term, that is . . . and you probably will. Heroin depresses the respiratory system so that the baby doesn't get enough oxygen. You're skin and bones, and you can be sure that your baby is, too. I've only known one addict who got as far as seven months. Her baby didn't look human. It hardly lived long enough to draw a breath."

I got to my feet, shaking uncontrollably. "I'll stop," I vowed. "I swear, I'll never do it again!"

He nodded sadly. "I hope so," he said. "I sincerely hope so, young lady."

That night when I left the doctor's office, there was a feeling of spring . . . a kind of sweetness in the air. I walked home slowly, looking up at the frosty twinkle of the stars. I thought about the baby that I was carrying in my body, and it seemed like a wonderful miracle . . . a human being, living and growing inside of me. I wondered whether it was a boy or a girl, and if it would look like Mark. I was happy with my thoughts, until I remembered what the doctor had told me. My unborn baby was a drug addict!

I went through horrible anguish then. I imagined the way that the drugs had seeped through my blood into the baby's body, infecting it with the same terrible sickness that I had. I stopped there, begging God to help me. It was funny that I should have called on God when I was frightened and suffering. I'd never called on Him for help before . . . I never thought that He could hear my cries of despair. But, that night, I fell down on my knees, and hardly felt the cold as I tried to find the right words to say to God.

"I'm bad," I whispered. "I know that I'm rotten, and that You hate me, but, please, don't hate my baby, too. It hasn't done anything. I don't want it to be sick like I am. Help me to get rid of the habit for my baby's sake. I'll take care of my baby. I promise I will. I'll work hard, and I'll love it. It won't ever be like me. Oh, God, help me . . . please, please, help me!"

I covered my face with my hands and the tears trickled through my cold, shaking fingers. Right then, I knew that I could never do it. The habit was too strong for me. It's almost impossible to explain how it was . . . trying to quit. It was like choosing between life and death.

I told Mark about the baby, and I saw in his face the same hushed wonder that I'd felt.

"A baby," he whispered. "I'll be a father. That's one thing that my parents can't take away from me."

He put his arms around me for the first time in days and we talked about the baby. We dreamed together, pretending for a little while that we weren't drug addicts and criminals . . . that we were fit to be parents of an innocent child.

But that was between hits. When Mark needed a fix, he didn't think of anything else but how to get it. He wanted to bring me another man, but I wouldn't let him. I told him that I'd kill him if he tried it, and myself, too. I guess he could tell that I meant it. It was the least I could do for my baby.

Mark sneaked into his parents' home when they were out, and stole everything that he could carry away . . . a radio, a camera, clothing, a VCR, books, and anything else that he could sell for a few dollars. He swaggered into the cabin, feeling good from a hit and with his pockets stuffed with drugs. Our friends were meeting at Rosalie's place and Mark was supplying the crank.

"They're going to pay me a bonus for it," he boasted. "Wilbert says that the heat is on him and he may have to close down for awhile. Man, don't think that everyone won't be bummed when they hear that."

His eyes were glittering and he looked very handsome in an excited, feverish way. My heart ached with love, fear, and a wild, desperate hope. It had been a week since I'd seen the doctor. It'd taken me all that time to work up my nerve to try and quit.

"I'm not going to Rosalie's place with you," I said softly. "I haven't had a hit since early this morning and I'm going to get along without it. I've got to, for the baby's sake. Please, Mark. Stay with me. Help me."

He knocked my hand off his arm. "You're talking like a fool," he said. "You can't kick the habit any more than the rest of us can. You're hooked, and there's nothing that you can do about it."

"Please, listen to me, Mark," I begged. "I didn't tell you this before, but the doctor told me that when I take drugs, it affects the baby. The baby's hooked, too. Our baby will die if I don't stop!"

Mark was looking at me with shocked pity on his face. Remorse, too, because he knew that loving him had done such horrible things to me.

"I warned you," he cried. "I told you to run a million miles away from me. Remember?"

Tears made it almost impossible for me to speak. "How could I run away from you when I loved you, Mark? When I thought you loved me and needed me, too."

"I did need you. I still do," he sobbed. He dropped to his knees, burying his face in my lap. "I should've left you with your stepfather. Whatever he might have done to you wouldn't be as bad as this. I knew what would happen when I married you, but I couldn't help myself. You were the only one who'd ever loved me, and I couldn't give you up. You should just kill me, Pamela. Why don't you kill me? I won't stop you."

"I don't want to kill you," I told him. "I just want to save our baby. I want to be normal again. I want to feel clean, like other people. Oh, Mark, we can both do it, if we stay together . . . if we help each other."

98

His body had stiffened against me. He didn't answer. When he got to his feet, the emotion was gone from his face and it was hard and calculating again. I wasn't surprised. I knew that his mind was set on his next fix. I was like that myself, except when I thought of my baby. I couldn't blame Mark, but the hurt of seeing him that way had spread all through me . . . throbbing and aching until I didn't think that the agony of drug addiction could have been any worse.

"You won't help me, Mark?" I asked.

"I can't," he told me. "I've got to go over there and sell this stuff so I can lay in a supply from Wilbert. Don't you understand what I've been talking about? The heat's bad. If the dealers get scared and leave town, we won't be able to get anything anywhere. I've got to get some ahead of time . . . I've got to," he insisted.

Sweat glistened on his forehead and I saw that he was in a panic at the thought of not having the drugs that he needed. I backed up against the table and gripped the edge with both hands.

"Well, I'm still not going," I said firmly. "I'm never going to do drugs again."

The sound that he made was more of a groan than a laugh. "You can't beat it, baby. When I come home, you'll be down on your knees, screaming for a fix."

I didn't move until the door had closed behind him. When I let go of the table, my fingers were cramped from hanging on so hard. I rubbed my hands together, trying not to notice that they were shaking.

I tried to fix myself some dinner, but the smell of food made me sick. I started yawning and then sneezing in hard spasms that sent pains shooting through my head. I couldn't sit still for a minute. I walked back and forth, trying to wear myself out so that I'd be able to sleep. My nose was running and my eyes kept filling with tears. I'd wipe them away and look at the clock, and it seemed as though the hands were standing still.

Then, the shaking began and finally, it got so bad that I couldn't walk anymore. I fell into a chair. My heart was pounding, and I felt as though something awful was going to happen to me. I was moaning.

"Please, help me," I heard myself whisper, but my lips were so numb that I didn't know that I'd spoken.

The hours dragged on as I crouched there, afraid to move. I felt as though I were coming apart, deep inside of me. I was sure that I was going to die, and that my baby would die with me.

When Mark came in at three in the morning, I was lying there, shivering and dripping with sweat. He didn't say anything . . . he just filled the needle. He came toward me, holding out the needle. I wanted to push him away . . . I swear, I wanted to! But, my body wouldn't do it. I held out my arm. My breath whistled through my teeth as I waited for the jab, the instant tension while the drug seeped into the bloodstream, and then, the wave of relief that washed all through my body.

The trembling stopped, and I got shakily to my feet. Mark's eyes were shining and I knew that he was high. His lips curved into a thin, cruel smile.

"How about it, Pamela? Ready to admit that you're hooked? Going to stop trying to knock that monkey off your back?" he taunted me.

That was what drugs could do to you. They could make you inhuman . . . make you rejoice in someone else's suffering. I was too crushed to care. I looked away.

"Yes," I muttered. "I'm through. I can't beat it. I wish that I were dead."

"Oh, come on, cheer up." Mark was talking in the quick, breathless way that meant he'd had a lot of heroin. "We're in good shape. I hit up our friends for plenty tonight. Tomorrow, I'll contact Wilbert and lay in enough to keep us going if the heat puts him under wraps for a while. I know what you need. Another fix. Baby, you're a big girl now. One hit's not enough for you. Fix your arm, and I'll shoot you up."

"No!" I protested. "I don't want it. I don't need it!"

But, even as I said it, I felt my nerves jerking, screaming for more. A sob tore at my throat as I pulled the string tightly around my arm and held it out for the needle.

Long after Mark had gone to sleep, I stared into the darkness. Forgive me, baby, I thought. Oh, my poor little baby, forgive your mother.

Beside me, Mark's body twitched and I knew that, even in his sleep, the hunger was beginning. Soon, it would wake him and he'd get up to shoot more drugs into his blood. The relief that he felt wouldn't last long. The hunger would begin to build up, and then, in a few hours, he'd be sneaking into the bathroom at work to shoot up again.

I began to shake. I rolled over and hid my face in the pillow, hanging on to it like I was drowning, but it was a rock and I kept sinking. God, we're lost . . . Mark and I, I prayed silently. We're trapped. Even You can't save us. We can't work or love or laugh. We're dying by inches now, so why don't You kill us? Why don't You put us to sleep forever . . . tonight? And our little baby, too. Please, God, end our misery.

Somehow, I thought that God would do it. I fell asleep almost peacefully.

The next thing I knew, I was opening my eyes to the gray dawn sifting through the dirty window. Mark was standing there. I heard the scratch of the match as he heated the spoon holding the heroin. I closed my eyes and clenched my jaws tight, trying not to think of what he was doing. The roof of my mouth went dry with longing, and I pushed my fingers between my teeth and bit down hard. I wouldn't ask for a fix. I wouldn't! But, of course, I did.

Time crawled by and my baby kept growing. But my boss was kind and didn't fire me. He let me wash dishes and even paid me the same wage as when I was a waitress. He gave me free meals, saying that I didn't eat enough. I knew that I should eat better for the baby's sake. I'd bought a book on pregnancy, but I couldn't do what the book had instructed. Good food, regular exercise, sleep, and fresh air . . . a junkie couldn't think about things like that. I was too busy wondering where my next fix was coming from.

I did try to eat sometimes, but my stomach wouldn't hold the food. The only things that I wanted were sweet things like soda, cookies, and candy. I thought that all of that sugar would put weight on me, but it didn't. I kept losing weight. My face, arms, and legs got thinner and thinner. Finally, all that anyone saw when they looked at me was my swollen stomach.

The police were cracking down still on drug dealers all over town. A few had been arrested, and the net was spreading. Mark had heroin hidden everywhere he could think of . . . sewn into the mattress, taped under a shingle on the cabin roof, behind a loose brick in the foundation. When he talked about Wilbert going underground and cutting off our drug supply, a wild look came into his eyes.

I'd just gotten home from work one day when he burst in, which was early for him. He grabbed my arm so tightly that his fingers had seemed to cut through the bone.

"Cut the drugs out of the mattress," he ordered. "I'll get them from the roof and the foundation, and then, we get the hell out of here. Wilbert tried to cut Bruce off, and Bruce killed him. They've got Bruce! Gary came to tell me. He'll spill everything he knows to the cops, and then, we'll all get dragged in. Hurry up! What are you just standing there for?"

In his terror, he hit me across the face, but I didn't feel the blow. The thing that we'd feared the most had finally happened, but I didn't seem to care. I did what Mark told me to . . . moving like somebody in a dream. I cut open the mattress cover and the heroin spilled out into my hand. Whatever stash was there wouldn't last long, and then what? Mark came in with the rest of his supply. We began to pack . . . . just one bag, so we could travel fast. I'd just closed the bag when I heard a car stop outside. Mark's head flew up.

"Look through the window," he whispered. "Quick!"

101

I flattened myself against the wall, easing myself around slowly so I could look without being seen. Four men were coming up the walk; three of them in ordinary, dark suits. Metal gleamed on the uniform of the fourth. In a stupor, I watched the leather gun holsters swinging at his hips.

I looked at Mark and saw his face go pale. "The cops!" His voice was close to a scream. He backed across the room until he was flat against the bedroom door. "They're not going to take me in," he vowed. "I'll never go through that hell again!"

He whirled around and the door slammed behind him. The police were banging on the outside door by then. I tried to close my ears to the noise, listening for some sound from Mark. The bedroom was very quiet, and then, suddenly, I heard a strange cry that was choked off into a bubbling sound. I rushed to the door and pushed it open. Mark was lying across the bed on his back. He'd cut his own throat.

I took one step toward him and then I screamed. After that, everything went black. When I came to, I was propped up in a chair and one of the men was bathing my face with a wet towel. "How old are you?" he asked.

He had a nice face and his voice was kind. "Seventeen," I whispered.

"What a waste." He looked at one of the other cops. "Seventeen, a junkie, and pregnant. How do these kids end up this way?"

The other man stared at me and I hung my head. I was a loser, just like Mark's mother had thought, and yet, I hadn't wanted to be. Everything had just seemed to happen without my looking for it . . . finding Rosalie for a friend, falling in love with Mark, and doing whatever they did. I tried to make sense of what had happened on the way to jail, but I was getting jittery for a fix and couldn't think straight.

Because I was so young, I was only in jail for a few hours. The juvenile judge had asked me if I wanted to be treated for my drug habit. I was shaking by then, and it was hard to stand up, but I pulled myself up straight with a tremendous effort. I couldn't believe that anyone would offer me help. I'd expected to get the same cold turkey treatment that had been such terrible agony for Mark . . . so bad that he'd killed himself rather than having to endure it again.

My mouth felt as though it were stuffed with cotton. "You mean . . . you mean, I can break the habit?" I asked quietly. I looked at the judge, and I began to pray silently.

"We can get you off drugs, and we can build you up physically, so that you're in good health again. But we can't make you quit your habit. You're the only one who can do that."

I didn't understand what he'd meant until I found out, at the hospital where I was sent for treatment, that the highest estimate for keeping drug addicts straight and sober is one out of seven. The other six addicts usually beat the habit and then go back to using drugs again . . . over and over. If someone has been on heroin as long as a year, it wasn't likely that they'd ever be able to stop permanently. Not until they died.

At the hospital I was searched for drugs that I might have hidden on my body. Then I was put in what everyone called the shooting gallery, it was where we got shots of methadone every three or four hours, to ease us off the heroin with as little suffering as possible. The iron gates of the shooting gallery were locked and guarded, they closed the ward off from the rest of the hospital. There was a lot of cheating by the patients. They soon found out which doctors were easy plays, and they pretended to be in terrible shape so that they'd get an extra hit.

That was what Rochelle did. It was her third time being clean and sober, and the last time, she'd stayed clean for almost a year.

"Why did you ever start again?" I asked, shocked and surprised. "You'd stopped . . . you'd kicked the habit. It was crazy to start again."

Rochelle had shrugged. "So, you're clean and sober. Then, you get out of here, and where do you go? Right back to where you came from, and your life's the same as it was before. Decent people won't look at you, and the other kind tries to hook you again. One day, something happens that's hard to take and you turn to the needle to help you over the hump. And then there are a lot of problems, and lots of needles . . . and you wind up here again."

Then she smiled. "Dr. Wilson is making the rounds today. Watch me get an extra shot out of him."

She grabbed the metal bars of her bed and started beating her head against them, howling like a crazy woman. When the nurse and the doctor had come running, she'd fought so hard that two orderlies had been forced to hold her while the doctor gave her an injection. It was such a good act that I was startled when she'd looked at me and winked.

I didn't pull any tricks, maybe because I had a lot at stake. I was honest with the doctors. I knew that they were trying to help me and my baby, and I did everything that they told me to do. They were honest, too. Like the other doctor had told me, they said that my baby would be born an addict and that he or she would have to go through the agony of withdrawal.

"It's easy to understand why your baby might not even survive," one doctor told me. "From the moment it was conceived, your baby has suffered from insufficient oxygen. You've also practically starved it to death."

I could see that he thought it would be for the best if my baby were born dead. But, I didn't feel that way. I wanted my baby to live. Mark was gone. I couldn't grieve for him, because his life had been a hopeless torment, but I wanted to have his baby. I wanted to look into my baby's face and see Mark there. Not the hard-faced junkie, but the young man that Mark might have been . . . sweet and gentle and lovable. If only his parents had understood him and accepted him as he was, things might have been different. If only I could have been stronger and wiser, I might have helped him, too. Those were the thoughts and regrets that were swarming through my mind as I lay awake, or paced up and down the ward trying to control my nerves.

The shooting gallery had been heaven compared to the ward where I was transferred to after a week. There, they cut down the shots that I was given, working up to the time when I could endure life without drugs. I had a bad time, though.

They were careful with me because of the baby. I was wild with nervousness. My body wouldn't hold a thing that I ate. I had pains that started in my back and spread out like a flash of light into every muscle in my body. My stomach cramped until I was bent over double, hugging my knees and groaning in agony. I tried not to ask for drugs, but sometimes, I couldn't help myself. I'd start screaming and I couldn't stop until I found relief.

I was in that ward for two weeks, and then I went into what is referred to as the population of the hospital, the part where the patients stayed who were receiving psychiatric help. We'd stopped our drug habit in a physical way; our bodies didn't demand it any longer. But if our minds weren't changed, we might go back to shooting up the day we walked out of the hospital. That's what they told us, and I had to believe them. I talked freely to my therapist, who was a woman. She was kind. She seemed to understand why Rosalie and Mark had meant so much to me, and that it had been easy for me to fall into their way of living . . . not understanding the evil and the danger.

Easy . . . but how wrong! I hadn't hurt just myself. I'd brought into the world a pitiful bit of life that none of the doctors thought could possibly survive. My baby was born six weeks early, a little girl. When I heard her crying for the first time, she sounded like a wounded kitten. They put her in an incubator right away, and I couldn't see her for two days.

Father Miller, the hospital chaplain, came to my room. He was a minister who'd spent many hours trying to help the drug addicts who were undergoing treatment. He wanted to baptize my baby because she was expected to die at any time.

"I think that you should be there when she's baptized," he said in his gentle voice. "You haven't seen your baby yet, have you, dear?"

I shook my head and tears filled my eyes. I'd had a rough time during the delivery and I felt exhausted and hopeless.

"Is she . . . do they have to give her drugs?" I whispered. I hadn't had the courage to ask anybody else.

He nodded. "They're afraid that she'll go into shock and die if they don't. She's very weak, Pamela. Would you like to name her after someone that you love? Your mother, perhaps?"

I closed my eyes and the tears ran down my cheeks. "No," I said. "Not my mother. You pick a name for her, Father."

He took my hand in his. "Let's give your baby the most beautiful name in the world. Let's call her Hope."

I looked into his face and something seemed to stir . . . to come alive inside of me. I didn't know what it was then, but I realized later that it was indeed, hope.

"Is that . . . alright Father? You know what I am. You know what my baby's father was."

"None of that matters," he told me. "This is a new soul that God has permitted to enter His world. There's not a blemish on it."

It's hard to explain what I'd felt then. Full of pride and a happiness that I was afraid to admit to myself . . . and there was something even deeper. My soul . . . the very soul that I thought I'd killed had dared to breathe again. Self-respect, courage, the will to live . . . Father Miller had given me some of all of those things in that moment. Suddenly, I felt stronger, and I was eager to see my baby.

A nurse helped me into a wheelchair and pushed it down the hall. Father Miller was waiting at the door of the nursery. Of course, I knew that my little girl wouldn't look like other babies, but I wasn't prepared for what I saw through the glass wall of the incubator. She hardly seemed human . . . more like a twisted bundle of bones, covered with bluish gray skin. She lay on her back, sleeping . . . my little daughter. Her doubled-up fists were bony knots, her arms and legs no bigger than a man's finger. I gazed yearningly at her face, but I couldn't see Mark there. It was the face of a dying child.

From a great distance, I heard Father Miller reciting the baptismal service. The nurse opened the incubator for a second while he touched her little forehead with holy water. My baby didn't move. Her chest barely rose and fell. I had the feeling that every ounce of her feeble strength was concentrated in a terrible struggle to draw air into her lungs and breathe it out again. There was no energy left for her to open her eyes, wave her fists, or cry like the other babies.

After I was back in my room, Father Miller sat down by my bed. I was crying, torn apart by pity and a crushing burden of guilt.

"I didn't know she'd look like that," I said. "I did that to her! I knew that I was hurting her, but I couldn't stop. I'm a murderer . . . I knew that I was killing my baby and I didn't stop!"

Father Miller waited until I'd finished crying out the storm of grief and remorse.

"That's the tragic thing about drugs," he said sadly. "Drug abuse is the most deadly thing human beings can do to themselves. It crushes their body and their willpower at the same time. It's a form of suicide, actually. Not many people can quit the habit without help . . . and nobody can stay clean and sober on his own."

"But, I want to stay clean," I told him. "And I haven't got anyone to help me. I can't stay in the hospital forever. Will you help me, Father?"

He smiled at me and there was a warm sweetness in his face that seemed to flow into my heart.

"I'll do what I can for you, Pamela, but I'm just a human being, too. You need somebody whose love, strength, and understanding are greater than mine are. I'm talking about God, Pamela."

"God?" I repeated. "I don't know anything about God, Father."

"If you believe that there is a God, that He loves you and watches over you, that's all you need to know," he told me. "When you're frightened, you can call on God for His help and He'll never fail you. Do you know the Lord's Prayer, Pamela?"

Ashamed, I shook my head.

"It's never too late to find God," Father Miller assured me. "Say these words after me, Pamela, and listen to them with your heart. God is listening, too, and He will answer your prayer . . . in His own time, and in His own way."

Father Miller knelt beside my bed and I repeated the Lord's Prayer after him. When we were finished, a silence filled the room. I felt at peace . . . as though a loving hand had touched me and quieted my fears.

"Will God help me to stay clean?" I asked.

Father Miller nodded. "Yes, Pamela, He will. If you believe in Him and let Him help you, you can have a good and decent life . . . one that will bring you a happiness that you've never known."

"If I pray to Him, will He save my baby?" My voice was trembling.

"We can't bargain with God," Father Miller told me. "He will do what's best for your baby. But, pray to Him, Pamela . . . pray and trust in His goodness and mercy."

"I will, Father. I will," I promised.

I was like a child who'd been lost for a long time, and who had finally found her way home. The protection that my parents had never given me, the love that Mark hadn't been capable of, I found in my faith in God. I came to feel that He was with me everywhere. During the long, black nights, when the loneliness was the worst, I talked to Him. I prayed as I sat beside my baby and watched her suffer for my sins.

They let me spend the days with Hope, because that let the nurses go about their other work. She was taken through the withdrawal period slowly and carefully. When her poor little body needed drugs, her legs and arms would twitch, and I'd see a cold sweat break out on her skin. I had to call a nurse then to give her a shot that would relieve her agony.

I'd stand by the window until it was over, shaking and sick, trying not to hear the weak wail that she'd cry when the needle had pierced the skin. Once, as punishment for the terrible wrong that I'd done my baby, I forced myself to watch the long, sharp needle penetrate the pitiful, trembling little body.

In that moment, it all came back to me . . . the horror of my life with Mark. I couldn't stand remembering. I ran out of the room and down the hall like a crazy woman. I'd have probably run out of the hospital in my gown and robe if an attendant hadn't stopped me. He held me until I was calm.

Finally, the withdrawal period was over. Hope was still living and she was getting a little stronger. She'd even gained a few ounces. Everything possible was done to build up her physical condition and her resistance to infection. She began to eat with an appetite like a normal baby. Her gaunt cheeks filled out and her color was better. The day I saw the tiny dimples on the backs of her hands, I cried with joy.

I was gaining weight, too. I woke up feeling good, and I ate my meals hungrily. I began to look like a young girl instead of a haggard, sick, old woman. It was wonderful to feel normal again. I went to the therapist for regular sessions. She helped me to understand why Mark had become a drug addict. His parents had made him feel inferior and worthless. He'd hated himself for his failures, and he'd turned to drugs as an unconscious means of self-destruction.

My own story was simpler. My background had given me no moral standards. I'd been lonely and naive, and my longing for love had betrayed me. It helped to understand those things, but it was in my prayers that I found the comfort and strength that I needed so desperately.

I also spent several hours a day in the occupational therapy room. The patients did all kinds of work there . . . painting, sculpting, and weaving. When the therapist found out that I liked to sew, she had a machine brought in and trained me for tailoring work.

I was grateful to God for sparing my baby and for helping me. We were both well and safe, but I knew that I was traveling a road that would soon come to an end. When that happened, I would lose my baby forever. I'd leave the hospital to make a new start, and my baby would be adopted and given a good home by some childless couple.

Nobody had told me that, but I knew that it had to be that way.

What kind of a mother would an ex-drug addict make? I wasn't worthy to be Hope's mother. I didn't trust myself. Even with God helping me, I wasn't sure that I'd have the strength to live the right way.

Hope left the incubator when she was about the size of a normal newborn. She was pretty . . . a bright, happy baby. When I picked her up, she gurgled and batted at me with her soft little hands. I loved her so much. There was a constant ache in my heart, but I told myself I had to do what was best for her. I had to let her grow up in a good home . . . protected and loved.

I was sitting in the nursery one day, holding Hope in my arms, when Father Miller came in. I saw him several times a week. We talked and prayed together, and at those times, God seemed very close. He'd brought his wife in to see me once. She'd been sweet to me, and had asked if she could hold the baby.

Father Miller had played with Hope a little and then put her back in her crib. "I've just had a talk with your therapist," he said. "She thinks there you're ready to leave the hospital. You've been here for a few months now, and everybody's pleased with your recovery. Tell me what your plans are, Pamela."

"I haven't done much planning," I admitted in a low voice. "I think that I can get a job doing some kind of sewing. Hope. . . ." I choked up and had to stop a minute. "I hope that whoever takes her will love her as much as I do."

"Do you mean that you want to give her up for adoption?" Father Miller asked.

I looked at him in bewilderment. "What else can I do, Father? I love Hope, but I know I'm not fit to be her mother."

"I'm going to tell you something that will place a heavy burden of responsibility on you," Father Miller said soberly. "Adoption agencies hesitate to place children with questionable backgrounds. Hope is the child of two drug addicts. She, herself, was born an addict. In all probability, she might never be adopted. If you give her up, she may very well live in an institution until she's eighteen."

I stared at him, trying to understand. "But then . . . that means that she hasn't got anybody but me!"

"That's right," Father Miller said. "If you don't make a home for her, she'll grow up with other unfortunate children who are fed and clothed, but whose hearts are hungry. You don't want that to happen to Hope, do you?"

My mind was whirling in a hopeful confusion. "Of course, I don't, Father, but will they let me keep my baby? Will they trust me with her?"

Father Miller smiled at my excitement. "If you have a sponsor, I think they will. I'm ready to be your sponsor, Pamela."

He outlined his plan while I listened with my heart beating

quickly; a whole world of happiness was opening up to me. He and his wife would give me and Hope a home in return for my help with the care of their four children. The juvenile court would have to approve Hope's custody, and Father Miller was prepared to pledge his word that I would be a fit mother. Of course, if I went back to drugs, Hope would be taken from me at once.

I didn't exactly know what happened right after that, I hardly knew what I was doing or saying. I just remember that I cried with joy and knelt to pray with Father Miller. As he was leaving, I was afraid that I hadn't said enough. I hadn't made him realize how grateful I was. I looked into his face and wondered what would have happened to me if he hadn't come into my life.

"Thank you, Father Miller," I said. "Thank you for giving God to me."

His smile was radiant. "I didn't give God to you, Pamela. God was there all the time . . . in your heart. He's in all our hearts, saints and sinners alike. Never forget that, Pamela. You're God's child, and He loves you."

That was three years ago. We're still living with the Millers, Hope and I. They're very good to us. Hope is treated like one of their own. She's still small for her age, but she's bright and sweet. I try hard to be a good mother to her. When I'm troubled, I don't think of turning to drugs. I couldn't do anything that would separate me from my baby, and leave her homeless and unloved. I know that drugs aren't an escape, but a deadly trap. I turn, instead, to God. God is my star, and my baby and I live in the light of His truth.

I know how lucky I am. I'm one of the very, very few who've actually remained straight and sober. I was young when I was caught in that deadly trap and I hadn't been an addict for very long. That's why they were able to help me. The others spend their lives stopping and then going back to the habit, over and over again until, mercifully, they die.

I learned the pattern of how drug addictions work. You start using marijuana because somebody tells you that it's safe. Pretty soon, you move on to harder drugs like heroin. Sometimes it's for fun, and other times it's to keep up with the crowd. Like I did as a young and ignorant girl who destroyed herself for love. No matter what the reason is, the story is always the same. Someone started down a long, dark corridor and as they walked, everything eventually fell away from them . . . their family, their friends, and any happiness they'd ever known. They stumbled along, clutching a glittering needle in their hand, and their eyes strained to see into the darkness . . . but there was no end in sight. There would never be another dawn in their life.

THE END

109

# IF LOVE CAN
# COME AGAIN

Compared to the housing project I'd been living in, ten acres looked like all the land in the world the first time Matt showed me his place. I knew that it had been his folks' and that the house was old. But as I walked through it that Sunday afternoon, the house didn't seem so bad.

Old, yes. Not much cupboard space and too few closets, but there was a built-in pantry with shelves that could hold a lot of things, not that my kids and I had many belongings. There was a screened-in back porch, missing most of its screening, a barn, and a woodshed. The patterned linoleum covering the floors was worn and rough, and the papered walls were darkened with age and dampness. The enamel was worn and chipped off the sink, and most of the rooms had bare light bulbs in the ceilings. But there were three bedrooms and two baths. Even enough old furniture to get us by.

"I told you it was old," Matt said quietly, looking a little embarrassed.

"It's all right," I told him.

There was all that beautiful land around it, and there sure wouldn't be any gang fights outside the windows at night, no drugs traded openly, or older thugs teaching my two boys the violent ways of the street.

"Like I said, we could rent a place in town," Matt offered, probably worried about what I thought of the house.

"No. No, this is fine," I told him. "Actually, I guess I'm surprised. I thought it would be nice, but I didn't know the country would be this beautiful," I admitted, raising the shade on a bedroom window and looking out at the rolling green pasture that ran right out to where the woods began. It looked like a painting, too peaceful to be real.

Matt stood close beside me, tall, angular, not really handsome but very masculine. He drove an eighteen-wheeler and had been frequenting the truck stop where I'd worked for over a year. He'd always smiled and seemed friendly, but we'd never really talked until just six weeks ago during a storm that was so bad I couldn't leave the restaurant after my shift was over. I'd gone to the front door and looked out at the solid wall of slashing rain.

"Might as well have a seat and wait it out," a deep voice had said, and I turned around and looked into Matt's eyes. He was sitting alone at the first table.

I smiled uncertainly. He'd always been so nice and hadn't tried to run a line on me like a lot of the other men.

"Coffee?" he'd asked.

I nodded and sat down. We introduced ourselves and talked a while. His wife had been killed in a swimming accident over a year before. He had a son, seven, and a daughter, nine. I told him about my sons who were also seven and nine, and that I'd been divorced nearly three years.

And now, here we were at Matt's place. I looked up at him. "I wish we'd brought my kids. They wouldn't want to go back," I said.

"You think you can manage out here then?" he asked, sounding relieved. "You can make do until I can get the place fixed up?"

"Oh, yes, I can make do," I assured him. Making do had been the story of my life!

He touched my shoulder. "Well, Cathy, I suppose we should be going."

I nodded. We'd planned to come out here and see the farm, and then we were going to pick his kids up from his sister's house where they stayed while he was on the road. I'd had less than an hour to look at the place where we were going to live. At the most, I'd have two hours with his kids—who I'd never met. Then, I would let him know whether I thought we should get married.

"If you need more time, we could take more," he said.

But I wanted to get my kids out of the projects before the warm weather, when gang fights seemed to break out with dangerous frequency.

A marriage of necessity—I'd heard that phrase somewhere. Maybe in one of the paperback novels I escaped into when I found them at the thrift shop. And that was what Matt and I were planning— more a marriage of necessity than of love.

In a way I did love him, because he seemed so good and kind and honest. Matt was offering to be a father to my boys if I'd be a mother to his children. He needed a wife and I needed a husband. That was what it really boiled down to.

I followed him back to the car, stepping over the muddy ruts in the driveway. Matt drove into the small town ten miles farther on, to his sister Mae's house. A little boy and a young girl sat on the front steps.

Matt introduced us and I could feel them looking me over. Lee was a slim little boy who could easily pass for my Danny's brother. And Joanie was a pretty girl who seemed quite shy.

We went inside, and I met Mae. She was a lot older than Matt. He said they'd come from a big family. She was very nice, and she and her husband insisted we stay for dinner.

I wound up helping Mae while Matt went into the living room

111

to talk to her husband Sam. Joanie came into the kitchen, but Mae monopolized the conversation so we really couldn't talk. Once, I felt her watching me anxiously, and I turned and smiled at her. She smiled back at me, her expression turning from worried to relieved.

After dinner, we sat on the porch and I still didn't get a chance to talk to Joanie and Lee. Finally, I got up from the porch swing where I'd been sitting and went and sat on the top step by Joanie.

"I wish we could spend more time together," I told her. "I'd sort of hoped that you and I could talk."

She pushed her hair out of her eyes and smiled at me. Her eyes were just like Matt's.

"What do you like to do?" I asked.

She shrugged awkwardly. "I don't know."

"Do you like living in town?"

"It's okay," she said with a sigh. "I like living on the farm better, but there's nobody there now."

"Your father took me by earlier. It's nice out there, isn't it?"

Joanie nodded. "I stayed there when my grandparents were alive, and I had my own dog." She looked down at her hands. "But we had to leave and I don't know what happened to him."

"I'm sorry," I mumbled.

I wanted to tell her that we'd all move out there and that she could have a dog again, which was my son's big dream, too—to have a dog. But Matt and I had agreed to tell the children nothing at all, not to get their hopes up until we made our decision. That was why we hadn't brought my boys.

I patted Joanie's arm. "Maybe someday you can live there again."

As we drove away, Matt glanced over at me. "Didn't get to know the kids much, did you?" he asked.

"Not as much as I'd have liked," I admitted. "Your sister and her husband seem like nice people, though."

"They are," he said. "They've been good to me and the kids. Their kids are grown and they talk about looking forward to retiring and taking life easy. They don't complain about keeping Joanie and Lee, but I feel like I'm imposing."

"I like Joanie and Lee," I said, not knowing how to tell him that I'd already made my decision. After I'd seen his place, the kids would have had to have had two heads to make me turn down Matt's offer. I was sure I could cope with two more children, especially with all that room out in the country.

"You want to stop for coffee or a soda?" he asked when we'd driven about half of the one hundred fifty miles back to the city.

"That would be nice," I told him, thinking it would be easier for us to talk that way.

We stopped at a drive-in in the next town and went inside. After we sat down in a booth, Matt reached across the table and took my hand. "Do you need more time, Cathy?"

"No, I don't think so." I met his eyes and he was smiling. "It would be nice if we could get moved out to the farm before much later in the spring," I told him.

"I hope you'll like it out there," he said. "I know it'll probably be lonesome for you, but I'll try to see that you always have a dependable car. There are neighbors and they're friendly once you get to know them."

"I'll be busy with the kids, and I suppose they'll want to have pets. I've always thought I'd like to have some chickens," I said with a laugh.

He looked pleased. "There's a good henhouse on the farm. Mom always raised chickens. She used to sell eggs when we had more than we could use. I didn't think to show you, but there are some fruit trees, too—apples, pears, and peaches."

We were both silent a few minutes. Matt cleared his throat and I knew we were both feeling awkward.

"Well, will you—should we get married?" he asked quietly.

"I'd like that, Matt," I said, hoping my voice wasn't as shaky as I felt. Oh, Lord, I prayed silently, don't let this be a mistake.

"I'll be good to you and your kids, Cathy," he said earnestly.

"And I'll be good to you and yours," I promised.

Matt and I were married two weeks later in a judge's chambers at the city courthouse. Matt was on his way through and would complete his run and be back for us two days later.

My boys were ecstatic at the idea of having a father, moving to a farm, and having another brother. They weren't too wild at the prospect of having a sister. Matt had talked to Lee and Joanie and told them we were getting married, and he said they had seemed happy about it. After the formalities of our wedding, I drove Matt back to the truck stop where his rig was, and he bought us all dinner. Afterward, he climbed back into his truck to finish his run, and I drove back to our apartment in the projects.

"Hurray, we have a father!" Danny yelled when he got out of the car.

"Yeah, we got a dad," Tim agreed. Then he turned and looked at me. "Are you happy we got a dad, Mom?" he asked hesitantly.

"Yes, I am," I said with a smile, and I was.

It was all so strange. Terry, my first husband, and I had both been eighteen when we married. I'd graduated from high school, but he'd dropped out several years before. We thought we were madly in love.

Terry promised he'd get a steady job. He said we'd save up so

113

we could own a house someday. I pictured a nice little bungalow with ruffled curtains and knickknacks on glass shelves. What we actually had were cheap apartments and eviction notices because we couldn't pay the rent.

Terry didn't hold any job long. I waitressed when I could find a job. We lived with other people when we didn't have rent money, or with my dad. My mom had died several years before, so Dad wasn't home much and had a two-bedroom apartment that he was happy to share.

Terry's folks had a nice home, but he'd been into some scrapes with the law and was arrested twice—though his lawyer had gotten the charges dismissed each time. Since then, they wouldn't have anything else to do with him, so we couldn't go there.

We had Tim before we'd been married a year. Terry thought he was cute, but he didn't develop any feelings of responsibility. It was harder for me to work with a baby, and my dad had remarried and moved away. I baby-sat and did some waitressing, just whatever I could get.

Tim and I lived in tiny apartments and rented trailers, usually shared with other people. Terry came and went as he pleased. Sometimes he'd give me money, sometimes not. He'd come back every so often and rent us a new place to live and make a lot of promises I kept hoping he'd keep.

It was during one of those periods that I got pregnant with Danny. I was pretty depressed all during that pregnancy, knowing that Terry was never going to do any better. Danny was born in the county hospital, the same as Tim had been, but this time, Terry was nowhere around.

It turned out that he was in jail for selling parts he and some other men had stripped off of stolen cars. He went to jail for six months, and I had no choice but to go on welfare. It was terrible for me.

I found a tiny place in an old house that had been divided into apartments. It was in the worst part of town—where Terry and I always lived. The friends I'd had drifted away because really they'd been Terry's friends more than mine.

I was alone in those two rooms day after day. I'd go to the supermarket a block away with the kids in the rickety stroller I'd gotten in the thrift store. Sometimes I'd go to the Laundromat, but mostly I washed our clothes in the kitchen sink and hung them out on the windowsills to dry. I took the boys to the park a few times, but then some of the guys hanging around there started eyeing me and asking me out and I was afraid to go there anymore.

When Terry came home, he promised that he was going to do better, that he'd learned his lesson. He got a job in a warehouse and we moved to a nicer apartment in a better part of town. But before long, he was bringing home the same friends. There was the drinking and the drugs, and I knew they were stripping cars and stealing anything they could fence.

I was terrified that they'd get arrested or that the police would search our apartment, find stolen goods, and charge me, too. I realized that if I wanted my boys and myself out of that nightmare life, I'd have to make it on my own. I'd gone back to working in a restaurant, but I always felt terrible because I left the boys with whoever I could find to keep them. I was afraid they didn't get good care or treatment.

Another waitress talked me into applying at the truck stop with her. She said the pay was better and that you could make a lot in tips if you worked hard. We both got hired and I managed to get an old car.

I applied for project housing, and after a three-month wait, I got an apartment. Terry didn't want to move into the projects for some reason. Since he wasn't home most of the time anyway, I moved the boys and myself.

At the time, the projects seemed like a haven. There was a low-cost nursery for the kids, with hot meals, a playground, and trained attendants. Our two-bedroom apartment seemed spacious enough, and there was a small yard around it and sidewalks along curving streets.

Right from the start, I knew you couldn't leave a toy, a stroller, or anything outside unwatched—it would be gone. And I had to watch that the older kids didn't take my boys' few toys or hurt them. But that was the way it had been wherever we'd lived.

Finally, I divorced Terry. The authorities tried to make him pay child support, but most of the time he couldn't even be found. And then, he was in jail a lot. He didn't pay any attention to the boys. The few times he came around, it was to try to bum money from me or see if I'd let him move in with us for a while. I wouldn't.

The work at the truck stop was hard, but I didn't mind. What worried me was the way things got in the projects: the fights, drugs, all kinds of rotten things going on, and my kids seeing it every day. I didn't want them in trouble or turning out like Terry. I tried to teach them right from wrong, but they heard and saw so much that was wrong all the time. I was already considering moving out of there when I met Matt.

The boys and I happily packed up our things, and Matt was back in two days with his rig empty. He put our belongings in the back of that huge trailer. The boys begged to ride in the cab, so he took them with him, and I drove my car the one hundred fifty miles to his place.

"I don't imagine we can stay here tonight," he said when we'd arrived. "We can't get the utilities turned on until Monday."

But the kids begged to stay, and there was an old wood stove that

Matt built a fire in. I saw that we could even cook on it. Then we drove my car over to get Lee and Joanie and pick up Matt's car.

We picked up Joanie and Lee, bought some groceries, and went back to the old house. I fried some bacon and eggs on the stove, then made beds and tried to start cleaning up the place. Matt and the kids carried in our things. The kids seemed to get along pretty good, and the boys were so enthused with exploring the place that they were soon friends. Joanie alternated between helping me and following after the boys.

Matt went to a neighbor's place and got some buckets of water so we could all wash up, and I made coffee in an old coffeepot I found in the kitchen. We got the kids off to bed and I poured us coffee.

"Let's go sit on the porch," Matt suggested.

We went out and sat on the worn wooden floor of the porch.

"It's so peaceful," I told him and thought to myself how strange this was. There were no traffic sounds, no TVs or radios blaring, no voices. There were just some birds and the soft swooshing of the wind in the pines around the house.

Matt grinned. "You really like it here, don't you?" he asked.

"I love it," I said with a smile.

He reached for my hand. "I do, too. I grew up here and I've always wanted to live here. I'm sorry it's so rough for you—no water or electricity."

"Oh, that's okay," I assured him. "It's only for a few days and we can manage." We were silent for a while and I knew we were both worried about the same thing—Matt and I had never made love. We'd had very little time together. Mostly we'd talked about our lives and what we wanted for our children. Matt had suggested that we should get together and make a home for our kids after we found we had a lot in common and thought alike on just about everything. And I had agreed.

Matt was five years older than me, sort of quiet and easygoing. Something about him had made me feel right from the start that I could believe and trust him—that he was a good man.

When we finally went back inside, it was dark out. I carried my nightgown to the kitchen and washed up with a pan of water and dressed there. When I returned to the bedroom, Matt was in bed.

"Cathy, I won't rush you or make any demands on you," he said quietly. "I know we don't know each other very well, and I'm not that kind of a man. Whatever is between us—well, it's up to you."

I slid into bed and he put his arm under my head. Impulsively, I snuggled against him. Neither of us was prepared for what happened next. I guess we'd both been alone too long. . . .

"Oh, Cathy, I love you," Matt kept whispering over and over afterward, kissing my face, holding me close.

"I love you too, Matt," I whispered shakily.

116

"I didn't know it would be like this," he said, burying his face in my shoulder.

The next morning, I could feel him watching me as I fixed breakfast, and I turned and smiled. When he smiled back, I saw love in his eyes. Everything was so good then that it was a little frightening, like it wasn't real or couldn't last. I told Matt how I felt after the kids had gone outside.

"We'll make it last, Cathy," he said, putting his arms around me. "If a rundown old house is all it takes to make you happy, we'll do fine," he added with a laugh.

"You make me happy," I told him.

He held me close and drew a long shaky breath. "You make me happy, too," he said. "I never expected this."

My eyes met his. "Neither did I."

We spent most of that day cleaning and working on the house. Matt fixed locks on the doors and windows and made a list of priority items, like a yard light and oil lamps to be bought in town. He'd arranged to have a week off before he had to go back on the road, but already he was making preparations for when we'd be alone. I was torn between feeling safe and happy that he cared that much, and wishing he wasn't leaving at all.

Monday morning, we all went into town and Matt made arrangements to have the utilities turned on and a phone installed. "Hey, it's trade day," he said. "Want to go?"

I had no idea what "trade day" was, but Matt told me I'd love it. He drove to a big lot out by the fairgrounds that was packed with cars and pickups. People were selling everything imaginable: antiques, fresh produce, chickens, ducks, pigs, homemade crafts. It was like a carnival.

The kids went wild and I just walked around, staring at everything. Matt bought us hamburgers that somebody was cooking on a barbecue grill and hot black coffee. We wound up with a puppy, three hens, a rooster, and twenty baby chicks in a cardboard box.

Everybody else had cages or little coops they carried poultry in and most of them had pickups. We hadn't brought anything, so I wound up carrying two chickens in my lap and the kids carried the other animals in the backseat. In the car driving home, we decided to trade my old car for a pickup!

Later, the weather turned cold and nasty, and I had to keep the baby chicks in the kitchen. The puppy stayed in simply because the kids refused to part with him.

The utilities had been turned on but almost nothing worked. The pump and well didn't work. The wiring in the house was in terrible shape. Matt seemed to know a lot about fixing things. He redid a lot

117

of the wiring, but he had to get some men to look at the well and the verdict wasn't good. It was going to cost a lot to have the well cleaned and buy a new pump.

"I'll have to borrow from the bank," he said with a sigh. "The well is going to be expensive, we need a washer and dryer, that old stove has got to be replaced, and the refrigerator—"

"Wait a minute," I interrupted. "I can manage with the stove and refrigerator and a used washer. There's already a clothesline. Just worry about getting us some water and we'll get around to the rest."

Matt looked surprised. "I don't want things to be so hard on you," he insisted.

By now I'd gathered that not only would his former wife Jackie not live on the place, but she'd expected a lot. He hadn't really said anything against her, but somehow I'd gotten the impression that she hadn't liked him being gone so much.

We got the kids enrolled in the county school and the bus would pick them up at the end of the lane. Matt borrowed enough money to have the well fixed. Then there were water leaks all over and he had pipes and faucets to work on.

"I bet you'll be glad to go back on the road and get away from all this," I told him as he worked on the kitchen sink.

He looked up at me then. "No, Cathy," he said seriously. "I won't be glad to be leaving. It's the only way I know to make a good living right now, but I sure don't look forward to leaving you."

I was a little flustered and didn't know what to say.

Somehow, Matt got almost everything working within the week and found me a used washing machine. Then the hot-water heater— which hadn't been doing too good—went out the day before he was to leave.

"Never mind," I told him. "I can heat water until you get back."

"Be careful," he cautioned. "I don't want any of you to get burned."

Matt left me numbers where I could call to have somebody get hold of him and he promised to call often.

After he left and the kids had gone to school, the house seemed suddenly quiet. Of course, I had a lot to do to keep me busy. I took the blinds and shades out in the yard and scrubbed them down to get the grime off. I washed windows and polished the furniture. I got out a sewing machine that was stowed in the hall closet and tried to get it to work, but it didn't.

I'd taken sewing in school and I was really anxious to make curtains for the house. I took the sewing machine to a repair shop in town, but the man said it was beyond help. He had some inexpensive used ones, though, so I bought one with money Matt had left me.

There was also a sale on material at the fabric store next door and I bought some for curtains. Sewing them kept me occupied for several days.

One afternoon two neighbors, Barb and Nancy, stopped by. They said they'd seen the cars and smoke from the chimney and decided to see if someone had moved in. They were really friendly and stayed to have coffee. Before leaving, they invited me to visit them and gave me directions to their houses.

Matt called regularly, and when he came home, I was surprised at the lump in my throat at the sight of him.

"Oh, Cathy," he said huskily, holding me close. "It's so good to have you to come home to."

We had a wonderful, busy week. Matt couldn't get over all I'd done to the house. Joanie and I had decided we could paint her room and the kitchen, so he bought us the paint.

"Now anything you need, just buy it," he told me. "Or let me know."

The kids seemed to be adjusting so well. They all called Matt "Dad" and me "Mom." I really enjoyed Joanie, and she seemed to take to me right away.

I decided to paint the bathroom the day Matt left again and the kids were in school. That's how I found the first letter. It was on top of the medicine cabinet, laid flat and so covered with dust that we hadn't noticed it. The envelope had no name on it and it wasn't sealed, so I took the two sheets of paper out. The letter was addressed to someone called Brian and I glanced to the end of it. It had been signed by Jackie, Matt's first wife! I couldn't help but read it.

"I live only for our times together," she wrote. "Matt has never understood me the way you do. His idea of life is to live out here in this backwater place raising kids and vegetables! I have to find someone else to keep the kids during our times together," she went on. "The last time I left them with Mae, she asked too many questions when I got back. Brian, I think we should do what we talked about the last time. You can find us a place in another state—for just the two of us—so we can be together.

"I can't wait for your next call, the next time we can be together. Being with you is everything. You must know what even the sound of your voice does to me."

She went on to describe some of the intimate details of their relationship, and I found myself blushing even though I was alone. I was shocked! She signed the letter with love.

It was clear that she was seeing Brian, whoever he was, and that she was planning on leaving Matt and the children. I felt as if I was snooping or invading someone's privacy, but the letter had been right there and open. I thought about burning it, but for some reason, I didn't. I put it in the back of one of my drawers and started painting the bathroom.

Mae had invited me to visit her anytime, so I stopped by their house when I was in town one afternoon. She was friendly and asked me how things were going, how the kids were.

"They all seem to be happy," I told her. "They all love living on the farm."

She nodded. "I know they always liked it out there. So did Matt."

"Did Jackie not want to live there?" I asked.

"Oh, honey!" she said, laughing. "Jackie was hardly the type for a farm! Matt always wanted to live there, but she never would. Our parents offered to give them a couple of acres to build a house on, and Matt practically forced her to move into the old house with them to prove to her that she'd like it. But she stayed only a little while, I guess three months or so, and he had to get her a place back in town."

"Well, I guess people like different things," I told her.

"I'm glad you like the farm." Mae patted my arm. "I'm glad Matt's got you! He deserves some happiness, and you two seem so right for each other."

I didn't ask her why she said that Matt deserved some happiness, but I couldn't help wondering what she meant by it.

When I'd told Matt about Barb and Nancy stopping by our house and inviting me to visit, he'd seemed pleased and encouraged me to go see them.

"They'll be somebody to talk to," he said. "Keep you from being lonely. Jackie didn't like any of the women out here. Maybe you will."

When I visited them, they were really pleased and friendly. Barb mentioned that Jackie had never visited.

"Well, she wasn't our kind." Nancy shrugged. "No offense intended. She just wasn't the right woman for Matt. He's always been so down to earth. Jackie thought she was too good for any of us."

So good, I thought to myself, that she took a lover and considered leaving her children!

One day when the kids had just come in from school and we were fixing snacks in the kitchen, someone knocked on the front door. When I went to answer it, an older woman stood there.

"Are you Matt's wife?" she asked.

"Yes," I told her. "I'm Cathy."

She stepped right inside. "Are Lee and Joanie here? I'm their grandmother." For a moment, I didn't understand. Matt's mother was dead. Then I realized that she must be Jackie's mother.

"Oh, Jackie's mother?" I asked.

"That's right," she said. "I've come to see the children."

I called Lee and Joanie, and their grandmother sat down on the sofa to talk to them. She didn't seem very friendly to me, so I went back to the kitchen with Danny and Tim.

Lee and Joanie didn't seem particularly happy to see her. I heard her ask them how they were and they said they were fine.

"And this new woman your father has married?" she asked. "Is she good to you?"

"Oh, yes!" they both chimed in, and I couldn't help smiling.

"Well, I hope she continues to be." She sighed. "I'll be coming by to check on you from time to time."

Then she came to the kitchen doorway. "I'll be on my way. I don't have time to waste," she said abruptly.

"Well, stop in anytime," I told her.

"How long have you been married to Matt?" she questioned.

"About a month," I answered.

"I hope you have better luck than Jackie did. As you've probably heard, they didn't get along very well."

"No, I hadn't heard."

"Well, they didn't," she said flatly. "No use mincing words about that. He's a miserly one. Scared to death he'll spend a dime. I see he's got you living in his folks' old house." She looked around disdainfully.

"We plan on fixing it up," I said weakly as I walked her to the front door.

"Don't hold your breath," she warned. "Won't be much fixing done if he has his way."

I didn't know what to say, and she looked at me as if she wanted to say more. Then she seemed to change her mind, said good-bye, and left.

"Mom, is she our grandmother, too?" Danny asked when I returned to the kitchen.

"No," I said.

"Oh, good," he admitted, "because Lee and Joanie don't like her."

"Why don't you like her?" I looked from Lee to Joanie.

"She doesn't like kids," Joanie said with a shrug.

There seemed to be more and more things I found myself wondering about. Lee and Joanie never mentioned their mother at all. Now, there seemed to be no affection between them and their grandmother. And her description of Matt didn't sound right at all. He was generous with the children and me. But then, I decided that maybe it was the difference in people. I'd always had to scrimp and make do; maybe Jackie had expected a lot more.

I found the second letter on the top shelf of the closet in the boys' room, clear at the back. I was standing on a chair scrubbing the gritty shelf and I found the letter—no name on the envelope, unsealed like the other. It, too, was to Brian.

"I can't wait to be with you again," she wrote. "The time we spend together passes so fast. I hope we can see each other soon."

She went on to say that she was bored and that things between her and Matt seemed to get worse all the time. And there was a little more, just telling Brian how much she wanted to be with him, how she loved him.

I slid the letter back into the envelope and put it away with the other one, wishing it could answer my questions.

When Joanie came home, I followed her into her room. "Do you remember staying here when your mother was alive?" I asked.

"Oh, yes," she assured me.

"Which room did you sleep in then?" I asked.

"This room," she replied. "Daddy and our mother slept in there." She pointed to the boys' room. "And our grandma and grandpa in there." She motioned toward the room Matt and I shared.

"How long ago was that?" I asked. "How old were you?"

"I think I was six—that would be three years. A long time ago," she said.

I didn't press her anymore, but it seemed odd. Two unmailed, unaddressed letters to a Brian, left lying around the house for three years! I couldn't understand why Jackie hadn't sent them, or why they hadn't been found before this. Of course, they'd both been in out-of-the-way places. Still, why had Jackie put them there?

When Matt came in the next week, I told him about Jackie's mother coming to the house. I could tell right off that he didn't like it.

"I suppose she has a right to see the kids," he said. "Though she seemed to have little enough interest in them up until now."

"Did you get along with her?" I asked.

"She never did like me," he admitted. "Guess she thought her daughter deserved better than a country boy. And we had some trouble after Jackie died. But I don't think she'll come around here very often, so don't worry about it. She doesn't want to be bothered with Lee and Joanie." The subject seemed closed as far as he was concerned, so I didn't say anymore. But on my next visit, I mentioned to Mae that Jackie's mother had come by.

"Don't pay any attention to anything she says," Mae told me. "She tried to make trouble for Matt. If I were you, I wouldn't put up with her. And like I said, pay no attention to anything she says."

"I know it's none of my business, Mae. But did Matt and Jackie have serious problems?" I asked.

She sighed. "I wouldn't wish on anyone what happened to her, the drowning, I mean. But Matt is better off rid of her, I don't mind telling you. She was nothing but trouble for him."

I was sure I wouldn't find any more letters. It seemed uncanny that I'd found two, at least three years old, in a house that Matt and Jackie had only stayed in a few months, and then with Matt's parents there. But I found myself looking.

Matt had a box of pictures that he'd put on a closet shelf when we'd moved in. I got them down and went through them. They were old family pictures, photos of Lee and Joanie when they were little— and Jackie.

No one had told me she was beautiful! She was tall with a figure like a model and long shiny hair. I'd thought Joanie looked like Matt. I saw now that she really looked more like Jackie. It was the kind of looks that seem to improve as a girl grows up. Joanie was pretty enough now as a little girl, but she would be a beautiful woman.

Looking at Jackie's pictures, I suddenly felt plain and unattractive. I put the photos away and told myself to stop thinking about it. Things were better for Matt and me than I'd expected them to be. The kids all had a home and family. Matt was good to us. I was happy.

Jackie's mother came again, finding me in the middle of soaking and scraping wallpaper off the dining-room walls.

"My, you mean you intend to live in this house after all?" she asked.

"Well, yes." I tried to laugh, but I felt like a mess.

"Matt offered to build Jackie a new house if she'd live out here with him," she informed me.

"Well, we thought we'd fix this one up," I told her, wanting to add that if Matt was as miserly as she'd said, I was surprised he'd consider a new house.

"Well, living here would suit his penny-pinching ways," she sniped, and I felt as if she'd beaten me to the punch.

"Can we go play now?" Lee interrupted. I nodded and Joanie and Lee both took off.

"Wild little things, aren't they?" she commented.

"Actually, they're very good children," I said brusquely. "Of course, you don't see much of them or know them very well."

She looked annoyed, surprised that I'd stand up to her, I guess.

"Well, I just wanted to see how things were going," she said, getting up. "Having known Matt, I feel I should check on Lee and Joanie."

"What do you mean?" I demanded.

"Well, dear, I know what a temper he has," she said. "When things don't go his way, there's a steep price to pay. Of course, he's probably not as jealous of you as he was of Jackie."

"I don't give him any cause to be," I replied coolly.

"Then maybe things will go well for you," she said and left.

That time, Nelda, as I'd learned her name was, had upset me. I couldn't really understand why. Maybe I was angry because she put Matt down. Maybe I was jealous. I decided it was both.

I cleaned up the mess in the dining room, took a shower, and made a cup of tea. By then I was calm again, and I thought: Matt? Violent temper? Well, I hadn't seen any evidence of it.

Matt was patient with the kids and never seemed to complain about anything I did or didn't do. Of course, maybe he did have his way about most everything. The only time he'd raised his voice at me was when I'd suggested going to work.

I'd learned that practically all the women where we lived worked at least part-time in the factories in town, so I'd suggested that I could do the same.

"I don't want you working, Cathy!" Matt had nearly bit my head off. "I thought that was the agreement we had, that you'd stay home with the kids and I'd earn the living."

I'd laughed and leaned against him. "Don't get so up in arms," I teased. "I'm perfectly content to stay home and scrape paint and pull weeds. Actually, I feel a little guilty sometimes, like some days I don't earn my salt!"

He'd laughed then and hugged me. "Just your being here with the kids is important," he said. "I never saw Joanie look so happy, or Lee, either. And this old house looks better all the time."

I told myself that Matt and I were a good combination. Whatever had happened between him and Jackie was really none of my business, and I should stop being so curious.

During one of his layovers, Matt bought a tiller, cut up a big spot for a garden, and planted early vegetables. Then, he and the boys fixed a chicken run. Later, he took us all to a watershed lake a few miles from the house to fish. Of course, the kids loved it and wanted to know if they could come back soon.

"Not unless I'm with you," Matt said.

"Mom can bring us," Danny began.

"I don't want any of you coming here without me," he said sharply. "There are too many snakes." He turned to me. "Maybe I'm being overprotective, but I'm afraid for you to come here alone. This is where—" He paused, then said, "Jackie drowned here."

I just nodded.

There were a lot of fruit jars on the back porch, and I mentioned to Matt that I'd like to use them but I didn't know how to can. He told me I could get pamphlets from the extension office in town. I'd seen a building with that sign on it, so I stopped in the next time I was there.

They gave me several pamphlets, and I noticed a poster advertising some classes on making slipcovers. There was a fee and

124

you had to buy your own materials, but the classes went on for a couple of weeks.

I mentioned the class to Matt on the phone, and he was all for my taking it. I ended up getting home each afternoon just in time to meet the school bus. One day when I drove up, Nelda was waiting.

She smiled knowingly. "Almost didn't make it home in time to be here when the school bus arrives," she observed.

I nodded, unlocking the door. "I'm taking some classes in town," I began, making conversation.

She just smiled that false smile, and I realized she didn't believe me. "Oh, I know how living out here would get on anybody's nerves," she said. "I don't blame you for finding other interests."

I did a slow burn and tried to think of what to say, but the school bus pulled up and the kids came running across the yard. Nelda talked to Lee and Joanie a minute, then they managed to get away from her with excuses about homework and having to feed the chickens.

"Well, be careful," she said to me pointedly as she was leaving. "I wouldn't want anything to happen to you."

"What do you mean?" I questioned her angrily.

"Hasn't anyone told you?" Nelda asked innocently. "They suspected Jackie's drowning wasn't so accidental." I was too stunned to reply and she turned to go. "So just be careful."

I was shaking. Did she mean that someone suspected Matt had killed Jackie? I had promised myself that I wouldn't even think about Jackie anymore—or anything pertaining to Matt's marriage to her. Matt and I had our own lives. But I couldn't seem to push Nelda's words out of my mind.

Matt had made it clear that he didn't like Nelda coming to the farm. Still, he hadn't said to try to keep her from seeing the kids. And I felt she had a right to see them. I just hadn't mentioned her visits to him after the first one.

I surely didn't want to mention this one. What I wanted to do was go to Mae's and ask her about the indirect accusation Nelda had made. But I had two more days of classes, and then it would be Saturday; the kids would be out of school and Matt would be home.

Instead, I called Mae and told her that Nelda had been to visit.

"I know I shouldn't pay any attention to the things she says," I told her. "But I can't help wondering about some of them. I mean, I don't know what to say to her because I don't know a lot of the circumstances."

"Like what, Cathy?" Mae asked.

"Like she said Matt has a violent temper," I told her.

"I suppose you could say he has a bad temper," she agreed thoughtfully. "But not violent! And it takes a lot to get him riled. Our

125

father was like that, but I only saw him angry a half-dozen times, if that many."

"Did Matt and Jackie fight a lot, or have a lot of trouble?" I asked.

She was silent a moment. "Well, yes, they did. You've probably guessed by now that there was no love lost between Jackie and me. But that has nothing to do with what I say about her. I wouldn't accuse her of anything she didn't do. She did seem to enjoy tormenting Matt any way she could. She went out on him," Mae confided. "Neighbors saw her leaving the house and meeting other men when he was on the road. She didn't even try to hide it. They had some big fights about that. And there were other things she'd just nag about and keep on and on until he'd blow up. She seemed to enjoy that."

"Nelda said something about Jackie's death being—being more than just an accident," I blurted out, unable to keep it back anymore.

"She had no right to say that!" Mae retorted. "I thought Matt probably told you about it. The police never even questioned him! Apparently, he and Jackie had a big blowup in town the afternoon of the accident. A lot of people saw it," she explained. "So when they heard that Jackie had drowned in the lake, well—they just assumed the worst. There was a story going around that Matt did it. Can you believe that? But you know how people will talk. Everyone knew how Jackie was carrying on. Matt may have been fed up with her, but he could never do something so awful," Mae assured me.

"I don't think so, either," I told her. "But I don't know what to do. I hate to tell Nelda she can't come here. I'll just have to try to make it clear that I don't want to hear any of her gossip."

"That's best, I suppose," Mae agreed. "Although she's shown so little interest in Lee and Joanie that I wouldn't feel bad about telling her to stay away entirely."

I was positive there was nothing to the things Nelda had insinuated, nothing that affected Matt and me in Jackie's old letters. Yet I found myself studying Matt's face sometimes, wondering. Was there a side to that gentle, patient man that I didn't know?

"I want to talk to you about something," Matt said quietly one evening after the kids were in bed.

I was putting the finishing touches on a blouse I was making for Joanie, and I looked up at him questioningly.

"I've got the chance to switch routes," he went on. "I could be home every weekend by Thursday evening or Friday. I thought maybe with the garden to keep up with, it would be a good idea. What do you think?"

I hated the weekends Matt was away. I could feel the smile spreading across my face.

"I think that would be wonderful, Matt!"

He stood up from the chair where he was sitting and walked to the darkened window.

"You don't mind?" he asked.

"Mind?" I cried. "Why in the world would I mind? I'd love to have you home every weekend!"

He sat down on the sofa by me. "Well, it's not really because of the garden," he confessed. "I'd like to be home more with the kids—and you."

I laid my sewing aside and slid into his arms. . . .

That Monday, when Matt was back on the road, I found the third letter behind the fruit jars on the back porch.

"Brian, I'm so afraid of Matt," Jackie wrote. "I know he suspects us and he's acting crazy, brooding. I don't know what he's thinking or planning. I don't know what he may do, what he's capable of. If we don't get a place of our own soon so that I can leave him, I don't know what he'll do."

There was more—again saying how much she loved Brian and wanted to be with him apparently at all costs. I slid the letter back into the water-stained envelope and stood with it in my hand, trying to figure out how the letter had gotten there behind the fruit jars in the first place.

Why would Jackie put it there, or anyplace where it could fall down there? I looked up. There was a ledge just below the ceiling of ate porch. If she put the letter there, it could have fallen down between the boxes of jars and the wall. The ledge was too high for me to reach, but probably wouldn't have been for Jackie.

I dragged a chair out of the kitchen and climbed up on it to search the ledge. There were several books of matches and cellophane that looked like it had come from a pack of cigarettes caught between the ledge and a board of the ceiling. I moved the chair to another spot and found a key.

The key looked vaguely familiar, and or an impulse I climbed down and tried it in the back-door lock. It fit.

Well, Matt's parents could have left key up there on the porch. That way if they locked themselves out or one of the family came while they were away, they could get in. That seemed reasonable enough. In fact, it seemed such a good idea that I put the key back and forced myself to forget about it.

Matt told me the family usually had reunion in June. "I was wondering about having it here this year," he said. "It would be nice to have it here at the old house. But I guess it would be a lot of extra work for you. Mae's been having it at her place, but it's crowded, especially for the kids."

I'd done some painting and cleaning, and Matt and I had papered

127

the dining room. The floors were still a mess and our furniture mismatched pieces left behind in the house and what Matt had stored at Mae's I'd reupholstered a few pieces, but nothing matched. What the heck, I thought. Matt and Mae are nice, down-to-earth people. Probably the rest are.

"I think that would be nice," I told him. "They'll just have to accept our house the way it is. I don't mind the work and I'd love meeting them."

Matt talked to Mae and she was all for it. She even offered to come out to the house to help me a day or two before.

"Everybody brings food," she said. "So it isn't too bad. It's just that there are so many of us. A lot stay overnight. Of course, some can stay here at our house. That way it won't all be on one person so much."

It was really exciting once we started preparing for the reunion. Matt bought a sheet of plywood, cut it in two, and made a table for the front porch and another for the dining room. He repaired a couple of broken chairs that were in the shed, and we rounded up every chair, stool, and wooden crate that we could use for seating.

I cooked nearly the entire day before the reunion. I baked a ham and made a huge bowl of potato salad and a tossed salad with the vegetables from our garden. Mae brought pies and baked beans and a chocolate cake.

Relatives started arriving Friday evening. I'd made the kids' beds up fresh for company, and we'd made pallets on the floor for them and other children who came. There were so many relatives and in-laws that I couldn't begin to keep them all straight. But everyone was friendly and helpful, and I could see that Matt was enjoying himself so much, showing off what we'd done to the house, telling everyone the plans we had for it.

Kate was the oldest sister, a lot like Mae. She came into the kitchen where I was putting on another pot of coffee and mixing another jug of punch for the kids.

"This isn't really fair to you, Cathy," she said. "All of us descending on you before you've even had a chance to meet us."

"Oh, I'm enjoying it," I told her. "Matt and Mae have helped a lot, and the kids, too. Joanie peeled a whole bucket of potatoes!"

"Do you come from a large family?" she asked.

"No, I was an only child. My mother is dead and my father remarried and moved to another state. I think this is just wonderful. Everyone is so nice."

"Everyone thinks you're so nice." She smiled. "It was really a surprise having the reunion out here at our old home. Most of us had heard that Matt was remarried. But—well, I might as well come right out and say it. Jackie wouldn't even bring a dish, let alone put on the whole thing."

"I've heard we're very different," I said.

She laughed. "To put it mildly!"

"I've seen pictures," I confided. "She was beautiful."

"Oh, yes." Kate's expression was suddenly sour. "She certainly was not a good wife or mother. Matt and the children deserve you. Joanie was telling me a while ago how much she loves you."

"That makes me feel good," I told her. "I love her and Lee, too."

Annie, a sister-in-law, walked into the kitchen. "Is this a private conversation, or can anybody join?" She grinned.

"Sit down with us," Kate invited. "I was just telling Cathy how happy Matt and the kids seem."

"Isn't that man just glowing?" Annie laughed. "I've never seen him like this! Well, I guess he never had reason before."

"I believe Cathy is more his type. And more ours," Kate said, and they both laughed.

"Is Brian coming?" Annie asked.

"I've been wondering." Kate looked at me. "Have you heard whether Brian is coming?"

"Who—who is Brian?" I stammered nervously.

"Our youngest brother," Kate said. "He's a trucker, too."

"I haven't heard," I managed to say, though I was afraid I was flushed with the shock of realizing just who Jackie's lover had been.

Kate and Annie looked at each other.

"Was there really anything to that—between Jackie and Brian, do you suppose?" Annie asked.

"I don't know." Kate looked sad.

"I think there was," Annie said thoughtfully.

"Brian hasn't been back here since the funeral," Kate mused. "Before that, he was always stopping by. In fact, he used to come out here to the house and stay. There was gossip that Jackie met him here sometimes, after Matt had gotten her a place in town."

I listened, fascinated. Then the letters might not have been three years old! Maybe she'd left the letters for Brian, but why scattered around like that? Why here?

"Well, I did hear that he and Lucy are back together," Kate went on.

I was picking up paper plates and breakfast scraps off the front porch the next morning, when still another car drove up. Matt had come out with a trash bag to help me.

"This was a good place to feed the kids," he said, grinning. But his expression froze as two young people got out of the newly arrived car, helped a toddler out, and started across the yard.

"What's wrong?" I asked.

"Nothing," he said quickly, hurrying to pick up the rest of the trash.

Just then, Kate came out onto the porch. "Brian and Lucy!" she cried. "And just look at how that baby has grown!"

They came up on the porch and greeted Kate, and then Lucy turned and took Matt's hand.

"Matt, it's so good to see you. You're looking great!"

"You're looking good too, Lucy. Oh—here, meet my wife. This is Cathy. Honey, this is Lucy, my brother Brian's wife."

We exchanged greetings and I thought she seemed really nice. Then Brian came over and held his hand out to Matt. I was sure Matt hesitated a second before he took it. He introduced me to Brian and the tension was so thick I could feel it.

More people came and I was busy with food and the endless cleaning up, but I found time to visit. Lucy put their toddler down to nap in our bedroom, and we sat talking quietly while she rocked her to sleep.

"Do you and Matt plan to have more kids?" she asked.

"Not really," I said. "Four's enough. Still, when we see a little one, we start thinking maybe—" We both laughed.

"It would be nice for you to have one together," she told me. "I swore I'd never have another. But now—well, things are better between Brian and me. He's not on the road as much, and he seems to care more about having a home and family."

I didn't know what to say.

Later that afternoon, someone put up a volleyball net in the front yard. There was a close game going on and everyone else was sitting on the porch, cheering the players on. I went to the kitchen to fix another pitcher of lemonade, when Brian came in, wiping the sweat from his face with the sleeve of his shirt.

"Maybe I'm getting too old for this." He grinned.

I smiled back, wishing I didn't know what I did about Jackie and him.

He got a glass of water and leaned against the counter. "So how do you like living here, Cathy?"

"I like it very much," I told him tightly.

"I'm glad." He took another swallow. "Matt always liked it here."

I didn't reply. I finished the lemonade and picked it up to carry it outside.

Brian caught my arm. "Cathy, wait. I—I have to talk to you."

I turned and looked up at him, wanting to tell him I couldn't imagine what we'd have to talk about.

"I have to ask you something." He was solemn and nervous. "Cathy, I don't know how to say this, but when I heard you and

130

Matt were moving into the house I was afraid he might come across something, some letters meant for me."

I set the lemonade down. "From Jackie?" I asked, not even trying to hide the disapproval in my voice.

"Yes," he admitted. "I did something very foolish. I met her out here a few times. Jackie liked to play games, especially if they were dangerous or if somebody was apt to get hurt. I can't imagine why I got involved now. But I did. She used to leave letters out here for me," Brian explained, "then tell me on the phone what she'd done. I'd have to come get them before anybody else found them. I know this doesn't make any sense. I was afraid I didn't find them all. I hope Matt didn't find them."

"I don't think he did," I told him. "But he probably suspected something. I'm the one who found the letters."

"You didn't show them to him?" he asked anxiously.

"No. I didn't know he had a brother named Brian until Kate and Annie mentioned you yesterday. I just didn't know what to think."

"You can think Matt has a brother who's a fool!" Brian said softly. "I've been sorry so many times."

"You know the gossip about Jackie's death?" I asked him. "That Matt—"

Brian interrupted me, waving his hand in a gesture of disbelief. "Jackie was never a good swimmer. She probably ignored Matt's warnings and tried to swim across the lake by herself. She was headstrong like that. Always trying to prove something—maybe to get attention," he said, shaking his head sadly.

I felt a little flood of relief.

"Look, Cathy. Matt's a great guy," he began.

"I know that, Brian," I told him.

"I think a lot of him. We used to be close. He was my idol growing up. He got me on driving trucks. I've got a great wife and little girl. I know I almost blew it all—our family, my own wife and child. Anyway, I'd appreciate it if you'd destroy anything you've found. And if you wouldn't mention any of what I've told you to anyone," he added.

I nodded. "Of course, Brian. There's no point in anyone being hurt anymore."

"Thanks. Thanks, Cathy." He pressed my hand and turned to go back outside. I followed him with the lemonade.

On the porch, I went and squeezed into the glider beside Matt. "You have a nice family," I told him, and he grinned proudly.

It was one great weekend, and by Sunday evening everyone had left. The kids and Matt helped me pick up what little the others hadn't cleaned up. Matt put the tables away for another year. The kids settled

131

down quickly, tired after all the excitement. Matt and I went out and sat in the glider after they were in bed. We talked about having a baby. . . .

On Monday, I burned those letters and never mentioned them to anyone. I hope that's all there were. The next time Nelda came by, I told her that I didn't really see any point in her coming to our house again. The kids weren't due home from school for over an hour that time, and obviously she'd only come to try once more to poison my mind against Matt. She hasn't been back.

We got a note from Lucy and Brian a few weeks ago thanking us for the good time they had at the reunion, and Lucy mentioned that she was expecting again.

"Should we tell them?" Matt asked.

"Oh, let's just wait and let them be surprised," I told him. "Everybody is talking about getting together here for Christmas, and our baby will be obvious by then!"

There are a lot of things in this world I don't understand—like what made Jackie and Brian do the things they did—and I probably never will. I'm just thankful for what Matt and I have—our home and family and the love we all share. THE END

# MY SIN COULDN'T
# STAY HIDDEN

My cousins said they were sorry to see me leave, but they didn't mean a word of it. Maybe Aunt Essie and Uncle Joe did, but they had enough kids to feed without me. Ever since my parents died when I was six and Aunt Essie took me to raise, I was conscious of being in the way. No wonder—for thirteen years I slept on a sofa made up in the living room, and never had a corner to call my own in their overcrowded flat.

All through high school, I made up my mind to leave my aunt as soon as I could stand on my own feet. The day after I graduated, I got a job as stock clerk in the interior-decoration department of a department store on State Street. And my big chance came only six months later. One February morning, Miss Lewis, the department head, called me into her office.

"I've been watching you, Lynn," she told me. 'You have a flair for style, and you'd be good in decorating, if you had a chance. I'm going to let you work with me and find out. There will be a small raise, and a future. But you'll have to work hard and do a great deal of studying."

I visualized Aunt Essie's crowded living room with the TV blasting away. You couldn't even hear yourself talk, much less study, in that flat.

"You're not hesitating?" Miss Lewis asked.

"No, I'm just a little overwhelmed," I said.

She smiled again. "Good. Then it's settled." She handed me a sketch. "Next week we're going to redecorate this apartment. If you get any ideas, let's have them. And, Lynn, one thing I hate is a yes girl."

I was in a fog as I went back to the stockroom. I touched the fabrics lovingly. Now I would get to do things with them.

Then it dawned on me. This meant more than a raise. It meant a chance to learn a trade I loved, to afford a home of my own, to eat when I wanted to, what I wanted, to be able to study in the evenings.

And two weeks later, on my day off, I found just the flat. It had a large living room, a kitchen, and a bath, and it was furnished.

I moved in the following Sunday. That first day in my own place, I felt like a queen in a castle. I kept running around to look at everything, to touch everything. The worn, shabby furniture and the rickety, rusted stove were beautiful to me. I cleaned and scrubbed the little place till it shone, and then I planned how I'd decorate it.

The next year flew by. It was like a dream—having privacy, and quiet, and freedom. No more wet diapers strung over the stove, no more gulping down my food to make room at the table for another child. And I was able to study all the books Miss Lewis suggested. I ate up her words, imitated her little gestures, and even copied the way she dressed. And at the end of that year, she made me her real assistant.

By then, I was full of shop talk and bright ideas about interior decorating. And by then, I had my big dream—about having my own shop someday. But I forgot about that on the day Miss Lewis asked me to see a salesman with a new line of drapery materials. "You can order as well as I can, Lynn," she told me on her way out.

I was thrilled with the responsibility, but my excitement changed to something else when the tall, handsome man strode over to my desk. "Miss Palmer?" he said. "I'm Larry Dahn." He lifted his sample case to my desk and snapped it open.

It was all routine, all businesslike, even his pleasant smile and courteous manner. But there was something smoldering beneath the businesslike air, beneath the handsome, smiling face. Something that keyed me sharply to an awareness of him as a man, so that I couldn't keep my mind on the swatches I was running through. And when I felt his hand on mine, I jumped.

"Hold it," he said, bending closer. "You passed up the best number. Blue is the color this summer."

The blood rushed to my face as I pulled my hand from his. "I was going back over them again," I told him.

He snapped the bag shut. "I'll leave them for Miss Lewis," he said. But he made no move to go. "We could talk about details over dinner tonight," he suggested. "Suppose you give me your address, and I'll pick you up around seven."

"Miss Lewis has the final word on all orders." My eyes met his. "Don't waste a dinner on me."

"It's not wasted. Besides, it goes on the expense account." I liked him even better with that boyish grin. He picked up a card, his pencil poised over it. "You can always put in a good word for me with Miss Lewis," he added.

I gave him my address, and even after he left, I still seemed to feel his hand, warm and tingling, on mine.

Dressing for that date with Larry was almost like the excitement I'd felt that first day in the flat. It was something new and wonderful. I'd gone out with several boys in high school, but there had never been anyone special, and since then, I'd kept pretty much to myself.

When I opened the door to Larry, I was repaid for the care I'd taken with my clothes and make-up, just as I was for the changes and improvements I'd made in the apartment. He didn't say anything—it was just the way he looked at me, approvingly, almost caressingly.

Being with Larry was wonderful. He knew places to eat in Chicago that I'd never even heard of. I couldn't figure him out, though. Sometimes he was like a wise old man; other times, a fun-loving, mischievous little boy. But one thing was sure: his charm. He knew he had it, and he used it.

During that first date, he talked about his job. "I've always liked the feel of fabrics, Lynn," he said. "But then, a good salesman should be able to sell anything. No holds barred when it comes to getting an order." He made a wry face. "At least that's my idea."

But later, when he took me home, he dropped business. "I'll drive you home the long way, around the Lake. I want to tell you about me, not textiles."

"I'd like to hear about you," I said.

He drew over to the side of a quiet road and parked. "It's a pretty dull story. I was born in Chicago and lived here all my life. Ever since I left school, I've been in the selling game. I've traveled a lot—been with this concern about two years. I do all right, only I hate my boss."

Suddenly, he gave me a searching, hungry look and, sensing what would come next, I shivered. "I'm cold, Larry," I said. "Would you mind taking me home?"

He did what I asked, but his eyes were cloudy. He didn't try to touch me before I got out of the car. He didn't mention another date, either.

The next day, I showed Miss Lewis the samples. She picked out several that she wanted. Then, Larry stopped by late that afternoon and I gave him the order. After he wrote it down, he reached over the desk and took my hand. "I'm not saying I don't take girls as they come, Lynn," he said. "But you're different. You kind of knocked the wind out of me, and that's pretty unusual."

I didn't pull my hand away. "Yes?"

His grip tightened. "May I see you tonight?"

It was as if I had no will of my own from that minute on. And after seeing Larry every night for two weeks, I was madly in love.

Not that I let him know it—I didn't dare. As Miss Lewis remarked once, "Women go for Larry Dahn in a big way and always will. Maybe it's the heel in him."

"He doesn't seem like a heel," I said.

She didn't bother to answer, but just went on looking at the sketch on her desk.

Well, I'll play it cool, I thought, returning to my work.

But how do you play it cool if your heart leaps when a man

touches you? When you jump to answer the phone, each time hoping to hear one voice? When you're sick with longing for him when he doesn't come to see you?

Finally, I broke down and asked him to dinner one Saturday night. He brought a dozen yellow roses and a box of candy.

"Anniversary," he said. "One month since we first met."

I hung his coat in the hall closet. When I turned, he caught me in his arms. "You're all I ever wanted," he whispered against my lips. "I love you, Lynn. I didn't want to fall in love. I fought it tooth and nail, but I'm in, up to my neck, and something has to be done about it."

I started floating on air. The blood seemed to sing in me. Then Larry kissed me, and I felt I'd suddenly come alive and was passing into a new world where loneliness didn't exist.

"I love you too, Larry," I murmured. "You'll never know how much."

"More than anyone?" he said.

"More than life itself," I told him.

"Will you marry me, darling?"

I held his head down to mine. "Yes, oh, yes! There will never be anyone in the world for me but you. Never!"

It was the smell of burning food that tore me from his arms, and I ran to the kitchen. "It's just charred around the edges," I said, laughing, as I pulled the overdone chicken out of the oven.

"Put that down," he said. "Kisses are more important than food." He held open his arms. "Come here, and I'll prove it."

I set down the pan. Suddenly, I was afraid. Not of him, but of myself. For the love that swept through me was like a terrible hunger. "We'll have lots of time for kisses, darling," I said. "You sit at the table, and I'll bring in the dinner."

That evening, Larry and I made plans for the future. "I'd like to keep my job," I told him. "We can save some money then. It would be wonderful to buy a house, Larry. I've always wanted a real home."

"Usual woman talk. You get a man, and then start tying anchors to him. A home, mortgages, washing machine, kitchen cabinets, a patio—" Larry wasn't taking it as seriously as I was. He was in one of his happy moods, and he pulled me closer to him.

"Larry, I want our marriage to be perfect," I said. "If there should be children—"

He let me go suddenly and got up. "For such a young thing, you travel fast, honey. We've just this minute got engaged, and you're planning for the children already." He leaned back and smiled down at me.

I went to the window. It was snowing, and the street below was all white except for the yellow circle of light the street lamp threw on it.

Larry came and pulled me around to face him. "I'll always love you, darling," he said, his voice deep and tender. "Your funny, scrious ways. You'll always be a part of my life. Part of me. I'll even get used to the idea of being a conventional husband in time."

I kissed him. "You're learning fast," I said.

He groaned. "The trapper is caught in his own little trap," he said, letting me go and reaching for his hat and coat. "See you next week. I'm leaving in the morning for Detroit on a selling trip. I'll be gone a few days." Then, without another word, he went out.

I shivered, knowing how I'd miss him, but the yellow roses on the table held the promise of summer, the happy time when I'd be Larry's wife.

On Sunday, I went to see Aunt Essie to tell her my good news. But her newest baby had a rash, and Aunt Essie talked a blue streak about her own affairs and I couldn't get in a word.

I realized then that in leaving their home, I'd gone completely out of their lives. And then, it struck me that I never was one of them at all—I had just lived there like some stray animal they fed and housed. The knowledge frightened me. For Larry was all I really had now. I was so deeply in love with him, it was as if I came alive only when I was in his arms.

When he came back from his trip, everything was brighter. I cried as he held me close. "Don't leave me again, Larry. I was so lonely without you," I whispered.

When I raised my head, his eyes were strange. And when he kissed me, I had no doubt that he loved me as I loved him.

"I'd better leave you," he said then. "I don't dare trust myself. . . ." For the next two weeks, the tension and frustration kept mounting. And then, on Tuesday night, the wave that had been building so violently finally broke.

Wednesday was my day off, and I always did the weekly chores the night before so I could be free on that precious day. That Tuesday night I cleaned the apartment, washed my hair, did my nails, and there was a line of clothes hung in the bathroom. Around eleven, I went to bed.

Sometime later, the doorbell woke me and my heart pounded in fright. Nobody ever rang my bell so late. I rushed over and pushed the buzzer, thinking of Aunt Essie and wondering if one of the children was hurt.

When I opened the door, Larry was standing there. He was hatless, his hair ruffled by the wind, and his eyes were bright. He pushed me aside, came in, and shut the door behind him.

"I had to see you," he said. Suddenly, I was conscious of my thin nightgown and ran to the chair for my robe.

137

But Larry got there first. He caught me in his arms and held me close, his hands warm and hurting. "I've almost gone mad wanting to hold you in my arms," he said. "I walked and walked, and then I decided to come and see you—talk to you—kiss you like this."

His lips were demanding now. And the hunger in him spread to me. Finally, I managed to break away from him, and clinging to the back of the chair, I said, "Larry, please leave now."

"Why should I?" he demanded. "Why should I go when I love you so? Why should I suffer, wanting you so, when in a few days we'll be married?"

Almost as if I had no will of my own, I waited for his arms to close around me again. "You're smaller, lovelier like this," he said, kissing my eyes, my lips—deep, demanding kisses that swept me into the tide of his passion, and swallowed me up, until there was no longer any of me. Only Larry, his hunger, his desperate need of me.

After a long time, I fell asleep. When I woke it was morning, and it was as if I'd dreamed all that had happened during the night. Except that I knew I was a woman now, and I belonged to Larry.

It was then the fear rushed through me like a dark tide. I glanced at the clock, and it was almost noon. Larry must have slipped out while I was asleep. Suddenly, all the things I'd heard about the foolishness of a girl giving herself to a man before she married him poured into my mind. Suppose Larry didn't want me any longer. . . .

I had to hear his voice. I slipped on my robe, went to the phone, and dialed his office number.

It was an eternity until I heard his voice. "Larry, I must see you!" I cried.

"Oh, Miss Palmer," he said, and I could tell that he couldn't talk freely. "Suppose I take you to lunch. We can talk over the order then."

"At lunch? Here, Larry?"

"Suppose I meet you. . . ." He named our favorite place, and then hung up. My legs were weak as I went to make a pot of coffee.

Later, at lunch, Larry was just the same. "Darling, you're more beautiful than ever," he said. "I love you more than ever."

Relief flooded me. "We've got to be married right away, Larry," I said. "I'm frightened. I mean—"

He laid his hand on mine. "Suppose you leave it to me." He smiled. "You surprised me, darling. Who'd ever suspect that a quiet little girl like you—" He broke off as the drinks came. "We'll talk about our wedding tomorrow night. In a few weeks, you'll be my wife, and no job, darling. I want you all to myself. You'll have enough to do to look after me."

All doubts left me. I was loved, wanted. And if I loved Larry yesterday, it was like I was floating in a sea of love now. "I didn't know I could love this much," I told him, when we'd finished lunch and gone outside.

He bent and kissed me. "Go shopping for one of those lacy nightgowns, darling. I'll phone you tonight."

During the next two weeks, I couldn't think of anything but Larry. Then, a week before our wedding date, he dropped in at the flat one evening, his face as dark as thunder. "That boss of mine is a dog!" he said.

I'd found out by then that Larry was moody and hated anyone who gave him orders. "What is it, darling?" I asked, hanging up his coat.

"Just before five, that big noise called me into his office. I have orders to take off in the morning for San Francisco." He kicked a footstool viciously. "So we can't be married next week. Unless I give up my job. And I've got a notion to do just that."

"No, Larry, don't do that." I put my arm around him.

He pulled me down on his lap. "We'll have to wait a few more weeks then. I'll be back as soon as I can, darling."

"I don't want to wait, Larry." I leaned against his shoulder. "I'll die missing you. Take me with you, Larry. Please take me with you!" I started to cry.

"Don't, Lynn. I can't take tears." He cradled me in his arms. "You'll always love me, won't you?"

"You know I will, Larry."

"You belong to me."

"Forever, darling."

"Never forget that, will you?" We sat there quietly for a long time. Then Larry set me on my feet and got up. "I'd like to take you with me, Lynn, but it doesn't make sense. We'd better keep our heads. I need this job if we're getting married, and I have very little money saved."

I smiled. "I'd better hold onto my job, too."

He sighed. "So we'll be married in May instead of April. It's as simple as that." He stood, looking at me like a forlorn little boy. "I guess I'd better be moving on. I've got some packing to do, and I have to get my car checked."

How could I let him go? How could I live without seeing him every day? "It's going to be terribly lonely, Larry," I said, crying again.

He turned me around. "Don't look at me when you say good-bye. I can't stand tears."

I stood there as the door closed slowly. And the loneliness I'd known as a child was back in me again.

From then on, I lived for Larry's letters and the cards he sent from the cities he visited. And when he described San Francisco, it was as if I were seeing it through his eyes.

"It'll take another few weeks," he wrote at the beginning of May.

139

"You'll be a June bride, darling." And then it was June—and July. And no more letters from Larry. Not a word. I waited endlessly, hurrying home to see if there was mail. I was heartsick.

Then one day, I went to his office to check up. I had visions of Larry sick in a strange city, maybe even dead. There were so many traffic accidents, and he was often a careless driver.

The girl who came out to see me looked at me oddly. "Mr. Dahn hasn't worked for us in over a month," she said. "As far as we know, he's still out West. The last we heard from him"—she scribbled something on a card—"he was stopping at this hotel, if that will help you any." She handed me the card.

"I can't understand it," I told her. "He suddenly stopped writing, and I was afraid something might have happened to him."

"We can't understand it, either," she said. "Larry was such a likable guy. He was doing fine out West. Orders came in from wherever he stopped. Then he sent his letter of resignation. Well, it was a shock to our sales manager."

I stood there, staring at the girl and gradually her face dissolved. I fumbled my way to the door, afraid I was going to faint, and somehow I was on the street again.

When the dizziness passed, I knew what I had to do. I had to find Larry I had to find out why he threw over his job like that, why he stopped writing me.

The next day, I asked Miss Lewis for a leave of absence.

"You look sick, Lynn," she said "A vacation will do you good."

I gave up the apartment, packed my clothes, and drew my savings from the bank. I called Aunt Essie to tell her I was going on a trip. Then, I went down to the bus terminal and bought a ticket for San Francisco.

As the endless miles rolled by, I saw hardly anything, for the tears kept welling up in my eyes. My heart was heavy as I thought of all kinds of terrible things that might have happened to Larry.

In San Francisco, I took a room in the hotel the girl in Larry's office had told me about, and then I asked the clerk if Larry was registered there.

"Larry Dahn?" he said. "Oh, no, not any more. He left about a month ago. But I remember him, all right. Couldn't forget that face—every woman in the place had her eye on him." He grinned, and I almost winced from the mixed pain and pride that shot through me.

"Do you have any idea where he went?" I said.

"I believe he headed for Santa Rosa. That's about forty miles from here."

I thanked him and escaped to my room. After a hot shower I fell into bed, exhausted.

I got up early, had a quick breakfast in the coffee shop, and then waited for the next bus to Santa Rosa. When I got there, I checked my bag at the station and started wandering down the main street.

The sun was hot and almost too bright. Then, as strange faces kept passing by, I wondered desperately where to start looking for a man in a strange city.

My first idea was that if he lived in Santa Rosa, he might have a phone. So I went into the nearest drugstore and looked through the phone book. He wasn't listed there.

Then I tried the department stores, inquiring after him in the fabric departments, hoping he would be working in the same line. But no one had ever heard of him.

All day, I tramped from one store to another. Finally, I came to a decorator's shop and, as a last resort, I went in and asked the proprietor.

She knew him! "Larry Dahn," she repeated. "He sells for a firm that deals in small lots. Choice stuff, too. You see, I have an exclusive trade. My clients are the best families in town."

"I am an assistant buyer in Chicago in your line," I told her. "I've had a lot of experience in the decorating field."

Her keen, dark eyes studied me. "I might be able to use someone like you. It's a little slow just now, but in the fall I'm almost crazy trying to keep up with the work. Tell me about yourself and your experience."

It was fun talking shop with her. I told her about Miss Lewis and said she could write to her for references.

"I don't need to," she said. "I'm a pretty good judge of women. When you're ready to go to work, come in and see me." She turned as the door opened and a woman came in. "Oh, yes, Miss Palmer," she added, "I expect Larry Dahn to bring in some samples in the morning. Around ten."

"I'll be here," I said, and left. Larry was alive! My heart lightened. Everything would be as before, I kept telling myself over and over as I went through the motions of living the rest of that endless day.

At ten the next morning, I was at Madame Helena's shop. My heart was beating wildly as I opened the door. Larry was there, holding up a sample of brocade, and laughing at something Madame Helena said.

When he saw me, his jaw dropped and his eyes darkened. "Lynn! It isn't possible!" he cried, coming toward me.

"I've been looking for you," I managed to stammer.

"Suppose you go next door to the diner and have coffee, Lynn," he said. "I'll join you as soon as I'm finished here."

I nodded to Madame Helena and walked next door. I took a table in the rear, away from others. I was staring into my empty coffee cup when Larry slipped into the seat beside me.

"I can't understand it, Larry," I said. "When you stopped writing, I didn't know what to think."

His hand closed tightly over mine. "I got into a jam, Lynn. A crazy, impossible thing, and I had to go through with it. It happened shortly after I got to San Francisco. But it had nothing to do with loving you. I do, and I always will. Only I have to get straightened out."

He was looking at me with that intense expression that I knew so well. The blood began to race in my veins. "What do you have to straighten out, Larry?" I said.

"I better start at the beginning. After I'd been in San Francisco about two weeks, I was as low as a worm. I' missed you, and I was lonely. You know how I am. Then, one night, I was in the lobby of the hotel and a man I knew who was stopping there came in with a woman. He asked me to join them for a drink. Catherine was very pleasant, and the three of us did the night spots together. It was early morning when we got back to the hotel. I found out then that Catherine was stopping there for a week or so. But that weekend she decided to go to a cabin she owned at some lake up north. She asked me to drive her up." His mouth twisted wryly. "Well, on Friday I did just that. Catherine is about ten years older than I am, and she's been around. A widow, and as lonely as I was."

His expression grew cold. "I never meant it to get out of hand, Lynn. I just went along for the laughs. I wanted to marry you. I never had any other idea."

"It doesn't matter, Larry," I said. "As long as we're together now."

"Darling—you're wonderful!"

His words were like a passport to heaven. All my love for him spilled over. "I'm here now," I said.

"It's not that simple, Lynn," he went on. "After a few weeks, Catherine told me she was going to have a baby. She insisted we get married. She was almost crazy, Lynn. She threatened to kill herself, made a terrible scene. Well, I married her, thinking that later I'd get a divorce." He took a ragged breath. "Catherine lost the baby—if there ever was one —and it was all for nothing. I've tried to get away, but she isn't buying it. She insisted I give up my job in Chicago. She has some money, and owns some property in Santa Rosa, too. She said she'd follow me, no matter where I went. Lynn, she's a devil when she wants to be."

Sitting there with Larry, his hand gripping mine, it sounded like some crazy nightmare. But I believed everything he told me. Because I still loved him. And I believed he loved me, too.

142

He begged me to stay in Santa Rosa. "I'll ask Catherine for a divorce," he promised. "It'll be all as we planned it, darling. Just give me a little time."

I agreed. I knew his desperate need for love, and blamed Catherine for trapping him.

Later, he drove me into the country. When we were alone in a quiet spot, he held me in his arms, and I promised over and over, as his lips took mine, that I would never leave him. It was as if those words of love we spoke made everything right.

During the next week, I settled in Santa Rosa. Madame Helena gave me a job in her shop, and she told me about a friend of hers who had a room for rent. "Alma Hadden is the best person who ever lived," she added.

Alma and I seemed to take to each other immediately. She was an attractive, lively widow in her middle forties, and the moment her warm smile beamed at me, the friendliness flowing out in her voice, I thought of her as the kind of woman I'd want for my mother—the mother I'd always longed for.

As she showed me the pretty little blue-and-white room she had to rent on the second floor, she said, "My son and I live here alone. The house is too large for the two of us. Dan is so handy around the place," she added. "He works in the lumber yard across town, and likes to build things. He built our cabin up at Clear Lake."

It was odd, but I didn't pay much attention to Dan at first. I suppose the only thing I noticed about him was that except for his coloring, he wasn't the least bit like Larry. For Dan was built on a big frame, and Larry was slender. And Dan was a simple, quiet man, with none of Larry's sophistication and charm.

Alma looked after me from the first. "What's a few more clothes thrown in the washing machine," she said, when I found my laundry in a neat, clean pile on my bed. "For heaven's sake, why should you run out for breakfast when I throw out coffee every morning? Besides, I hate to eat alone. Dan goes to the yard so early."

Alma was truly like a mother to me. I told Larry that a week after I'd moved in with the Haddens. But he wasn't pleased. "I know Dan and Alma Hadden," he said. "I think you'd better look around for another place to live, Lynn."

"I don't think your knowing them will matter in the least, Larry, because you won't be coming to see me there," I said. "Besides, in a small city you get to know a lot of people, so it won't seem strange that you and I know each other. And I'm happy there."

He shrugged. "You may be right," he agreed.

It seemed easy at first. Larry and I met in out-of-the-way places each day, if only for a little while. Sometimes he would take me to lunch in a place off the beaten path. Or after work, we'd drive to Russian River and sit among the pines. And when he took me in his arms, it was as if there was no one in the world but us.

There were times when I longed to talk to someone about Larry, about our situation. Because soon, it became as if I were living two separate lives, and it disturbed me. I kept asking Larry about his plans to get a divorce so we could be married. His answer was to kiss me into forgetfulness.

But finally, one day, I pushed him away and insisted on a direct answer.

"I've asked Catherine, darling." He hesitated. "You'll have to know sometime. Now don't blow your top. The answer is no. She won't hear of a divorce. So we'll have to wait."

"Wait for what?" I pulled away as he reached for me. "To go on like this endlessly?"

"How else? I'll be free someday. In the meantime, we have each other."

But we didn't have each other, not really. Because from that day on, I had an empty feeling in the pit of my stomach. I wasn't built like Larry—to him, it didn't matter at all. He took life as it came. But I hated to sneak around the way we did, feeling guilty most of the time.

It was especially hard when I went home to Alma and Dan. I wanted to die of shame remembering Larry's kisses. Because beside their simple goodness, I was a cheap phony.

"You're invited to the best grilled steak you ever ate," Dan greeted me one day. "Change to something comfortable, and you can mix the salad."

Sitting in the garden with Alma and Dan, I found something I'd never known before—togetherness, family warmth. And they accepted me as a girl who worked for a living, a girl as simple and honest as they were.

"Lynn, you belong with us," Alma said, later, after Dan insisted on carrying the dishes into the kitchen while she rested. "You've brought me so much, dear. Dan is different too. Before you came here, he was so restless. Forever driving up to the lake."

"And speaking of the lake," Dan said, returning, "Lynn hasn't seen it yet. Let's drive up this weekend. They say the black bass and perch are really biting."

I remembered Larry speaking about the cabin Catherine owned at some lake. Larry acted strange when I asked him about it—about what he did weekends, when I didn't see him. He always changed the subject. But that was the way Larry was.

"Is it far to Clear Lake?" I asked Dan.

"Just a couple of hours' drive. Lots of people in this part of the country have places up there. It's a big lake, and lots of room for everybody. The most beautiful spot in the world, to my mind. They say Switzerland hasn't anything on the scenery around there."

"I'd love to go," I said. At least I wouldn't have to sit around and wait for Monday, the way I usually did.

The next morning, when I went down to breakfast, Alma was all smiles. "A perfect California day!" she said.

"We can start as soon as you're ready, Lynn," Dan said, reaching for his leather jacket. "Everything is already packed, including the food."

Dan was different that morning. In jeans and a dark-blue shirt, he looked bigger than ever, but much younger and happier.

As I drank my coffee, Alma said, "I've baked a ham. We'll have fish, of course, but there's nothing like ham for sandwiches."

Dan picked up the picnic hamper and started for the door. "You'd better lend Lynn some warm clothes, Mom," he said. "It gets cold up at the lake."

"I'll take your Mackinaw, Dan," Alma told him. "And next week, we'll buy Lynn some jeans and a wool blouse. Jumping in and out of boats is no place for those skirts."

Suddenly, I wanted to be like Alma and Dan, who had nothing to hide. And as we prepared to leave, I had an urgent wish to know where I stood with Larry.

Two hours later, we drove around the lake shore, to a grove of pines with small houses scattered among them. Dan's cabin was larger than I'd expected—a living room, kitchen, and two bedrooms. There was a path that led to a narrow dock where several small boats were tied.

"All the folks up here use the dock," Dan explained.

Just then, a truck drove up. A man jumped out and walked toward us. He was built like Dan, and wore jeans and a cowboy shirt, too. His eyes took me in boldly from head to foot. "You're new up here, aren't you?" he asked as Alma came out of the cabin to greet him.

"First time up, Harry," she said. "Meet Lynn Palmer."

He stuck out a huge red hand. "Pleased to know you, ma'am. Jackson is the name."

"Harry does trucking for folks up here," Alma told me.

"That's right. I stopped by to see if you wanted anything from town."

"We could use some melons," Alma said. Then she added, "Who's up this week?"

Harry was willing and eager to tell the news. He leaned against a post and lit his pipe. "Not many this week end. Catherine and her new husband drove up Thursday. She's ready to jump the gun, she's so nervous. What do you suppose makes her like that, Alma?"

"Some people are made that way." Alma said, settling down on a rocker on the porch.

My heart was pounding crazily. So this was the lake Larry spoke of! I went to sit down on the steps. I was shaking so, I was afraid the others would notice.

"Catherine is thinking of selling her house in Santa Rosa and living up here all year round. She says she feels good up here. That with her husband away so much, what's the use of keeping up two places."

"It makes sense," Alma agreed.

"I sure was flabbergasted when Catherine married that fellow." He knocked the pipe ashes against the pole. "He's some younger than her, too. That spells trouble when a man's that good looking—and a woman has a wide streak of jealousy in her."

"Could be she's keeping him up here so he won't be tempted," Alma said, smiling.

Harry grinned back. "Guess I'd better get a move on." He turned to Dan, who was coming out of the cabin. "The bass are biting like they're itching to get themselves in a fry pan, Dan. You should get a good mess of them for supper."

"I aim to try," Dan said.

When Harry drove off, I could scarcely get up from the steps. Larry was living close by with his wife, the woman who wouldn't give him a divorce. . . .

But an hour later, when Larry dropped in to see Dan, he didn't look like a downtrodden victim. He was tanned, and there was a glow of health about him I'd never seer before.

"Catherine sent me over to borrow some eggs until Harry gets back with her order from the store," he said.

Alma put her arm across my shoulder. "Meet our Lynn, Larry,' she said. "This is her first visit to the lake."

Larry smiled impersonally "You'll love it," he said. "It's very peaceful and quiet up here."

There was nothing peaceful about the way I felt. Even Alma noticed it, "You're shivering, Lynn. You need a sweater."

I'm dying inside, I thought watching Larry walk away.

Later, when Larry's wife, Catherine, wandered down to the dock to admire the string of fish Larry and Dan had caught, I hated myself even more. Because I could see by the possessive way she acted that she wasn't going to let Larry go.

Where does that leave me? I wondered. And later, after dinner, when it was dark, I slipped away and walked down to the end of the dock, hoping to find some peace in the solitude.

146

I saw all shades of dark as I looked at the mountains etched against the sky. The stars seemed so close I was sure I could touch them. The only sound was the lapping of water on the shore and the rustling of the wind in the treetops. If there was peace to be found, it was here. But there was no peace in me. The loneliness I'd known as a child overwhelmed me, till I felt I'd die of it.

Then, a voice came out of the dark. "Don't speak, darling. I've tried to get you alone all day."

"Larry—oh, Larry!" I whispered. He knelt beside me, another shadow in the dark. A shadow I'd been running after, only to find it faded and shabby.

"I pretended I didn't know you, darling, because I didn't want you hurt," he said. "If Catherine suspected I knew you, it might cause trouble. She can be very ugly at times." He pulled me against him, and the soft wool of his shirt, the soap-and-water smell of him, so familiar, so dear, made me cling to him.

"I love you, Lynn," he whispered.

For a long moment I let myself feel the comfort of his arms tight around me. Then I pulled away. "I've got to go, Larry," I said. "This is sheer madness."

He moved so quickly that he faded into the dark, as if he had never been there at all. And then I heard Dan calling my name.

"I'm on the dock, Dan," I called back, getting to my feet. "It's so wonderful out here. So quiet."

Dan's face was a white blur beside me. "I love it that way too, Lynn. I'm so glad you feel like I do about the lake."

I didn't dare speak. My mind was seething with crazy thoughts. It had been like that ever since I met Larry, I realized later, when Dan took my hand to lead me back along the narrow walk.

That night, things seemed to change. It was as if a veil were torn from my eyes. I knew Larry meant all he said to me—at the time he said it. I believed he loved me. But I also knew now that he was a weak man. He'd drifted into what he thought would be a momentary affair with Catherine, still proclaiming love for me. He married her without any intention of being true to her, as the easiest way out of trouble. He'd drift along with me too, taking my love, with no responsibilities. . . .

But even as I recognized that truth, my heart cried out that I loved him, that I couldn't face life without him.

Then you are as guilty as he is, something deep inside me said. And besides, you're a fool.

The next morning at breakfast Alma started talking about Catherine. "I'm not sure it's right for her to stay up here all year, Dan. It's lonesome when the summer folks leave."

"Harry Jackson lives up here all year round, and some of the

147

folks around the bend of the lake," Dan said. "It's not far from town, either. Catherine has a good house and a big stove in the kitchen." He stirred his coffee thoughtfully. "A lot of us come up off and on to fish and hunt all winter."

Alma buttered toast for him. "I don't think Larry will like it. He's an outgoing sort of man. He likes fun, has to have people around. He's really a city man, Dan."

Dan pushed back his chair. "That's his hard luck," he said. Then he smiled at me. "I'd like to take you on a hike, Lynn. If you're up to climbing, the view of the lake from Konocti is wonderful. Whenever I have a problem, I go there, and my puny little troubles seem to fade away."

My eyes met his, and it was as if I were seeing Dan for the first time. His features were strong. There was strength in the line of his jaw. His mouth, wide and generous, could grow strong too. He'd never hurt anyone he loved, I thought, as we got up from the table.

"I'd love to climb your mountain, Dan," I said. "I have a few problems to solve myself."

Later, as we climbed up the winding road, Dan didn't talk. When we reached the top of Konocti, my breath caught sharply. The lake, stretching for miles, was in full view. It was incredibly blue, framed in tall pines, with a background of mountains. I'd never seen anything so beautiful.

Suddenly, I knew what Dan meant about things coming clear up there. It was as if the vast expanse of beauty released something deep inside me. For the first time since I met Larry, I seemed to be thinking straight. It was like fitting the right pieces in a jigsaw puzzle and finally seeing the picture. And breaking my heart at the same time, I thought, fighting to keep back the tears.

Dan's face blurred, and for the first time in my life I knew I'd found a real friend. "It makes me feel like crying too," he said, taking my hand.

A warm contentment rose in me as my fingers curled around his. This wasn't the wild frenzy of emotion I felt for Larry, making life a living hell. It was a still and lovely feeling that Dan's strong hand gave me.

"I'd like to stay up here forever, Dan," I said.

"The air is too rare to live in all the time, Lynn. This is only for once in a while."

"I don't ever want to go down," I whispered.

We stood with our backs against a tall pine, and we were silent for a long time. But there was no loneliness in me then.

Around noon, when the sun grew warm, we went down the mountainside, and I knew what I had to do if I wanted to keep that peace in my heart.

But Larry's voice, coming from the porch, shattered it. No matter what I felt in my mind, my body betrayed it. It was all I could do not to run to Larry, because the hunger to feel his lips on mine was almost painful. I realized then that that was what it was like to be a drunkard—Larry was like some drug that had taken hold of me and wouldn't let go.

"I brought you some fish I caught this morning," Larry said, looking at me.

"Then you must eat with us," Alma said. "Get Catherine, Larry." She turned to me. "Lynn, will you set the table on the porch?"

I was glad to do anything to hide my agony. I moved about mechanically, wondering how I could live through the next few hours.

Larry came back with Catherine clinging to his arm. She was wearing a faded blue cardigan over a shapeless cotton print. The pain in me grew, because Catherine went out of her way to show that Larry belonged to her, and that she wasn't going to let him go. Her thin hands were greedy in their hold on him, and her dark eyes, too large for her narrow face, darted from one person to the other as she talked a blue streak in her high-pitched voice.

No, Catherine wasn't an easy woman to like—but she was the woman Larry married, and I was sick with shame at the role for which Larry had cast me. It was as if I were awakening from a dream, and recognizing the ugly truth—the reality every woman content to live on the fringe of a man's life and take the crumbs of his love sees when she comes out of the spell he cast!

I knew I couldn't go on fighting inside myself all the time. Even love wasn't big enough to blank out the sordid side of my relationship with Larry. In that moment, I knew I had to choose between him and the decency I wanted so desperately.

My eyes were open at last, and knew if I went on with Larry, I could no longer find excuses for myself. But there could be no halfway decision—I had to go all the way, no matter what I suffered.

Later, when I went to the kitchen to get the coffeepot, Larry followed me. "I'm not seeing you alone any more," I told him. "Please help me Larry. Don't call me at the store again. I can't take it any more."

"I knew meeting Catherine would spoil things for us!" he said. "I should have known."

"You were engaged to me where you married Catherine," I reminded him. "She is your wife. I'm—"

He leaned over and kissed me. "I love you, no matter what I did. I always will."

Everything in me longed to kiss him back, but I clenched my hands at my sides and resisted. "Please leave me alone!" I begged.

"Please!" Then I broke away from him and ran back to the others.

But I knew that resisting Larry wasn't going to be easy. At first I refused to see him. Then he grew furious, but later he kept away. My heart started easing when, around Thanksgiving, he stopped calling. And as the New Year edged in, I was sure it was all over. I resolved to tie up the loose ends and start a new life—a life in which Dan had begun to play a big part.

On New Year's Eve, Dan took me dancing, and as the bells rang in the New Year, he told me he loved me.

"I know I'm just an ordinary guy, Lynn," he said, "but I'm very much in love with you. Ever since the day we took the hike to the top of Konocti, it's been like that with me."

It wasn't the frenzied kind of love I'd known with Larry. I was happy and so much myself with Dan, and the companionship and real affection we shared made what Larry and I had known together seem like madness.

That madness was over, but a new problem arose: do I dare marry Dan? After all, he knew Larry—they were neighbors at the lake. Fear clutched me, and I turned away from Dan's eager face.

Suppose he found out about Larry and me? Suppose he discovered I wasn't the girl he thought I was? It wasn't fair to marry him without telling him the truth, and yet I wanted desperately to hide my shame from him and take the chance that he would never hear about it from someone else.

Dan was staring at me. "Why are you so worried, Lynn?" he said. "Take your time to decide. Like Mom says, I'm pretty blunt at times. I guess I sprang this on you too fast. But how can a man lead up to the way I feel?" He took my hands in his. "Gosh, I'm out of words, darling."

I made my decision in that moment. I couldn't spoil the way he felt about me. "I know you are the best, Dan," I said then.

"Is there anyone else?"

For a second my heart stood still. Then I said it, and it was true. "There's no one else but you, Dan."

His lips brushed my cheek, and I reached up and kissed him. "That's for the New Year, and all the years to come," I said.

His arms closed around me, and he held me close. "This is the happiest day I've ever known," he said. "And it will be for Mom, too."

"I'm glad, darling," I said. "Let's go home and tell her."

Alma was waiting up for us. "Well?" she said, when I ran to her. "Did he finally get enough courage to ask you?"

"Yes, Mom, and she's willing," Dan said.

"A daughter!" Alma cried, hugging me. "All my life I've been praying for one. It's like my life is now complete."

I felt so humble. "I'll try to be a good one," I said.

"I know that, Lynn." She brushed her fingers across her eyes. "I've been thinking about a lot of things, sitting here—waiting and hoping." She smiled. "Young people should be alone. I'm going to leave you the house and go up to Seattle to live with my sister."

"I won't have it!" I cried. "I've always wanted a mother, and now that I have one, I'm not letting her go." I held her hand to my cheek. "Please, Mom. Why can't we go on as we are? You keep on running the house, and I'll go on working for a while."

"I make enough money to support my wife," Dan said.

I turned to him. "For now, Dan, I'd like it."

But even as I said it, I knew why. Deep inside me I knew if I worked in town, I might run into Larry. I hated myself as I thought it, but there it was in my mind. I couldn't deny my feelings to myself—but I could try to conquer them. And I felt, with a burning faith, that if I married Dan, my feelings for Larry would surely die.

After Dan and I were married, we drove up often to the lake, and I was careful never to be alone with Larry.

It's all over between us, I told myself whenever I heard Larry, Dan, and Harry Jackson talking together, as they did so often. I could even sit quietly, with my heart not missing a beat, when my eyes met Larry's.

The summer was almost over when I discovered how wrong I was. It was a Saturday afternoon, and Alma had gone to town to buy some blankets that were on sale. I had a yen to be alone and decided not to go along.

After I finished some chores, I went for a walk along the lake. As I turned at the bend where the tall pines were, I heard someone running. I stepped behind a tree, thinking whoever it was would pass. I didn't feel in the mood for small talk.

Then I saw Larry.

"I followed you," he said. "I must talk to you." His face was dark with anger.

"Please, Larry, go away," I said.

"Why couldn't you wait for me?" he demanded. "Why did you have to marry Dan? You sure were in a hurry to get yourself a man, weren't you?"

"I waited a long time for you, Larry."

"You didn't believe me, did you?" he said.

"How could I?" I was amazed at the way I could talk to him, as if he were a stranger. It seemed incredible to me that once I'd longed for his kisses and almost died of it—that my happiness had hung on his passing moods.

How strange, when there was nothing there to cling to, I thought. Larry has nothing—he's as weak as water.

151

In the few months I'd been married to Dan, I'd learned about men—strong men, who don't change with each passing mood. And I knew so surely in that moment that what Dan and I had was so much more important than what Larry called love.

Larry reached out and gripped my shoulder. "Words, words, words—women are forever talking! They keep handing out reasons for everything they do. They yell about morals and make a man's life a hell on earth." His hands bit into my shoulders. "Why don't you tell the truth? You married Dan to spite me! You married him to show me." He shook me violently. "Well, we're even now. You have a husband, I have a wife. But it doesn't change anything. It doesn't change us!"

I tried to get away from his hands. "You're hurting me, Larry!" I cried. "Let me go."

"I know you love me. You're not the kind to change. You're still the same. I'm taking no more of your nonsense. People go on being lovers for years. It works out fine. It will with us."

His hands slid downward, and he pulled me against him. My throat closed with fear as his lips found mine. The kiss was deep, cruel, demanding.

"We're going to be the same lovers we were, from now on," he said. "Someday I'll be free, but for now, I'm not letting you go."

He was like a madman. His arms were hurting me as he bent me against him. "You love me! Say it! Say it!" he cried.

My decent, happy life hung in the balance—I realized that, and the knowledge gave me the strength to fight Larry. I pounded his chest with my fists, and the pain of his hands tightening on my flesh was like a symbol of all the hurt I'd suffered through him. He forced me to my knees, but I managed to get my right hand free, and I rammed my fist in his face. I hit him again and again, and he let me go to cover his eyes with his arm.

Somehow I got to my feet, and I ran, my lungs fighting for life. When I got to the dock, I threw myself face down, gulping in the cool air. Then the sobs came. My body shook with them, and it was as if all the torture of my days with Larry was in them. "Lynn—darling!" It was Dan.

I was in his arms, my head buried in his shoulder. "I want to go home, Dan. I'm afraid!" I sobbed.

He lifted me up and carried me down the dock. "There's nothing up here to harm you, honey," he said. "This is the one safe place in the world."

But, even so, we went home the next day. Dan and Alma had talked over my outburst, I knew. As soon as we got back to Santa Rosa, Dan said what obviously had been on his mind:

"Being a wife is a full-time job, Lynn. You're thin and worn out.

152

I want you to stay home with Mom. You tell Madame Helena you've got a decorating job to do right here."

"It's slack time," I said. "I'll be glad to stay home, Dan." I sighed wearily. "I didn't know until now just how tired I was."

"What you need is a hot bath," Alma said, coming into our room. "I'll run the water. Then to bed with you, and no back talk!"

My body was bruised. My shoulders ached when I moved my arms. "I think I'm coming down with a virus," I told her. "Would you lend me one of your long-sleeved nighties?"

"Now you're getting some sense." She smiled. "I'd freeze to death in one of those flimsy things you wear."

Dan grinned. "I like them."

"Oh, you!" Alma giggled. "I'll get you the gown, Lynn. And after the bath, right into bed."

Later, as I lay in the hot bath, I saw the marks of Larry's fingers on my body. I had to keep Dan from seeing them.

When I was in bed, dressed in Alma's blue flannel, she fussed over me like a hen with a chick. She brought me tea and toast, and sat there while I ate it. "All of it," she insisted.

After I finished, I lay back on the pillow. "I've never been so tired in all my life," I said.

Alma turned out the lights then, and I closed my eyes, certain I would be all right in the morning.

But I wasn't. The next morning, I couldn't get out of bed. It was a week before I could creep around again. I looked like my own ghost.

Something seemed to happen to me deep down inside. It was a fear eating at me. Fear of meeting Larry, mostly. When Dan spoke of driving up to the lake, I didn't want to go.

"You go, Dan, I'm not up to it," I told him.

Alma seemed to understand. "The summer is about over. What woman wants to wait all day for a man to come back with a mess of fish to cook? I'll stay home with Lynn. I want to can some things, anyhow."

"Like mustard pickles, I hope," Dan said, grinning. "But I sure would like your company, ladies."

So, that late summer and fall, Dan got into the habit of driving up to the lake alone. He'd drive up Saturday afternoon, stay the night, and come back Sunday.

It was October when the fear that haunted me came to a head.

Dan was reading the newspaper one Wednesday evening, and Alma and I were discussing a dress pattern she'd bought that afternoon, when the doorbell rang.

"Now who on earth can that be at nine o'clock?" Alma said.

Dan shrugged and went to the door.

153

It was Larry. He came in, followed by a man I'd never seen before.

"Sheriff Gardener!" Dan put out his hand. "Glad you and Larry dropped in. How are things up at the lake?"

They shook hands. Then the sheriff said, "I heard you were up Saturday and Sunday."

"Sure was. Got in some good fishing, too."

Larry just nodded. He wasn't like himself at all.

Dan invited them to sit down, and Alma offered to make coffee.

"Don't go to any bother, Alma," the sheriff said. "I just dropped in to ask Dan a few questions."

Dan pulled up a straight-backed chair and straddled it. "Be glad to tell you anything I can," he said.

The sheriff's face was troubled. "I'm just following down a few leads, Dan. I heard you were at the lake. About what time did you get there Saturday?"

"Offhand, around three, I'd say. I started from Santa Rosa right after lunch and drove straight to the cabin."

"What did you do up there?"

Dan's eyes widened in surprise. "I went fishing."

"Off the end of the dock?"

"No, as a matter of fact, I didn't. I walked around the bend, where the rocks are, thinking maybe I'd get some bass."

"And then what did you do?"

"Well, when it was dark, I went back to the cabin and ate. I was tired, so I went to bed, and slept like a log. Sunday I drove home. That about wraps up the weekend."

"Who did you talk to, Dan?"

"Come to think of it, I didn't talk to anyone. Most of the houses are closed for the season. You know that, Sheriff." Dan turned to Larry. "Where were you? I looked for you, but nobody seemed to be in the mood for fishing."

Larry's eyes were very dark in his pale face. "I was up north on a selling trip. On Sunday I was in Crescent City. I didn't get back to the lake until last night."

An odd silence hung in the room, and tension seemed to grow. Dan broke it. "Maybe if I knew what you're after, Sheriff, I could help you more."

Sheriff Gardener cleared his throat. "Well, when Larry got home last night, Catherine wasn't there. He called me to find out if I'd seen her. I hadn't. So I drove out and found—" He paused, frowning. "It was kind of funny. Catherine had set out her dinner in the cabin. It was still on the table, just as she left it. Now, Catherine isn't the kind to just go off and leave a mess like that in her kitchen. Any more than you would, Alma."

"Maybe she just took a notion to go somewhere," Dan said. "It's lonesome up there for a woman alone. She could be visiting a friend right here in Santa Rosa."

The sheriff got up. "Larry and I have checked that. We've been to see all her friends. Everybody she ever knew, as a matter of fact. Nobody has seen her. Believe it or not, Catherine just vanished into thin air."

"Nonsense!" Alma said. "She's got to be somewhere!"

Larry's eyes met mine. For a moment I remembered how much he wanted to get rid of his wife. A strange fear seized me. Did he know where she was?

"I was over three hundred miles from the lake," he said, as if he'd read my mind.

"Catherine will show up." Alma's voice broke the spell of Larry's words. "She was always temperamental."

"She was that." The sheriff walked toward the door. "Well, after all, she's a grown woman, and she might have taken a notion to go somewhere, as Dan says—especially being the nervous kind. Any woman might get restless and get out." He put on his hat. "Thanks, Dan, for answering my questions."

"I haven't been much help," Dan said, opening the door for them. Larry turned around. "I just can't understand it." He looked straight at me. "Catherine knew I'd be back Tuesday night. She always waited up for me. No reason for her to go off like that."

Was he trying to tell me something? It was as if there was a warning for me in his eyes.

After they went out, Dan said, "This worries me, Lynn. I've always liked Catherine. I wouldn't want anything to happen to her." It more than bothered me. But the next morning, Alma decided to do some house cleaning, and Saturday Dan started to paint the kitchen. By then, I forgot all about Catherine. Since we hadn't heard from Larry or the sheriff, we figured she had returned.

It was November when Alma heard from her sister in Seattle. "Hilda is very sick," she told us after she read the letter.

Dan insisted Alma get the next train up there to look after her, and by eleven, she was on her way.

It seemed strange to be all alone in the house. For the first time since Dan and I were married, we were by ourselves. And after Alma had been gone a week, I told Dan at breakfast one morning that I was sick with missing her.

"Your mother-in-law?" he teased, pulling me down on his lap. "But to be honest, I miss Mom, too."

I kissed the tip of his nose. "Dan, we're such a happy family, aren't we?"

155

He held me close. "I do believe you're getting to appreciate your husband, darling." He set me on my feet. "The job is calling. Let's have steak for dinner to celebrate."

"Steak it is," I said, following him outside.

It was a beautiful day, and I hurried inside and breezed through the housework so I could have the afternoon free. Around noon, I finished washing and cleaning, and had a quick snack. Then, I dressed and walked over to the shopping center. I looked over some cottons on sale, dropped in for a chat with Madame Helena, then picked up some groceries and a steak and strolled home.

It was almost four when I got there. As I opened the gate, I noticed a man sitting on the porch. My heart lunged as I went up the path —the man was Larry. When he stood up, I stopped.

"Don't act as if I were an unwelcome guest, Lynn," he said. "I thought you might be interested in what happened to Catherine."

I climbed the steps and dropped into Alma's rocker. "Sit down, Larry. Naturally, I'm interested."

His eyes narrowed. "She hasn't come back yet, Lynn. I dropped in to warn you not to let anyone know about us. I'm sure Catherine didn't suspect a thing."

"But, Larry, Catherine's got to be found!" I cried.

"I'm sure in my heart that she's dead," he said. "Catherine wasn't the kind to go away like that. While she was alive, she'd never let me go. When I asked her for a divorce that time, she said just that." He leaned closer. "I was afraid for you, Lynn. Because Catherine threatened to make it hot for any woman who tried to take me from her."

My eyes closed against the bright sunshine. It all seemed unreal. Even Larry did.

His voice sounded far away as he went on. "She must be dead." His hand touched mine. "Someday, when her body is found, we can start where we left off."

"Larry, it's all over," I told him. "Completely."

His hand closed hard on mine. "If we were both free, would you marry me then, Lynn?"

My eyes flew open, and I pulled my hand from his. "How can I answer a question like that? You aren't free, and neither am I."

Larry got up, an odd expression on his face. "When that time comes and we are, I'll ask you again," he said. He bent and kissed my hair. Then, before I could speak, he was hurrying down the path.

I went into the house. And, God help me, I didn't realize until then that I'd let Larry go away believing that someday I'd leave Dan for him! And then I realized that Larry always believed what he wanted to believe.

Why should he still want me? I wondered. The answer was obvious now: Larry always wanted what he couldn't have. For the first time, I realized that I'd never have lost Larry if I'd played hard to get when he first made love to me. But Larry was so sure of his charm when it came to women. He couldn't believe it possible that any woman he had possessed could forget him. Why couldn't I have told him, so there was no mistaking my words, that I was through with him forever? Why hadn't I the strength to slam the door on the past, so he could never doubt my meaning? Those were the questions I asked myself, but I had to push them from my mind then. It was almost five, and Dan would soon be home for dinner.

He came at quarter after, grinning like a boy. "I've got good news," he said. "Mom is coming home Friday. She called me at the yard—said she tried to get you, but you were out gadding."

"Buying you food, darling," I said, keeping my voice light to hide my troubled heart. "I sure will be glad to see her."

"I'd hate it if you and Mom didn't get along," Dan said. "I'm a lucky guy to have two wonderful women like you."

I served his dinner, but all the time I hated myself for being so weak. I always would be, I knew.

Then Friday came, and Alma was home again. Her sister was fine, and Alma was her cheerful self once more.

The next afternoon, she decided to cut out her dress. Dan was working in the garden, and I was watching him, when Alma came out on the porch. "I just remembered, Lynn," she said. "I have an old pattern that's right for me. It's in one of the boxes stored in the garage."

Dan wiped his forehead with his sleeve. "Here we go again. Look, Mom, I'm not going through that routine again. These bushes need cutting back—"

"I'll look for it," I said, and walked through the open door of the garage.

"It's in the box where I keep cloth scraps," Alma called. "The one on top, I think."

I reached up and pulled the box off the shelf. I set it on the floor, and then lifted off the lid.

Everything in me jolted to a stop. On top of the bits of cloth and patterns was the blue cardigan I'd last seen on Catherine—and a woman's handbag! I opened the bag with shaking hands. In the wallet was a picture of Larry, Catherine's driving license, and a credit card.

A cry escaped me, and I ran outside to where Dan was, holding up the things for him to see. "They're Catherine's!" I cried. "Dan, how on earth did they get into that box?"

His face stiffened into a hard mask as he took the bag and sweater from me. I followed him as he ran into the house. When I got to the living room, he was already picking up the phone.

After a moment he said, "Sheriff Gardener, this is Dan Hadden. Can you drive down here at once? Lynn has just found some things of Catherine's in our garage."

"What!" Alma cried when Dan hung up. "Catherine must have put them there! That means she'd been around—"

"But why our garage?" Dan said. Did Catherine know about Larry and me? Was she trying to frighten me? I asked myself as I huddled in a chair by the fireplace. It was as if an old scar had opened in my heart, and it was bleeding. Fear ran wild in me. All I'd held inside me for so long might be uncovered.

Two hours later, Sheriff Gardener hurried in. He studied the bag and sweater for a long time, and then slipped them in a plastic bag. Slowly, he questioned Dan once more. Over and over, he made him repeat what he'd said the day Catherine disappeared.

Finally he said, "Dan, you haven't any alibi. You say you slept in your cabin that night. But your car was seen in town. A woman swore to me that a man answering your description was in it. We're now sure the woman with that man was Catherine."

I was stunned, as he went on. "Your brown leather jacket and cap were found half buried in the sand down by the lake," he said.

Dan's jaw tightened. "I left the jacket and cap hanging in the closet like always. Anyone could have taken them, Sheriff. You know we don't lock doors up at the lake."

"But you were seen in town with Catherine Saturday evening, Dan."

"That's impossible. I never left the cabin. I was sleeping like a log."

"But it was your car," the sheriff said. "The woman wrote down the license number."

"Could be. I left it back of the cabin, and the keys were in it"

Sheriff Gardener got up. "It's a nasty business, Dan. But until we find Catherine, nothing makes much sense—least of all, finding these things in your garage. A lot of pieces are missing in this picture."

"I'll say," Dan said.

"They will all fit when we find Catherine," the sheriff said. "If we do," he added, and his eyes were like granite.

When they find Catherine—the words hung in the room long after the sheriff left. My horror rose then, as events started to fit into a pattern—Catherine's disappearing the weekend Dan was up at the lake alone—Dan having no alibi—Catherine's things in the garage.

Larry could have put them there! Anyone could have, for the door of our garage was never locked. For a wild moment, I thought of telling Dan about Larry and me. But as I looked at him, sitting there

158

with his hands dangling between his knees, a line cutting his forehead, I knew I couldn't hurt him like that. Telling my secret would make it too easy for me.

You'll hear it the hard way, I thought, my eyes filling with sudden tears.

Two days later, the sheriff found the pieces that fit into a picture of horror. That morning, Catherine's body was found in the lake. There were bruises on her body, and her neck was broken. She was dead before she was dumped into the water, the coroner's report said.

And that afternoon, Dan was arrested on suspicion of murder and put in jail. Everything pointed to him.

"It's too pat!" I cried. "Someone is deliberately framing Dan."

"Why should they?" Alma demanded. "Dan never did a mean thing in his life, and he has no enemies. It's impossible! Dan couldn't kill a defenseless woman."

Words were whirling in my brain now—Larry's words: "Catherine is dead! I'm sure of it, Lynn. We'll both be free."

Did Larry kill Catherine? Was this his way of freeing himself of her? Implicating Dan? But I knew he couldn't have. Because at the time Catherine disappeared, he was three hundred miles away—and could prove it.

So it was Dan who was in terrible trouble. A woman was already swearing she saw Catherine and Dan together. He had no alibi. His jacket and cap had been found by the lake.

When I visited Dan in jail the first day, he was bewildered and miserable.

"I can't figure it out, Lynn," he said as he paced up and down. "I was up at the lake the weekend Catherine disappeared. Everything I told Sheriff Gardener was true!" He smashed his fist into his open palm. "I can't prove anything. Nobody believes me!"

"Someone wants the sheriff to think you did it," I said.

Dan stopped pacing and studied my face. "But who would want to do a thing like that, Lynn? Who would want to kill Catherine?"

My eyes shifted from his to the bars at the window. Every nerve in me protested at this terrible thing they were doing to Dan. It was as if I were living in some nightmare and couldn't wake up. There weren't any answers to Dan's questions—at least none that I dared answer.

Deep down inside me, I felt that Larry was somehow involved in Catherine's death. He could have hidden her belongings in the garage the day I came home to find him waiting for me on the porch.

Did he? I wondered. Was Larry thinking that in this way he'd get rid of Dan as well as Catherine?

Dan's hand rested on mine. "Honey, I'm so sorry for what this is doing to you," he said.

I rested my head against his shoulder. "I'm so worried, Dan—scared to death, too."

"I told Mom to get a lawyer from San Francisco. Never mind how much it costs."

"But we haven't much money saved, Dan."

"Mom can put a mortgage on the house and sell her bonds," he said. "It makes me sick thinking of it, but then everything about this does."

Tears came to my eyes. I knew how hard Dan had worked to pay off the mortgage so no one could take Alma's home from her. Ever since he was sixteen, he'd worked hard to give her security.

"I feel so helpless, Dan. So lost."

"It will work out, Lynn. Don't worry so, darling."

He was comforting me. My throat was a throbbing ache as I kissed him and went out.

After that, my mind was filled with Larry. I had to find out what he knew. I had no illusions about him any more. So I walked out to the mill where his office was. He was there, and came right over to me when I went in.

"This is a surprise, Lynn," he said.

I sat down in the chair he pulled out for me. A dead, cold feeling hit me as our eyes met over his desk. The flame had gone out forever—I no longer had any doubts. And my certainty made me careful, gave me strength:

"Larry, I came to ask you one thing," I said. "I have to be sure about it."

His lips kept smiling, but his eyes were cold. "Ask," he said.

"Did you put Catherine's bag and sweater in our garage the day you waited for me on the porch?"

He didn't move a muscle. "I had nothing to do with that, Lynn. I swear it."

"Or with Catherine's death?"

"I was three hundred miles away at the time. And I can prove it."

"Do you have any idea who put her things in the garage?"

Did he hesitate a fraction of a moment? I held my breath waiting, straining every nerve to catch some thread of hope.

It was as if he were weighing every word. "I wish I knew, Lynn." Play it dumb, I thought. Make him think you believe him. I got up to leave. "Do you think Dan did it, Larry?" I asked.

"It looks like it, Lynn. Sheriff Gardener is pretty sure, at any rate."

I said it slowly, as if driving each word home: "If Dan did this terrible thing, he deserves to die."

Larry came around the desk. "You were always one to face the truth, Lynn. It isn't as if you were in love with Dan. After all, you only married him to spite me, didn't you?"

I hid all the sudden contempt I felt for him, and even managed a smile. "Thank you, Larry, for answering my questions so honestly."

A gleam of triumph lit up his eyes. "I'm glad you believe me, darling. But after all, I told you the truth."

I nodded and left. Outside, I blinked in the bright sunshine. "You're lying, Larry, you're lying," I whispered as I walked down the street.

I passed the familiar places I'd seen a hundred times—the market where we bought our food, the street where Dan and I walked sometimes in the evening to window-shop. Homey, everyday things that I had no idea could mean so much brought tears to my eyes. Wonder filled me as I walked home that day—because I knew that, without being aware of it, I'd fallen in love with Dan. A quiet, deep love that had nothing to do with the wild frenzy I'd known with Larry.

When I got home, Alma was waiting for me. She was dressed in her best clothes, and her eyes were calm and clear.

"Dan is fine," I told her.

"I hope you're not too tired to go out again, Lynn," she said. "I made an appointment with Jeffrey Barnes. I was thinking about getting a lawyer from San Francisco, like Dan told me to do, but then I remembered Jeff. He and Dan went to school together. Maybe I'm wrong, but I've asked Jeff to defend Dan. She picked up her pocketbook. "Matter of fact, Jeff called me on the phone and asked if he could help Dan. So right then and there, I hired him. He knows Dan didn't kill Catherine. That's a good start, I think."

Later, huddled in a chair in his office, I studied Jeffrey Blake. He was a slender, quick-moving man, and my first impression was that he was quick thinking too. After he questioned Alma and me, I was sure of it. It was almost like a third degree. And when Alma got up to go, he said, "You run on, Alma. But I'd like to go over a few things with Lynn. I'll drive her home later."

When Alma left, he stood with his hands in his pockets and rocked back and forth on his heels, studying me. "What are you hiding?" he asked suddenly.

"Nothing." I was startled, but tried not to show it.

"Suppose you tell me all you know, Lynn. If you want to save Dan, you've got to."

"I've told you—"

"What you wanted me to know," he interrupted. "You're hiding something. If you don't tell me, I won't be able to help Dan."

I sat silent a long time. "It's something that has nothing to do with this case," I said finally.

"I went fishing and hunting with Dan when we were boys," Jeff told me. "Dan isn't a killer. Someone is deliberately framing him." He paced the office, paused at the window, and then came back to my chair. "I think you know who it is."

Something broke inside me. Then, slowly, as if the words were torn from me, I told Jeff the truth. About the day Larry came to the house and spoke of us both being free sometime.

"I don't think Larry killed Catherine," I finished. "He was three hundred miles from the lake when she disappeared. Anyway, he hasn't got nerve enough to kill anyone. But Larry is one to turn anything to his advantage, and if he could get rid of Dan this way, he wouldn't hesitate."

"Why should he still want you?" Jeff said. "He's the kind who could have plenty of women."

"I've asked myself that, too," I said. "I think it's because I turned him down. Because I married Dan. He hated that."

Jeff studied me. "I can see why a man would want you. You're an attractive woman. A man like Larry, once possessing you, might fight to get you back."

"But by not telling him I wouldn't go back to him—even if he were free, I drove him to plan this," I said. "I'm guilty, too."

Jeff patted my shoulder. "We all do foolish things," he said. Then he walked toward the door. "Don't repeat a word of this to anyone, Lynn. Tomorrow morning, you and I will drive up to the lake. I want to have a look around myself. This frame is too pat. Let's see firsthand if Larry Dahn had anything to do with the murder of his wife. And if he didn't, maybe we can find out who did." He opened the door. "Come on, I'll drive you home. You look pretty worn out."

That night, I lay awake trying to figure it out, but no matter where I turned, the evidence pointed to Dan.

The next morning, Jeff and I drove up to the lake. We started out by searching the cabin.

"Think hard, Lynn," Jeff said. "Is there anything out of place?"

It hit me. "Dan's gray flannel shirt and Mackinaw aren't in the closet."

"Are you sure?" he asked.

"I put them there myself."

"What else is missing?"

"Dan's leather jacket and cap," I said. "The Sheriff has them. But why should anyone take Dan's old clothes?"

"That's one thing I'm going to find out." Jeff was going over the living room inch by inch. He even poked among the ashes in the fireplace. When he straightened up, he said, "If we find out where Dan's clothes are, it might help."

After ten minutes, we found them. We had walked to Harry Jackson's cabin. His truck was parked in the back. The Mackinaw was lying on the seat.

Jeff knocked at the cabin door, but there was no answer. He opened it, and we went in.

Harry was lying in a bunk over in one corner of the room. His mouth was open, and he was snoring. The odor of whisky seemed to fill the room. And on Harry, we found Dan's gray flannel shirt.

Jeff took my arm and steered me outside. "We're going to call on the sheriff, Lynn, right now."

It all happened so fast, I was in a daze. I waited in the sheriff's office while he and Dan drove out to have a talk with Harry Jackson.

A half hour later, they brought Harry in. He was still drunk and was muttering under his breath. His hair stood on end, and he flopped into the chair they set out for him as if his legs were made of rubber.

"Black coffee," the sheriff told his deputy. "We'll sober him up first, then let him explain how he came to be wearing Dan's shirt."

Four cups of black coffee later, Harry Jackson came out of the whisky fog. His speech was a little thick, but he could answer the questions the sheriff shot at him.

At first, he was hostile. "Since when is it a crime for a man to get drunk in his own house?" he demanded. "You ain't got no call to drag me in here and talk like this, Sheriff, and you know it. So I borrowed Dan's shirt and Mackinaw. I'd have put them back before he came up to the lake again. Besides, Dan's in jail, ain't he? And Lord only knows when he'll be out again."

"You'd put them back like you put his leather jacket and cap back?" Jeff's voice was brutal as he bent over Harry. "You left them down at the lake, didn't you? You didn't have the decency to tell the police you borrowed them and forgot to give them back."

Harry shrank back in his chair. "You got nothing on me. I didn't do nothing!" He was trembling. "All I did was get drunk. That's no crime, Sheriff. That guy can't talk to me like this. I didn't kill Catherine. I never laid a hand on her."

It was terrible from then on. Voices asked questions endlessly, voices that grew hard as Harry suddenly slumped in his chair. Inch by inch they broke him down. He began to admit things, damning things that were dragged from him. His replies grew more broken, as if his befuddled brain couldn't stand the strain.

Finally, he admitted he had taken Dan's jacket and cap, and that he had left the jacket by the lake where it was found. He said he'd been drinking a lot since Catherine disappeared, but that he always drank a lot. He swore he didn't know Catherine's body was in the lake. He figured Catherine went with her husband when he took that trip up North.

163

Sure, he borrowed clothes from the cabins when the folks were away, he said. He looked after them, didn't he? And folks paid him by having him haul things and giving him odd jobs. That's how he managed to get along. Everybody knew that.

The questions went on. Perspiration sprang out on Harry's face, and he kept wiping it off with his sleeve. Now and then, he shook as though he were having a chill.

Jeff's questions started following a certain pattern, and with each answer, Harry's face grew more haggard. He began to look really frightened.

He admitted he'd been drinking heavily the day Catherine disappeared. He'd told them that before. Then suddenly Jeff's voice lowered. "Why did you kill Catherine, Harry?" he asked.

The room was very still. My heart pounded madly, and I wanted to scream—anything to break that accusing silence.

Suddenly Harry broke. "I didn't kill her!" he cried. "It was an accident. I'll tell you everything!"

He told the sordid story. As he spoke, I thought I'd die of shame. Because I was part of the horror that in the end killed Catherine. His gasping voice was like an accusing finger pointed at me. It sounded as if I were as guilty as he was when he told about Larry wanting to get a divorce from Catherine.

As Harry told it, there was a woman back East whom Larry wanted to marry. The woman had followed him out West. Harry guessed that if the woman hadn't showed up, Larry might have made a go of his marriage with Catherine. They were getting along real well before that, he said.

I was that woman! I sank to a new low as Harry spoke. Because I knew his story was based on truth. It was seeing me again that had made Larry turn against Catherine, when she wouldn't give him his freedom.

But I hadn't known that. I hadn't known Larry was married when I followed him. Tears burned my eyes as Harry went on with his story.

Larry was set on getting free of Catherine, and he gave Harry a hundred dollars to help him. Harry was to get friendly with Catherine and get her to trust him. And then one night, Larry would come in and find them in a compromising position. Harry agreed to the bargain, and even got a kick out of it. Catherine, who was lonely when Larry was away, seemed glad to see him when he dropped in.

Then the day came when Dan went up to the lake—the day that was to bring tragedy to all of us. Around four, Harry saw Dan go down to the lake to fish. He dropped in to see Catherine, and she asked him to drive her to town to match some cotton she needed. Harry went to get his truck, but he couldn't get it going. That's why, he explained, he decided to borrow Dan's car.

164

It was standing in the back of Dan's cabin, and the keys were still in the ignition. It was chilly, so Harry borrowed Dan's jacket and cap. He then drove Catherine to town and sat in the car while she went in the general store. She took her time, so Harry pulled the cap over his face and took a nap.

On the way home, he stopped to buy a bottle of whisky. When they finally got to Catherine's cabin, she invited him in to have dinner with her. He left the car where he had found it, and walked over to Catherine's.

At that point in his story, Harry buried his head in his hands and his shoulders shook. When he lifted his head, his face was white and stricken.

The story grew more sordid as he went on. He and Catherine had some drinks, and Harry felt pretty good. Catherine started cooking dinner, and while she was at the stove, Harry had more drinks. In a few minutes, he went over to Catherine and kissed the back of her neck.

She turned, laughing. Then Harry kissed her on the mouth, and suddenly he couldn't seem to stop kissing her. Catherine got scared and hit him. He got mad and tightened his hands on her arms—that was what caused the bruises. He didn't mean to hurt her. He lost control of himself and didn't know what he was doing.

Then Catherine, fighting wildly, got loose and ran out the door. She tripped and fell down the porch steps, rolled down the hill, and hit the big pine at the bottom. She lay there, her head twisted in a funny way.

I gasped in horror, and Jeff's hand on my shoulder warned me. Harry's eyes were like a tortured animal's. "Catherine was dead," he said. "Her neck was broken."

Again, there was that terrible silence in this room, until the sheriff said, "What then?"

The rest came in broken whispers. Harry had carried Catherine's body to the lake. Nobody was around, and it was dark as pitch. He put her into a boat and rowed out. Then he slid the body into the water. When he finally got back to the shore, it was as if he had a fever. He tore off Dan's jacket and cap, staggered back to his cabin, and got drunk. He kept drinking steadily from then on.

He went on to explain how the sweater and bag got into our garage. When the woman swore she had seen Dan in his car with Catherine, Harry panicked. He'd taken Catherine's things, figuring people might think she had run off. He felt they would never find her body. But when he heard Dan was under suspicion, he drove over to our house in Santa Rosa. He wanted to know what the sheriff had asked Dan. He meant to get rid of Catherine's things that day.

165

No one was home, he said, and he started snooping around. He was in the garage when Alma drove up suddenly, and he threw Catherine's things in a box on the shelf and hid until Alma went into the house. He was scared silly. "And when a man is scared," Harry said, "he does foolish things."

He cried then—the way a man does who hasn't cried since childhood. I couldn't stand any more, so I got up and went outside. The sun was bright and the air was sweet, but it was a mockery to me. I couldn't forget that I was partly to blame for Catherine death. No matter what they did to Harry, I'd remember that as long as I lived.

And that wasn't going to be easy to live with. As I leaned against the wall, waiting for Jeff to come out, I felt as if my heart would break.

Later, as we drove back, Jeff told me they were holding Harry for the coroner's jury. But he felt the verdict would be accidental death.

Larry was in the clear. He had had nothing to do with Catherine's death. And I knew, too, he'd swear he had nothing to do with paying Harry to get evidence for a divorce.

"I'm going to get Dan out of jail this afternoon," Jeff told me. "You needn't tell him or Alma that you're the woman in the case, Lynn. It may not come out at all."

I stared ahead at the road. "I can't go on without telling Dan the truth, Jeff," I said.

"You love Dan, don't you?"

"I never believed I could love anyone so much," I said.

"Maybe it's best you tell him then. Dan is big enough to forgive."

I wasn't sure anyone could be so forgiving, but I knew I had to follow through to the end, no matter what happened. I couldn't live a lie any longer.

Dan came home the next day. I told him and Alma the whole story, and I didn't whitewash my part in it.

"I love you, Dan," I finished. "I should have told you about Larry and me before I married you. Then none of this would have happened. I have no right to expect you to forgive me—to want me now."

Dan looked stunned, staring at me as if he were trying to grasp the whole thing. When he didn't speak, I turned and walked down the hall to my room.

I'd pack my clothes and leave in a little while, I thought. I had no idea where I'd go, but I'd work it out. But in the meantime, I sat on the side of the bed and looked around the familiar room I shared with my husband. It was as if I were trying to imprint it on my mind, to give me something to hold to all the rest of my lonely life.

Then the door opened, and Alma came in. Our eyes met, and tears spilled down my cheeks. I loved her and I couldn't bear to think of the sorrow I'd brought her.

"Dan is trying to pull himself together," Alma said, crossing the room to me. "It's a shock, Lynn. You see, Dan is the kind of man who puts a woman on a pedestal." She sat down beside me. "Maybe it will be better for him to love you as a very human woman—one who can make mistakes, the way we all do."

"You never did, Alma," I sobbed.

"Not the way you did, Lynn," she said, putting her arm around me. "But in other ways. They haven't invented a perfect human being yet."

"I'm going away," I told her.

She shook her head. "You can't run out on trouble, honey. You see, both Dan and I love you. You can't turn love on and off."

Dan suddenly appeared in the doorway, his eyes bleak, and his mouth tight. "Mom is right, Lynn. No matter what you do, you still go on loving."

I got up and walked over to him. "I never knew I could love anyone as I love you, Dan. Nothing can change that. If you can forgive me, I'll try and prove it."

It isn't going to be easy to do that. It takes time to heal wounds as deep as those I gave Dan. The only thing I can do now is be as honest as I know how, with Dan and with our love. And someday I hope to win Dan's forgiveness completely, and his trust once more.

### THE END

167

# I CAN'T RUN
# FROM THE PAST

It was one of those perfect days in October . . . warm and golden, with the sun shining bright from a deep-blue sky and the leaves falling leisurely to the ground. I dallied as I walked down the street to the corner mailboxes. It was that kind of a day, a time that you wished would last forever. Everything was beautiful.

Edna Ferguson met me at the box and invited me over for a cup of coffee. "My fresh rolls are just out of the oven," she said, laughing good-naturedly. Edna was always going on a diet but kept right on baking food that was so delicious she couldn't resist eating it.

I reached in the box and grabbed the stack of mail, knowing most of it was junk. But suddenly my heart began to pound. There was a letter addressed to me. There was no return address in the corner, but it was post-marked Cottage Grove, Wisconsin. That was where Bruce was . . . my stepfather. I felt hot and weak and the tears just came as memories flooded through me . . . memories I'd buried when I married Brian.

"Come on," Edna said.

I tried to be natural and keep the nervousness out of my voice. "I think I'll just run home with the mail," I said. "I've had a headache all morning."

I walked to the front door and headed for the kitchen. As soon as I got inside, I tore open the envelope, letting the other mail drop to the floor. The words blurred through my tears as I read them, and I had to go back to the beginning and reread it all:

Dear Stephanie,

You don't know me, but I know all about you. I really need your help desperately. It's going to mean either the beginning of a new life or the end of one for me. I would not want to live if the world doesn't know the truth. Bruce always talked about you when he was drunk. He was, and still is, a cruel man. Everybody believes him because he's got money. Would you help me please? My lawyer will be contacting you. Please!

Sincerely,
Cindy Hanson

I walked over to the window. Across the street I could see my son,

168

Dylan, and all the neighbor children playing in the sun. They were so carefree and untouched by the dark side of life . . . far removed from the world that I came from. I had finally been able to leave that nightmare life when Brian came back into my life. . . .

It had all started on a day like this nine years ago. My dad and my brother Greg were going to the woods north of town to do a little hunting. Actually, it was mostly for the companionship . . . being together in the woods, sharing lunch. That's why they went, Mother said, to be together. They seldom brought any game home.

We were living north of Madison at the time, in a small town that was built on the edge of a lake. Dad had bought some cabins and was trying to renovate them so that they could be rented. The lake had fish in it and had a good beach for swimming. We lived in town, though; Dad had a small repair shop and Mother worked in the drugstore.

Mother was sewing a skirt for me that day, and I'd just finished trying it on when the sheriff's car drove up. I remember Mother dropped the skirt right on the floor and looked at me with urgency in her eyes. "Something must have happened or the sheriff wouldn't be coming here," she said.

I didn't move. I couldn't. Mother opened the door, the sheriff said something to her, and she screamed and opened her arms to me. "Not both of them!" Mother cried.

The sheriff's face was like a mask. "Sorry," he said. "A drunk ran into them. Smashed the pickup right into the culvert. They were killed instantly."

Mother kept screaming and the sheriff called the doctor and a neighbor. But nothing could dull the pain or fill the loss. Dad and Greg were never coming home again. No more teasing from Greg, or support from him when I needed it. No more hearing Dad talk affectionately to Mother or watching him hold her close. No more dreams about a trip to the coast when they got on their feet with the cabins . . . nothing. Just emptiness and grief.

Dad had insurance, more than Mother had ever imagined. When she got the check she wept. "He was such a good man," she said. "We were all that ever mattered to him. That was all the counted."

Somehow time passed. After awhile Mother went back to work. I went back to school and we both tried to get on with life. I'd noticed, a few months later, that Mother had started getting her hair styled, wearing makeup . . . looking younger than she had when Dad was alive, happier, too. I figured it was good for her.

Then one day in school Jenna Murphy nudged me and said, "What's this about your mom's new boyfriend?"

My face felt hot. I was shocked, but I just shrugged and said I didn't know anything about it.

Jenna put her books in her locker. "Well, my mom says his name is Bruce Reid. He's from Springfield. Nobody seems to know what he's doing around here, but he's been seeing your mother. He took her to Madison a couple of times. Someone saw them in a restaurant. Hasn't she even told you yet?"

I was disappointed and hurt to think that after all we'd been through and how close we'd been, that Mother wouldn't say anything at all to me. My eyes filled with tears and I felt a terrible lonesomeness for Dad and Greg. Jenna noticed and right away she tried to make excuses.

"She probably thinks you wouldn't approve," she said quickly. "Like Mom says, it's good if she can find someone. It was pretty terrible, losing a son and a husband both at once. Please don't say that I said anything."

Jenna was probably right, but it hurt anyway. I kept waiting for Mother to say something . . . there was plenty of opportunity . . . but all she ever said was she was so glad I had a lot of friends, that I got out.

It was in February when Jenna said that my mother had asked her mother if I could spend a weekend at their place. My face felt hot and I just stared at Jenna. "You mean she asked your mother if I could stay overnight at your place? What is she going to do, bring him home for the night?" Anger and embarrassment went through me like a knife.

Right away Jenna told me I shouldn't say anything, that her mother told her she should just ask me over for the night. Then she shrugged indifferently. "If you don't want to, it's okay," she said. "Just don't get huffy with me. I can't help it if your mother wants to shack up with that guy."

The words whirled around inside me. "I'll see," I mumbled.

We hardly talked the rest of the way home, but I said I'd go skating with her that evening. She said she'd pick me up.

When I got home, I noticed a note from Mother taped to the kitchen cupboard. It said she'd gone to the city for dinner and there was food in the refrigerator for me to heat.

I wasn't hungry. I wasn't anything but heartbroken. Of course she was with that guy. And I hadn't even met him yet.

I wandered through the house, and for the first time I noticed that all the reminders of Dad were removed. His pipe rack, his books from the bookshelf, even their wedding picture . . . all were gone.

Later, Jenna came by and waited while I changed clothes. She told me she was sorry, that she knew how I felt.

I told her how everything of Dad's was gone. "I'm all mixed up, I guess," I said.

"Listen, I talked to my mom," Jenna replied. "She says your

170

mother was a good wife to your dad . . . that even your dad wouldn't want her to be unhappy and lonely, It's better to see someone laughing than crying all the time."

I realized she was right, and I did feel better after that.

We had a good time roller skating. We met a couple of guys from Springfield, Dennis and Barry. Afterward we had something to eat at the cafe next door and Dennis took my phone number. He was older, mature, and nice. Jenna really liked Barry, too. We laughed all the way home.

When Jenna's car turned the corner of my street, I saw the big car parked in front of the house. My heart pounded and I felt scared. I knew it was him, whoever he was!

Jenna parked out front and said, "There. She's brought him home to meet you. You should feel better about that."

I did and I didn't. I thanked her for the ride and got out slowly, walking in the deep snow to the walk. It was freshly shoveled . . . I figured he had done that.

When I got in the house, I could hear soft music and gentle voices. They were in the living room. I hung my coat in the closet and walked into the hallway. Mother heard me and came over. Her cheeks were flushed and she reached for my hand. "Stephanie, I want you to meet a special friend of mine," she said.

A man stood up and came toward me. He was big. Much bigger than my father. His eyes burned into mine and made me feel uneasy. "Bruce Reid, this is Stephanie," Mother said. "I want you to be friends."

He was waiting, like he was reading my reaction. Bruce was not about to bend my way. He just nodded carefully. "Pleased to meet you," he said. "I've heard a lot about you, Stephanie." He wasn't exactly friendly, but he wasn't unfriendly, either. He glanced at Mother, who put her hand in his.

Mother chattered on about where I had been and if I'd had a good time. Suddenly she put her left hand out in front of me and I noticed a large diamond ring on her finger. Mother looked at Bruce adoringly. "This is what Bruce bought me. We're engaged, Stephanie. It's going to be a whole new life for me."

He sat down on the couch, opened a can of beer, and looked at me with a kind of satisfaction in his eyes. "That's right. It's going to be a whole new life for your mother. After we're married we're going to Europe. I think we'll sell this place and keep an apartment so we'll be free to travel, to pick up and go when we want."

Mother looked stunned. "I never intended to sell this house," she said. "It's Stephanie's home, too. She can live here for as long as she wants."

171

He shrugged. "Okay, keep it. It's up to you, hon. Of course Stephanie is staying with us. I wouldn't have it any other way. I never had children of my own so I'm going to enjoy her."

The way his eyes went up and down my body unnerved me, and the look in his eyes sent shivers through me.

I excused myself and went to my room. I kept thinking about what was going on downstairs . . . what my dad would think . . . and I cried until I fell asleep.

In the morning, Mother was up first. Thankfully, Bruce had left. She'd made coffee and was looking bright eyed, cheerful, and happy. "Well, isn't he nice?" Mother asked. "I'm so lucky. I think I'd have died, Stephanie, if I hadn't met him. I missed your dad and Greg so much. If I didn't have you, there's no telling what I'd have done. You have a right to your own life. I knew that when you graduated you'd leave and then I'd be all alone." She paused. "I really love him . . . not like your dad, of course, but in some ways it's much better. I can't explain it."

I wanted to say I didn't like the look in his eyes. I wanted to say that she was desperate and that's why he looked so good. But it would only have hurt her and caused trouble between us. She was seeing Bruce the way she wanted him to be. Nothing I could say or do would change her mind.

I sipped my coffee. "What does he do for a living?" I asked.

Mother looked startled. "Oh, right now he's between businesses. He's looking at property to start something new right now. He says there's a time to get in and a time to get out, and if you know what you're doing you'll make money. He's been all over the world, so he must know what he's doing."

A little voice inside me said that Bruce had probably been around all right, but I suspected it was on someone else's money. "But what business?" I pressed. "You must know what he's into."

Her cheeks flushed. "Stephanie, did I ever bother your father about business?" she asked. "I don't bother Bruce, either. It isn't a woman's business what a man does so long as he's good to her. Why do you want to needle me? Are you jealous?"

Was that what she really thought? That I was jealous of her happiness? I wasn't jealous, I was afraid!

With tears brimming in my eyes, I got up from the table and went for my jacket.

Mother got up and followed me to the door, putting her hand gently on my arm. Her eyes were wet, too. "Stephanie, I didn't mean that. It's just that it isn't all happiness. I keep thinking about your dad and Greg. They're with me all the time, but theygone. I talked to the pastor. He said I had to let go and I have to believe that. I love you and

172

I want you to have everything you want from the insurance money. Haven't I let you buy all the clothes you want? I let you use the new car. I'm trying to be fair, Stephanie. Give me that much credit."

"Okay, I give you credit. Let's just forget it," I said, leaving the house.

When I turned the corner, I looked back and Mother was standing in the window watching me. Seeing her there alone sent pangs of hurt through me. Maybe she was right. Maybe Bruce was nice and maybe I did resent him for coming into our lives.

Jenna met me at the corner as she did every morning before school. "Well, did you meet the man in your mother's life last night?" she asked.

I shrugged. "I met him," I said.

"Well? What do you think? Do you like him or what?"

I knew I could be honest with Jenna. "I guess I don't care for him much," I admitted. "It isn't anything he says. I just don't care for him. Maybe when I get used to him I'll feel differently. If not, it won't be long before I can move out."

The weekend was coming up and Jenna invited me to stay over at her house Saturday and Sunday. When I told Mother later, she got real fidgety and nervous. "Sure you can, if you want to," she said. "I think I'll ride with Bruce into the city then. He's going in on business and we can take in a movie, go to a dance or something."

The lump in my throat grew. "You're going to a motel with him, aren't you? Just as if you were married." My heart pounded hard.

She looked at me. "Yes, I am," she said finally. "Stephanie, one day you'll really love someone and then you'll understand. I love Bruce. He's everything to me. He could have lots of women. You should see how the women flirt with him when we go out. It hurts me and scares me. I don't want to lose him. I couldn't stand it. Please, Stephanie, don't hassle me. We are getting married, you know."

What could I say? Nothing would change her mind. But it sickened me to think of her degrading herself like that. My mother, a wonderful, respectable woman, chasing him like she was a young girl who didn't know better.

Jenna's folks were wonderful people and they didn't mind my being there all weekend. On Sunday night her dad went to visit his father in the nursing home. Mrs. Murphy, Jenna, and I were in the living room watching TV. Mrs. Murphy cleared her throat. "I hate to say anything, Stephanie," she began. "You know I've always thought the world of your whole family, and you know how rumors are . . . how people talk and think later. But Pearl Hasely knew Bruce back when he lived in Springfield. She says he doesn't have a very good reputation. She wouldn't say much except that he left town suddenly and there was a lot of talk about him . . . talk that was hushed up somehow. I don't want to hurt you or meddle in what isn't my business, but I just hate to see your mother or you get hurt. You've both had enough trouble."

In a way, I was almost relieved that she brought it up. At least I could talk about it with someone. But as we sat talking, I felt guilty, as if I was betraying my mother. My life was in an endless, get-nowhere circle. I couldn't ask mother too much about Bruce and I couldn't tell her what Mrs. Murphy had heard. I just had to wait and hope that somewhere along the line he slipped up and Mother would catch on by herself. I just hoped she'd be strong enough to handle it.

When I was leaving that night, Mrs. Murphy walked me to the door. She said I could come over any time I needed to talk or cry, and what we said would never go beyond her house. I needed that, needed a port in the storm of my life.

Mother didn't come home until after midnight and then Bruce came in with her, laughing. They weren't quiet at all and from my room I heard Bruce say he was staying all night!

In the morning, I got up for school and they were still in bed. Mother had left a note on the kitchen table, saying that she was going to work at noon that day. She wanted to know if I'd had a nice weekend and said hers was fabulous!

After school Jenna and I met Dennis and Barry, the guys we met at the skating rink. They wanted to take us for pizza and to the rink afterward. Jenna had to go home and tell her folks and we both had to change clothes, so they left us off at our houses and said they'd pick us up at six-thirty.

I went rushing in the house and Bruce came out of the downstairs bedroom. He looked at me and grinned. "Surprised?"

Surprised? I was scared. Mother worked until nine on Monday evenings. "What are you doing here?" I asked. I hadn't seen his car out front and I hadn't noticed if Mother's car was in the garage.

There was satisfaction in his eyes as he answered me. "I live here, Stephanie. Your mother and I got married. She said you didn't like her shacking up with me, so I figured why not tie the knot and keep little Stephanie happy? And we did."

I ran upstairs, locked my door, changed clothes, and combed my hair. I forgot about taking a bath and dressing leisurely. No way was I going to sit in a tub with him downstairs.

I kept crying and smearing my makeup. How could Mother do something like that . . . run off and get married and let me come home to him living here? He'd be sleeping in my father's bed . . . a man like Bruce with evil in his eyes.

I'd been excited about going out with Dennis. I'd wondered if I'd

174

ever see him again. But now my happy thoughts were all mixed up with anger and pain.

They'd picked up Jenna first. Both Barry and Dennis were so nice. It was like we'd known them for years. Some people are like that. They give you a feeling of trust and comfort.

Jenna and I had pizza and sodas and they had beer. I didn't like that much because they drank two pitchers. When they were paying the bill I told Jenna, but she said they were older and we had to remember that everyone drank beer, even if we didn't.

They kept trying to get us to have some, but neither of us would. By the time we got to the skating rink, they were acting a little loud. I managed to tell Jenna I didn't want to go out with them again and she just grabbed my arm and said to be patient, that she really liked Barry.

Afterward, Barry drove to Jenna's house. He walked her to the door and they went in the house for quite a while. I knew her folks were out.

Dennis put his arm around me, pulled me close and kissed me. I kind of liked it. He said he really liked me a lot and he hoped that we could have a "special" relationship. We sort of talked about our lives. He and Barry worked together at a factory in Springfield.

Finally Barry came out, winking at Dennis, and they drove me home. Right away Dennis looked at me when he saw the big car that belonged to Bruce.

"Hey, isn't that Bruce Reid's car?" he asked.

My mouth went dry and my throat felt tight. "Do you know him?" I asked, adding quickly, to stop any bad things he might say that I wouldn't want to hear, "because he married my mother."

"Well, I wish her well, that's all," Dennis replied. "He's a handsome jerk. That's all I'm going to say because I couldn't prove anything else."

He walked me to the door and kissed me good night. He held me too close so I pushed him away and said I had to go in. He said he'd call me.

Mother was home, dressed in a satiny robe and fluffy slippers. Bruce was wearing a robe, too, and they were having a drink together. Mother's eyes were glowing, searching my face for approval. She snuggled next to Bruce, covering his big hand with her small one.

"We got married, Stephanie," she said. "I didn't want a big wedding, it wouldn't have been appropriate."

I wanted to cry, but I didn't. I just stood stiffly in the doorway of the living room, blinked back the tears, and managed to say, "Good luck."

Mother got up and put her arms around me, hugging me. "I'm so happy Stephanie, happier than I've ever been."

I felt Bruce's eyes staring at me. A strange uneasiness went through me, leaving me with an awful, heavy feeling.

I can't say that Mother didn't try to make things easy for me and I can't say that Bruce interfered with what Mother and I discussed because he didn't. He agreed with her that her new car, the one she'd purchased with Dad's insurance money, could just as well be mine.

They actually went on a honeymoon to Europe. When they left, everything was wine and roses, but when they came back, Mother was pale and Bruce was restless. He kept coming and going at all hours, always taking his briefcase and going to Madison for "business." But when I asked Mother what it was all about, she just said it was something to do with construction.

Jenna kept calling Barry and finally he said they'd be coming to town on Saturday. I don't know why, but I was uneasy. I felt that they wouldn't have come at all if Jenna hadn't been so insistent. But for her sake I agreed to go.

When they picked me up I could smell liquor on their breath. Jenna was in the front seat, snuggled close to Barry, and Dennis was in the back waiting for me. The minute I looked at him I thought: He doesn't look as nice as he did before. His eyes never really met mine, but went up and down me . . . like Bruce.

I closed the car door, staying close to my side of the seat. "I have to be home early. I promised my mother," I said.

Barry looked back, laughing. "Early in the morning, you mean."

"No, early this evening," I said firmly.

Dennis pulled me toward him. "Oh, I'm stuck with a wet blanket. Well, I can dry you off soon enough," he whispered huskily.

Barry turned off the main highway and headed north.

"Where are you going?" I asked nervously.

"Relax, we're going to my uncle's cabin. It's only seven miles from town, not seventy. We're going to have steaks, a fire in the fireplace, listen to some music," he said.

The cabin was a comfortable one, and the steaks were good. The moon riding the waves on the lake looked like a picture. I relaxed until Barry took Jenna in the bedroom and Dennis pulled me down beside him on the couch. When he reached for me, I pushed him away and his eyes filled with anger.

"Don't," I said. "I mean it. Leave me alone. I'm not that kind of girl."

He threw his head back and laughed. "Not that kind of girl? How stupid do I look? Anyone who lives in the same house as Bruce Reid has been through it all. Don't kid me. I didn't drive all the way here from Springfield to be a nice guy. What do you think Jenna is doing? Playing checkers?"

176

Suddenly, he reached out, pulled my shirt, and tore it. He came toward me and I kicked him hard and he fell back.

I ran out of the cabin and down the road. It was light enough to see in the moonlight. I remembered the way from being there before many times as a child. I knew there was a farmhouse coming up . . . if only someone was home!

When I got up to the house, two big dogs came out of the shed and started barking. Suddenly the back door opened and a woman stood in the doorway. "Who is it?" she called.

"I need help," I replied. "I don't have to come in. I need to call for a ride home."

She stepped outside, calling back to someone inside, "It's just a young girl wanting to use the phone." Then she looked back at me and told me to come in.

I stumbled in and sat down on the chair by the door. She looked at me. "Looks like you got away just in time," she said.

I nodded. She said the phone was on the other wall and I was welcome to use it.

Bruce answered my call. "Could I talk to Mother? This is Stephanie," I said.

"Your mother has an upset stomach. What do you want? I can tell her," he said.

"I just want a ride home. I'm up at the lake, the first farm at the turnoff. The place on the hill, by the apple orchard."

He sighed. "Okay, we'll pick you up and ask questions later."

Relief flooded through me. I was safe!

When Bruce got there, I thanked the woman and said I'd mail her money for the phone call. But she said it wasn't necessary.

I got in the car and then noticed that Bruce had come alone. "Where's Mother?" I asked.

He shrugged. "Like I said, she doesn't feel good." He started the car, looking at me, at my clothes that I was trying to hold together. "Who were you with, anyway?" he asked.

I looked at him, watching his face for a change of expression. "Someone who knows you . . . or of you. Some guys from Springfield."

The words hung in the air and left a silence. "So they know of me," he said. "And they know of you. We have something in common. We've both been around. Right?" He looked at me, grinning.

Suddenly I was aware that we were not headed back to town . . . we were going north again. I leaned toward the door, touching it with my back. The moon had gone behind the clouds and the night was dark. The only light came from the car's headlights. I closed my eyes. "Bruce, please, I want to go home. Right now!" I begged.

He laughed. "Oh, so you want to go home? Well, we're going

177

home. We're just going for a little ride first."

I was crying, but he just ignored me. He turned the radio on and sang with the music. Desperately, I asked, "What about Mother? She loves you, Bruce."

"Your mother drives me nuts. I think I'll like you better," he said.

He turned onto a side road and pulled up in front of a house. I looked around. The house was abandoned. The windows were boarded up.

Bruce looked at me and grinned. "Come on in. It's nothing fancy, but it will do."

I leaned against the car seat, but he grabbed me, his strong fingers holding tight to my arm, and pulled me out with him. I stumbled behind him, crying all the way.

He pushed me through the door and through a couple rooms to a dusty old couch. It was filthy in there, dark and creepy.

I made a final plea. "Please, Bruce, I won't tell Mother. I won't tell anyone. Let's go home."

He pulled his belt off and tossed it on the floor. "We're going home in just a little while. And of course you won't tell your mother, or anyone else. Who'd believe you anyway? Running around with those two strangers from Springfield."

I closed my eyes and cried. I kept wishing I could die, that fear would stop my heart and the pain would end forever. But I didn't die . . . and nothing stopped Bruce.

Afterward he dressed himself, combed his hair, and said, "Now we'll go home. And you can tell your mother how lucky and happy you were that Bruce came to rescue you. No telling what might have happened if I hadn't come along."

When we pulled up in front of the house, he turned and looked at me. "Listen Stephanie, you'd better not say anything to your mother about me. She wouldn't believe you, for one thing. And if she did, it would kill her. So let's keep this to ourselves."

I didn't move, so he came around and opened the door and took my arm. I stumbled beside him, weeping . . . I couldn't stop.

We went in and Mother was sitting in the recliner, looking worried. "Where have you been?" she asked. "Jenna called. I've been almost crazy."

Bruce was a master at deception. He went over to Mother and kissed her. Her body relaxed and I watched the tenseness go out of her face. "Hon, we were out in the middle of nowhere and I got a flat," he said. "You remember that the jack didn't work right in your car. Well, I had the same trouble with this one. I had an awful time fixing and changing tires. And Stephanie was crying all the time . . . that didn't help matters."

Mother looked at my torn clothes. I started to go upstairs and she stopped me. "What kind of boys did you go out with anyway?" she demanded. "I just can't imagine you going with strangers like that."

My heart pounded hard and anger filled me. "Why can't you imagine it, Mother?" I asked. "You married one, didn't you?"

Her hand dropped from my arm. She looked at Bruce.

He quickly crossed the room, put his arm around her shoulder. "Sandy, let the girl go to bed," he said.

I didn't sleep that night. I cried till I couldn't cry anymore, until my body was exhausted. I listened to Bruce moving around downstairs early in the morning. My body ached and I felt dirty.

The phone rang and I heard Mother answer it. She came to the stairway and called up to me that it was Jenna.

I put my robe on and went downstairs, keeping my back to Mother and Bruce. Jenna's voice was urgent. "Where'd you go?" she asked. "Listen, can I pick you up? I've got to talk to you so we get our stories straight."

I told Jenna she could stop by in about an hour. Then I took a long, hot bath looking at my body and remembering why I hurt so much. I dressed slowly, making my bed, timing it so I wouldn't have to be near Mother and Bruce for too long.

Bruce was outside puttering around the yard. He looked at me when I came out, his eyes going up and down my body. "Take care, Stephanie. Don't ride with strangers," he said.

I ran to Jenna's car and got in. She drove around town telling me how much she loved Barry. She said she couldn't disappoint him or she'd lose him.

"I think they're coming around next week. He promised he'd call," she said.

I was empty inside except for the hurting. Hot tears burned my eyes. "Well, count me out. I don't ever want to be with Dennis again," I told her.

Right away, Jenna got angry. She wanted to know what he was supposed to do when they came.

"I don't care what he does . . . as long as it isn't with me," I said.

"I told my mom you really had a crush on Dennis, that Dennis and Barry were super guys," Jenna pouted.

I looked at her. "Jenna, you are my best friend and I'd do many things for you. But going out with Dennis again isn't one of them. If Barry likes you, it won't matter."

She stared ahead, her lips set in anger. I opened the car door when we got to my house and she said, "Okay, stay at home with Bruce. Maybe he's more fun!"

I felt like the blood was draining out of me. "What do you mean by that?" I asked.

179

She shrugged. "I suppose I shouldn't say anything, but Barry says that Bruce is a real slob. And my mother heard that he's seeing other women. He's been in trouble before, Stephanie. He almost went to prison once, but somehow managed to get off."

I just got out of the car. I couldn't stop thinking about my dad and Greg. Why did they have to die? I thought. We all loved each other so much.

Bruce and Mother didn't hear me come in. They were in the bedroom and my mother was crying, pleading, "Bruce, if you'd just stay home tonight, please. Don't go."

"Listen, Sandy, what should I hang around here for?" he growled. "To be nagged at for one lousy check I wrote? I told you, as soon as I get my money from my business I'll return it to you with interest. But that's not enough for you. Then I find out you talked to the bank about the money in the savings account. I thought I was your husband. I thought we were equal. Well, I can get along without you. But what would you do without me?"

Mother was crying hard. I sat down at the kitchen table and listened.

"Bruce, I didn't call the bank. They called me at the drugstore," she said. "They asked if I wanted money transferred to the checking account and I said I didn't have any such plans. When the man said you'd been in, I said that whatever Bruce wants is fine with me. I swear that's what I said. You can have that money for whatever you want. I don't ever want anything or anyone to come between us. I love you, Bruce, more than anything."

"Okay, Sandy. Let's forget it. But I am going out tonight. My old friend John is up in Madison, visiting his sister."

Bruce came out of the bedroom and went into the bathroom, whistling. He came out later smelling of cologne and looking pretty sharp to go visiting some old friend.

Mother stood by the door, wanting for a sign of love and affection. He bent down, his lips brushed hers and his eyes met mine. I read what was in them . . . the horrible memory of the other night. "See you," he said, grinning at us both.

She went to the window and watched him leaving. There was a look on her face that hurt me.

"Mother?" I asked. "Why don't we move to the city? I could get a job. You could start a new life away from here."

She turned around with a strange look on her face. "Stephanie, do you really think I'd leave Bruce? He's my husband and I love him. I know you resent him and the good times we have. Maybe you can't help it, but you aren't going to come between us, so stop trying."

"Listen to me," I begged. "Jenna says her mother heard that Bruce

180

sees other women up in Madison, and Dennis and Barry both said he was in some trouble in Springfield. If he's trying to get your money maybe you should check into some of the rumors. What would Dad say?"

She waved her arm impatiently. "Listen, Stephanie, I don't want to hear any more of this nonsense. Don't you think that Jenna's mother might be jealous? Bruce is so handsome, so charming. He can have anything I have. I don't care. Not one thing or one person in this world means as much to me as he does. And don't bring your father into this. He's gone. He lived for himself, his hunting and fishing and friends. If you think about it, I did a lot of sitting here alone."

I went upstairs . . . angered by what she said about Dad. There was no use talking to her. I knew she was waiting for Bruce.

The next morning I met Jenna at the corner as usual. She wasn't friendly like she used to be, but at least we walked together and there was comfort in that. In front of the school entrance, she turned to me and apologized for what she'd said about Bruce.

I needed her friendship, so I said it was okay. I told her we'd just forget it.

When I came home from school, both cars were gone and the house was quiet. Mother would be working, but who knew where Bruce was. I drank some milk, ate a few cookies, and got to thinking about the metal safe that Mother kept under her bed. The key was in the top dresser drawer. Before she met Bruce, Mother showed me the certificates she had purchased with the insurance money. She explained where everything was in case something happened to her.

I went into the bedroom and found the key, but the safe was gone from under the bed. I looked on the shelf in the closet . . . sometimes she kept valuable items there. I saw a manila envelope and I took it down. The safe was behind it, but for some reason I looked in the envelope first. My fingers trembled as I pulled out the contents . . . pictures of naked women! Bruce's pictures!

My stomach churned inside. It was true what they said about him . . . he was evil. I recognized the background in the pictures . . . it was that empty farmhouse.

I put the pictures back, took down the safe, and unlocked it. The savings account passbooks were still there, but inside they were stamped "Account closed." I put everything back and sat on the bed in shock. Mother was buying Bruce. And when everything was spent and gone, he'd be, too.

I was sitting there crying when Bruce suddenly appeared. "Taking a nap on my bed?" he asked.

"This is my mother's room. I can come in here if I want. She's going to be home in a little while, so I'll go get some supper started," I said, getting up.

181

He pushed me down with one swift movement. "No, she won't be home in a little while. Her friend Hope had a heart attack and your mother left for the city," he told me. "She left a note on the table but I took it. No telling who might come in with the doors unlocked. I've locked them now. So nobody will bother us."

The room was whirling around. I kept wishing I could just pass out because I knew Bruce was going to rape me . . . and I wanted to die.

I started crying and he laughed. Then the phone rang and Bruce grabbed my arm, his fingers cutting into my flesh. He put his face next to mine and muttered, "That's going to be your mother. You tell her everything is just fine, and it will be."

I took the phone and said hello. Bruce was watching, his eyes intent on my face.

"Stephanie, did you get my note?" Mother asked. "Is Bruce home with you?" Her voice sounded so far away.

"I got your note, Mother. How is Hope?" I managed to ask.

"They think she's going to be all right," she replied. "The first seventy-two hours are critical, but I have a feeling she'll make it. Is Bruce there?"

I said he was and handed the phone to him. Then I ran to the front door and out of the house as fast as I could go.

I ran across the street to Mrs. Sander's house and asked if I could use her phone. She said sure, and I called Jenna. I asked her if she could pick me up and she said she would.

When she got there, I thanked Mrs. Sanders and ran out. I leaned against the car seat and Jenna's eyes widened. "Did he hurt you?" she asked.

I looked away. I couldn't tell her what had happened. "He tried, but I got away," I told her. Then I explained about Mother's friend and that I didn't want to stay at home. Jenna said I could come to her place and that her folks were in the city with friends for a couple of days.

It was after eight when Jenna's doorbell rang. I ran upstairs to hide . . . I was sure it was Bruce! But as I listened, I realized that it was Barry and Dennis.

Jenna came up in a little while and said, "I called Barry as soon as my folks left. Please come down. We'll go for a pizza or something and then come back and listen to records."

I went to the window so my back was to her. "Jenna, I'm sorry," I began, "but I can't go anyplace tonight. Can't I just stay up here? You just go out and have fun."

She snapped, "Listen, Stephanie, you messed things up for me once and caused a whole lot of trouble between me and my folks. If you don't want to go with us, you can go back home . . . with Bruce."

I had no choice, so I went to the bathroom and combed my hair. I heard Jenna go back downstairs, heard her say sweetly that I'd be right down. Her folks had a phone in the bedroom, so I went in there and called an old friend of Mother's who was a widow, Agatha Thorton.

It took her forever to answer the phone, and when she did I just blurted out that I needed a place to stay for the night because Mother was away and I wasn't comfortable staying with Bruce. Right away she said I could, and I said a prayer of thanks.

When I went downstairs, they were having drinks from a bottle that Barry had brought. Dennis looked at me with a smirk on his face. Barry put his arm around Jenna and hugged her close. The whole scene made me sick. I told Jenna I was leaving, that I had found a place to stay for the night.

Dennis stood in front of me. "Oh, no, you don't. You owe me, remember?" he asked.

I shook my head. "My friends are expecting me," I said. "If I'm not there in ten minutes, they'll be over."

Dennis put his hand on my face. "Who cares if they come over? We'll just say you left."

But Jenna looked frightened. "Dennis, don't. Let her go. I'll call someone else," she promised. "I know plenty of girls who like to have a good time."

Outside, the air was crisp and cool and the tears that fell were cold on my cheeks. I walked the back way to Agatha's place, in case Bruce was looking for me.

When I got there, I could tell Agatha had changed her mind . . . that she wasn't comfortable having me there. I thanked her for letting me come over and she kept fidgeting with her hands. "You're sure that Bruce won't come over here?" she asked. "I've heard so much about him . . . not that I'd ever say anything to your mother. Probably it's all talk. . . ."

"Agatha," I began, "he won't come looking for me. I'm sure he's back in Madison by now. He doesn't care where I am. I just don't want to be in the house alone when he comes. I'll leave in the morning, so don't worry."

I couldn't sleep most of the night, reliving it all in my mind . . . thinking until I couldn't think anymore. I cried until I was empty.

Agatha was up before dawn, wandering around downstairs. Finally I washed up and went down.

She seemed relieved when I said I'd leave; she didn't ask me to stay for coffee or anything. I heard her bolt the door the minute I was outside.

When I got near my house, I saw Bruce's car was gone, so I hurried inside and locked the door. I ran up to my room and changed into fresh clothes.

The telephone rang and I was afraid to answer it. Finally, though, I picked it up. It was Mother.

"Stephanie, where is Bruce?" she asked.

"I don't know," I said. "Probably in Madison. He isn't here."

"Wasn't he there last night?"

"For a while he was. Then he left," I said. "When are you coming home?"

She sighed. "I was going to stay another couple days, but maybe I'll come now."

Relief flooded through me. "I wish we could talk when you get home," I said. "I've learned some things you should know about."

It was as if she already knew. Right away there was harshness in her words, an edge. "Stephanie, I don't want you causing trouble between Bruce and me," she snapped. "He has a right to some privacy. I don't want to quarrel with him about anything. Do you understand? I don't want you causing trouble for us."

No, I didn't understand. Was she so desperate for love and companionship that she would turn on her own daughter?

When I came home from school late that day, Mother's car was out front. I went inside and saw she was drinking coffee and pacing the floor. "I called a couple of places but no one's seen Bruce," she said right off. "I can't understand it. He was here last night, wasn't he?"

I only nodded and she stared at me.

"You didn't have words with him, did you?" she asked. "You know he knows you don't like him, and he resents it. Stephanie, can't you understand that soon you'll be out of school and on your own and I'll be all by myself? That's how it should be, but I have needs, I need Bruce, need his love, need him coming home to me. If only you would stop looking at me as if I was doing something terrible." Suddenly she went for her purse and her jacket and she said she was going to drive around and see if she could find him.

"Mother, please don't go," I said. "Do you want to know what Bruce is really like? Did you see the pictures in the closet . . . in that envelope on the shelf?"

My words hung in the air. There was silence, stunned silence. Her face went white and her eyes filled with tears.

"What's wrong with that?" she asked. "It's just like a girlie magazine. Why do you want to turn me against him when I love him? Or do you find him attractive?"

Her question cut me to bits, I shouted, "Mother, he took those pictures himself and I know where. He took me there, the night he came and picked me up. Mother, Bruce raped me that night!"

I thought she'd break down and take me in her arms and comfort me. But all she did was shout and yell and tell me I was afraid that he was going to get all the money and that was all I was concerned with.

I leaned against the kitchen wall, feeling trapped. Mother sat down by the table sobbing. Her body looked so small and thin. I kept remembering the good times, the good years, the times of love and laughter.

It was love that moved me to walk over and touch her shoulder with tenderness. "Mother, I'm sorry," I said. "I won't bother you about Bruce again. I'll stay out of your affairs. Like you say, soon I'll graduate and then I can be on my way."

Jenna hadn't been in school that day, but she called me around seven. She asked if I would go for a ride with her. I could tell she had been crying.

We went for a ride and she said she was upset because Barry was moving to California with Dennis. He didn't tell her until just before they were leaving. She wanted to go down there after graduation, but he said he didn't want to be tied to anyone, that it was better that they go their separate ways.

"Why did he come up here to be with you if he didn't care?" I asked, wanting to comfort her.

She looked at me strangely. "He said he wanted to have some fun."

What could I say to that? It was what I'd figured all along.

When I got home, Mother was happy because Bruce was there. Strewn all over the table were brochures of the business he'd purchased in Madison. Mother's happy voice cut through the storm inside me that kept reliving the memory of what had happened the night before.

Bruce laughed and I looked up to see him standing by the living room doorway looking disgustingly confident. He was dressed very nicely in a new shirt and trousers. "Your mother and I will be moving to Madison," he said. "I think things will be much better for us there."

Mother touched my arm. "Won't it be nice, Stephanie? We need a change, all of us."

I stared at her. How could she just ignore what I'd told her about Bruce raping me?

I walked away to the window, staring out into the night. "When I graduate, I'm going to move away," I said. "I'm not moving to Madison."

Bruce popped open a can of beer and the sound sliced through the tension in the air. "Well, now, you aren't going to be eighteen until . . . let's see October, isn't it? You're still a minor until then, so of course you will come with us."

I turned around and stared at him. We had no secrets any longer.

I'd told Mother everything. If she wouldn't believe me . . . well, I couldn't help that. My voice trembled as I said, "I'm not going, Bruce. I'll tell about you first."

My words got to him, but he remained outwardly calm. I caught his look at Mother and saw the determination in his eyes. "Tell? What is there to tell?" he scoffed. "That you went with a fellow you hardly knew and he took you to bed? That now you want to blame it on me? Oh, no I've got too many good friends to vouch for me. You've been making a play for me all along."

"I saw your pictures," I said.

He laughed. "Pictures? Where? Show me. I'd like to see them . . . see if I recognize anyone."

A coldness went through me, but I went to the bedroom, stood on a chair, and rummaged around the shelf in the closet. The envelope was gone!

Bruce had followed me into the room. He reached in his billfold and took out a photo and handed it to me. "This is the only one I have," he said.

Tears blurred the image, but I could see it was me . . . my face above a naked body. "It isn't me and you know it!" I cried. "It's some kind of trick photography—"

Bruce just smiled. "You want to try to prove it?" he asked.

Bruce put a for-sale sign in the yard the next day. When I came home from school, there it was, telling the world that our home was going to belong to someone else.

It was hard dodging Bruce's advances, but Mother must have believed me because she quit her job at the drugstore so she was always there when I got home from school. But there were times . . . like when she went to mail a letter and Bruce came up to my room, shoved the door open, and grabbed me. He held me, his lips hot on mine, his body pressing hard against me. Then he heard Mother come through the front door and he let me go. I went downstairs. She asked where Bruce was and I said boldly, "Up in my room. He followed me." But all she said was that I had no business wearing a sweater like the one I had on . . . it was too revealing! I guess that's when the love I'd felt for her started to melt away . . . to disappear and harden my heart.

I graduated soon after that and Mother invited all the relatives. Bruce invited a few people I'd never met. He introduced me as his daughter and it disgusted me.

It was toward the end of the evening when Bruce's younger brother Brian came over. I'd never met him, but I liked him right away. He didn't look a bit like Bruce and he didn't act like him either. He was gentle and nice and had only a kind of tenderness rather than evil behind his eyes. I gave him some cake and punch, and he kept looking at me like he was interested. He asked if we could go out on the porch. Most of the guests were done eating, so it wasn't impolite to go out.

Brian filled me in on his life. He'd gone to college and had a degree in business. He'd been engaged and the girl had died in a plane accident a month before the wedding. Bruce was his half brother, and they'd never been very close. . . .

I hung on every word Brian said. I felt a tingle of excitement go through my body, when his arm brushed mine. He was so nice . . . so warm and friendly.

He leaned back and asked, "Do you think Bruce is good to your mom? She seems like a nice person."

"I don't know," I said vaguely. "When my dad and my brother died, she didn't want to live anymore until she met Bruce. I can't wait to get away, though, when I'm eighteen."

His face looked tense. "You stay away from him," he warned. "Once Bruce's been after a girl, no one wants her, believe me. I'm glad I met you. But I'm sorry that he's in your life. He's never been anything but bad news, I'm sorry to say."

Suddenly, Bruce walked out on the porch. Right away, Brian stood up and glanced at his watch. He said he had to leave because it was getting late and he had to drive back to Milwaukee. His eyes met mine as he said, "Maybe I'll drive around some Sunday and we could go out to dinner or take in a movie or something . . . if you'd like that."

My heart went to my throat. "Oh, I'd love that," I told him. "I'm almost always home."

Bruce cut in and said, "Well, you don't have to drive way out here for that. We're going to be plenty busy with moving."

Brian sort of smiled. "Well, we'll see," he said. Then he left.

Bruce put his face close to mine. I could smell the liquor on his breath and I felt his hand running up and down my back. "I ought to show him how well you photograph," he whispered.

I just walked away.

Brian called me the next evening, and we talked for some time. Mother and Bruce were out somewhere and it was a relief to have the house to myself. Brian said he was coming through town on Wednesday and asked me if I could go out for dinner. Of course I could, I told him.

All night I dreamed about Brian . . . dreams that sort of covered over the memories of Bruce. But the memories were always there . . . the awful humiliation when I remembered how he hurt me, how he abused me. I kept praying for forgiveness, as if I had done something wrong.

When Mother and Bruce returned, I didn't say a thing to them about going out with Brian. They were going out to look at an apartment Wednesday evening so they weren't even going to be home.

I'll always remember when Brian came to get me for our date. He looks so handsome, I thought, as I walked out on the porch to greet him.

To my surprise, he hugged me and a tremor went through me as I remembered Bruce coming close to me like that . . . his hands, his arms, determined, and rough.

Brian sensed my discomfort and he pulled away. "Did I offend you?" he asked.

I looked away. "No, you just surprised me, I guess."

"Okay, we'll take it slow," he said easily.

I loved him right away! I know it doesn't sound possible, but I did! And I could tell he cared for me. Brian even told me he felt something special for me that night, over coffee in a cafe outside of town. He also said he was pretty sure he was going to get a job he'd interviewed for nearby. His hand went over mine and he smiled. "Who knows? Maybe I'll settle down in that town, get married, and have a home," he said. "I think you'd like it there. It's near a lake. I'd like to take you there sometime. But of course you probably want to go to school and be free for a while. I don't blame you for that. Everyone needs some time to find out who they are. But there's no harm in dreaming, is there?"

Four days later, I got a letter from Brian . . . a letter that said he really cared for me and that he didn't want anything to spoil what we had going for us. He said he knew I was young and that if I cared for him he'd wait until I was older, because I was worth waiting for. My tears blotted the letter as I read it over and over. I could just imagine him sitting down writing that letter, sincere, honest, and caring.

After that I saw Brian a lot. And he called every night. He got the job in Blooming Grove and then he was closer to us . . . close enough to drive over and take me to a movie and still get back home at a decent hour.

Bruce was occupied with his new "business," and Mother spent a lot of time going with him. The house didn't sell so I got a job at a nursing home for the summer; Jenna worked there, too. Life settled down nicely . . . but then I started feeling sick in the morning. I knew what was wrong and I didn't need a doctor to tell me that I was pregnant.

Who could I talk to? Not Mother. It was Bruce's baby! Not Brian, who thought he loved an innocent, sweet young girl.

It was my mother's friend Hope who happened to call one morning. I'd been crying and I tried to cover it up because I knew she was still recuperating from her heart attack. But Hope asked me point blank, "What's wrong? I know you've been crying, Stephanie. But why? Your mom said you've been so happy, that you've been dating Brian and he's such a nice fellow."

The tears kept coming. "I don't know what I'm going to do, Hope," I blurted out. "I don't know where to turn."

"Stephanie, why don't you come down here for a few days?" she suggested. "We can talk it over. I'd love to have you . . . it's been ages since you've been to see me. You take the bus and I'll meet you."

It was like a door opening . . . as if going there could change things. "Maybe I could see a doctor down there," I said.

There was silence. She was putting it all together. Suddenly she said, "Sure. I know several good doctors. I'll make an appointment. When can you come?"

I looked at the calendar. I had two days off, but I had worked one day for another girl the week before. I'd ask her to fill in one day for me. "Are Wednesday, Thursday, and Friday okay?" I asked.

"Sure. I'll pick you up Wednesday. I think the bus gets in at around eleven. We can have lunch," Hope said.

Brian called me that night, saying he wanted to come over. I asked for a rain check, saying I didn't feel well and he believed me. He said I should take care of myself and he'd call the next day.

Mother came home later in her car . . . without Bruce. She said she wasn't feeling well. I felt like she was shutting me out . . . going around in silence, pacing the floor, anxiety alive on her face. I knew it had to do with Bruce, but she'd never say anything against him to me.

We were in our own little worlds, my mother and I. She went in the kitchen and after awhile I heard her calling around trying to locate Bruce. Finally I heard her tell someone she'd be there in a while, that if he arrived he should be told everything was going to be all right.

Then she went into her bedroom and came out all dressed up. With eyes that avoided meeting mine, she said, "I'm going up to Kimberly Wallis's. Bruce will be there soon. Stephanie, he and I had words. We got an offer for the house. I didn't think it was enough, but Bruce said we should grab it. Maybe he's right. Everything is so good when we get along. Better for all of us!"

I made a stab at reaching her and said, "Mom, don't give him everything you have. When the money is gone, he'll leave and you won't have anything. Don't you know that?"

Her face became a mask of coldness and she suddenly slapped my cheek. "Why do you resent his loving me?" she shouted. "You have his brother, don't you? Or do you want them both for yourself?"

My face felt the sting of her blow and tears sprang to my eyes. I ran up to my room, closing the door and throwing myself on my bed. I heard my mother leave the house and drive off.

I was dozing there when I heard someone at the front door. I got up and went to the window. It was Bruce! I shivered as his footsteps sounded on the stairs and he appeared in the doorway.

"So Mother has gone looking for me," he said. "She shouldn't leave you home alone. There's no telling what could happen to a sweet girl like you." He tossed his jacket on the floor, unbuttoned his shirt, and I backed away.

"I'm going to have a baby, Bruce," I told him. "Your baby."

He laughed. "My baby? You're not going to pin that on me. After all the guys you've been with? I might have been first, but I sure wasn't the only one . . . or the last."

"Mother will come back soon. She's at Kimberly Wallis's. She told me that. She could be driving in any minute," I said quickly.

He shoved me down on the bed. "Well, I'll listen for her. You don't have to worry."

I closed my eyes and tried to think of other things . . . tried to drown out the pain and humiliation, the cruelty of the man who lived in my parents' home, slept in my father's bed, and made love to my mother. . . .

Afterward he looked at me and laughed. "Now I'll go up to Kimberly's and see if I can catch your mother," he said.

It was late, almost midnight, but I called Hope anyway, and asked if I could come down on the morning bus. She said I could, so I packed what I could into two suitcases and then sat downstairs on the couch and waited for morning. At seven-thirty I walked to town to the bus stop.

Hope was waiting when the bus came in. She said she was glad I had come. We got into her car and I leaned back against the seat. When Hope asked me, in a warm, caring voice, if I was ready to talk, I blurted everything out. I told her everything. . . .

When I finished, I just sort of crumbled inside. "I'm sorry I've bothered you," I said. "I just thought you were the one person in this whole world who I could talk to, who would believe me."

"I do believe you," Hope insisted. "And I'm going to help you all I can."

We went to her house and I had toast and hot chocolate. Hope gave me a bedroom with a lot of south windows and said it could be my room for as long as I wanted.

Hope made an appointment for me to see her doctor at four that day. He told me what I already knew . . . I was pregnant. The doctor wasn't aware of how I became pregnant, but seeing that I was so young, single, and unwilling to talk about the father he assumed it wasn't a welcomed pregnancy. He gave me some pamphlets about the process of giving a child up for adoption and few about what an abortion entailed. Even though the baby growing inside of me was created from a violent and hateful act, I didn't have the heart to get rid of it. It was an innocent being that deserved a chance at life. There was also something healing about carrying the baby to term, like it was expelling the horror of Bruce from my body.

When we got home, the phone was ringing. I knew it was Mother. Hope answered it, looking at me. "Yes, she's here. I think you should just let her stay, it's what she wants." She listened for a while, then said, "I don't know if she wants him to have my number or not." Hope cupped her hand over the phone. "Brian has called for you. What should she say?"

Brian? Brian was from what seemed a lifetime past . . . a dream that was shattered, a hope smothered out. I got up, walked to the living room, and looked outside. "I don't want him calling here or coming around, either," I said. "Just tell him I've found a good job and I don't want any ties with anyone."

When Hope hung up, she looked at me. "You could have talked to Brian. If you care about him, if he loves you, he'd understand."

I looked away. "Maybe sometime I'll talk to Brian," I said. "But not yet. Not until I've got some sense of direction to my life. Okay, Hope?" I asked, tears spilling out. I needed desperately to feel close to someone . . . to have a friend.

Hope came over and put her arm around my shoulder. "Listen, Stephanie, you think everything over and then you do what you think is right for your life," she told me.

The next day Brian called. Bruce had given him Hope's last name and he called information. It was as simple as that. When I answered the phone, he said, "Stephanie, I want to see you."

I sat down on the chair in the kitchen, my mind racing. "Brian, I'd rather you didn't come here. I'd rather we just don't see each other anymore," I said.

"Is there someone else?" he asked.

I fought for control, to keep my voice even. "Sort of, I guess," I said.

"Did I do anything?" he asked. "I thought you really cared about me. I was making all kinds of plans."

"It was nothing you did, Brian," I said. "I'm getting a job here, because I didn't want to move with Bruce and Mother."

He sighed. "Well, maybe I can call you. Maybe absence will make the heart grow fonder, you never know. I wish you the best of everything. If you ever change your mind, call me."

I guess I said sure, but I remember I never said good-bye because I was crying so hard that I just hung up.

Hope came in from outside. "I heard you talking," she said. "Was it Brian?" I nodded, and she touched my shoulder. "He loves you.

Maybe if you talked to him about it, told him the truth. . . ."

Never! I thought.

Hope heard about a job opening at a grocery store two blocks away. They needed a cashier. I got the job and started work the next day. I called the nursing home, too, to say I wouldn't be back.

By the end of August I was beginning to show my pregnancy, even though I'd eaten very carefully so I wouldn't gain weight. But the baby grew anyway. It even moved inside me . . . gentle little flutters at first and then determined movements that said, , I'm here!"

It was cool in the store where I worked but the air outside was stifling. When I stepped outside to walk home one day, my breath came hard, my heart pounded, and my head throbbed. I walked home slowly passing all the people walking back from the lake . . . families, children, and babies in strollers. I was weary and tired and longed for the cool quiet of Hope's house.

Hope's voice sounded nervous when she called, "Stephanie, guess who's here!" when I walked onto the front porch.

Through the screen door, I watched as Mother came into the kitchen. She stopped short and stared at me. She was pale and much thinner.

I didn't move when she said hello. Pretty soon Bruce came in and put his arm around Mother. "Putting on some weight, I see," he said smugly. "Well, you look mighty good to me. Your mother here has gotten too skinny. A slight wind would blow her over."

Hope looked first at me, then at them. "I was telling them about the new Chinese restaurant downtown. I said I'd treat them to dinner. Do you want to go?" she asked.

I shook my head no, and they left soon after, getting into Bruce's new car. When Bruce opened the door, he turned to look toward the house, his eyes searching for me, and it all came back to me . . . the horror of that man.

I went to my room and closed the door. I pulled the shades down so that only an outline of the late-afternoon sun peeked through, and I lay there, listening to the neighbors outside talking, to Mr. Potter clipping the hedge, and to the birds chirping in the trees. I'd never felt so alone.

I thought a lot about Brian as I felt my baby move inside me. I thought about what it would be like if we were married and this was his child. I pictured him beside me, planning what we'd name our baby . . . planning our future. I thought about the kind of home we'd have. It'd be a little house but a warm, friendly, and loving one . . . somewhere the baby would always feel safe and loved, not cold and afraid and alone.

It was a long time before Hope got back. She came over and sat

192

on my bed. "They went home," she told me. "I didn't even ask them in. I can't stand the sight of Bruce."

I looked away, just the sound of his name filling me with dread.

"Your mother isn't well," Hope went on. "She's been to a specialist, but had to take the bus, mind you. Bruce couldn't find time to drive her there. Anyway, she wanted you to know that the house is sold and that if there's anything you want, you're welcome to it. Otherwise, it's all going to be auctioned off."

I mumbled that I didn't want anything at all, and Hope reminded me that what I didn't take, Bruce would get. I didn't want anything, though . . . anything that he had touched.

It was October when Hope had to go to a heart specialist in the city for a checkup. Afterward, I drove her home and she asked me if I'd mind going out to the shopping mall to get her prescription filled. I was tired and uncomfortable, but I'd do anything for Hope.

I stood in line for some time before I was waited on, and then I had to wait for her prescription. I had just paid for it and turned around when I saw Brian! I knew it was him right away; I recognized the way he walked. I watched as he disappeared into a mass of people going onto the escalator. I realized then that I still loved him . . . more than I had remembered.

My feet seemed to move automatically, and I followed him down the escalator. But I couldn't find him downstairs.

I was going out the big front doors when I heard, "Stephanie? Stephanie, please wait!" The words were so loud that other people looked at me.

Brian ran to catch up and grabbed my arm. He looked into my eyes, deeply, as if he could see into my heart. "Where are you headed?" he asked. There was a glance downward at my cumbersome-looking figure, and the smile left his face, but only for a second.

I looked away. "I'm going to Hope's. I live there," I said.

"Let's go across the road to the coffee shop. We can talk there."

My heart was in my throat. "Brian, there is nothing to talk about," I told him.

He sort of looked away. I thought I saw tears in his eyes and noticed that he seemed thinner. "Maybe not as far as you are concerned," he said, "but I'd like to get some things settled in my mind. Maybe then I can forget you and let go."

Would it hurt to see him for a little while . . . to have the luxury of his nearness? Or would it be torture to be close to what I wanted and would never have? I shrugged tiredly. "Okay," I said.

We went to the coffee shop and sat down in a booth. I said I'd better call Hope to let her know I'd be late.

Brian had ordered coffee for us by the time I got back. His

expression had changed from concern and love to a look of anger and resentment. He looked beyond me when he said, "Maybe this wasn't such a good idea. After all, you broke it off with me and obviously there was someone else. So what am I doing here now?"

I reached out and touched his hand. "Brian, I couldn't stop him," I began. "Believe me, I didn't care about him at all . . . I tried to stop him."

He looked away. "Now you're going to tell me you were raped, I suppose. You were with him, but you didn't want to be. Sorry, Stephanie, I don't buy that. Why didn't you report it then? You could have seen a doctor and done something about it." He reached in his pocket, took out some change, and slapped it on the table. Then he got up and said, "Well, good luck with everything. It was nice to see you."

I leaned back in the booth as I watched him go outside, get into his car, and drive away.

There was no place to go except back to Hope's. I drove slowly; traffic was heavy. People were heading home to their loved ones and families . . . to someone who cared. The baby moved inside me and I felt a lonesomeness and longing for the days when Dad and Greg were still alive and I'd come home to a house that was cozy and warm, to home-cooked food, to sharing and love.

Hope was waiting anxiously for me "Well, how did it go?" she asked.

"He didn't believe I'd been raped," I said tonelessly. "I guess I don't blame him. I couldn't tell him about Bruce, so you know what he must think about me."

Hope's eyes were filled with compassion and she came over and put her arms around me. "Stephanie, I know it's a bad time for you, but I believe in God and I'm sure He's got something very special planned for your life. You just believe that and wait and see. Someone will come along to love you."

October slipped away. The golden leaves left the trees and the first frost of November killed all the late-fall flowers. It seemed like everything had settled down to wait for the blanket of snow.

Mother wrote brief notes with bits and pieces about their new life. They were living in an apartment because Bruce didn't want to be tied to a house in case they decided to travel. Bruce's business was doing okay and Mother had made a few friends in the building where they lived. When she got to feeling better, she wrote she planned to find a part-time job to keep her occupied.

I was up at five on Thanksgiving morning, shivering as I dressed because we always turned the heat down at night. I had promised Hope I'd make us a real holiday dinner since she and I were practically family. And I was thankful to have her as my friend.

194

After dinner, it started to snow. It looked so pretty that Hope and I decided to go for a walk. When we came home, the telephone was ringing. Hope hurried to answer it. She looked at me and told me it was my mother.

"I tried to call you several times," Mother said. "When neither you nor Hope answered, I was worried something might have happened."

"We went for a walk," I said.

"I was hoping you and Hope could drive up to visit us. I get lonesome for you," she said.

"I'm pregnant, remember?" I practically snapped. "I can't come up there. And I don't want to see Bruce. Never again would be too soon."

"Honey, don't talk that way," Mother told me. "I love you. You're still my daughter . . . the only family that I have left."

How come I'm worth so much now? I thought bitterly. Not too long ago Bruce was number one and I didn't even count.

I handed the phone to Hope and said, "She'd like you to come up, but I'm not going."

I went in the living room and turned on the television set, listening to Hope's hushed words. When she came into the living room, her face was ashen and her eyes heavy with tears but she didn't say anything.

I got so depressed after that. And as time went on I felt worse. The doctor kept asking me what I was going to do about the baby and I kept putting off a decision. I knew what I had to do, but I couldn't bear to face it, to think about it. There was no choice. I had to give my baby away.

Time passed quickly. Soon Christmas music filled the air downtown. I could hear it out in the streets from inside the grocery store. It snowed often, leaving thick, high icing on the pine boughs. The air was cold and crisp and everyone seemed so busy. Hope and I bought a small tree and we put a few gifts under it. I bought her a pair of slippers, a nightgown, and some nice perfume. I kept thinking about Brian . . . had he found someone yet? Were they going to share this Christmas?

It was two days before Christmas and I came home from work to find Hope waiting with her coat on. She looked at me with weary eyes and said, "The hospital in Madison called. Your mother has been admitted and she wants you to come down. We have to go right away."

My mind whirled and I felt a little dizzy.

"Stephanie," Hope went on, "she has cancer."

The drive to Madison seemed an eternity long. When we got to the hospital, Mother was lying on the bed, her eyes sunken and darkly circled. She raised her arm and her fingers reached for mine. I took off my coat and put my hand in hers; it was cold. She was dying! Tears

195

filled her eyes as she looked at me. I was due to have my baby any time now. "Oh, Steph," she whispered, "what have we done to you?"

I put my face close to hers. "Mother, you didn't do anything. You only wanted love. You missed Dad and Greg so much. I don't blame you."

Her eyes seemed to be looking beyond me. "Bruce wanted everything," she went on, "and he almost got it. But not all I had. You go to the bank when I'm gone. I've put money in a trust for you . . . my girl." She closed her eyes. "You believe in God, donyou?" she asked. "Remember, He'll always be with you, no matter what happens."

I looked away . . . outside at the dark sky. The barren trees held snow in their branches and the lights from the street shone on the snow-covered roofs. Then I reached over and covered Mother's thin hand with mine. "I love you, Mother," I said.

She nodded. There were no more words between us.

The nurse came in and took Mother's pulse, glanced at me, and shook her head. "I'm sorry," she said.

My body ached. The wooden chair was uncomfortable and Hope looked weary . . . and almost angry. I knew what she was thinking: Bruce hadn't even come to be with Mother as she died.

Hope and I made all the funeral arrangements. I'd never intended to go home while I was pregnant, but I couldn't miss my mother's funeral. I felt the staring glances of my old friends and neighbors, and I imagined the talk that was going around. But what difference did it make now? All I'd loved was gone.

Jenna came to the funeral with her folks, and afterward they came over and talked to me. Her mother hugged me and said what a wonderful mother I'd had. Jenna put her hand out to show me the diamond ring she'd just gotten from a nice man who was going to dental school. She was going to move to the city to be near him and she said she already had a job with an insurance company. Then she added that maybe she would call me at Hope's sometime. It was a lukewarm offer and I closed my eyes around the tears and played the game, saying that would be nice.

There was nothing to stay in town for. I didn't want to see any more of Bruce . . . he'd been playing the bereaved husband at the funeral and that sickened me. But before Hope and I left, he reminded me that he was Mother's rightful heir and that he was going to get what was coming to him.

I closed the car door in his face. But the sound of his threatening voice echoed through my mind. You haven't heard the last of me. I'll be around again one day.

I felt scared. Hope reassured me that he wasn't going to be able to do anything she'd see to that.

When we got back to Hope's, I was surprised to see the Christmas tree and the presents just as we'd left them. Christmas had come and gone and I hadn't even realized it.

In the week after my mother's funeral, a man from her bank called me. His name was Mr. Riley. He confirmed what Mother had told me before she died . . . that there was a trust fund in my name. Mother had left me thirty-five thousand dollars. Mr. Riley said that there had originally been fifty thousand dollars set aside, but that my mother had started withdrawing from the trust before the house was sold.

I was certain that it had been Bruce who'd convinced my mother to give him the money. If Mother hadn't died when she did, I was sure he would have gotten every last penny she had.

When the mail came one morning, I saw that I'd gotten a sympathy card from Brian. Even before I read the return address, I recognized his handwriting. Brian would do that . . . send me a card. He was still kind and thoughtful, in spite of how I'd hurt him.

I read the card, then put it away in my dresser drawer. I remembered how it felt to be in his arms, to feel his lips against mine, to look into his eyes and see the love glowing there.

My labor pains started early one cold January morning . . . short, sharp jabs cutting through my back. I told Hope, and then I called my boss and told him I wouldn't be in to work for a week or so. Then Hope called the doctor and drove me to the hospital.

Hours passed . . . and still no baby. The pain was almost unbearable. Finally, one of the nurses called the doctor. When he examined me he said he was going to have to have a cesarean section. Everything whirled around for a while and then there was relief because there was nothing. . . .

I awoke sometime later to hear a voice saying, "Okay, Stephanie, it's time to wake up. It's all over. Everything is fine."

I opened my eyes and saw a nurse. I mumbled something and blinked back tears. I had made arrangements while I was in labor for my baby to be given up for adoption. But I had to know something about it. I needed closure.

"Was it a boy or a girl?" I asked the nurse. "Was it all right?"

"Better you don't think about it," she said.

I stared at her. I knew she probably had someone to love her . . . someone to dream with. "I want to know," I insisted. "I have that right. The doctor told me so. He even said that if I wanted to I could see the baby. And that's what I want."

"Well, then, you talk to the doctor," she said. "I don't know what he told you."

Hope came to my room later on. She seemed nervous. She went

to the window and made some remark about the snow. I looked at her and asked, "Hope, was the baby all right? Was it a boy or a girl?"

She turned around, then walked over and took my hand. "Stephanie, it was a beautiful baby boy. He's perfect in every way."

Her words brought relief. I had prayed that the baby would be perfect and beautiful, that someone would want that baby.

In the evening the doctor came in to examine me. I told him I wanted to see the baby. He looked at me for a moment, then patted my hand. "Of course," he said. "But first we need to talk." Then he told me he'd had to do emergency surgery . . . I had been bleeding profusely and he'd had no choice. I could never have another baby, he said.

I looked away, dying inside. I felt all alone in my grief. They were taking away my baby as well as any others I might have had someday.

It was a sleepless night . . . a night of memories of Brian, Bruce, Mother, Dad, and Greg. It was a night of thinking about the future. Now that I was no longer pregnant, I felt as though I was floating in space, with no destination, without any dreams.

Before breakfast, a woman came in with forms for me to sign. She asked me if I understood what I was signing. I looked at her and my eyes filled with tears. "Yes, I'm giving my baby away," I said.

She handed me the pen. Her voice held no emotion as she said, "All right, then. Just so you understand."

I signed my name and stared at the signature. Just like that, it was all over.

The woman left and they brought my breakfast. Life just went on.

Around ten, a nurse came in with a little bundle. Her eyes held mine and I knew she must have been wondering: How can you give this child up? But she said nothing. She just bent down and placed my baby in my arms.

He was soft and pink and beautiful. When I put my finger in his little palm, he closed his fingers around it and held tight. I kept looking at him, etching his face in my mind. It would have to last a lifetime. I would never see him or hold him again. But I would always love him . . . the innocent beautiful little boy who'd brought me a peace I couldn't explain.

I kissed his soft cheek and he reached out to stretch, touching my chin as he did so. The nurse reached down and took him from my arms, telling me that there was a good program on television . . . that I should watch it. She walked out, closing the door so people couldn't hear my sobbing.

Hope came to visit right after supper. She was apprehensive and hesitant, her eyes watching my face. "Are you all right?" she asked.

I nodded. I told her the doctor had been in to see me and had said I could go home in a week. Normally, he'd discharge me almost immediately, but the emergency surgery I'd had would delay things.

"By the time I can leave, my baby will probably be gone," I said. "But don't worry, Hope. I'll be all right."

There was never any mention of my baby after that. When I was discharged from the hospital, I went back to work. I tried not to feel or think. It was the only way I could survive.

One Saturday about a month later, I got up to find a note on the kitchen table. Hope was going to be gone for the day, it said, to do a little shopping.

The day passed slowly . . . a long, empty day. The sky remained clouded over and it was dismal outside. I had cleaned everything there was to clean, so I went into the living room and tried to read a magazine.

When the doorbell rang, I got up to answer it, expecting the paperboy to be there to collect. But to my surprise it was Brian!

He smiled. "Hello, Stephanie. May I come in, or do I have to freeze out here?"

I let him in. He took off his jacket, tossed it on a chair, and then turned around and faced me. He opened his arms! I went to him in a trance and he held me close, his heart beating against mine.

"I talked to Hope about you," he said quietly. "She said I shouldn't come here until I'd thought everything over and decided whether or not I could forget about the baby . . . put it all in the past where it belongs. She said if I really loved you, I could do that. If I didn't, it would never work. So here I am with my heart in my hand. I don't want to talk about what happened before. I just want to know if you love me and if you will marry me."

With tears in my eyes, I told him yes . . . I had always loved him and always would.

When Hope came home, Brian told her the news . . . that there was going to be a wedding soon. Hope hugged us both.

It was unbelievable that I could be so happy. Brian really accepted me and loved me just like before . . . with trust and gentleness, with an open heart. But my baby still lived secretly inside my heart . . . the baby I thought about every day. Every time I saw a little one in someone's arms, it was my private heartache . . . a hurting that no one would ever erase, a pain that only God knew.

Then one evening Brian came over with a diamond ring. I looked at him and said, "There's something you have to know before you give me that ring. I can't ever have another child. When I was in the hospital, I almost bled to death and they did surgery that made it impossible for me to get pregnant again."

There was an expression on his face that I will never forget, a hesitancy that almost stopped my heart. Then he said angrily, "If I knew who raped you, I'd kill him!" It was then I that realized he didn't know it was Bruce . . . and I knew that I could never tell him.

I walked away from him, my heart full of pain. "We don't have to get married," I said. "I'd understand why you wouldn't want me. Every man wants to have his own child."

Suddenly Brian's arms were around me and he was holding me close. "Honey, we'll have a child," he said. "We'll adopt one . . . maybe two. I don't ever want to lose you again. No one ever has to know about any of this. We'll settle down like other people, have a nice home, be a family."

We were married in Brian's church, with just Hope and a couple of Brian's friends present. We lived in an apartment until we had enough money saved to put down a deposit on a small home . . . Brian insisted we save the money Mother had left me. Then we applied for adoption and a social worker came to check our home. We filled out numerous applications and time passed.

Finally, though, the phone call we'd been waiting for came. They had a son for us! I cried with joy . . . and with sadness, remembering my son. I wondered again where he was. He was nearly three years old already.

When they placed Dylan in my arms, a feeling jolted through me. I knew that someone had received my baby in this same way, and that another mother was crying because she had given Dylan up.

Brian put his arm around me and hugged us both. "Well, Mother, let's go home!" he said.

So that's where we were the morning I received the letter. We were a normal, happy, busy family. Brian was active on the church council, was a Sunday school teacher, and was doing well in his job. He was a respected, loving, wonderful husband and father. Dylan had grown as fast as corn on a summer day and was filled with mischief. The past with its nightmares seemed dim and far away. But now there was this letter, linking the present with those dark days and nights . . . reaching out like the flames of a fire burning, destroying.

My mind whirled . . . I couldn't even think. I remembered Brian saying that he'd run into Bruce once in a restaurant. They had talked briefly. Bruce was married again, to some woman who owned a hardware store. Bruce said he was doing very well, that he was finally respected and had amounted to something. I remembered feeling cold when Brian spoke of him. I'd asked him not to invite him to our home and Brian said he wouldn't do that, not after the way Bruce had treated my mother. I had looked away because I was afraid that it might show in my eyes . . . the hate I felt for Bruce. Little did Brian realize it was more than my mother that Bruce took from me.

So all this time I had tried to forget Bruce. Whenever something happened to remind me of him, I'd just quickly think about something else. I didn't ever want the darkness of the memories of Bruce to dim the bright life I shared with Brian and Dylan.

I locked the doors, went to the telephone, and dialed Hope's number. "Oh, Stephanie, how nice to hear from you," she said.

I started to blurt it all out, telling her that Brian didn't know about Bruce and me, telling her about the letter.

She was as shocked as I was. She advised me to do nothing yet. She would drive over the next day and we could talk about it.

I felt trapped, like an animal pursued and caught in a corner. I tried everything to remain calm . . . I started to iron, turned on the television set, and planned lunch for the next day. I tried desperately to blot out the letter . . . what it meant. Suddenly I remembered we were supposed to be going out for dinner with Faith and Mike Fischer. Mike was Brian's supervisor. Brian respected him so much. It was up to Mike if Brian got a promotion or a raise.

I shuddered. Why did this have to happen on such a beautiful day, such a wonderful time in my life?

Dylan came pounding at the back door. He was crying because he'd fallen and skinned his knee. Brian came in the front door looking irritated.

I patched Dylan's knee and sent him back outside. Brian tossed the daily newspaper on the table. My heart pounded hard and my hands trembled as I picked up the paper.

"Bruce sure has made headlines this time!" he said. "The fool had everything going for him, but he had to mess it up."

The newspaper headline glared at me: Businessman Charged With Sex Abuse Of A Teenager.

Brian paced the floor, mumbling that we weren't going out to eat . . . he'd already called Mike. Then he opened his arms and I went to him. "I'm sorry," he said. "Everyone knows I have a brother. I hope they realize I'm not responsible for his actions. Our good friends will understand. The rest . . . well, they don't count."

Guilt went through me. I knew I had to make a decision about the letter, about whether or not to tell Brian. I decided to wait and see. Maybe if I didn't answer the letter, that would be the end of it.

It was a long and sleepless night for us. No one called. No one stopped by. We knew that everyone must have read the paper. By now most of the town knew about Bruce. The article had revealed past arrests and counseling sessions Bruce had been ordered to attend. His defense lawyer was quoted as saying there was no truth to the new charges against Bruce, he was a gentle and good man. That Cindy Hanson, the teenager, was bitter because Bruce's wife had fired her from her job at the hardware store because she was suspected of stealing.

The article continued on, but I couldn't read it because the tears were blinding me. I could just imagine how Bruce had cornered that girl and abused her. And I could hear him telling his wife that he'd done nothing wrong.

In the morning, Brian tried to act unconcerned, but his eyes showed his worry. When he was ready to leave, he bent down to kiss Dylan, ruffled his hair, and forced a smile. "Have a good day, you two," he said.

Around ten, the phone rang, sending shocks through my body. Was it Cindy Hanson calling? Her lawyer? Finally I answered. It was my neighbor Edna. Her voice was light and friendly. She wanted to know if I wanted to drive to the city with her. I said I couldn't, that Hope was coming over.

"I read about Bruce in the evening paper," she said. "It's too bad the papers are so desperate for news that they have to embarrass a whole family. Poor Brian. Tell him we all understand and sympathize."

I thanked her and hung up. When Hope arrived, she told me she'd called Cindy's attorney and asked him if they couldn't just leave me out of the whole thing. He told her that everyone doubted Cindy's story as it was, and that if I wouldn't come willingly, he'd subpoena me to court.

I knew then that I'd have to tell Brian. I was scared, but I told Hope I'd call Cindy's attorney myself. Then, when I had to, I'd tell Brian.

Hope wasn't feeling very well and she didn't want to drive home too late so we had an early lunch. She played with Dylan and waited while I put a call through to Harrison Kingsly, the attorney.

He wanted to know what I knew about Bruce's past, and if what Cindy had been told was true. My heart skipped a beat.

"What did he tell Cindy?" I asked.

The lawyer said Bruce told her I was another girl who'd tried to accuse him of molesting her . . . and failed. He'd mentioned he had "evidence" that could prove I was no good. The lawyer was hopeful I had things to testify to against Bruce . . . facts that would stand up in a court of law. Otherwise, he was afraid Cindy's charge would be thrown out.

I was crying by then. It was in my hands now. I could say it wasn't true. I could say Bruce was a decent man. But then he would be free to hurt more people, destroy their lives. The only choice I could live with was to cooperate. Mr. Kingsly said there would be a hearing on Wednesday of the following week. He asked me if I could come in a few hours before court convened. I'd be there, I said.

Hope forced a weak smile when she heard that. After I'd hung up, she said I did what was right.

But would Brian understand?

On Tuesday evening, the night before the court date, Brian came home from work and announced that Mike wanted him to go up to the lake with him to get the cabin winterized. Maybe they'd stay for the rest of the week, he said. Brian stared at me, watching me, as if he already knew something. His look made me uneasy, but I managed to say I thought that would be nice.

"He's doing it because he heard the hearing on Bruce is tomorrow," Brian said. "He knows how hard it is on me, how rotten I feel. I'm grateful that he thinks enough of me to ask."

I didn't move. I watched Dylan rolling in the leaves outside. His cheeks were rosy from the brisk fall air, and he had a happy, carefree smile. I wondered about another little boy . . . wondered if he was getting the same love I gave to Dylan.

Brian came over suddenly and put his arms around me. "I'm sorry, honey," he said, "that you have to be hurt by all this. I love you so much."

I wanted to tell him then . . . let him know the secret I'd kept all these years . . . but the words just wouldn't come out.

Soon Mike arrived, and he and Brian left for the cabin. I went to bed early, exhausted.

On Wednesday morning, I dressed slowly, dreading what I knew was ahead. I had arranged for Katie Simmons, a neighbor, to baby-sit for Dylan for the day. She arrived at nine.

Dylan was playing with building blocks on the floor in the living room. He looked up at me and grinned. A wave of love floated through me and warmed my heart as I realized how much I loved my son. I bent down, scooped him up in my arms, and held him close before I left.

Hope met me at a little cafe. We were both nervous and I felt guilty because she had to come with me. She'd been through so much for me already . . . it wasn't fair. But when she had offered to come, I was so scared that I said I'd appreciate it. But sitting across from her, seeing how weary she looked, I almost regretted the decision.

We met Harrison Kingsly inside the courthouse. He came right over to me and put his hand on my arm and led me to a small room off the hallway. I thought longingly of home . . . of Dylan and Brian. They seemed a million miles away! I felt like the world was closing in on me . . . that I was going to come out of there with my whole life exposed.

Mr. Kingsly was strong and determined and never wavered. He set his briefcase down on a wooden table and looked at me. "We are going to put Bruce Reid where he belongs once and for all," he said. "All you have to do is tell the truth."

Mr. Kingsly asked the questions and I gave him the answers. When he was done, I was filled with the same remorse and shame I'd felt a long time ago. Now it lived again inside me.

I was told to wait in that room until someone came for me. I could have waited in the courtroom if I wanted, but Bruce was there and I didn't want to see him.

The morning dragged on. Just after eleven, the door opened and Bruce came in! "I thought it would be you when I heard there was another witness," he said. "I just knew that you'd be fool enough to come here. Well, you hurt me, I'll hurt you. You've got a kid now, haven't you? When you're shooting off your mouth, just remember that."

From out of nowhere someone came in and grabbed his arm and pulled him away. Hope reassured me that everything would be all right, but she added that she wasn't feeling well so she thought she'd drive to a drugstore and fill a prescription.

There was a lunch break and Mr. Kingsly had sandwiches and coffee brought in for me. Outside the wind was blowing strong and hard and the sky had clouded over and rain pelted the windows.

Finally, around two, a man came in and told me to follow him. I walked like a sleepwalker behind him, not seeing the people on either side of the courtroom. But I noticed the young girl sitting next to Mr. Kingsly at a long table. She was around sixteen and had eyes that looked frightened. I could just imagine Bruce cornering her, hurting her, laughing at her tears. I knew that no matter what price I paid to testify, I had no choice.

I was sworn in, and then Mr. Kingsly asked me to tell in my own words what happened between Bruce and myself. I felt all the eyes in that courtroom burning on my face, and I felt Bruce's glare. I looked away as I told what had happened . . . to me, my mother, and my baby.

When I finished, Cindy was crying. Bruce's attorney got up slowly and approached me. As he questioned me, he tried to imply that I was bitter because my mother had left Bruce nearly everything and that I had actually become pregnant by some other man. Then he asked if I really thought anyone would believe that Bruce's own brother would marry me if I'd had a child by Bruce.

"My husband never knew," I said. "And that is the only thing I've ever done that I'm ashamed of . . . not telling him."

I was told to step down then, and everything after that was a blur . . . Cindy sobbing . . . the lawyers quarreling . . . Bruce . . . the judge . . . all of it was unreal.

Later, court was adjourned and Mr. Kingsly said I could go home. I walked outside and there were reporters following me. I got in my car and locked the doors. I looked around for Hope and saw her heading for her car.

Hope decided to follow me back home. As I drove, I went over everything in my mind, dreading the time I would have to face Brian and everyone else in town.

As I pulled up to the house, I noticed that it was dark. I got out of the car slowly, the tension mounting. I turned the key in the door and went inside. The house was empty! There was a note on the table from Katie, saying I was to call Faith Fischer, Brian's boss's wife.

With nervous fingers I dialed the number. Faith answered immediately, as if she was expecting my call. She sounded different, not friendly.

"Brian called here," she said. "He heard on the news about your testimony. Why didn't you tell him? He was terribly upset."

I was crying, so all I could ask was where Dylan was. Faith said he was in bed there and that I should wait until morning to get him, or wait until Brian came home. Brian had said he'd pick him up.

I hung up, then looked on our phone list for the number at Mike's cabin. I dialed and Mike answered. When I asked for Brian, he hesitated, then called, "Brian, it's Stephanie."

I waited. When he finally came to the phone, I was crying.

"Thanks a lot," he said in a tight voice, "for sending me packing and then going to court and spilling out your whole life. Thanks for letting me get the facts straight from the news that my brother fathered your child! And I thought you were so wonderful, so decent."

He hung up, and I went over and sat down at the kitchen table. I looked at Hope . . . I'd forgotten she was there. She looked ill; her skin had a pasty color and her eyes looked weary and tired. I was exhausted, too. I could hardly think sensibly but I knew that in the morning the reporters would come. There would be cameras and prying questions. I couldn't face any more of it.

Hope seemed to read my mind. "Stephanie, why don't you stay at my house tonight?" she offered.

I sighed tiredly. "Why not?" I said. "The way Brian sounded, I don't think he'll be wanting to see me. Anyway, I don't want to be here tomorrow morning."

I packed some clothes, then called Faith Fischer and said I was going to Hope's. I asked her if she would tell Dylan that I loved him very much. My voice broke as I said I was sorry for what had happened. She said she'd tell Brian I'd called.

When we got to Hope's house, she took some of her medicine and went right to bed. But first she said, "Stephanie, if Brian loves you, he'll come to you . . . he'll stand by you. Now try to get some rest, okay?"

"I will," I promised, and then thanked her again for all her help.

For a long time I sat in the living room and listened to the wind outside. We weren't that far from November and winter . . . like the winter in my heart. Finally, I dozed off from exhaustion.

The next morning a loud pounding at the front door awakened me. For a moment I'd forgotten what had happened . . . even that I was at Hope's . . . and then it all washed through me. I got up and went to the window. There was a van out front from a television station.

I heard Hope's faint voice calling me. I went to her room and saw that she was still in bed. She looked ill.

"Stephanie," she whispered. "I've got to go to the hospital, I'm so very sick. Please call my doctor right away."

I called the doctor and he said he'd send an ambulance. He muttered something about expecting this for a long time.

I rode with the ambulance. When we arrived at the hospital, they took Hope to the intensive care unit and said I could wait in the lounge. They promised to let me know how things were going.

After awhile, a nurse brought me a cup of coffee. I watched the sun break through the dark clouds and felt its warmth through the window. My heart was heavy. How many times had I been to this hospital before? I remembered my mother . . . and my baby. Where was he now?

Someone walked down the hallway with a little boy about Dylan's age. He was chattering happily and a wave of loneliness went through me. I closed my eyes. I was afraid to think about the future . . . without Hope, without Brian and Dylan.

It was evening before the doctor came to me and said they were moving Hope into a private room. He told me that when they had her settled, I could go in and sit with her. She'd had another heart attack.

I was looking out the window in the lounge, watching cars stop, people getting out, when a woman came up to me and said, "Hey, are you that woman who's been on the news . . . the one testifying at that bum's trial?"

I looked at her, amazed. Then I nodded.

She put her hand on my arm. "If you haven't seen the six o'clock news, you won't want to miss the broadcast the next time it comes on." She smiled warmly. "Your husband was on!"

I went in and sat by Hope, the woman's words echoing in my mind. At ten o'clock I told her I was going out to the lounge for a little while. The TV set was turned on so I sat down.

When the picture of my home flashed on the screen, I almost jumped up. Brian came out of the front door and looked straight into the camera. The reporter asked him what he had to say about the notorious case involving his wife and his half brother.

Brian's voice was strong and firm as he said, "My wife is the most wonderful woman in the world, and I resent anyone making a victim feel guilty. People like my half brother should not be allowed to go free to hurt more innocent people." He paused. "And one more thing," he went on. "Steph, I love you."

After that I sat in the lounge, praying . . . thanking God that Brian had realized that I couldn't tell him about what had happened because of my own fears.

Shortly after midnight, Hope died. I was with her, holding her hand. I hoped she heard me when I told her how grateful I was for all she'd done for me.

I was just leaving her room when I saw Brian coming down the hall. I ran to him and he held me close. It wasn't a time for anything more than a few whispered words of love, but when we finally got home, we talked everything out. I told him how sorry I was that he'd had to learn about Bruce and me from someone else, but that I had been too afraid to tell him. He apologized, too, for not being there when I needed him.

Hope's funeral was hard for me. I said good-bye to a dear friend, knowing that I would miss her terribly. Afterward, Brian took me home. . . .

In the days that followed, I was scared and nervous when I thought about Bruce's trial. What if he was let go? Brian told me everything would work out for the best and I wanted to believe him.

Then the call came from Cindy Hanson's lawyer . . . Bruce had been convicted! I felt so relieved and so vindicated.

Eventually, our lives went back to normal. Our friends and neighbors told us how glad they were that everything went well for us. I knew there were some people who would choose to believe the stories rather than the truth. But we held our heads up high and talk soon simmered down.

So the dark days are over . . . forever. The sad, hurting past has finally been laid to rest. There will always be bittersweet memories of the little boy I held in my arms just once, but I have Brian and Dylan to ease the pain . . . to fill my life with love.

THE END

Made in United States
Troutdale, OR
01/12/2024

16909347R00120